MAIN___

Robert McCrum has written four novels: *In the Secret State*,
which was made into a film starring Frank Finlay and Natasha
Richardson, *A Loss of Heart*, *The Fabulous Englishman* and
Mainland. He also wrote the award-winning television series,
The Story of English. He lives in London.

ROBERT McCRUM

MAINLAND

PICADOR
PUBLISHED BY PAN BOOKS

First published 1991 by Martin Secker & Warburg Limited

This Picador edition published 1992 by
PAN BOOKS LIMITED
a division of Pan Macmillan Publishers Limited
Cavaye Place London SW10 9PG
and Basingstoke

Associated companies throughout the world

ISBN 0-330-32100-5

Copyright © Robert McCrum 1991

1 3 5 7 9 8 6 4 2

A CIP catalogue record for this book is available
from the British Library

Printed in England by Clays Ltd, St Ives plc

PART

ONE

I

On the mainland it was the beginning of spring, but here it might have been the dead of winter. The airport was like a prison. Arc lights, watch-towers, closed-circuit video cameras, and men in uniform: everything was under surveillance. The rain was coming down hard and the earth and the sky were confused in the dusk. As the engines were shut off, the Muzak came back and the passengers got to their feet. Already the flight attendant was levering the door open for disembarkation. Stephen waited alone at the head of the queue: remote, watchful and lost in himself.

When he was a small boy growing up in the hot countries where his father had supervised engineering projects for various Western governments, his mother sometimes spoke about her childhood home in the wet green islands of the north, but it was only later that Stephen, remembering the tears that sometimes came into her eyes at such moments, began to understand exactly what it was she had lost when she married his father. 'And they all lived happily ever after,' she would say with a sigh. 'The End.'

As he grew older, Stephen found this sad, well-meaning lie pushed aside by other, more significant deceptions, and in the uncomfortable list of subjects that could not be mentioned between his parents it became a faint, almost forgotten, memory of a time now distanced by years of reserved but easygoing retirement among the avenues and copses of the prosperous mainland. By then, in the mysterious way of family, Stephen himself was criss-crossing the troubled parts of the world, a high-flyer for an international operation that advertised itself as a 'strategic think-tank'. For many of his clients, such vagueness was preferred and the 'political consultant' of his business card was accepted without difficulty. He

3

had come to like that. In the complexity of the shadows he could remain elusive, unchallenged, free. To the cynical, he could be cynical; to the dreamers, idealistic; to the pragmatists, a man of business.

'The End.' Stephen remembered his mother's time-for-bed voice and acknowledged that 'home' was a collection of bedtime stories and some awkward weekends away from boarding-school with grandparents he hardly knew. Perhaps that explained why when he was finally home he felt foreign. He had told himself, in the middle of his recent depression, that all his life he had been running away, but perhaps coming back to settle down in a place that was little more than a mother's fantasy was just another kind of escape. An end or a beginning? He could not say.

That was his mood just now: frustration, frustration, frustration. There were inexplicable moments of rage, and others of mindless euphoria. Occasionally, he felt he was going mad. He had told head office that he was not ready to make this trip today, but they insisted he see the so-called 'risk department', the security end of the business, in action. The future of 'risk' was in question they said, and it was an opportunity to observe and take notes. They had reassured him that he would have no duties. 'Nothing hands-on,' said his boss.

One look at his colleague as they had checked in for the short flight told him that this hope was dead. Smith was an ex-serviceman, as anonymous as his name, no doubt skilled in survival techniques but out of his depth on this assignment. Even his mufti was ill-judged: with VIPs you wore a suit. Stephen had found himself taking command. Part of him resented this, but he was intrigued to discover he was not entirely displeased.

The door was now fully open. He watched the ground crew in slick yellow anoraks manhandle the steps towards the nose of the plane. When that gangway locked into position, he realised, he would be committed to five days of responsibility, and for a moment, seeing Smith's hopeless expression and his ridiculous sports jacket, something inside him almost lost control.

His collapsible umbrella, catching the wind, tugged in his hand and the weather shook itself over the tarmac like a great wet dog. The VIPs crowding behind him seemed taken unawares by the rain, as though travelling first class gave them diplomatic immunity to the laws of meteorology.

A liaison officer in a camouflage jacket, a big game hunter with a soft brown shaving-brush moustache, was clattering up the steps. 'Major Potter.' The handshake was firm and professional but there was a weariness in the voice and the sombre eyes were pink with exhaustion.

There was momentary confusion about who was in charge. 'Dr Mallory?' Stephen nodded. 'Not really the kind of doctor you need here, I'm afraid,' he replied. 'I don't save lives.'

Major Potter looked at him, not sure how to take this, and Stephen gave him no help. He liked to test the people he encountered with an air of enigma. In his line of work it helped to be unaccountable, hard to pin down; it was also an approach that suited his temperament perfectly.

If he had supposed that here, so close to his own country, there would be a different response to his presence, he was mistaken. The experienced part of him knew he should not be surprised. Every touchdown was the same. There were ground rules to be settled, local sensitivities to be understood, and a temporary authority to be established. In some parts of the world, a doctorate was as influential as a loaded weapon. Among the hoodlums and racketeers he had worked with during the emergencies in the Far East, it had become his trademark. There, he was simply 'Doc', and he used to enjoy the mild frisson of travelling unarmed through the lawless states of his self-appointed jurisdiction. Here, with a Who's Who of dignitaries at his heels, it would have suited his fancy to be an ordinary footslogger, a mister; but he was not concerned.

Smith, asserting himself, had been conferring with Potter, and was now looking indecisively to Stephen while the major watched with a hardboiled expression that said, This is not my problem. Smith knew he was failing, but he tried, unsuccessfully, to find some lightness. 'I'm afraid we have a little local difficulty, sir.' Stephen considered him with nonchalance, enjoying the panic in his eyes. There was always something small but oddly significant about these trips that became the antidote to the numbing predictability of the Xeroxed schedule in his briefcase. Potter seemed to be enjoying Smith's discomfiture as well; he became confidential. Close to, Stephen noticed a tiny smear of lipstick on his cheek. Wife or mistress, he wondered. 'We have received a threat, Dr Mallory, and I am advising your colleague,' he nodded contemptuously at Smith, 'to relocate.'

Stephen looked at Smith, who began to bluster.

Potter broke in, explaining the alternatives. Stephen considered Smith frankly. 'We'll keep this to ourselves, won't we?'

The ex-serviceman looked relieved. 'Thank you, sir.'

They turned. A coach, with a police escort, was sweeping through the rain. They watched it park at the foot of the steps. There was a squawk and a burst of chatter from the short-wave radio on Major Potter's lapel. 'Well then,' he said. 'Shall we?' He gave a flourish with his clipboard, a second lieutenant urging his men over the top. As the VIPs buttoned their raincoats and began filing out, Stephen studied the list of names over his shoulder. The half-familiar, elderly features, craggier, purpler versions of their television and newspaper images, lumbered past, exchanging the cryptic conversation of the privileged. Influence had its own special language, as Stephen, who had grown up with many advantages, was well aware. Behind, penned in by the stewardess, the economy class passengers looked on with curiosity.

Stephen took his place at the front of the bus next to Smith while his party settled in their seats, nursing their briefcases like schoolboys. He glanced at them as he sat down. There was a collective quietness that he recognised. Fear was too strong a word, but there was something more than nervous anticipation registered in those experienced faces, and when he mentally skimmed their collective dossier he was not surprised.

Now the coach was hissing through the rain. Across the airfield, beyond the lights of the runway, there was the shadowy outline of military warehouses, the shape of parked tanks and tiny figures filing into the black belly of a troop transport. As he watched, Stephen saw one, two, three helicopter gunships dropping in out of the cloud, coming to rest by a rank of fighter aircraft. The bus bumped over security ramps, approaching a sandbagged checkpoint. In the cinematic glare of the arc lights, Stephen noticed the ugly blotches on his companion's skin. Two soldiers, one black, the other sickly-white, were strolling up and down with automatic weapons lowered. They were very young. An officer stepped forward, but it was only to wave them through. Now they were gathering speed down the main road to the city. The short spring day was nearly over and even the lights of the oncoming cars seemed drowned in mist and water.

Once the bus was cruising and there was no chance of being generally overheard, Smith began to seethe with dissatisfaction. Stephen, half-listening, wondered if this was an odd kind of defensive self-justification for the cock-up, or a late appeal for sympathy. He noticed that across the aisle Major Potter, browsing a local newspaper, was eavesdropping Smith's complaint.

It was time he got out, Smith was saying. He hadn't joined 'this outfit' for trips to places like this. He had been posted here three times before leaving the forces. It was, he said, the arsehole of the world. It wasn't that he was really scared, though enough of his mates had been killed or wounded to make him careful, it was simply there was no one you could trust. 'They're not like us,' he said. 'What they say and what they do are quite different things. At the end of the day, you have to treat them all as the enemy, and that's that.' He made it sound so simple. The so-called policy of 'normalisation', he went on, indicating the VIPs behind them with a jerk of his head, was just an abdication of responsibility that would be

7

dearly paid for in blood. Getting tough was the only answer. That way, he reckoned, you could end it within a year. 'Have the boys home by Christmas, I'd say.' The troops would love that. When he'd been here all he'd thought about was getting out, and at the time he'd sworn never to return. He gave a cynical laugh. 'The road to hell is paved with good intentions.'

The windscreen wipers swished back and forward, regulating his grumbles like a metronome. From time to time, Stephen prodded the conversation along with a question, but mostly his mind remained detached and neutral.

This was so often the tone of first landings. Discontented stooges he would never meet again letting their hair down in front of an outsider, an oddly painless confessional. Peacekeeping was the same drudgery the world over. A low-level violation of local freedoms paid for with high-level boredom punctuated by moments of sheer terror. No wonder everyone always angled to get out. The dreams of leaving didn't change much. In the Third World, the jittery guardians of the state wanted a fish-farm or an American visa. In other crisis zones, they talked about early retirement, long weekends and a condo by the sea. He wondered vaguely about the pipe-dreams he was going to find here in the clapped-out West.

'What about Australia?' he asked, with the same unreadable expression.

'Are you kidding?' Smith's response was pure delight. His garish jacket seemed right for a golf course or a barbecue.

'Well then,' said Stephen, 'perhaps you should go for it.' His grasp of this mood, and his sympathy for it, was new. Until recently, he had been so absorbed in the challenge of his work he had often said he would not know what to do with leisure.

His career was successful. In those years since he had left the archives, he had acquired a reputation for master-minding Third World election campaigns. 'Political consultant' came to mean steering fragile political craft through the rough waters of semi-democratic polls to the safe harbour of office.

Then there had been a catastrophe. The opposition had

killed one of his candidates, gunning him down on the platform three days before the vote, the vote that he had been certain to carry. He had been so close to Federico. They had flown the length and breadth of the country together in the campaign jet. They had spoken of women, jazz and favourite reading. They had joked about Federico's inauguration. For the first time, Stephen felt that in victory he would not be discarded as the embarrassing representative of electronic manipulation or media capitalism.

The after-shock of Federico's death had disturbed him for longer than he could have imagined. Once the immediate pain had become a memory, there was still the bitterness and the despair. He felt weary and disillusioned, and nothing seemed to matter. He sought alternative explanations, and the word he applied to his persistent low spirits was 'homesick', though 'home' was something he hardly knew, and could scarcely define, beyond a certain accent of speech.

In the early days, he had got a buzz from what the office liked to call 'troubleshooting', but now he told his superiors, when they summoned him for debriefing, he was sick of it all. He was tired of waking in strange beds, not knowing where he was. He was tired of the pills he was taking to get to sleep and the pills he was taking to stay up. He was not xenophobic (no one could be more at ease in alien territory), but he was tired of abroad. He'd had enough of foreign airports, foreign hotels and foreign clients, even ruthless fascinating ones whose campaigns gave him such a vicarious thrill. He was tired of being provisional, for hire. He was tired of that lightweight suitcase and his drip-dry suit. He wanted routine. He wanted to be mundane, to have news-papers delivered on successive Sundays, to walk in the park and go to the theatre with friends like an ordinary person, not watch the in-flight movie, half-drunk, five miles up, alone in first class. He wanted, as a recent girlfriend had put it, 'to get in touch with himself'.

His office was co-operative, the director understanding. Alan Wagner did not want to lose a valuable colleague, and

Stephen was reassigned to domestic duties. Shortly afterwards, he was commissioned to look into all aspects of the company's current business and write a hard-hitting report for the board. 'After all,' said Wagner, as he concluded his briefing, 'that's what you're supposed to be good at.'

'I'm a little rusty,' he'd replied.

'Time to shape up, Steve,' said Wagner, and something in his voice said his sympathy was a scarce commodity on which Mallory could not rely indefinitely.

The evaluation of the risk department in action was his first trip away from the office since that conversation. Staring out of the window at a queue of cars filtering past a military road-block, he wondered how much was always missed, how the true story escaped casual, even thorough, scrutiny. He sighed. If I was in love, he thought, none of this would matter.

'Don't you love your wife?' he asked, tuning recklessly into Smith's complaint.

'I do – now that she's left.' He gave a weak laugh of shame and regret. 'That's life I suppose.'

Stephen was briefly grateful not to be married. He had always preferred solitariness to rejection. He was about to pursue the question of loss, but the moment slipped by. Major Potter was folding away the newspaper and the coach was pulling up outside another wire-netting security gate. Through the rain streaming down the window, he watched the shouted exchange between the driver and the attendant on the video monitor in the guard-house. Then they were swinging under the boom into a blaze of security light in the hotel forecourt.

Stephen stood up and turned to face the passengers. Now he was on. For a moment, he saw himself through their eyes: tall, boyish, hesitant, and slightly aloof. Then he was welcoming them to their destination. He explained the evening's pro-gramme, assuming that nothing else had been changed. Drinks at seven, dinner in a private room, followed by an illustrated talk from the local secretary of the trust. 'I'm sure I don't need to advise you that it is not sensible to leave the hotel premises.'

He imagined they would favour an early night. 'We have quite a full day tomorrow,' he concluded.

The distinguished faces listened attentively. He might have been making a maiden speech or an appeal to a trial judge. He watched them as he spoke. They were still just an audience with an obedient collective personality. They behaved as one, like an animal. By tomorrow night, he would know the animal's moods, its fears and preferences. For the moment, it was a tour party getting to its feet and filing after him towards the hotel foyer.

As he pushed through the double doors there was a muffled thud in the distance. It was sufficiently indistinct to escape the notice of the inattentive, but Stephen did not look back to see how many of his party had registered alarm.

Isabel heard the bomb while she was still in the Ladies, freshening up after the broadcast. The blast was quite near, but such a routine event that the journalist in her did not consider covering the story. Already, others would be racing to the scene; she could have filed copy without leaving the building. The usual hijacked car; the usual plastic explosives; the usual military or government target. Occasionally there was an 'own goal'. Usually there was a warning, often to the newsdesk down the corridor; usually there were few, if any, casualties. Still, she was glad to be living out in the country, away from the worst of the violence.

She was alone in front of the mirror; she could take her time. Isabel never liked to be hurried, especially when it came to her appearance. She knew she was vain and dreamy and inclined to be lazy. In certain moods she could be harder on herself than her most critical friend. It was her habit to speak her mind. She also knew that she was considered attractive, a gift she found at once annoying and delightful. It gave her a power she despised herself for using almost as much as she despised those who responded to it. Now she dropped her hairbrush into her bag and smiled, as if at a private joke. She

II

lit a cigarette. It was very quiet. The water prattled in the cistern. In the distance there were sirens.

It was often this way after the broadcast: the slow release of tension, preferably in solitude. After the chaos of the previous year, her life was beginning to take on a pattern again, a pattern focused upon the weekly drive from the country to the recording studio. She blew smoke at herself in the glass. She was well aware that she had got the job because the producer, whom she knew slightly, claimed to feel sorry for her. Sympathy soon turned to desire, as she had feared. 'Tom's a fool and a shit,' he had remarked, at the end of a long evening's drinking. 'Will you sleep with me?'

Isabel had laughed. 'I can't sleep with you, Charlie. I'm a married woman.'

'I've always wanted an affair with a married woman.'

'Perhaps when I'm divorced,' she said. 'You're drunk, and so am I. When you're sober you'll see the error of your ways and realise I'm dangerous to know.' As she spoke the words she knew she was lying, to herself as much as anyone, and the truthful part of her acknowledged that in recent months it was only such fantasies of sexual power that had kept her going.

'That's why I love you, Isabel.' Charlie was a lonely radio producer with a frustrated desire to be a foreign correspondent, and in conversation he always reported the news he imagined you wanted to hear.

She had resisted his attentions but kept the commission. Now, when he blew kisses at her through the soundproof glass as she sat in front of the microphone with her script spread out on the baize in front of her, it was just a game, but with enough residual feeling in it to make her feel, temporarily, less bereft.

At first, she had been nervous and unconfident, but quite soon Isabel looked forward to her visit. Her writing, once stiff and didactic, became relaxed, personal, and at times even witty. The programme controllers on the top floor were pleased, Charlie told her. 'They like something from over here that's not political.'

'You know I loathe politics,' she said.

Now, stubbing out the cigarette, Isabel took her pass out of her bag. Before she went home she would economise with a couple of long-distance phone calls from the newsroom. She sneaked a final glance in the mirror. It was certainly an improvement on her ID photo, her Frankenstein's daughter look. That had been less than a year ago: a bad time; the worst. Surviving on chocolate bars; hardly sleeping; waking up in tears; living like a zombie. In retrospect, getting the ID card was a first step on the road to recovery. At least she'd got her own name back.

She passed through the swing door into Reception. 'Evening, Miss Rome,' said the duty officer. 'The boys are busy tonight.' She nodded back, flashing her pass. The man was known to be 'unreliable'. It was better to say nothing.

There was a distraction. Two folksingers, one with a guitar, came towards her, flushed with drink and companionship. Some months ago they had all three shared a complicated joke about 'fiddling while Rome burns' and now, when they met, a raised eyebrow and the exchange of 'Miss Rome', 'Mister Young', 'Miss Rome', 'Mister Carpenter', was the code for their friendship. So she greeted them, smiling now, and moved on down the corridor to the newsroom, stepping lightly. She found a quiet corner of the office, put her feet on the desk and picked up the telephone.

This Wednesday call to her parents was part of the weekly ritual. Somehow it was easier to handle their tender solicitous inquiries in the heartless openness of the newsroom. Her drama was nothing to the stories breaking here. At home, alone in her bed, or by the fire, she might just give in and say, Yes, I'll come back. Here, where she was known and respected, and where she had a role, she could identify with a successful version of herself and pass it on to her parents without feeling deceitful. The substance of this call was mutual reassurance: she was coping, she was not making a mistake, the work was going well, she was right to stay put, she had friends here, and yes, she was happy on her own.

13

Isabel told herself she had lost none of her independence, but she always had the same thought as her fingers found the number: you're thirty-two and in your head you're still half at home. But she had to share her news with someone and this was comparatively risk-free. She was still afraid of love that was unfamiliar. And when, on the fourth ring, her call was answered, these thoughts vanished and her performance began.

It was always a long call. Her mother, more agile in the home, was usually first on the line. Then she'd be handed over to give a brassier, chirpier rendering of the same stories to her father, chain-smoking in the corner of the living-room. Next, after an argument at the other end, her mother would come back on the line, sometimes on the kitchen extension, and would ask her again if she was all right. Finally, she'd have a few closing words with her father. She was all they had, and they must be given equal time. Each week she had to describe her latest broadcast, though they could hear it easily enough the following day. Sometimes, when she was feeling cruel, or depressed, or angry with her situation, she would scare them with local news. Today, she felt good about things and did not even refer to the bomb.

Her censoring caution never made much difference. Part of this call was always devoted to her parents begging her in their faultless middle-class accents to be careful. There was something so thin and clipped and lifeless about mainland speech: when she heard it on the line each week it conjured a blameless landscape of suburbs and complacency she was glad to have escaped. This, she knew, was one of the reasons why, initially to her surprise, she liked it here. It was darker and stranger than the cosy world in which she had grown up. Even the speech was different. (She believed it was Tom's voice she had fallen in love with first.) The weight and value of words was somehow larger and richer here, and the experience they gave voice to seemed more serious as well.

Now the telephones in the newsroom were coming to life as the report of the bombing hit the wire. It was getting noisy and distracting. 'Time to go home,' she said, a catch-phrase from childhood.

Her father's farewell never varied. 'Look after yourself, darling.'

After she put the phone down, she paused. She looked at her watch, reminding herself that Tom lived abroad now. She still had trouble with the time gap, but calculated it would be one o'clock with him now. He might well be in, but if he was in he would be through the first drink of the day, and heading towards belligerence. There was nothing to be gained, not now. She would put her queries about the insurance premium in writing.

Isabel pulled her things together, wrapped her coat round her against the cold, and took the elevator to the underground car-park. She hurried through the echoing shadows to her regular space, stooping to check under the chassis as usual. Outside, the city sky was thick with rain clouds and smoke, and the light was orange. If she hurried, she could be home for the seven o'clock news. It amused her to notice what a creature of habit she was becoming. Soon, she told herself, I'll be having my best conversations with the cat.

2

It was nearly dark when Curtis came out of the house, but over to the west, where the street rose with the slope of the land, and the older children of the township were larking about on bikes in front of Mr Hu's brightly lit window, there were still flags of sunset in the sky.

Curtis paused, and breathed in deeply to clear his head, his smoker's lungs hurting with the evening air. He looked round, watchful yet confident. He had been born here and, now that he had inherited the family business, expected to die here too. It was his territory and he was known to one and all as the fixer, what the local people called 'an ear', someone who could arrange anything from a new word-processor to a child's birthday surprise, someone from whom there were no secrets.

Much of his information came from his shop, the biggest general store for miles around. Curtis's, as it was known, stocked everything: cotton wool, screwdrivers, seasonal fruit, parrot seed, videos. The pay-phone by the door was always busy with incoming and outgoing calls. Despite local rivalries, and the constant tension with the army, whose mainland recruits tramped up to his counter, Curtis manoeuvred skilfully through the minefields of conflicting loyalty and managed to be acceptable to all sides. If the Martians had landed in the wasteground beyond the ruined church and asked for a spokesman, nine out of ten would have directed them, without hesitation, to Curtis's door.

Curtis was unmarried and lived with his sister. At work or at leisure, his interests did not vary. He had to know; he had to find out. He was, he sometimes joked, the Recording Angel. He told people he was writing the history of the place, and during the long, dark winters when nothing stirred he would spend his evenings tape-recording interviews, teasing out memories and marvelling over photographs and souvenirs. Mary, his faithful ally, would transcribe the tapes and file the results in a library of ring-binders. Sometimes she would come home and find her brother standing by the bookshelf, running his fingers down the even row of black spines, and she could see he was savouring the power of his knowledge. 'Don't,' she said once. 'Don't what?' 'Don't frighten me.' He had laughed, but his laughter said he knew what she meant.

He never passed up an opportunity for a better source of news. He was one of the first to eat at Mr Hu's when his restaurant opened across the street. Mr Hu was honoured and delighted. Mr Curtis, he understood, could arrange anything. His guest glowed with a mysterious pride. That was what people said. Well then, Mr Hu wanted to know, with a fierceness that Curtis came to know as enthusiasm, where could he obtain food for his tropical fish? He pointed to the tank by the counter. Curtis was intrigued by the challenge. Two days later he presented Mr Hu with a packet containing three kinds of fish-food. Mr Hu was impressed. Here was an ally in a hostile land. Soon Curtis found that, alone in the neighbourhood, he had unique access to the local Chinese and their secrets. When, to celebrate the New Year, the year of the dragon, Mr Hu gave Curtis his own aquarium, their friendship was sealed.

Through Curtis's patronage, Mr Hu's became a popular meeting point. Smiling Mr Hu in his saffron shirt was so impenetrably foreign that even the most suspicious-minded customer felt able to speak freely there and the restaurant became an important junction on the network of Curtis's influence. Teenagers crowded in at all hours; hard-pressed mothers would order time-saving takeaways on Saturday nights; sometimes you would see foot patrols lounging against the wall outside, eating spare ribs; and late at night, when Mr Hu's fluorescent light flooded into the darkened street, the young men of the area might assemble there before heading on to an illegal dog- or cock-fight or an all-night disco.

The secret of Mr Hu's was its size. Apart from the red

plastic counter and the tropical fish in the corner, there were seats for a maximum of eight, two tables of four. People were always informally on the move, waiting for takeaways, or standing in line for a place at table. No one dawdled much over their food; no one complained. They made up for the inconvenience with talk. Meanwhile, Mr Hu and his wife hurried to and fro, obliging, unintelligible and utterly remote, witnessing every kind of transaction. Perhaps only Curtis knew how much they understood of what passed.

Now he hesitated on his doorstep in one last moment of indecision. If he had not been already late he might well have accepted the invitation of that brightly lit window and strolled up the road to gossip with Mr Hu about his plans for redevelopment while Mrs Hu and her two daughters hurried about the steaming kitchen. But Mary was keen on punctuality and tonight was an important occasion for her. He turned down the hill towards his car.

The day's rain carried a hint of new growth in the surrounding woods and fields but this did not lift his spirits. He yawned and looked up and down the pavement. Isabel's car was not there, and her light was off. Then he remembered that it was Wednesday. Curtis walked over to his own vehicle and opened the driver's door with a sigh, casually checking, front and back, before he did so. An outpatient from the hospital shuffled past, mumbling in a mad private language. This was a common sight. Sometimes they came into the house. Once he had found a couple making love on his bed.

For a moment, he could not even find the energy to switch on the engine and sat staring stupidly at the dashboard. He tried to remember when Isabel had been simply Mrs Harris, the wife of the man next door.

Tom Harris was a poet, but Curtis's interest in his new neighbour (what the older people, translating, called a 'blow-in') was not literary. In Harris, he had found a congenial drinking partner, someone of learning and connections with whom it was good to talk things over. They would sit for hours in local bars sharing brilliant, impossible schemes for the future regeneration of the town; it was one of Tom's fantasies that he would write and direct a film here, a slow, loving study of ordinary lives in which his good friend Joseph Curtis would play a special part.

In those days, to be honest, Curtis had not paid much attention to Isabel, probably because he found her reserved and, unlike her husband, whose family came from these parts, rather foreign. Her looks and intelligence made him nervous. So he stuck to pleasantries and treated the Harrises as a happy partnership, a common response among the locals in whose hearts poetry always had an honoured place. If he had examined his deeper feelings towards them he would perhaps have found a pang of envy for their domestic harmony: he, writing poems and reviews, giving readings and visiting literary festivals; she, apparently absorbed in her life with him, a cultured woman fully satisfied by the unexpected complexity, as she once put it, of country life.

And then this picture began to disintegrate before his eyes. Mr and Mrs Harris – Tom and Isabel as they had become – had moved into the little terraced house with the picture postcard back garden in a final attempt to save a marriage that was already on the rocks. Isabel's edgy, bright-eyed politeness, that many had put down to metropolitan nerves, was now explained as a face-saving mixture of anxiety and embarrassment. Occasionally, Curtis and his sister could hear Isabel's tearful entreaties to her husband through the party wall. People began to talk. It was such a shame; of course it had been too good to be true; if only she could have children; if only he would drink less, etc. Curtis, the man of secrets, heard it all, though never from Isabel.

Then, one day during the autumn, Curtis's habitual Sunday afternoon snooze had been interrupted by a faint knock at the door. He sat up, curious. The house was always open and the neighbours came in and out of it all day long. Such a knock was a cry for help from a stranger: he knew it would be her. He called out, but her reticence held; when he pulled open the front door she had come in like a bird with a broken wing.

19

Even in the gloom of the late afternoon he could see her face was swollen and flushed with crying. 'He's left me,' she said, and threw herself into his arms.

Curtis was scarcely equipped for this moment. As his many confidants knew well, he could find sympathy for anything, but there had to be distance too. Yet here was a reserved, self-possessed woman shaking convulsively against his shoulder. At first he was at a loss, and then he realised that this soft, warm creature with the smudgy wet eyes was hugging him as a child hugs a father and something deep inside him began to break down.

He seated her by the fire and made tea, as his mother would have done, and they began to talk, admitting to each other how slight their contact had been, up to this moment. 'That's how it is on the mainland,' she said. 'Neighbours are always the people we know least.' He asked her if she was homesick, and was startled by the directness of her reply. 'Home makes me sick,' she said, with a ghost of a laugh, 'but that's because I hate it over there. All that money and arrogance and stupidity and vulgarity.'

He had hardly poured the tea before she was speaking of herself, putting her thoughts into words without hesitation. She spoke as though she had not had a chance to speak in this way for ages and he guessed she had been lonely. Curtis, who found even the simplest emotions hard to express, whose upbringing had been devoted to not saying what he felt, and whose skill as an 'ear' depended on a chameleon tact, found himself fascinated by her candour. Hesitantly to start with, and then more freely, he began asking questions and then sharing mild confidences in a way that his sister would have considered impertinent, even rude.

He made more tea. She lit a cigarette. He could see she was already recovering at least some temporary composure, and he asked her why it had all gone wrong.

Hoping, she said, not to embarrass him, she described her life and marriage. He realised, as she spoke, the tea growing cold in the pot, the cigarette smoke rising between them, that although she had lived next door for over a year this was the first time they had talked alone together. He spoke this thought aloud.

'When I found Tom's letter I didn't know where to turn, I really didn't,' she replied. 'I'm sure Tom's told you terrible things about me – '

He protested.

' – but you always seemed sympathetic.' He recognised her ironic smile. 'So I thought I'd risk going over to the enemy.'

He said, quite seriously, that he was bad at taking sides. 'I'm glad you came here.' He smiled back and their eyes met briefly.

When Mary came home from the hospital he found himself suppressing a pang of regret. His sister, of course, read him like an open book, and told him he was crazy even to think of it. Isabel had gone, and they were sitting in the kitchen as usual. Mary referred to the local girls from whom it was generally expected that, in due course, her brother would make his choice.

Wide-eyed, fair-minded Mary would always be a spinster of the parish, the ubiquitous angel of mercy, so good she could walk on water, as the country people put it. As well as her work at the hospital, there was no charity she did not assist, no benefit she could not organise. When the latest atrocity sent shudders of fear and vengeance through the community, it was always Mary who, regardless of no-go areas, comforted the bereaved and visited the wounded. To the spreading of local goodness she was as indispensable as her brother was to the gathering of local intelligence, and there was hardly a soul who could not picture her wavy cornflower hair bobbing at bedside and graveside alike.

Curtis, whose unconscious heart told him he had no interest in those girls, scowled at his sister. 'It gets on my nerves sometimes, the idea that people know you better than you know yourself.' He got up to go.

'No one knows you, Joe. No one but me. That's why they think they trust you.' Mary began to clear away; moodily,

Curtis went and sat in the living-room, still thick with Isabel's cigarette smoke. Sometimes he felt oppressed by his sister's love for him.

He sighed now, as he had sighed then, started the engine and switched on the headlights. His beam caught flints of granite in the local stone. A half-blind old gentleman with a hat and stick was tapping along the road towards the light, but did not flinch.

Ignoring Mary's warnings, he became the self-appointed mainstay in Isabel's life. There were nights when she seemed so forlorn that he insisted she sleep over in the spare room at the back, the room his father had occupied during his last years. The courtesy of her brother's attentions persuaded Mary that this was only friendship, and she too began to find a satisfaction in the slow amelioration of Isabel's distress. Her own patients were so far beyond the reach of help it was rare to make any headway. With Isabel, she and Joe could detect almost daily improvement and take pleasure in that.

At first, they had half expected Tom Harris to return. He had not, Isabel told them, left her for anyone else. But when, one day after Christmas, she came round carrying an airmail letter with a row of foreign-looking stamps, Curtis knew they had reached a turning-point. It was shortly after the news that Tom had settled abroad that he defied his sister's wisdom and, choosing his moment, asked Isabel out for the evening.

She was, as he might have predicted, both nervous and self-possessed. They were standing on the pavement and she had been teasing him about his new car.

'Perhaps,' he hesitated, 'perhaps you'd like to risk a ride one day. With me.' He could see his reflection in the shiny red paint and the polished glass. A certain crumpled shabbiness made him more acceptable in the poorer parts of his territory: he was not exactly the image of the dashing young man spinning the girls about in an open-topped sports car.

She looked at him shyly. 'I'd love to,' she said, without elaboration.

'Perhaps,' he hesitated again, though the sentence was one

he had rehearsed, 'perhaps we could go to the new place that's just opened. They say it does good traditional cooking.' He paused; she said nothing. Had he gone too far? He almost panicked. 'What do you think?'

Now she smiled, as though making up her mind about something. 'That would be great,' she said.

When the evening came, they had taken the road he was on now, driving down the main street, past the school and the deserted factory, past the war memorial, and past the locked-up Institute, his latest acquisition. He had so many ideas about the building now that it was his, he said. If she was interested, he could show her the plans one day. She replied she would be delighted, and they drove on down the lane, past the ragged football pitch and up the hill towards the south. Here, the land became a rolling green maze of tracks and roads mapped only in the memories of the country people, the front line of the conflict. Turn a corner and you were as likely to run into an army road-block as a herd of cows and a boy with a stick.

The 'new place' Curtis had selected was the restaurant of a family hotel, recently reopened after a bomb attack. There was a strong smell of paint and everything about it was brand-new. The patron and his waitresses fussed over their customers, hill farmers in their Sunday best, with exaggerated hospitality. Curtis, clumsy with anxiety, stumbled over a chair. He seemed large and out of place. Isabel was the only person who did not seem ill at ease. They had hardly given their order before the door opened and a local politician, his wife and their two bodyguards came in and took a reserved table at the back of the dining-room.

'Joe Curtis.' The geniality was as much an advertisement as a greeting. Part of his jaw had been shot away in a botched attempt on his life and his miraculous escape gave him an air of invincibility that challenged Curtis's own self-esteem.

The restaurant fell silent. Curtis made the introductions, feeling awkward and annoyed. Always discreet, he had hoped, this evening, for some privacy in which perhaps he could speak his mind. Now here he was chatting to a man universally known as 'the Mouth'. It always disturbed Curtis to meet someone who shared his passion for information, and in a public place it made him tight-lipped and resentful.

Eventually, they settled down to their dinner, but Curtis's secret had been discovered and his confidence thrown. He found himself struggling through the conversation, speaking of everything but his real thoughts. After the main course had been taken away, he apologised. 'I'm sorry,' he said, 'I'm not making sense.'

She seemed to understand. 'It's allowed.' It was as though she was looking into him. 'You're not used to losing control.'

'Losing control?'

'Of the situation,' she added, with a silvery flirtatious laugh.

He blamed that laugh when, later, as they stood outside her front door, with the orange sodium light buzzing overhead, he suddenly managed to express his true feelings and make what he now considered to be his big mistake.

Curtis had that moment in his head now as he swung the car into the grounds of the hospital. Once, before scandal, decline and bankruptcy, this had been the home of the local grandee. Curtis had in his possession sepia photographs of the place in its heyday, a fine greystone mansion with young men and women of leisure posing on the lawn before the mystery of the wet-plate camera. Even now, the house and its uncared-for garden could not shake off the memory of those better times. Occasionally, as he came up the driveway, bumping over the rain-filled potholes and winding past cedars and rhododendrons, he liked to imagine himself a Victorian bigwig being driven to a candlelit soirée crowded with handsome women.

He sighed again, regretfully. If he closed his eyes, he could still recover the sensation of her kiss. Even now he could only half believe that she had not pushed him away. Then he heard her say: 'Why don't we go inside?'

He managed a joke. 'Your place or mine?'

Mary was away on a refresher course; both doors were open; there was a choice. A dark, angry, confused part of him wanted to defy all that he had been taught, to turn his back on his sister and her wisdom. As he crossed Isabel's threshold, leading her by the hand, the words of the Ten Commandments jangled in his head and he answered back that he did not care. There was something in his blood he could not stop, something about the weakness of it all that made him feel temporarily strong and free.

The next morning there was a knock on his door as he was preparing to go out and open up the shop for the day. It was Isabel, fresh and smiling as though nothing had happened. 'I just wanted to thank you for a lovely evening,' she said.

Curtis began to mumble an apology.

'Don't be silly,' she said. 'It was very sweet of you.' She put her arms round him and gave an affectionate hug. 'It was my fault,' she said. 'Don't even think about it.'

Then she had gone, as elfin as ever, and he had been left alone with his doubts and his desires and his regrets. He had spent the day, indeed every day since then, obsessively turning over his actions in his head, trying to tell himself he was not in love, a soul in hell.

When Mary came back from her course and asked him his news she saw instinctively what had happened. 'She's a sad, weak woman and you're a great big fool,' she said. 'Don't say I didn't warn you.' He looked at her miserably. 'You'll get over it,' she added, with the decisiveness of one who has long ago given up all hope of romance.

There she was now, closing the front door behind her. Inside, distantly, he could hear the cries of the patients. She came towards him, a woman who knew her own mind and usually spoke it, her every step full of certainty. Tonight, she was wearing anxiety like a reproach. 'We're late,' she said, kissing him good evening. He replied that it was only just after six, but she brushed him aside. 'You know how that place fills up. I want a good view.'

'We'll be all right. Don't fuss so.' Sometimes, in his worst moments, he had a vision of this exchange becoming the pattern of the rest of their lives.

Now she was putting on make-up in the mirror. He turned on the radio. '. . . is just coming in of a bomb explosion . . . no one has yet claimed responsibility, but the authorities believe – '

She switched it off.

'Is there no end to this?' she said.

Curtis did not answer. His thoughts were elsewhere.

Isabel did not like driving; she liked being driven. One of the worst practical features of Tom's departure from her life was the necessity of getting behind the wheel again. Her answer was to become a driver of habit. She always took the same route to the studio, and the same route back. A routine journey minimised her anxieties and allowed her the time for her own thoughts.

Tonight she was thinking about Curtis. She reflected: am I so lost I did not know where to go next? So poor I cannot enjoy the simple things? I want love; why should I deny that? Why should he? It was only a moment. I said, Why not? and he said, I'm weak too. That was all. It was no big deal. I thanked him. Somewhere we all need someone. If I made a mistake, it was to underestimate the feelings of a shy person.

It was in such a daze of introspection, steering through the dark, that Isabel realised that the road ahead was blocked. Looking in her mirror, she could see headlights snaking behind her. The traffic was now almost at a standstill; there was no backing out; she was going to miss the news. She put the car into neutral and tried to find a mood of patience in herself. She wondered if the delay was connected to the bombing: the army often exploited the rush-hour to make random searches.

That was the odd, slightly exhilarating, edge to living here. The familiar experiences of home – a traffic jam, a siren in the night – had unfamiliar explanations, usually associated with violence. A street that might have been the setting for a television sitcom could turn out to house a terrorist with half a dozen murders to his name and conscience; a landscape that epitomised the pastoral might conceal a remote-controlled culvert bomb capable of blasting a ten-ton truck a hundred yards; that harmless lay-by on the clifftop might be a dumping ground for the death squads' mutilated victims. Some people talked about a war, but if it was a war it was only partially declared, with many on both sides trying to keep the peace, pretending there was no trouble. Was it possible, she sometimes wondered, that they needed this trauma in their lives just as the tortured and the torturer are said to need each other?

The car inched forward down a long avenue of Spanish chestnuts. Isabel's destination was three miles away, on the other side of town. The only short-cut was through a no-go area littered with burnt-out vehicles that even armoured personnel carriers preferred to avoid. She fumbled for a tape in the glove compartment but when the voice of the poet began chanting through the darkness (her old life with Tom still popped up at surprising moments) she ejected the cassette in a hurry, and this time found Haydn.

It was not a road-block. There was something happening in one of the churches. She could see families of up-country people in rough clothes hurrying through the darkness like the medieval faithful. Muddy farm vehicles were pulling up and dropping elderly passengers. There were cripples in wheelchairs; an old woman with a walking frame was inching painfully through the crush; a small girl with a lollipop was leading a blind man down the middle of the road. Two policemen were trying, unsuccessfully, to direct the traffic.

A young man in a donkey jacket, his face blue with acne, was passing down the line of waiting cars handing out publicity. Isabel put her hand out of the window and took a flyer. 'Russ Hickey's Ministry,' she read. 'The country and western gospel of hope and salvation.' She had never heard of Russ Hickey, but she was curious. On impulse, she parked her car in a cul-de-sac and joined the throng, wondering if this was not perhaps the subject for her next week's broadcast.

Isabel shuffled with the crowd through the door into the church, drawn by the distant radiance of the altar. In the expectant, fervent hubbub, her complicated agnostic feelings seemed almost in bad taste. As she took her bearings in the fug of damp winter clothes, wondering where to sit, she realised with dismay that she was standing only a few feet from Curtis and his sister. She was about to move away from the main aisle when he turned and saw her. She could not escape his eye. There was a moment of mutual panic and then his defiant, wounded smile spread across his face and she, determined to encourage an air of normality, smiled resolutely back.

Isabel made her way across. No other move was possible. Curtis was bending down, warning his sister. As they all met, the organ began playing 'Onward Christian Soldiers' softly in the background. She and Mary shook hands. There was a fractional awkwardness and then he kissed her politely. Mary said: 'Why are you here?'

'I was just passing. I was intrigued.'

'Yes, I suppose you would be. Will you be telling us about it on the radio?'

'I might,' said Isabel, unable to stop herself, 'if I'm short of material.'

Mary glanced protectively at her brother, as if to say, I told you so, and then added: 'It must be so hard to write about a place you don't know.'

Curtis intervened with a few distracting comments about Russ Hickey. As she listened, taking in the scene around her, Isabel recognised (it was awkward to admit this) that he was still in love with her. Looking into herself she knew she could not find half his persistence.

Curtis was explaining Hickey's career. He was a country and western singer, a minor American star who, having seen the light and been born again, was now dedicating his music to God and his life to his mission. This was his third visit. His plangent ballads of exile, loss and separation had always been popular and, as a preacher, he was credited with several minor miracles.

The organ began to swell, joined by snare-drums and the rattle of tambourines. The tempo quickened. In front of the altar, massed behind banks of plastic flowers, a fresh-faced choir in magenta surplices rose to its feet, followed by the congregation. As the hymn reached a crescendo, Isabel was aware of a lean figure in a cowboy hat, carrying a guitar, moving modestly through the crowd from the back. The last notes surged with a clash of cymbals, and the choirmaster took the microphone. 'Ladies and gentlemen, brothers and sisters, I ask you to clap your hands joyfully together to give a big welcome to that mighty missionary for the Lord, the Reverend Russell Hickey!'

There was a spotlight on the podium and now Hickey was standing in it, blinking slightly, an oddly diffident, uncertain figure, fiddling with his guitar strap and quietly acknowledging the waves of applause breaking over him from every side.

As the clapping died away, Hickey seemed to find a new confidence and power. He stretched out his arms towards the light and lifted his face to the heavens. 'Brothers and sisters in Christ – ' The church was abruptly hushed. 'Brothers and sisters in Christ, let us praise the Lord.'

The congregation mumbled back: 'Let us praise the Lord.'

A smile of satisfaction passed across Hickey's face. 'Amen.'

The people settled in their pews and Hickey stood there watching. He was quite still; he said nothing. Perhaps a minute passed; he shuffled his notes; he waited. The church was deathly still. When the tension was becoming unbearable, Hickey leant towards the microphone and spoke, almost whispered. 'Fellow sinners,' he said.

Then he began.

Isabel took notes, scribbling on the back of her programme, ignoring Mary's frown of disapproval.

He was glad, he said, to be among them once again. It was a privilege to do the Lord's work here. The children of light were at war with the armies of the anti-Christ and it was both an honour and a responsibility to bring his mission of hope and salvation to these shores. Yes, the eyes of the world were on them, each and every one, and it was their duty to listen. 'I say unto you tonight that man is born in sin, but the word of the Lord offers us all a vision of salvation: "Marvel not what I say unto ye, ye must be born again."'

Here Hickey broke off and invited the congregation to offer their voices to God and their pockets to the furtherance of his good work. Volunteers with plastic buckets fanned out through the church. Hickey played a chord on his guitar. Organ, drums and tambourines took their cue and the faithful clapped in time to the music. The refrain echoed down the nave, and Isabel felt the rhythm and the excitement resound through the darkness. She looked about her. Hickey had begun to reach his congregation and there was 'revival' in the air. The hymn ended, their offerings were dedicated to the Lord, and Hickey launched into his main address.

'Make no mistake, my friends. There is a hell.' He looked down at the silent rows, and emphasised the words with his battered scripture. 'The hell that I preach is the hell that Jesus preached, the hell this Bible speaks of, the hell that's revealed in all its terror and torment in the word of God.' He paused impressively. 'Only the fool says there is no hell. At the end of every life, there is a reckoning. Galatians six, seven: "Whatsoever a man soweth, that shall he also reap." At the end of every life, there is heaven with Christ or hell without him, and let me tell you God's truth: we are all sinners on the way to hell. And when I pray, as I shall pray for you-all tonight, I pray: "Lord, save us from hell."'

Isabel could sense the congregation growing absorbed in Hickey's words. Here was a voice from on high, a voice from across the sea, from the world to which so many aspired, a voice they trusted, telling them they were God's chosen. She watched the expressions on the faces round her. Dour, meaty-faced town burghers in shiny suits next to loyal wives in floral dresses; country people with broken veins and sunburns; tired-looking mothers and fidgety children: a thousand separate thoughts united by the figure of the Reverend Russell Hickey.

How many sorrows can you hide? Within a month, or a week, or even a day, there were people in this church who would be violently dead, cornered at a road-block, or blown up in an ambush, or executed at home in front of their wives and children. Many of this congregation would walk in the funeral procession, as they had walked in countless processions before. These faces were like stone walls, refusing to admit defeat, and when they smiled it was like the light of a winter sun on a granite tombstone. She sensed the volatility of their pride and pain.

Hickey's invigorating words were resounding in their ears. 'This, my friends, is the necessary sacrifice, the final sacrifice, the great tide of Calvary, the blood of atonement.' Isabel looked about her. Yes – a thousand times yes – they were the footsoldiers of the Lord, the armies of the Apocalypse wrestling with Satan and the forces of darkness, and one day soon they would march into the Promised Land . . .

Suddenly it was all over. Hickey had finished. There was music again, triumphal and all-conquering. Hickey stepped down into the front row of his audience and began to pass down a line of cripples and old people, laying on hands and speaking softly to each in turn while the stony faces behind opened in a roar:

> Would you be free from your burden of sin?
> There's power in the blood, power in the blood.
> Would you o'er evil a victory win?
> There's wonderful power in the blood.

3

Stephen lay in his hotel bed and listened to the music floating
up from the disco downstairs. He was sweaty and sleepless
with the heat of the room; the thermostat was broken and the
window behind the dusty grey muslin was painted shut. There
was not even the solace of darkness; a constant movement of
cars in the yard outside threw floating rectangles of light across
the ceiling, trapping his thoughts.

It was strange to be back on the road again, but he was
beginning to enjoy the impersonal solitude of his hotel room,
and he could feel himself being drawn back into his old ways.
When he had checked in earlier he had phoned the office with
the new contact number, deciding to save his comments about
the risk department's planning skills for later. 'All well?' said
his assistant brightly. 'Just fine,' he replied, and rang off. After
a moment's hesitation, he resolved not to call Louise. After
all, she was, in her own words, 'only a sort of girlfriend', an
arrangement that seemed to suit them both. He sat on the edge
of the bed with a plastic beaker of scotch from the mini-bar
and wondered what she was doing that night. He told himself
he did not really care. He was about to join the pre–dinner
reception party when he heard singing in the corridor outside.

Curious, he pressed his face to the peep-hole in the door and
found three of his distinguished charges serenading their
colleague, the general. 'Happy birthday to you, happy birthday
to you . . .' The singers were in lounge suits. The general, in
a blue blazer and grey casuals, was trying to shush their
serenade. 'Please, gentlemen.'

As Stephen watched, a waiter passed between them and the
singing faltered. There was a flutter of applause, and a voice
out of sight said: 'Speech.'

'Gentlemen.' The general tried again. 'I have to pay a brief visit to this fellow Mallory. I will see you all in the bar.'

The general's face loomed before him; there was a polite knock. After a calculated pause Stephen opened the door.

The singers had moved away towards the elevator and the general was now alone, cutting the dapper, composed figure of a quiz show host. 'Sorry to bother you, Mallory. I just wanted to introduce myself. Richard Windermere. If you don't mind I'll come in for just a moment.'

Stephen had hardly stepped back before he was pushing into the room, as if inspecting the mess. Windermere had a reputation as something of a military intellectual, and had published a number of books, including a strategy for counter-terrorist warfare. He was an obvious target. Stephen wondered if his peremptory manner had something to do with this anxiety.

'I hope my colleagues didn't disturb you.' He seemed slightly embarrassed. 'It happens to be my birthday, you see, and – well, enough of that. This isn't a social call.' He paused. 'I expect you heard the bomb.'

'I thought it best to keep quiet about it.'

'Absolutely. We don't want to alarm the civilians.'

Stephen offered him a drink, apologising for the label. 'I'm afraid this isn't exactly five-star service, but we decided to switch hotels at the last minute.'

'A tip-off?' Windermere looked concerned.

'Just a routine precaution,' Stephen lied.

'Fair enough.' The general raised his glass. 'Cheers.'

'Good luck,' said Stephen, repeating the old formula. Memories of his time in the East came briefly to mind, the hours he had spent at the bar with old Asia hands, drinking brandy and ginger and hearing tall stories about wars and coups.

The general tasted his drink and frowned. 'God knows why I agreed to join this committee. Frankly, the idea of sipping sweet sherry with those Heritage Trust poofters is my idea of hell. I suppose I was afraid retirement would be boring.' His humourless laugh was like a bark. 'Boring? I've never been

33

busier. Charities, boards, lectures, you name it.' He directed a curious look across the room. 'Aren't you down to give a lecture somewhere soon?' Stephen admitted this was so. The general was searching his memory. 'I've also seen your name in one or two bibliographies, haven't I? Some book about the military and the media?'

'They published my thesis.' He became evasive. 'I don't have much time for writing now.'

'I seem to remember it was rather good.'

'When I started this job I found that theory is rather different from practice.'

'My dear boy, never forget the old Chinese proverb. No military plan ever survives contact with the enemy.'

Stephen poured another finger of scotch.

'I remember,' the general went on, settling comfortably into his chair, 'when I first came here back in – well, back in the good old days – I had a neat academic theory for what was happening, and was full of nonsense about winning hearts and minds. In fact, I made quite a bloody fool of myself trying to make the facts fit the theory. Then I realised it was simply a roughhouse like anywhere else and I began to make sense of things. In those days, you knew who the enemy was. You respected him and he respected you. Now – who knows? Anything could happen.'

'So you don't believe in "normalisation"?'

'Balls to "normalisation".' He almost glared at Stephen. 'No offence, but if it wasn't for so-called "normalisation" the army would be handling this little trip of ours. In my time we wouldn't have given you freelancers the time of day.'

'Of course, we didn't exist then.' Stephen wondered, with a tiny prickle of irritation, where the conversation was leading.

'My point exactly. There's simply no room for the serving professional any more. Everything's been privatised and that means putting profit before duty. In my day, we'd never have allowed a lot of old buffers like me on the loose here. Much too risky.'

Stephen felt his professional calm pierced by a sudden shaft of annoyance. 'If you're saying that the ministry should not have given its approval – '

'What am I saying?' The general was commanding but still affable. 'I suppose I'm saying I hope to God you know what you're doing, Mallory.'

'Perhaps you'd like to check with my superiors,' said Stephen, coolly picking up the bedside telephone.

Windermere's retreat was swift and tactical. 'Look here, I don't want to make waves but you need to know that mine is the one scalp out there those boys would really like. It's a sort of accolade, of course, but it means I do have to be careful.'

'Let me reassure you, general,' Stephen replied, now at his most conciliatory. 'I'm well aware that you are the most important person on the tour.'

Windermere's pleasure sweetened his anxiety into modesty. 'Well, the most vulnerable. Let's put it that way.' He put his glass down. 'When I was here before one of my duties was to tour the hospitals after a big blast. Until you've visited a plastic surgery unit, you can have no idea what high explosives can do to people. It's not a pretty sight.'

'No, I don't suppose it is.'

The general found his stick and grappled to his feet. 'Well, I must join the party. Glad we had our little chat. No hard feelings, I hope. If you need any advice, just let me know. I'll be pleased to help. Keeps my hand in, if you know what I mean.'

Stephen watched him turn towards the door. He supposed this was the way with fear, that it reached everyone in the end. Once you plant a thought it quickly becomes a worry. He found himself wondering if he had not been too nonchalant with Major Potter. The idea that the risk department thought Smith could have handled this assignment was astonishing. A memorandum was already taking shape in his head. As Windermere reached the door, Stephen picked up his pocket dictaphone.

'Happy birthday, general,' he called out.

'Happy bollocks,' said the general good-naturedly, and moved into the corridor.

Now it was late, and he lay in bed restlessly revolving phrases from his dictation in his head. He poured another miniature scotch, and then another, and wondered whether it was too late to ring Louise. And what if . . .? Only the other day she had said: 'You can't always assume I'm alone when you call.'

Louise. The woman he had known, on and off, between trips, for five years. The woman whose clothes and make-up were scattered through his flat, whose scent was on his sheets. The woman he did not love . . . Once they both started cheating, he knew it was over. He wondered who she was with tonight. Did she say the same things? Did she 'honey' and 'baby' and 'darling' all her men? Was this jealousy? He had made no real claim on her and she had asked for none in return. That, of course, was the problem.

The room was oppressively hot and stuffy. He switched on the bedside light and looked at his watch. A few minutes past midnight. A rhythmic bass was still thumping away down below. He got up with a yawn and went over to the mirror by the dressing table. He studied his nakedness and decided he was getting flabby. A new exercise regime was called for. His years in foreign hotels with time to kill by the pool had left a trace of a suntan, a biscuity discoloration that ended just below his navel. There was a trick he often used in the East. He went into the bathroom and turned on the shower, cold tap only; then, gasping with shock, he stepped into the icy jet. One, two, three . . . He counted to twenty, and then he was rubbing himself down with the rough white hotel towel, refreshed and tingling with a Spartan virtue.

On duty, so to speak, he always wore a suit, but for this trip he had also packed some casual clothes – a pair of jeans, a soft designer shirt and a sweater – and now, certain that all the members of his party would be in their rooms, he rummaged gratefully in his hold-all, dressed quickly, and followed the noise downstairs.

Even at this hour, the hotel foyer was jammed with teenagers. One or two stared at him, but once he had a drink in his hand he could linger by the bar and survey the scene at leisure. He had always been good at becoming part of the background.

The girls were in party clothes, in groups. He was no fashion expert, but there was something provincial and out-of-date about their get-up. A few of the boys were roaming about with beer glasses, eyeing the talent. Others had collected in a gang by the route to the toilets and as the girls passed they cracked jokes and made predictable suggestions. It wasn't Friday, but most were still looking for a result. The incessant beat of the disco, a hell's mouth of strobe lights guarded by a sullen-looking DJ, kept the dance floor crowded. In the darker parts, a few couples were engaged in desperate kissing.

He was reminded of wartime newsreels, off-duty soldiers and their girlfriends going cheek-to-cheek in the jive halls of blacked-out cities. In its own way, this was a war zone. What blasted streets did these revellers come from? How many bricks and Molotov cocktails had they thrown at the security forces? He liked to think that he had seen everything, but these faces were young and old at the same time in a way that disturbed him. They were kids whose experience of the world was expressed in fire and blood and tears. Was it just his fancy that he saw in their eyes as they danced a reckless frenzy of enjoyment?

Two girls, blondes, came up to the bar and ordered Coca-Colas. When he smiled at them they looked at each other flirtatiously and smiled back. 'You staying here?' said one. She was wearing a sweetheart necklace with 'Barry' picked out in turquoise.

'That's right.'

The girl said something to her friend, as though Stephen was not there, then returned to him, with a quick glance over her shoulder at the crowd. 'You a journalist or something?'

Lies came easily. 'Yes,' he said.

'Will you put us in your paper?' asked the second girl, lowering her eyes.

Stephen shrugged non-committally and changed the subject. 'Do you like it here?'

'It's okay,' said the girl with the necklace. A serious, defensive look came over her. 'Of course we like it here. It's our home.'

'And where do you come from?' asked the quiet girl.

Stephen hesitated. How should he answer? He did not exactly feel part of the mainland, but he was no longer an expatriate. There was a time, before his recent crisis, when he had spent so much time in the air that his accountant had suggested, only half joking, that his principal residence for tax purposes should be the first class cabin of a jumbo jet. 'Me?' he said, after a moment's thought. 'Let's just say I'm from all over.'

They seemed disappointed. 'All you people are the same,' said the first. 'You never give a straight answer.'

The quiet one asked, daringly, if he had a girlfriend.

'Yes,' he said.

'Missing her, are you?'

'Does it look like it?' He looked at them frankly. 'What about you?'

The two girls thought this was very provocative and amusing and whispered together for a few moments. 'What about us?' challenged the one with the necklace.

'Well – who's Barry?' He saw the look of panic and surprise and realised he had gone too far. 'So you're here on your own?' he said, quickly addressing her friend.

She looked up from her drinking straw. 'Oh yes, we're just cruising,' she said, and laughed.

'She lives here,' said the first, coolly. 'Her dad's the manager.'

'I saw you arrive this evening.' The girl watched his surprise with amusement.

He was about to explain himself when they were joined at the bar by two young men. They seemed to know the girls. They both had close-cropped hair and wore identical leather jackets and blue jeans, very tight. One had LOVE/HATE tattooed on the back of his hand and played with a bunch of keys like a rosary. He appeared to be the leader.

'Does he want a massage?' asked the boy, kissing the girl with the necklace, but not looking at Stephen. His friend stood behind him, the light of hero-worship in his eyes.

'I haven't asked him yet.'

The boy was incredibly young, but his expression was dead. Even when he turned to Stephen, he seemed not to see him and his voice was cold and flat. 'We've got a place where you can have fun,' he said. 'You look like a bloke who could handle a bit of fun,' he observed neutrally. 'Doesn't he?' he added, turning to his friend and punching him in the solar plexus.

'Fuck you.' He was winded but laughing. The girls looked on, hugging each other in mock-horror.

'On the house,' said the boy, confronting Stephen directly.

He was puzzled, doubtful. What was happening? He felt hustled and apprehensive. 'I'm not sure I quite understand,' he began.

'It's okay,' said the quiet girl, with a confidential smile.

The boy with the keys took him by the arm, quite firmly. 'We'll have to hurry,' he said. 'They'll close soon.'

'Sure,' said Stephen decisively, putting his glass down. Memories of nights in the East crowded back. The deliciously unbearable surrender of the senses. 'Why not?' The question was for himself, but rhetorical. It was a stupid risk – his colleagues would call it crazy – but he was bored and he didn't care. Besides, he fancied an adventure and tonight he felt lucky. Secretly, he wanted to prove to himself he was not fortune's fool. He smiled inwardly: if anything happened to him, the irony would not be lost on the office.

The group broke up. 'See you later,' said the girls. 'See you, doll.' 'Later, babe.' 'See you.'

Stephen followed the two boys behind the bar into the darkened hotel kitchens. Once they were alone, the boy with the tattoo put out his hand. 'Skylark,' he said, speaking with something like animation for the first time. 'And this is my good friend Mister Speed.' They both shook hands. It was rather odd, but Stephen felt better.

They came out into a cul-de-sac at the back of the hotel. The rain had stopped; it was a cold night with stars. Stephen tensed himself for danger, but the two boys seemed quite at home in the shadows and their manner did not threaten.

Within a few hundred yards they were lost in a maze of backstreets, blocked by crash barriers, the only evidence of the emergency. They turned a corner.

'And this is where the fun starts,' said Skylark, pointing.

The house they were approaching was like all the other houses in the street except that at the edge of its heavily curtained windows there was a faint glow of yellow light. Stephen and his two escorts walked quickly up to the front door.

Speed, the junior, pressed his mouth confessionally to the intercom. 'It's Skylark,' he said. On the buzzer, the door clicked open and they went in.

'If it isn't Mister Speed himself.' A short, bespectacled, elderly man with a bald head and lugubrious jowls, dressed in a maid's uniform, stepped forward to greet them. He seemed completely at ease among the bric-à-brac and conservatory plants cluttering the hallway. A lurid oil diptych, a representation of cunnilingus and fellatio, was hung like an icon over the fireplace. There were coals in the grate, glowing quietly. It was very hot; there was a dew of perspiration on his wrinkled pink forehead. 'The one and only Skylark,' he said, kissing him on the cheek.

'Evening, Philip.'

Philip looked over his glasses at Stephen. 'What's on the menu tonight, boys?'

As in a comic routine, they both pointed to their visitor. 'Over here on a trip,' explained Skylark, 'and looking for a bit of fun.'

'They offered me a massage,' said Stephen, interrupting. It seemed easier to comply with the mood of the place than insist on being taken back to the hotel.

40

'Oh ho,' said Philip, 'the Queen's whatsit.' He gestured with a soft, jewelled hand. 'Step up this way if you please, sir. Step this way.'

He pulled aside a faded blue velvet curtain and Stephen, following, came into a long, bleak corridor with two or three doors, all shut. A dusty gilt Buddha and some chipped mirrors attempted an atmosphere of oriental mystery, but the effect was cheap and tatty. There was no one about. As they crossed into an annexe, a chilly prefab extension to the house, there was a strange, joyless laugh from somewhere close at hand, and Stephen was involuntarily reminded of the fairground ghost trains of childhood outings from school.

Philip stopped at a half-open door. 'Monica, my dear,' he said. 'This is Stephen. He's come for a bit of fun.' He turned to his client and pointed him forward.

Stephen went in alone, closing the door behind him. Like the corridor, the room was strangely functional, comfortable but not plush, with a linoleum floor. There was a chinoiserie screen in front of a plain white porcelain hand-basin, a large couch heaped with chocolate-brown pillows, and a low light burning in the corner.

Monica was standing by the couch in a Red Cross outfit, pale and silent and exhausted. She was, he guessed, hardly thirteen. She handed him a towel without a word and indicated the chair behind the screen. This was a long way from his expectations, but again, it seemed easier not to protest. He undressed quickly, wrapped the towel round his waist, and walked in his bare feet across to the couch. He shivered. The one-bar electric fire by the screen did little to take the chill off the room. In the absence of instruction, he lay down on his stomach, resting his head on a pillow. The linen carried the stale smell of hair oil and perfume. Monica bent over him, apparently indifferent to his nakedness. Her fingers were cold and inexpert; she was embarrassingly bad. She gave little of the usual pleasure, the elusive luxury of anonymous comfort. He tried to make conversation but her replies were monosyllabic. After a few minutes of awkward squeezing and rubbing,

41

he sat up and asked her how long she had been working for Philip. 'I don't work here,' she said. 'It's my mum comes here really, but she's off sick.'

She seemed unmoved by her admission. She was like a child actor with lines in a grown-up play she did not understand. After a while, overcome by the sense of absurdity, he asked her to stop. She did not seem upset.

'What about Skylark?' he said, getting up.

'He's Philip's pet,' she replied, almost chatty. 'My mum says he's good.'

'I suppose he's gay.'

She shrugged. 'He's whatever you want, Philip says.' She smiled. 'That's why he likes him.' She rubbed her finger and thumb together. 'More money.'

Stephen finished dressing, thanked her again, and creaked back down the corridor to the hall. The two boys were playing cards together and gossiping with Philip. Skylark glanced up. 'Nice bit of fun, then?' It was impossible to know from his expression if he was being ironic.

Stephen looked at him coolly. 'She says I should have had you.'

'Now there's a proposition,' said Philip.

'Shut up, you silly old queen,' said Skylark.

'One of these days, my dear, I'm going to have to speak to your superiors about you.' He winked at Stephen. 'Sometimes I think you forget that we're both kept women.'

Skylark's eyes were like cement, but he did not retaliate. 'Don't pay any attention to him,' he said finally, throwing in his hand.

To change the subject, Stephen fumbled for his wallet. 'How much do – ?'

Skylark cut him short. He seemed offended. 'I said it was on the house,' he said, getting up. 'Don't you trust me?'

It was a strange challenge. 'Of course I trust you,' Stephen replied.

'Good,' said Skylark, with an odd smile. 'You never know.

One day I might need a reference.' He showed Stephen to the door. 'Mister Speed, will you take our guest home?' He was recovering his sense of humour. 'I hear he has an early start tomorrow.'

4

Isabel loved country houses. She liked the marriage of nature and civilisation. She knew about the pain and squalor of the past, but show her a well proportioned room and her imagination turned to elegance and luxury. She was pleased with the idea of restraint that concealed passion. In her fantasy life, she was the mistress of such a place, orchestrating witty and dangerous liaisons, entertaining the circle of her intimate friends with the leisured woman's indifference to night and day.

As she rattled down the drive in her old yellow Volkswagen, past a standing lake and through a mile or more of rolling parkland, she was joyous with anticipation. When she caught sight of the great white façade, gleaming like a wedding-cake in the pale spring sunshine, she felt her spirits lift again. She was going to enjoy herself today.

Years ago, as students, she and Tom had spent an idyllic summer cataloguing the library at a stately home on the mainland. They were given rooms in the converted stables and ate with the family retainers. At weekends they were free to do what they liked. Tom learned to fly-fish with the gamekeeper's son, developed a taste for black pudding, and wrote some of the poems that first caught the attention of the literary establishment. Isabel had simply enjoyed the wilderness of the gardens, the mysterious rural tranquillity, and the windy reaches of the surrounding purple moor.

There was a maze in the garden, with high, dense privet hedges and in the middle of the maze an open space with a bench, facing south. Sometimes, when her work in the library was done for the day, and the sun was still slanting high in the summer sky, she would find her way, not easily, to the heart of the maze, and sit and read and ponder her happiness with

Tom and think, Here I am in the middle of this puzzle, making sense of things. We shall get married and have children, and he will be a famous poet and I shall be his loving wife and best critic, and we shall live gladly together, strong, intimate and successful. There were moments in this dreamy solitude when the music of her hopes drew her to her feet and she would float in a slow dance down the long green confusing corridors, full and vacant and airy with happiness.

Looking back on those days, she could see now that they were innocents. In their careless ignorance, they thought they were immortal. They had walked as children through the woods and seen none of the demons – boredom, disappointment and infidelity. Isabel was an optimist, not given to regrets, but it was impossible not to reflect on the ironies of growing up, the poignant mixing of knowledge with desire, ambition frustrated by experience.

Had their difficulties started when Tom decided it was his obligation to come back home? The military occupation's remorseless grip on his people's lives persuaded him he was needed here. Isabel acknowledged that the crisis was good copy and that he was missing the story. At first, it had been an adventure. What neither of them anticipated was the impact the return would have on Tom. It brought out moods she had only glimpsed before, awakened preoccupations that fed a dark vein of fantasy, stirred loyalties that she could neither share nor understand, made him increasingly morose and unreachable, and sent him back deeper into drink. It was only then that Isabel realised she was a foreigner here.

The little car crunched on the gravel as she followed the freshly painted arrows towards the car-park, a deserted area to the side of the main house. The press release on the seat beside her stated that the restoration would not be made public until the end of the month. Journalists were welcome to have previews 'by arrangement'. This turned out to be more difficult than she expected. Whenever she telephoned, the curator was away; when, finally, she had proposed arriving unannounced, the voice at the other end had made no objection. So here she was.

There was no one about, even now. She locked the car and strolled towards the back of the house for a view. The sky was as clear as a diamond. She wandered down an avenue of stripling limes. Even the formal garden was new. Tiny plants and shrubs, carefully labelled and bedded in nests of woodbark and manure, indicated the pattern of a horticultural blueprint. Someone, miraculously, was building for the future and thinking of generations as yet unborn. She paused to take in the scene. The stonework on the balustrades and terraces of the great house was bone-white in the sunshine. After the ugly monotony of towns and villages protected against terrorist attack, the sandbags, barbed wire, and corrugated iron, it was like stepping into a dreamscape, a lost world of harmony and peace.

Suddenly there was a shout. Someone was leaning out of an upstairs window and appeared to be waving at her. She turned without haste and walked back towards the house, wondering what would happen now. This was precisely the pleasure of getting out and about, the unexpected.

Now she could see a figure on the terrace. He – she assumed it was a he – was not hurrying; in fact, he was standing there, as if expecting her to come towards him. As she drew closer, intrigued by his stillness, she decided this must be the curator. He was rather short, with a friendly beard. In his hunting green duffel coat, he looked a bit like a cartoon dwarf. There was an obedient young Labrador at his heels.

'Hello,' said Isabel, putting out her hand and taking the initiative. 'Isabel Rome. I rang a few times to arrange a press preview but you were away on business.' She smiled sympathetically. 'You must have been very busy getting everything ready for the opening, Mister – '

'Bennett. Christopher Bennett.' They shook hands. The dog bounced round them.

'Your office said to come anyway – '

'Who – who said?' He was appealingly vague and forgetful.

46

'I'm very sorry, Miss – er – ' His eyes were darting beadily backwards and forwards, as if a closer inspection would surrender a clue.

'Isabel Rome,' she repeated, with careful emphasis.

Now, as she had hoped, a look of recognition came into his face. 'On the radio?' She nodded. 'Oh – how interesting. My wife and I – ' He interrupted himself. 'Look, I'm terribly sorry, Miss Rome, but you really can't come here today. The house is closed.' He seemed to disappoint himself with his words. 'We've got a very special party and I've been told there are strict security arrangements. You'll have to come back another time.'

There was a side of Isabel that welcomed such moments. The challenge to get the story. She adopted her most crestfallen expression. She regretted the early start and the long drive. She referred doubtfully to her unforgiving producer. If Mr Bennett had heard her broadcasts he would know how topical she had to be. She paused to let him repeat his wife's enthusiasm for the programme. 'She will be sorry,' he said. (They were strolling across the gravel towards her car.) It did seem a shame, he was saying. She murmured something about good publicity and not staying long. He looked at his watch. It was just eleven. 'I suppose . . .' Isabel fixed him with a bright, expectant smile. He was hesitating; he was lost. 'How long would you need?'

'If I could walk round with you – I have my tape recorder in the car here – I'm sure we could do it in half an hour.'

Bennett's good nature and a certain curiosity towards his surprise visitor got the better of his discretion. 'Come on,' he said.

When the front door closed behind her and Isabel looked up at the hammer-beam ceiling in the gloomy hallway, with her guide murmuring informatively at her side, she thought to herself that it was not perhaps the greatest victory, but it was something.

The curator soon forgot that he was supposed to be otherwise engaged. The house and its restoration was really his life and he was delighted to have 'a woman of culture and intelligence', as he put it, with whom to share his enthusiasm. Isabel, not immune to flattery herself, was careful to nourish his pride. Soon she was also settling his anxiety. She discovered, as they passed into the first of the formal rooms – a magnificent chamber hung with Flemish tapestries – that the imminent visit was an inspection by the trust that had sponsored the refurbishment. So there was a lunch to host, security to worry about and a guided tour to conduct. 'I just hope I don't forget my lines in front of all those distinguished people.'

'This can be your dress rehearsal,' she replied. 'I find it's easy to talk about things you love.'

He seemed reassured by this and escorted Isabel into the library, a spacious, sunlit room with a fine drum table and an antique globe in the window. The books, a country gentleman's collection, filled every wall: leatherbound editions of the classics sleeping in ordered rows. Isabel looked around enviously. 'Very inviting,' she said.

'Do you think so?' He seemed grateful. 'I suppose it is rather splendid.' He shook his head. 'You should have seen this place before we started.'

The house had been badly damaged by fire seven years ago. Rumour pointed the finger in various directions, but responsibility was never claimed and nothing was ever proved. The rebuilding had gone ahead without the feared-for intimidation, perhaps because the family who had lived here for the last two hundred years had bequeathed the charred skeleton of its inheritance to the state and moved abroad.

Christopher Bennett, an outsider like herself, had been appointed by the trust to administer its patronage here. By profession, he was a picture restorer. He had his own studio at the back of the house. ('I'll show you if there's time.') He had no interest in politics ('A plague on both your houses, that's what I say'), but he agreed, when pressed, that politically it was considered important to keep the local heritage alive.

'Who finances this trust?' she asked.

His eyes moved evasively. 'The ministry of the interior,' he said, as if admitting something he would have preferred to keep to himself.

They were admiring a nineteenth-century landscape of the estate. Isabel asked about the family. Bennett seemed glad to get away from the subject of money. 'Fine people. Good landlords. Everyone was sad when they went.' They passed into a long gallery hung with portraits. 'It wasn't just the fire, apparently. There was a lot of pressure before that. Petty vandalism, boycotts, even death threats, I'm told. Most of the land around here is owned by a few old families. The terrorists want them out. There's been a lot of killing and a lot of fear. In the end, I think the old man got fed up. I can't say I blame him.' He seemed reluctant to say more.

Isabel strolled over the squeaky parquet floor to inspect the ancestral faces. Simple, no-nonsense, God-fearing folk with nothing to hide, they sat at desks, or on horseback, or stared out of plain wooden frames. There was nothing sophisticated or fashionable about them. Their idea of frivolity would be a piano duet or an impromptu quadrille. They were just land-owners who knew the value of a good acre or the price of corn, holding down hostile territory, making a living where others were too lazy or cowardly. These were people for whom life was early rising and the endless negotiation between man and nature.

She found herself sneaking a sidelong glance at her guide. The pride Bennett was taking in the regilded splendour of the house was the pride of the loyal retainer. Although, like her, he was an outsider here, he was dedicated to conserving a way of life that now seemed as vulnerable as the new shoots in the garden.

They climbed a staircase 'wide enough to take a coach and four', as Bennett put it. In the kitchens below stairs they could hear the clatter of preparations. The curator glanced at his watch. 'I won't take much more of your time,' said Isabel.

Bennett asked her about her work and expressed the hope that she would allow him to introduce her to his wife before she went. 'We are both such fans,' he said again.

They were in a large bedroom with hunting prints on the wall and a Japanese lacquer table. The sky-blue satin on the four-poster caught the pale winter sunshine and Isabel's mind went to the countless moments of intimacy evoked by an old bed. She walked over to the window. There was a view over broad yellow lawns to a ha-ha beyond, then ragged brown fields, then a black wooded slope, and then the land rolling free and wild in all directions. It was a magnificent position and the phrase 'lord of all I survey' came into her head.

She thought of her parents in their anonymous terrace, remembered the ridiculous garden, the dusty laurel tree and the litter thrown over the fence from the street. When she described this splendour on the phone next week she knew she would hear a note of fascinated envy. How she hated the suburbs and how she hated her childhood there; the narrow, insular lives of their neighbours and their prying, censorious ways. No wonder she had married a poet and chosen to live across the water. And yet, when she stood here, surrounded by the emblems of lineage, her childless, lonely self that she did not like to recognise felt a pang of regret for what she had, for the moment, turned her back on. 'What happened to the younger generation?' she asked, idly moving the repainted rocking horse under her hand.

'There was only one boy.' He hesitated. 'He was killed.'

She challenged his instinctive discretion. 'You mean murdered?'

Bennett nodded. 'That was the real reason why the old man sold out.'

'Does he keep in touch?'

'I get the occasional letter. I've sent him photographs. He tells me he's pleased with everything.' His gesture was vague but quite lordly. 'He's getting on now.'

The line was going to die out and none of the other branches of the family would dare to take it on, not with the risks involved, the bombings and the shootings.

'So now you're the king of the castle,' she teased.

'Yes, I suppose I am.' His modesty returned. 'But only a stand-in.'

There was a faint sound behind them and they turned. A middle-aged woman in a long, shapeless dress floated into the room with whispering footsteps.

'Sarabeth,' said Bennett, speaking her name like a charm. 'My wife,' he added proudly, making the introductions.

It was strange, but at one glance Isabel felt she was already known to this woman, known and understood. She had an air of other-worldly calm and, even more than her husband, she conveyed an extraordinary and soothing peacefulness. Isabel noticed that her fingers were speckled with paint, and asked about her work. As they chatted happily, without consequence, Isabel noticed that the curator and his wife were actually holding hands.

They stood looking out of the window in a reflective, companionable silence. Isabel heard the noise of a helicopter, getting stronger. As they watched, a military troop carrier landed on the lawn and a patrol of soldiers in combat gear carrying automatic weapons jumped out and fanned across the lawn.

'What on earth,' said Bennett, his agitation returning. 'What on earth is going on?' Isabel wondered if he would shout from the window as he had done before, but instead he whistled for the dog and hurried to the door. 'Will you excuse me?'

Sarabeth said of course he should go down and see what was happening. She seemed quite removed from the intrusion, as if translating it into another consciousness. After he had hurried away, she looked at Isabel in the alcove. 'Perhaps,' she said, with a weird, almost flirtatious, smile, 'they have come to rescue the princess in the tower.'

5

Stephen sat in the front of the coach listening to his Walkman. Smith was asleep beside him, lolling like a grotesque baby. Behind them, the VIPs were reading or chatting or looking out of the window. The coach was passing through fenland, trailing its police escort at an obedient fifty. Occasionally, they overtook a horsebox or a tractor; once or twice they saw an army patrol with blacked-up faces making a routine search of a roadside village.

He felt unrested, distracted. When day broke, he had been first into the dining-room. He sat alone in a corner and read about last night's bombing in the local paper. A remote-controlled device; an army patrol; three serious injuries and one death. The headline asked: How Many More? The other front-page story was a report that the rock star, Troy, described here as 'the notorious hell-raiser', was planning a charity concert in aid of widows and orphans. Stephen frowned cynically; another bleeding-heart pop millionaire with publicity-conscious susceptibilities.

'Did Andrew give you a good time, then, Dr Mallory?'

He looked up from his newspaper. It was the manager's daughter, the quiet blonde, smiling.

'Andrew?' he queried.

'You know, Skylark.'

For a moment he was confused, and then he realised why she seemed so oddly familiar. 'Your brother's quite a character.' He studied the menu. 'What's your name, then?'

'Harriet – but everyone calls me Mouse.'

Looking at her, he could see why. Mouse and Skylark. Pet names, he thought, and the same surreal detachment. She was still there, without embarrassment. 'So you're leaving today,' she said. 'Now where?'

'I'm afraid that's rather confidential, but – ' He broke off. The dining-room door had opened and the chairman of the trust, a university professor whose name he'd momentarily forgotten, was hurrying towards his table. The professor was a classical archaeologist, intense but cheerful, with the pointed, inquisitive movement of a desert bird. Stephen, who had been opposite him at dinner, found his frank, breezy manner a welcome contrast to the general's pomposity. As he sat down now he was already halfway through a vigorous complaint about 'that bloody disco'. He looked at Stephen. 'Who chose this place?'

'The ministry.'

'I see.'

Mouse took their order. 'Chatting up the local talent,' he remarked as she went to the kitchen. 'A bit young for you, I'd say.'

Stephen leant forward. 'Not as innocent as she looks. When you came in she was quizzing me about our itinerary.'

'These people.' The professor paused to scan the newspaper headlines. 'There's nothing they won't worm out of you if you give them a chance.'

'So I've been told.'

'It all goes straight back, of course.' He had been a visiting lecturer here, he explained, and had decided views on 'these people'; he had decided views on everything. 'Basically, it's the survival of the tribe. A bloody costly kind of atavism if you ask me. Look at poor old George.' An elderly man with a stick was shuffling painfully towards their table. Stephen recognised the former minister. 'Caught it badly when they blew up that hotel. Wife killed. Quite ga-ga now.' He lowered his voice. 'Between you, me and the gatepost we use him to touch the government for the extra million now and then. Morning George.'

His colleague's faltering reply was interrupted by another arrival, the only woman on the committee, Lady Jacqueline Lyon, a well-known legislator. Stephen had sat next to her the night before and found himself challenged to debate almost every aspect of contemporary politics. She nodded graciously at him now. 'Good morning, Dr Mallory.' Her accent and exquisite clothes added to her indefinable air of foreignness. Turning to the waitress she said: 'I should like a cup of weak tea, without milk.' She sat down. 'The food here is disgusting.'

'What you and I, my dear Jacqueline, have to suffer in the cause of conservation,' observed the professor.

'If it were not for mad classicists like you and cultivated outsiders like myself,' she replied, 'this philistine country would turn everything into a freeway or a shopping precinct.'

Gradually, the party assembled. One or two natural alliances had already declared themselves but generally it was without inner discord, perhaps because the majority of its members were in retirement. Everyone seemed to defer to Lady Lyon, even while some joked about her behind her back; and everyone accepted the professor's chairmanship, though without affection.

Stephen made his excuses and left the breakfast table early. He found Smith waiting for him outside, like a chauffeur. He was at least wearing a suit, but he still had the shifty, ingratiating manner of the disgraced policeman. Stephen answered his eager 'Good morning' with a curt inquiry about the revised security arrangements.

'Over there, sir,' said Smith, nodding discreetly in the direction of the reception desk. 'A stuck up so-and-so, if you ask me, sir. Typical intelligence type.'

Stephen said nothing, but walked across the foyer, shadowed by Smith, and introduced himself to a young man in a tweed jacket and highly polished brown shoes, an off-duty captain.

They shook hands and Stephen explained why he had requested the meeting. 'You know General Windermere?' The captain nodded. 'I don't want to alarm you, but if anything happened –'

'It would ruin his entire day.' Smith blurted out the old joke, then stared at the floor with embarrassment.

Stephen sensed the intelligence officer's distaste for private security guards, and drew him to one side. His appeal was simple. He'd had to take charge of this Mickey Mouse operation – he rolled his eyes in Smith's direction – and was trying to get a grip. He described his conversation with the general.

'It's true that he's on their list,' said the captain. 'By the way, was there a Major Potter waiting for you at the airport last night?'

Stephen nodded.

'I guessed as much.' The captain seemed put out. 'He plays a deep game, I must say.'

'He said he was worried about our security.'

'He would, wouldn't he?' He glanced round, as if expecting the major to appear at any moment. 'He's just another empire-builder like the rest of them. You'd be amazed at his network.'

Stephen affected unconcern. 'Well, at least he's on our side.'

'If only it was that simple,' said the captain. 'There's an awful lot of freelancing going on over here.'

Stephen, remembering the general's words, asked what he meant.

The captain's expression was opaque. 'Let's just say that our people were unaware of his request for police protection.' From the stress of his words, 'our people' were plainly not 'Potter's people'.

'It was Potter who put us up in this hotel,' Stephen explained.

The sympathetic captain had been making a note. 'That's no surprise,' he said, looking up. 'It's run by his team.' He frowned. 'Potter's tastes are notoriously unconventional,' he murmured, as if to himself. Now he was scanning the guest list. 'Looking at the top brass in your party, I'd say his response has been, shall we say, rather low-key.'

Stephen sensed an ally. 'If you could do something . . .' He let the idea hang in the air.

The captain was about the same age as Stephen. 'I'll see what we can do.' He winked. 'Show Potter who's in charge round here.'

Stephen thanked him and went to join the others, now assembling by the reception desk. As they filed out into the morning sunshine, he noticed Mouse, the manager's daughter, watching them from the window of the dining-room, but when he caught her eye she moved back into the shadows and he was left staring at the reflection of a blustery day in the bullet-proof double-glazing.

The bus, braking suddenly at a junction, brought him back to the present. How often on long international flights he had sat with the music of the headphones in his ears, worrying over his assignment, staring stupidly at the in-flight maps and surprising himself with the world's geography. Not much had changed. Here he was now, music pounding, a road-map open on his knee. Only the free champagne was missing.

Stephen turned the place-names over in his mind. To the local people, every aspect of their history was coded into these topographical microchips, but even to an outsider some places had a special meaning. Here was the scene of a recent shoot-out with the army. A judge had been blown up here, two policemen there. Arms and explosives had been discovered on this mountainside. That was the home of a notorious interrogation centre. It was a landscape of a thousand memories and a thousand perils.

He looked out of the window. In the spring sunshine, the country looked like a place where you might go for a walk after lunch on Sunday, or in the summer take an apple and a good book. Yet hardly an acre of it was free of bloody associations. The thought flourished in his imagination. In a certain light the heather in the distance could be the colour of dried blood. His inner eye filled with a vision of the damned, like a crowded, medieval morality painting: shrieking ghosts in the heavens and the air filled with screams and groans.

The driver was signalling to attract his attention. He pulled off the headphones. There was, said the man, a service station coming up, 'by the monument – a good place for a breather'.

'The monument?'

In answer, the driver pointed ahead. In the near distance,

standing alone on an open heath, was a featureless grey slab the shape and size of a high-rise building. In its shadow, so to speak, by the roadside, was a tiny isolated settlement, a cafeteria, a small tin church with a cross, and a garage with an illuminated sign – 'Last Fuel for 50 Miles' – blinking monotonously next to a scrap-metal graveyard of wrecked cars from the highway.

Stephen asked about the monument as they pulled into the forecourt, gears crashing. 'I dunno, mate,' said the driver. 'It's just a monument.'

The professor, coming to the front of the bus, overheard. 'They were putting it up when I was here last,' he explained, as they stepped outside. 'It's supposed to represent the spirit of the place. You know, the will to survive.'

As they stood looking at the absurd concrete immensity across the heath, they heard the sound of singing.

Between the church and the cafeteria, dwarfed by juggernauts and tractor-trailers, was an old white camper van. It had the appearance of a vehicle that has been resprayed many times. RUSS HICKEY'S MISSION OF HOPE AND SALVATION was painted in amateur red lettering along the side. Over Hickey's name, floating like cherubs, there were scarlet grace-notes; a blood-red crusader cross emphasised the purpose of his mission.

Stephen and the professor walked over. Standing in front of the camper van was a small figure in a cowboy hat, a guitar slung over his shoulder, singing into a microphone. Next to him, a long-haired girl was beating a tambourine. Behind, in a menacing chorus, half a dozen middle-aged men in shiny black suits, holding bibles, stared fiercely past their leader at the ragged circle of spectators.

The hymn ended. The girl with the tambourine crossed herself ostentatiously and began to pass through the congregation with a box. One or two VIPs, who had strolled over to stretch their legs, now joined the circle. In their tailored suits and city overcoats, they attracted curious looks from the congregation.

The evangelist was quick to notice a better class of audience. He quickly blessed the offerings in the box and then, looking over his shoulder at the cafeteria, began to address his remarks in the direction of the VIPs.

'Yes, my friends, man is born with his back to God and his face towards hell. He is born in sin and shapen in iniquity.'

Here the girl with the tambourine emphasised the preacher's words with a spontaneous 'Hallelujah!'

'This is the word of the Lord, my friends. "Whatsoever a man soweth, that shall he also reap." Galatians, six, seven.' Glancing behind again, he waved a small black bible. 'Put your trust in the Lord, my friends. Put your trust in the blood of the Lord Jesus Christ and you will be saved. Only the fool says there is no hell. At the end of every life there is a reckoning.'

As if on cue, an angry-looking man in a blue boilersuit came banging through the screen-door of the cafeteria. Like a hard-pressed sprinter, Hickey took one last backward glance and raced for the finishing line. 'Marvel not what I say unto ye, ye must be born again. This is the word of the Lord. Thanks be to God.'

The man in the overalls was almost running himself. 'I told you to clear off out of here,' he shouted.

The black suits crowded protectively round their leader. Hickey himself remained calm. 'God bless you, my friend.'

'Go to hell.' He glared at the preacher. 'I told you before, I'm not having you on my land. Now clear off before I call the police.' He stormed back inside.

The little band of spectators watched him go, but they seemed indifferent to Hickey's fate and began to drift back to their cars.

Hickey turned to the few remaining faithful. 'The Lord's work is carried out in adversity. We must move on.'

A small boy with a toy gun came up and asked him for an autograph. 'God bless you, son. Go and live in the fear of the Lord.' He took the child's toy. 'Cast out evil not with the weapons of destruction but by faith and prayer.' The boy began to cry. Hickey looked awkward, made a joke to the child's mother and returned the gun.

Stephen walked back to the coach. The driver was drinking tea out of an old yellow Thermos flask. 'Hope and Salvation, I ask you.' He glanced sourly across at the camper van. 'Bloody Yanks. Always telling us how to be saved. Haven't they got enough of their own problems?'

Stephen found his curiosity about Hickey spurred by the surprising degree of hostility he seemed to inspire.

'He comes here every year now,' explained the driver. 'I don't know why someone doesn't just shoot him in the head.' He climbed back into his seat and switched on the engine. 'Save us all a lot of bother.' He seemed disinclined to specify the nature of the trouble.

The VIPs boarded the coach and they set off again, refreshed. The route was climbing, and the land became hilly, almost mountainous. Soon the horizon was bright with the promise of the western sea. A military Land-Rover with armed soldiers on the tailgate passed in the opposite direction. Stephen sensed journey's end.

Now they were approaching an ornamented stone gateway, rattling over a cattle grid and following a long drive through well tended parkland. There was a small lake and a herd of longhorn cattle by the waterside. The VIPs were pointing out the sights to each other, stirring in their seats and making jocular comparisons with the country houses of their acquaintance. The coach slowed down to pass a soldier in combat gear, and then another. Clearing a rise, they came in view of a spacious lawn with a helicopter parked in the middle, rotors spinning idly.

Stephen stood up next to the driver. There was a voice behind him, a voice used to congratulating efficient staff officers. 'Well done, Mallory.' The general was observing the security with obvious satisfaction. 'It's good to see the lads in position.'

The coach swept up to the front of the great house. The

distinguished visitors filed out onto the gravel with appreciative comments about the magnificently restored object of their patronage. Stephen found himself intercepted by the curator. 'Dr Mallory? Could I have a quick word before we go in.'

6

Each morning, driving Mary to work, before the rhythm of his own day began, Curtis conducted a private battle with his inner fears. He could not admit this, even to Mary, but somewhere, deep inside him, there was a voice that said he was no different from her patients. He had this fantasy, as he turned past the gate every morning, that in her caring way she was acclimatising him for the moment when he, too, would be taken in. He had heard her remark that hopes and fears were sometimes the same and, as he struggled to define his demons to himself, he occasionally wondered whether all the secret stories in his head were not the beginnings of something more than nightmares.

Today, in the sunshine, his spirits lifted, and there were no shadows. He dropped Mary at the front door with a goodbye kiss. A patient, watching from a distance, might have mistaken them for a long-married couple. A girl in a flowered night-dress was waiting on the steps, astride a broomstick. Curtis watched his sister take her capably by the hand and lead her back indoors.

The hospital looked after about seventy adolescents in various states of mental and emotional incapacity. To the outside world, it advertised itself as a 'Special Care Unit', but that, like so much of the language employed by the authorities, was a euphemism. To a greater or lesser extent, its inmates were insane.

The wards were colour-coded. 'Blue' was relatively normal, its occupants free to mix in the community under supervision. 'Green' was intermediate. The patients in 'Red', all boys, were technically labelled 'challenging'. They lived in a fractured, claustrophobic world of restraint, incontinence and childlike chaos. At any moment, the hazy tranquillity of these distracted minds could be interrupted by sudden storms of violence, inexplicable rages and gusts of manic laughter. The incoherence of life here was usually depressing, but then one day a lunatic teenager with the face of an old man and a jersey covered in sick would put his hand in yours, follow you with serene obedience, call you Dada, and for an instant of weird clarity an odd kind of human contact would be made. It was like watching a foreign television channel and finding a story transmitted in your mother tongue.

Curtis, who coded his own words so carefully in public, discovered that even here, within these flaking walls, there was meaning to be found. Language was often the key. Slowly, like someone learning to write with an unfamiliar hand, he taught himself to decode its distortions and compensate for its absence. Partly to help his sister, and partly because he wanted to confront his fears, he unofficially adopted one boy, Paul, for himself.

Paul was in 'Blue' and, at nineteen, preparing to move on to an adult unit. He was a schizophrenic and, on occasion, so lucid, forthright and objective it was hard to imagine what he was doing in care. His problem – and it was one that could reduce him to gibbering hysteria – was the intolerable painfulness of the English language. In his worst moods, he would refuse either to speak it or listen to it. In his time, he had been known to rip up books and newspapers, and he habitually carried a Walkman loaded with classical symphony music to block out the unbearable intrusion of everyday speech.

Paul would spend weekend afternoons at Curtis's house on what was known as 'outpatient parole'. Curtis bought a high-powered short-wave radio and together they would tune into foreign language broadcasts. The odd thing, Curtis found, was that he sympathised with his loathing of mainland speech. Then he had an inspiration. He would gratify his own anti-quarian enthusiasm and extend the boy's repertoire by teaching him the dead language of their own land. This joint study was a great success. Back in the hospital, Paul would sit in a corner of the ward, his Walkman on full blast, happily tracing the unfamiliar hieroglyphs into his notebook. He was a great favourite with the nurses, some of whom believed he was a kind of genius. Both Curtis and Mary dreaded the approaching day of his transfer, but he was long past the age of adoption and there was no way they could keep him.

Curtis was thinking sadly about Paul's future now as he drove back to the road. In truth, his impending move was in the nick of time. The inspectors had visited the hospital last year and their damning report had described the conditions as 'poor'. They had singled out 'Red' for special censure; in their words, 'as bad as anything we have seen in our experience'. They had recommended that 'the unit is closed down as soon as possible'. The verdict had upset Mary. 'What do they expect on the money we get?' she demanded angrily. 'A five-star hotel?' Curtis had calmed her, pointing out that her dedication had been commended. Privately, he was pleased. He hoped he could persuade her to exercise her philanthropic spirit in a less depressing environment.

Now he paused as he reached the head of the drive. Today his routine was interrupted by Peter Dobbs hurrying out of the former gatekeeper's lodge, a gingerbread house set behind bright green railings. Dobbs was known throughout the neighbourhood as Curtis's right-hand man. He was both furtive and ubiquitous. He liked to say that he had not a bone of ambition in his body, but he always had the satisfaction of knowing that Curtis, who listened to him carefully, often acted on his word. Dobbs was a short man and when Curtis opened the driver's window, he spoke, secretive as ever, almost without bending. 'If you have a moment, Joe, I have something to show you.'

Curtis recognised the quicksilver smile and the hushed inquiry, and saw there was something on his mind. 'And what could that be, I wonder?' he replied, lightly, as he parked the car.

Inside, there was the familiar, unruly warmth of the Dobbs household. Two small boys were fighting in their pyjamas on the sofa. Mrs Dobbs, feeding her youngest, was shouting at them to be quiet while her daughter, not yet three, marched round the kitchen tunelessly blowing into a toy recorder. Curtis was a regular visitor and his appearance made little impression on the scene. The boys greeted him like an uncle and then, ignoring their father's pleas, renewed their fighting. Dobbs rolled his eyes. 'Holidays,' he said, though Curtis knew perfectly well that it was always like this here, school or no school.

Dobbs had the poor man's love of bargains: pictures, statuettes and souvenirs cluttered the walls and shelves of the little house. Each of these items was the fruit of some deal or scheme, usually a long story with many implications. It was never exactly clear what he did for a living, but somehow, through a mixture of odd jobs and government handouts, he survived. The Dobbses were the people you called if you wanted something fixed, and a house or a child minded. Although they had next to nothing, they were always generous with the little they had, especially to Curtis. Now Mrs Dobbs was offering him a cup of tea.

He would never say no, but he couldn't stay long. He had to get up to the shop.

Dobbs disappeared briefly and came back into the kitchen with a dirty roll of canvas. For the first time his children were almost quiet, crowding curiously round the table.

'Seeing as how you are the acknowledged expert on all matters relating to this area,' Dobbs began, speaking so formally that Curtis suspected his words had been rehearsed, 'I thought I would take the liberty of exhibiting this unique treasure to you at the earliest possible opportunity.'

Curtis acknowledged the honour with satisfaction while Dobbs unrolled the canvas with a flourish. The family crowded closer. It was a portrait of a couple, presumably man and wife. A very dirty, dusty portrait, it seemed to Curtis, as he bent over the table to get a better look.

'I expect,' Dobbs went on, 'that you are wondering how such a treasure came into my possession.'

'Well,' said Curtis amiably, 'that is a question.'

'I'll tell you,' said Dobbs. 'I was up at Birch's place buying chicks for the yard – '

His wife interrupted to ask their guest if he would like a piece of seedcake with his tea. Curtis declined, noting with curiosity the nervousness in her voice.

'Well then,' Dobbs continued, 'we had completed our negotiations, when he stopped me dead in my tracks. "Wait on," he said, "I have something for you, something I found in a drawer." The next thing I know, he's showing me this canvas. "What do you make of that?" he said. "It's a lady and a gentleman," I said. "But who?" I said. "I'd say it was a question of identification," he said. And he looked at me in this funny way, as if he was expecting my wisdom in the matter.' Dobbs seemed suddenly apprehensive. 'I hoped you'd not mind, but it was then that I took the liberty of mentioning your name.'

Curtis did not demur. 'Not at all,' he said thoughtfully.

Dobbs seemed relieved, nodding encouragement to his wife. 'Mr Birch seemed pleased. "Take the picture," he said. "Show it to Joseph Curtis by all means. There's nothing he doesn't know about our district. Tell him it's just a question of identification." Those were his very words, Joe.'

Curtis frowned, but concealed his displeasure by peering closely at the surface of the picture, pointing out the artist's signature under the dirt. 'I'm sure,' he said, 'that research will give us the answer.'

'What did I tell you?' said Mrs Dobbs. 'Didn't I say – ?'

'You did, my dear, you did.' Dobbs smiled at Curtis. 'A woman's intuition and no mistake.' He congratulated his family, who were watching with childish mystification. 'My dears, we are lucky to have such a friend so close at hand. In fact, if you would like to have the picture, Joe, as a small and inadequate thank-you from a grateful family . . .' He pushed it across the table. Curtis knew it was pointless to blame Dobbs – in many ways he should be grateful for his naïvety – and quickly said he was happy to accept the gift.

'Thank you,' he said. 'I'll take it away for closer examination.'

'There,' said Dobbs. 'The best possible outcome.' He looked at his wife again. He seemed to be hesitating. 'Mr Birch will be so pleased.'

Curtis rolled up the picture and went to the door. The Dobbs family followed, a ragged troupe in cast-off costumes. As he turned to say goodbye, Curtis looked hard at Dobbs. 'Well now, Peter?'

Molly Dobbs gave her husband an encouraging prod, bobbed a goodbye to Curtis and ushered her children inside. The two men stood alone on the step in the early morning light. Dobbs seemed unhappy, but did not speak.

Curtis could not control his suspicion any longer. 'So what's the trouble with Birch?' he asked. It always annoyed him when outsiders tried to put pressure on his circle. He could feel his anger rising.

Dobbs poked a stone with his shoe. He was silent for a while, and Curtis knew better than to press him. He had the canvas rolled up under his arm like a map, and stood looking out across the fields in front of the gatehouse, a general sizing up the terrain of battle. There were rooks cawing in the beech trees down the road. Otherwise, it was still. Finally, Dobbs spoke. 'He says you went too far,' he said.

He did not have to say more. Curtis knew what he was referring to.

Curtis stared coldly into the distance, keeping his annoyance down. 'Does he have any authority to make that remark?'

Dobbs was almost inaudible. 'He says he does.' He shrugged. 'Of course,' he added, 'you never know.'

'No,' said Curtis, 'you don't.' He paused. 'A question of identification.' He tested Dobbs. 'What did he mean?'

'You know what he means, Joe.'

He squinted down the rolled-up canvas, pensive. 'If I hadn't leaked those files that operation would have gone ahead.'

'He says you went too far,' Dobbs repeated, with sudden

boldness. 'He predicts you'll have blood on your hands, he says.'

'Is that so?' Now Curtis was angry. He did not like his position challenged. 'What does he know?'

'He's well connected, Joe.'

'In case you had forgotten, Peter, so am I.' Sometimes he could only just restrain the violence inside, but then the mood passed and he was calm again. 'No need to worry, Peter. I'll speak to him this morning.' He walked over to his car, waving the canvas. 'I'll be happy to identify his likeness in the files that have yet to reach the newspapers.' He laughed grimly. 'Then he'll really know how far I can go.'

7

Isabel saw that Bennett was enjoying himself at last and was pleased. The tour of the house had gone well, Lady Lyon had pronounced favourably on the project, and her colleagues had taken their cue. 'Money well spent' was the phrase that now circulated – as Bennett himself was circulating, decanter in hand – among the guests in the library. Isabel saw the success of the party mirrored in his face and told herself he would never have invited her to stay to lunch if he had been apprehensive of further difficulty. The visit, so long expected, so minutely planned, so full of pitfalls, was passing off as well as anyone could have hoped.

She glanced across at him now. He was talking to the anxious young man in the grey suit who had given her such a lecture about security. There was always something ridiculous about professional minders, especially when they took themselves seriously. She smiled.

Bennett smiled back. 'No problem with Miss Rome, I trust?' he murmured confidentially, beaming up at his guest.

Stephen shook his head. 'I had a few words with her,' he replied. It was wildly unprofessional, but what else could he do? He could hear Wagner saying that it sounded like amateur night at the zoo, but Bennett had put him in an impossible position. The best he could hope for was that they were all on their way before the general started asking questions. 'No,' he said, 'there's no problem.'

Bennett, oblivious to these concerns, was happily describing Isabel's weekly broadcast. He and his wife were regular listeners and were, he said, always completely charmed. He looked across the room again. 'A most engaging person.' There she was now, in conversation with his wife, so poised

68

and attractive, socially at ease and yet not glib in that tiresome metropolitan way.

'I'm sure,' said Stephen indifferently. He felt tired and irritable. This trip was fulfilling all his fears. A word like 'engaging' always struck a false note with him; he loathed charm and he was suspicious of poise. He could feel the temptations of rudeness coming on. He excused himself and went to check that Smith, who seemed for a moment reassuringly charmless, was not getting into trouble with the platoon outside.

Bennett, abandoned, made his way across the room, refilling his guests' glasses. He found Isabel and Sarabeth in a corner by the window, laughing together like women sharing confidences. 'Well?' he said, looking for approval.

'They're having a wonderful time,' said Isabel. 'Who,' she added recklessly, 'is that armour-plated old mastodon with the stick?'

'That's General Windermere.'

'I might have guessed.'

Bennett's anxiety returned to plague him like a wasp. 'What did he say?'

'Not much,' she replied. 'I didn't let him get a word in edgeways.' She made no effort to conceal her satisfaction. 'I told him I thought that the military occupation would never work. He seemed quite put out.' When she saw the look of alarm on her host's face she realised that, for the first time since Tom had left, she felt completely herself. There was a word they liked to use here. Glad. She felt glad.

Bennett was trying to be indulgent towards his protégée. 'It was probably good for him,' he said doubtfully.

Sarabeth said, in an absent voice: 'Of course it was,' as if coming out of some imaginary conversation.

At this point a gong sounded in the distance and Bennett turned to invite his guests to follow him to the dining-room. As the committee filed in, Stephen found himself next to Isabel. 'Enjoying the great and the good?' he asked lightly, wondering if he was going to receive any of the famous charm.

Her reply was cut short. 'Trust you, Mallory, to sit next to the most attractive woman in the room.' It was the professor, tactless and self-possessed as usual. He took the vacant seat next to Isabel. 'May I, my dear?'

As he watched her smile of invitation, Stephen wondered what was going through her mind. There was something composed and private about her that aroused his interest, against his will. She was quite small, but stylishly dressed in rather boyish clothes. The professor was right: she was attractive, but in an unexpected way. He was still in full flight. 'You've met Mallory, I take it. He's here to see we don't get blown up. He's a bright fellow. You should talk to him.'

'I don't know what made you think I wouldn't,' said Isabel.

'Ah-ha.' The professor was amused. 'Almost rude.'

There was still an empty chair on Stephen's right, and now Bennett, nervous with apology, was at his side. 'I'm afraid I should have had a seating plan,' he said, looking for encouragement, 'but they did say they wanted to be informal.' He lowered his voice. 'Is everything all right?'

Isabel, overhearing, leant across. 'Everything's fine, Christopher,' she said. 'You can relax.' She glanced at Stephen, and a note of teasing came into her voice. 'Leave it to the professionals.' Spontaneous and direct, she steered the conversation back to Stephen, turning to ask him if this was his first time here. Her right hand was resting on the table a few inches from his. She was wearing a man's watch and her fingers were so fragile and white they were almost translucent.

Stephen, answering, noticed she was not wearing a ring, and wondered in reply what she was doing here herself. He put this so tentatively that she did not feel threatened or intruded upon.

There were few things that Isabel hated more than having to rehearse her autobiography to strangers. That was the worst part of being single again, the loss of the known world of friends and family, people who knew you exactly as you were, knew your story and for whom any artifice was pointless. As a single woman, cut off from all that, Isabel found that she could suddenly re-invent herself if she chose. At times, when the conversation pressed too close to her feelings, this was quite an appealing subterfuge. She could catch herself saying that she was working on a screenplay, or doing research for the government, or 'seeing' a married man on the mainland – anything but the truth about Tom Harris and her broadcasting. The odd and surprisingly pleasant thing about Stephen Mallory was that, though in many ways he seemed her opposite, she found, as they chatted, that she didn't have to worry about explaining herself as she usually did in these situations. With a faint thrill, she heard him echoing these thoughts. 'I mean,' he added, as a kind of coda, 'it must be a bore to have a voice or a name that people recognise.'

She laughed, and leant towards him. 'People are so intrusive. They always come up and argue.'

Stephen felt her breath on his cheek and the pressure of her hand on his arm, and he wondered, because it was a while since he had found himself flirting, whether this was her usual manner. 'You wouldn't like it if they said nothing.'

'I suppose not.' He was much less serious than he seemed at a distance.

'I mean we all have our vanity.'

She was too proud to admit this, and to cover herself she fired back: 'So what's yours?'

He paused for a moment. Her eyes were brown, amused but watchful. Her honey-coloured skin, slightly freckled, was soft and clear, with a suggestion of sunshine. 'I suppose it's to do with self-sufficiency.'

'Oh.' She found the intensity of his concentration almost alarming.

'My vanity is that I don't need anyone.'

Now it was her turn to be ironic. 'You're not going to tell me that you're a cat who walks alone.'

'That's it.' They both laughed, and something good passed between them.

She looked down, suddenly shy, and momentarily without a response.

In the lull, Stephen, looking across at the row of distinguished faces in various attitudes of conversation, became concerned that he was forgetting himself.

Isabel was speaking again. 'The professor was boasting to me about the dangers of your work abroad.' She indicated the lunch table ironically. 'This must be rather a come-down.'

'It makes a change.'

She seemed disappointed with his reply. 'I must say, I find politics terribly boring.'

He could see that she was trying to provoke him. 'I don't think you mean that,' he said. 'In my experience, people who say such things are usually rather boring themselves.'

'That's me.' She laughed. 'Dull as ditchwater.'

As he listened, enjoying her irony, Stephen realised he was looking at her properly for the first time. When she smiled, her expression lit up, as though the inspiration of the smile ran right through her.

'So, like most journalists, you have to make everything up, I suppose.'

He was surprised to hear himself teasing her, but was even more surprised at her response.

'If you're still that paranoid about the press,' she said, with sudden irritation, 'I think I should talk to someone else.'

She turned away from him; Stephen felt ashamed, dismayed. He imagined the others secretly noting his embarrassment, and was grateful when Bennett leant towards him in confidence. 'Do you think I should say a few words?' Stephen, leaning back in the hope of drawing Isabel into the conversation, repeated the question rhetorically.

Isabel, apparently absorbed in the professor's conversation, paid no attention. He heard himself foolishly answering his own question. 'A few well-chosen words? Oh, definitely.'

The curator fiddled with his notes under the table. Then he was on his feet, tapping his glass with his knife for silence. The guests, mellow with food and wine, looked up politely. Bennett was devoted to this great house and he was glad to have an opportunity to say so. His anxiety disappeared; he spoke as master of the place. He thanked them all for coming here at such personal risk and ventured that perhaps the house and its new splendour, a reminder of happier times, might also be a symbol of regeneration, a sign to one and all that there was always hope, even in the darkest days.

Stephen tried to listen, but his thoughts were at war with his concentration. He had known it was an error of judgement to let Isabel join the party in the first place, and now he had compounded that mistake in a far more personal way. He could scarcely believe his lack of finesse.

He came back to the present. Christopher Bennett was asking them to raise their glasses.

The professor, answering for the guests, was obviously a man who liked giving speeches on such occasions. From the way he beamed round at the assembled company, from a dozen self-important mannerisms – repetitions, pauses-for-effect, cheeky references to colleagues, joking self-congratulation – and from the light of satisfaction that flowed from him, it was clear that he, at least, was enjoying himself. Today, he was also valedictory. His stint as chairman was coming to an end, and he was, as he put it, 'passing on the Olympic torch'.

'I would, I think you will all agree,' he went on, 'be neglecting my duties if I did not also thank our attentive colleague, Dr Mallory, who has set our minds at rest with such excellent security arrangements.'

A murmur of gratitude ran round the table. Stephen indicated his appreciation of this tribute, though his pleasure was chilled by the coolness on his left.

'Finally,' the professor concluded, 'I should like to say what an unexpected delight it has been to have the journalist and broadcaster, Isabel Rome, among our number today. I look forward, as I'm sure we all do, to hearing her account of our visit on the radio next week, thus bringing our humble efforts to the audience of millions we so richly deserve.' A ripple of laughter went down the table, and Stephen tried gamely to share in it. 'Ladies and gentlemen, I give you a toast to our heritage, a toast to ourselves.'

As the good and faithful servants of the trust lifted their glasses, Stephen, glancing across the table, saw the evil eye of the general's displeasure standing out among the bonhomous establishment faces. He realised, with a sinking heart, that he had some explaining to do. Sneaking a quick glance to his left, he was not sorry to have an excuse to move away from the table.

The helicopter pilot knew the general's reputation. 'He was always known to the lads as "Windy". The sort that likes to talk tough but can't hack it when the chips are down. Stupid bastard.' He was shouting over the noise of the rotors, chewing gum and throwing his comments to Stephen as they watched the patrol hurrying across the grass. There was a young lieutenant leading, bending low, instinctively placing his hands to his beret in the whirling wind.

'Scandalised' was the word the general had used, over and over. He had paced up and down in front of the fire in the library, and with each circuit of the hearthrug, and each repetition of his astonishment, his sense of the 'scandal' increased.

'I cannot imagine how you could be so lax,' he said. 'I simply cannot imagine how you could allow a reporter to infiltrate this occasion.'

Stephen had remained detached. His experience told him that the general's anger came from fear. He stood by the window watching the rest of the party strolling outside on the terrace in the spring sunshine. He had already decided that attack was the best form of defence and was refusing to concede a mistake.

The general had come up close, speaking slowly. 'You allowed a member of the press to witness what was supposed to be a private visit and you did not even have the courtesy to warn me.'

'It was the curator's invitation, and I established at the outset that everything was off the record.'

'Off the record! I must say, young man, you are being

exceedingly cavalier with the lives of some very distinguished people.'

'I'd be surprised if this woman's presence amounts to much. What are you suggesting will happen now?'

'I'll tell you what will happen now, Mallory. Little Miss Muffet goes back to her newspaper – '

'Actually, she works for a radio station.'

The general waved him aside. 'She goes for a drink with some fellow journalists. She's chatting at the bar. Guess what? she says. I saw General Windermere today. Walls have ears, Mallory. In next to no time, every sniper and bombmaker in the district will have the story.'

Stephen pointed out that Isabel's interests appeared to be limited to heritage and conservation. 'She told me herself she had no interest in politics.'

'For a woman with no interest in politics, she has some fairly decided views about the military.'

Stephen was curious to know how 'decided' she had been. 'She told me she wanted to do a piece about this house. Full stop.'

There was a long silence. Stephen was intrigued by the irritation he felt towards Windermere's attack. He could recognise the injury to his professional pride; what surprised him was the strength of his defensive feeling towards Isabel. His chief concern now was to find a way to defuse the general's smouldering anger. If this row rumbled on throughout the tour, his critique of the risk department would be over-shadowed by a dozen awkward questions from the office. Wagner loved post-mortems. Would they be in the morgue with this one!

He said: 'I suppose I could have another quiet word with Miss Rome.' In the circumstances, the chance of success seemed slight, but he felt obliged to make the suggestion.

'Now that is the first sensible thing I've heard you say all afternoon.' The speed of the general's satisfaction suggested that his annoyance had been merely tactical. 'Fix her, Mallory, any way you like, and you'll hear no more of this.'

Stephen came out of the library in a bad mood. If he had not exactly enjoyed his interview with Windermere, he had even less pleasure to anticipate in another meeting with Isabel Rome.

Bennett was waiting for him. He was about to speak but Stephen, preoccupied, cut him short. 'Where's Isabel Rome? I have to see her urgently.'

Bennett seemed startled. 'She asked me to say goodbye,' he began. 'She said she had to get back – '

'She's gone?'

'Half an hour ago. What's the matter?'

Stephen shook his head in dismay and went outside to look for Smith. It was always true – why had he forgotten this? – that the assignments promising nothing but difficulty turned out to be smooth, while the operations that were routine on paper put everyone on the rack. It was like parties: the ones he dreaded were often the most enjoyable.

Smith was in the car-park discussing football with the coach driver. Stephen explained his predicament. Smith seemed grateful to be taken seriously. 'Leave it to me, sir.'

Stephen said he expected to be back in the evening, and almost ran out to the helicopter on the lawn. In action again, he thought. It was not an unpleasant sensation.

The pilot was fighting a major war in his head; he was so cool he was hyper. There would be no problem. 'We can put you down like a baby wherever you want.' His eyes were slightly bloodshot and he had a two days' stubble. To Mallory, who had seen military commanders high on cocaine joyriding over peasant villages, he seemed comparatively normal. As Stephen elaborated his story, the pilot said he would radio ahead and have a car waiting. There would be just one stop, en route, to pick up an injured man at a surveillance post. 'A small detour,' he said, 'but you might find it interesting.'

The tune of the engine went up an octave and the fuselage began to shake. The young lieutenant was shouting orders and the last of his platoon was scrambling aboard. The troops were big and boyish and their camouflage-dirty faces were streaked with sweat. They had a strong animal smell about them and their bulky weapons were black and greasy. Stephen, who had forgotten how physical warfare could be, felt small and out of place in his suit and tie and overcoat, but they looked at him with the eyes of men who are no longer capable of surprise. As the last man in slid the door into place, the lieutenant gave the thumbs up and the helicopter rose unsteadily into the air and began to move fast across the ground, flying low. Looking out, Stephen could see the coach moving slowly down the drive towards the main road, following the police escort. He felt a sense of temporary release from the VIPs; he was relieved to be on the move again.

The lieutenant climbed over piles of military debris, and sat next to him. He seemed anxious to talk. 'The place we're going to first, it's tough. We never drive there.' Stephen nodded appreciatively and the lieutenant carried on, shouting over the noise of the rotorblades. 'The guys we're up against, they're good. They got two of my men on our last tour. A very professional job. They're probably the best in the world when it comes to this sort of fighting.' He was like a player discussing a rival team. 'Funny things happen, too, you know. Dead funny.' He started to tell an involved story about a pig, a scrap-metal dealer and a terrorist suspect.

The helicopter began to zigzag, to avoid the threat of ground fire, the lieutenant explained. They skimmed through the fading light, with the land spread out below like an old brown skin. The lieutenant was still talking. 'A minute or two before touch-down, my sergeant flicks the door open ready for the landing. The chopper banks, the pig panics and slips his lead. I make a grab, miss him and he goes hurtling out. The young bloke, the suspect, he's never been in a chopper before, he thinks he's next and he's packing shit. And we're all raging because we've lost the pig. When we get in it turns out that the bloke was the wrong bloke after all and we had to release him the same day.' He shook his head. 'This bloody country.'

There was a shout from the pilot. They were descending. The helicopter came to rest in a concrete yard surrounded by concrete bunkers; a narrow hilltop observation post bristling with electronic gadgetry. Stephen was invited to step out and take a look. It was a relief to be in the fresh air. Now the sun was down, the wind was sharp; there was an acute sense of isolation in enemy territory. The watchers on duty peered into the twilight with tense grey faces; they seemed sombre and uncommunicative.

In the valley below, working beneath arc lights, behind corrugated iron screens, two bulldozers were grinding backwards and forwards, uprooting low trees and scrub, scarring the silent earth with deep black wounds. This, Stephen supposed, was also part of 'normalisation'. If there was only wasteland, went the reasoning from the bright sparks in the ministry, there would be nowhere for the enemy to hide, and thus fewer incidents to keep the emergency alive. Just to see the theory in practice made him smile; it was as ludicrous as 'provincialisation', 'pacification' and all the other buzz words.

The lieutenant came over and stood next to him. 'Dangerous work,' he said as they watched one of the bulldozers shunt a tree aside like a pot-plant, 'especially at dusk.' He paused, no longer the raconteur. 'We're ready to go now.' They turned back towards the helicopter pad. 'I suppose I should warn you. I'm afraid the man is dead.'

As they came out of the bunker, they were joined by a heavy-eyed young man in an anorak and jeans, an undercover soldier according to the lieutenant. No one said much as they climbed back on board.

In the confined space on the hilltop the noise of take-off was thunderous. The body bag was stretched unceremoniously across a heap of weapons. Stephen supposed there was nowhere else for it to go. The soldiers stared, but did not speak. 'Okay,' shouted the lieutenant. He put his mouth close to Stephen's ear. 'Only twenty minutes to base camp from here.' The helicopter rose into the air. Pinpricks of light showed in the dangerous fields below. Stephen asked how the man had died.

'Sniper.' He did not seem to want to say more, perhaps inhibited by the silent young man in the anorak. There was no need to ask the officer what he felt; he knew the answer. Somewhere, sometime soon, he and his men would even the score. Stephen looked at the soldiers sitting round him. If there was any life in those expressions it was from the unconscious satisfaction that they could shoot to kill with a clearer conscience, tracing the words 'an eye for an eye' in the blood of the enemy, whenever he came into their gunsights.

At the base, they came bumping in through low cloud, and landed next to the other helicopters on the grid. Stephen climbed out and followed the lieutenant across the tarmac into a poorly lit cluster of portacabins. A military policeman was waiting to meet them. 'The car is here, sir, whenever you're ready.' He was holding a buff folder. 'This is the surveillance dossier. Not much I'm afraid, but we do have an address and phone number. Shall I try and get the young lady on the line?'

'It's probably worth a try,' said Stephen.

After a long pause, the officer put the phone down. 'No one at home.'

'Is it far?'

'An hour at the outside, sir. I'll be glad to take you.'

Stephen said goodbye to the lieutenant, and soon they were slipping past the heavily guarded checkpoint and out into the darkness.

Stephen's mind was on Isabel. Would he find her? What would he do if he did not? And if he did, what would he say? She had tried to say goodbye: what did that mean? Absently, he asked where they were going.

'It's a small town in the country, sir. Very pretty in spring. A bit of an oasis, I'd say. Nothing ever happens there.'

8

Isabel sat at Tom's typewriter distracting herself with the bent Q. Lately she had come to enjoy the solitary light of the Anglepoise and the invitation of blank paper, but this evening she was lost in thoughts she could not easily find words for. The fire stirred and settled in the grate behind her, sending a glow into the darkness. She lit another cigarette.

Q: the key jammed again with a dead click. She prised it free and tried again, Q. Click. She sighed. She was supposed to be typing up her notes from the day with the impressions still fresh in her mind. Instead, she was fiddling with Tom's geriatric machine, thinking it was high time she bought a word-processor, and trying not to linger too moodily on Stephen Mallory.

She had failed to police her thoughts in that direction on the journey home, indulging herself with longing and regret. The cheap music on the tape filled her heart with doubtful emotions but for once she was not ashamed to be sentimental. Being on your own was sometimes like being on holiday; you should wallow a bit. She felt it was somehow typical of her that just as she was getting to feel at home with her solitude she had allowed something to threaten it.

Anyway, she had escaped. As soon as lunch was over, Mallory had become taken up with an urgent discussion involving the bad-tempered general, and she had broken away from the table, thinking, I must go now, I must go before . . . it gets dark! That was the pretext she'd used with Christopher Bennett, and she could see that the hospitable curator was startled by her determination to leave. Sarabeth, standing watchfully beside her husband, seemed to understand. 'Come and see us again when there's less on your mind,' she said, kissing her goodbye.

As soon as she set off down the drive, Isabel repented her haste and wondered if she could not find another excuse to take her back. For a mile or two, she could glimpse the house across the moor. She hesitated, but kept on. She would never see him again, but she could still imagine what it might have been like; besides, she told herself, he was probably not her type and she must not make the mistake she'd made with Curtis. The truth was that she was still nervous of her emotions, and it hurt her to admit it. Involuntary tears came into her eyes, but she could not say if they were tears of sadness or relief. The road itself, windswept and romantic, riding through mountains and moorland, echoed the drama in her mind.

When she got home, she drew the curtains, switched on a few low lamps, and had a long slow bath listening to Mozart's Requiem in the soothing darkness. The Lacrimosa filled the house as she treated her body to the luxuries on her dressing table, and it was to the Sanctus that she crawled under the duvet for a reflective and occasionally tearful snooze. At six o'clock she pulled on her tracksuit, made tea, and sat down in the parlour to try to concentrate on her work.

Q. This time the key jumped back into place. She added a question mark. And then another: ?

The cat was purring by the fire. No question marks there. She listened to Bennett's voice on the tape. Was there really enough for a story? Who cared about old houses? Apart from Curtis, of course. Curtis. She hit the key again: Q. There was no story. She would forget about Mallory, do as she had intended, and write about Hickey instead.

The phone rang. She was about to answer but then became fearful it would be Tom. It rang and rang, and the more it rang the surer she was it would be him. Finally it stopped and she returned to her thoughts.

He was not exactly handsome, he was rather more middle-class than she would have liked, and he was obviously into politics, but he listened to what she said, and engaged with it properly, unlike so many of the men she encountered. There was, she detected, an unacknowledged desire for intimacy that cancelled out the off-putting distance in his manner, and it was this she found appealing. He was also, she discovered, confessing to the rage in her heart, able to be serious about the things that mattered and flippant about those that did not. She'd commented, as Bennett's Labrador sniffed at their feet, how much she disliked dogs.

'What about cats?' He smiled. 'Not just the ones who walk alone.'

Her sense of his shyness faded when he looked at her. 'I've always liked cats,' she said.

He said he liked cats, too. 'But only in other people. I have enough trouble running my own life without that responsibility.'

'I have one,' she said. 'He's no bother.'

'I suppose if I wanted I could have a stuffed cat. For show.'

'He would still need dusting.'

They had laughed at this idea, not in a polite, disconnected way, but reaching deep inside. He said: 'It would make a perfect excuse. I have to go home now to dust the cat.'

It was then that Isabel realised that she was enjoying herself more than she expected, and that he was in danger of making her feel good about things. In a mild panic, she made up her mind to leave as soon as possible. Shortly after this, she had picked her moment and taken offence. Now she felt vile, stupid, and full of remorse.

There was a light, familiar knock, followed by Curtis's footsteps in the hall. Isabel came grudgingly out of her reverie. 'Hello Joe,' she said, not turning round.

'Am I interrupting?'

He was wearing his old red anorak and had a roll of newspaper under his arm, a shambling figure who invited confidences. She imagined that he'd brought something he'd want to discuss in due course. She noticed that he generally gave himself a reason for his visits now.

'Yes,' she said, welcoming him with a forgiving smile. 'It doesn't matter. I don't seem to be able to work tonight.'

He was standing in front of the hearth idly checking the cards on the mantelshelf. 'You were away early today.'

Sometimes Isabel found the know-all side of his nature getting on her nerves, but tonight she was not affected by his habitual nosy-parkering. 'I went towards the coast.' She began to describe her day, and as she talked Curtis grew calm and easy, stopped pacing, and stretched himself out in Tom's armchair. 'It's quite a different world out there,' she said. 'Not what I expected at all.'

'We used to go there for holidays as children. Mary and I used to sit on the rocks by the sea, wonder how far it was to the horizon and argue where the mainland was.'

'Emigration dreams?'

'In our hearts we all want to leave, and in our hearts we know we never will.'

Isabel felt her own heart going out to him. This was the off-duty, sympathetic Curtis, dropping his guard and speaking freely for a change. 'I didn't actually see the sea,' she said, rehearsing a line from her rejected broadcast, 'but there was ocean light in the sky and seabirds on the lawn – altogether I had quite an adventure.' Curtis was naturally curious to hear everything, and she unfolded her story, hesitating in her mind about how and when to introduce Mallory.

Curtis saved her the awkwardness. 'Talking of restoration,' he said, interrupting, 'would you like to see what Peter Dobbs gave me this morning?'

Of course she would. Politeness was her best armour against the inescapable fact of his love for her. He was already unrolling the portrait on the floor. She sat on the edge of her chair and peered down. 'Who are they?'

'It's hard to say until they've been cleaned.'

'It needs more than cleaning.' She bent down to examine it. 'Look. It's torn.' A plan was forming in her mind. 'Who's going to restore it for you?'

Often, when he hesitated, it was to protect a source or to compose the right coded sentence, but now, she saw, he was simply unsure of his answer. 'To be honest, I've no idea.'

'At a loss, Joe?' she teased. 'That's not like you at all.' She held the portrait up to the light and saw that the canvas was worn threadbare. 'It really does need expert treatment.' Then she saw an opportunity. 'As a matter of fact – ' She described her meeting with Bennett and Sarabeth.

'If it was properly restored,' Curtis became enthusiastic, 'I could hang it in the Institute.'

This was an invitation to ask how his plans were going.

'I was on my way there just now – perhaps you'd – would you like to come and have a look?'

Yesterday she would have made an excuse. Tonight, she wanted to be taken out of herself. She put the canvas aside. It would be through such projects that they would rediscover their friendship. She could even begin to imagine a day when they might be secure together. She said she would be pleased to go with him. He seemed surprised, and then pleased himself.

It was her habit, sitting at her desk, to curl her legs under her. She extracted herself from her chair. 'Give me a minute while I put on something presentable.'

'We won't be seeing anyone.'

'You never know,' she called, as she went upstairs, but censored the rest of the thought.

The Institute was an imposing red-brick building set back from the road behind wrought-iron railings, next to the deserted factory on the edge of the town. When there was prosperity, it had been the focus of everyday life, at once a club, a theatre, an indoor games hall and a place to meet. The main auditorium had seen political rallies, ballroom dancing, trade union debates, film shows, amateur theatricals, boxing matches, revivalist meetings and victory celebrations. Upstairs, there had been billiard tables, slot machines and a long bar where the men used to drink and gossip. When the factory closed, the Institute closed with it. By the time Curtis acquired the freehold, it had become dusty with disuse.

Curtis fiddled with the lock. Isabel looked up at the darkened, forbidding exterior. The silence of the evening was broken by the faint but insistent throbbing of a military helicopter in the distance. The door creaked open. Inside, Curtis switched on the lights. Their feet rang out on the stone floor as he led the way down the hallway to the auditorium. The emptiness and the sense of a world just ended was eerie. There were unsteady pyramids of metal chairs piled along the walls and faded curtains half-drawn across the platform. A slogan from the last rally hung limply from the flies. In the wings, heaped in wicker baskets, there were musty piles of military uniforms. As Curtis knew only too well, the Institute's less publicised political activities had been one reason why the authorities had not discouraged its closure.

Isabel shivered. 'There are a lot of ghosts here.'

'I'll soon blow away the cobwebs,' he said proudly, spreading his plans on the front of the stage. He was going to put the place on the map, make it a conference centre, the only one of its kind, attracting business from all over. Perhaps she would help him write the prospectus. Tourism was the one industry that would surely bring prosperity back to the town. 'People will come from miles around.' Now he was boasting. 'It's a great opportunity we have here. Mr Hu agrees with me.'

'Is he involved in this too?'

'We're talking.' An unexplained reticence came into his voice. 'That's all I'm prepared to say at this stage.' He sounded like a politician. 'You see, Isabel, we have to open up new horizons, and find new perspectives. I want the Institute to promote peace and harmony.'

Isabel was curious to know where he would get the investment for such an ambitious scheme.

'No problem. There are loads of government grants for anything that sounds like 'normalisation'. Everyone wants to bring a smile to the face of these parts. Look at your country house. It's just a question of going to the right sources.'

'You're very confident.'

'In the property game you have to be. It's a question of keeping all the balls in the air.' He was growing uncharacter-

istically forthright. 'It's a new challenge for me. I'll enjoy it.'
As they went upstairs, Curtis developed his ideas. Perhaps the
new building should bear his name. 'I can't decide. What do
you think?'

'If you want permanence, you should stick with the Institute. That's how it's known, Joe.'

'You're right. It's the community that matters.' He pointed
to a bare patch on the wall. 'We'll restore that canvas and hang
it there in the place of honour.'

Isabel did not interrupt. She was pleased to hear him so full
of plans.

The Institute would, Curtis said, aspire to an ideal of
community. It would harmonise, inspire and unite. 'The
community,' he repeated, like a pledge. His optimistic reverie
was interrupted by a loud banging on the door downstairs.

As Stephen stepped inside, the door behind him slammed in
the wind, sending a premonitory echo through the empty
stone hallway. He looked up at Isabel. She was leaning over
the banisters. The gloomy institutional light over the stairway
swung in the sudden draught and threw her shadow across the
wall. She seemed to tower above him, but when she spoke,
breaking the silence, her voice was small and hesitant.

'What are you doing here?'

'I was sent,' he replied.

He saw she had lost her self-possession and he wanted to
take charge, but he was on her territory, and there was an
unfamiliar figure standing behind her on the staircase.

Curtis was like a spectator in a drama he couldn't understand. 'Who is this?' he challenged.

'Dr Mallory and I,' Isabel began, mastering herself at last,
'met just recently.' Her nervous smile darted between the two
men as if unsure of its loyalties. 'But I did not expect to see
him again so soon.'

She hurried down the stairs to meet him as she spoke. He
was here; he was hustling. But she had no anger left for him.

Curtis followed at a distance, as if he knew he had walked into the wrong scene.

Stephen and Isabel shook hands. He wanted to laugh out loud at the absurdity of the gesture; then he dropped his voice. 'There's something I have to ask you.'

She flew from his discretion, and turned nervously to add Curtis to the circle. Stephen glimpsed another Isabel, naturally poised, as Bennett had said, but naturally self-protective too.

'Joe Curtis,' she said. 'The new proprietor of this Institute.'

Stephen stepped forward to introduce himself. 'I think I just met your sister,' he said. 'She directed me here.'

'One of yours, I see,' said Curtis resentfully, ignoring the visitor and looking at Isabel.

She only half heard him. She was still digesting her surprise. 'Why? I mean – what have you come for?'

'I need to speak to you alone for a moment.' There was urgency in his voice – a man with a mission – but he managed an easy smile towards Curtis. 'Mainland talk, you know.'

'I see,' said Curtis.

Isabel recognised his instinctive suspiciousness coming into play. Curtis hated other people's secrets, and this was his nightmare, a story in his own backyard he knew nothing about. 'I won't be a moment, Joe,' she said. 'Promise.' Stephen followed her into the empty auditorium and closed the door.

'What are you doing here?' She heard the anger creeping back into her voice with dismay. She didn't like to be caught off-guard, and she was torn between so many feelings. Coming in, she had seen herself in the glass in the hallway and had momentarily wished for a fairy godmother.

'I'll explain,' he said. 'Give me a minute.'

They paced slowly across the darkened floor. Looking at Isabel in the orange glow of the streetlight beyond the neo-Gothic windows, Stephen was conscious of being quite alone with her, and for a moment he felt in danger of forgetting the purpose of this mad dash across the countryside. His anxieties about security seemed suddenly tedious and irrelevant.

Almost before he realised it, he said: 'You left very quickly.'

'I had to get back.' She became defensive again. 'I have a piece to write, or should I say – ' she paused and smiled forgivingly, ' – to make up?'

'I'm sorry,' he said. 'It was a thoughtless comment.'

In the silence, there was a mutual truce. Then she said: 'I don't believe you've come all this way to apologise.'

He admitted this was so. She stopped. 'What's the matter?'

Stephen summarised his meeting with Windermere.

'D'you know, I guessed he would be trouble.' Isabel described her own encounter with the general. 'Does he really think I'm a threat to his safety?'

'Well, it may seem absurd, but that's why I'm here.' He hesitated. 'Mainly.'

'Of course,' she murmured, answering the playful look in his eye. 'I won't forget.'

They paced in silence for a moment, then the journalist in her reasserted itself. 'So you're saying, or he's saying, that I'm not to be trusted.' She sounded crisp and professional. 'What does this mean in practice?' She stretched her arms out wearily, as if flexing her strength. 'You see, I have a job to do. It's called broadcasting.'

'It means – look, I know this is ridiculous, but – '

'You also have a job to do.' For a moment, he couldn't decide if she was genuinely disappointed or just teasing, but then she yawned and said, quite sharply: 'God, I hate politics.' Now she was confronting him, and there was no amnesty in her expression. 'So, go on, tell me. What does all this shit add up to?'

He knew he seemed awkward; he wished he had more of her cool; with him, it always seemed off-putting not manipulative. 'The general's request is that you keep his story to yourself.'

'This sounds like news management from the paranoid tendency.'

'It was a private visit.'

'You knew I was there from the start.' She could be very unrelenting. 'Bennett was most punctilious about that.'

He didn't want to have this conversation; he felt tired; he heard himself losing patience. 'All I'm asking is that you keep the general's name off the air.' He hesitated, but could not stop himself. 'And perhaps you could also find it in your heart to be discreet about the trust as well.'

'I'm not sure I appreciate sarcasm from someone who's asking a favour,' she said coldly.

Isabel saw his dismay, and this time it was her turn to apologise. She admitted what he already knew, that her anger was always closer to the surface than she realised, and try as she might she sometimes couldn't stop herself.

He was touched by her frankness. 'It's been a long day,' he said. The apparent lack of artifice or calculation in her emotions, he decided, gave her a kind of innocence.

She found she liked him for his sympathy, and spoke the thought aloud. 'I think you are probably rather nice,' she said, as though discussing an absent friend. When he demurred, she said she always used to be against niceness. 'Now I can see that it has its uses,' she said with another smile.

He forced himself to bring up the other worry in his mind. 'Did you mention anything about your trip to – to – ?' He searched for the name.

'Curtis?'

He nodded. 'Who is he?'

'Joe's a big wheel around here, but anyway he's my neighbour and friend, really.' She realised as she spoke that she had never described her relationship with Curtis to another man before, and it was odd to hear the summary in her inner ear. 'He once – ' She stopped.

'Once what?'

'It doesn't matter.'

Stephen wondered about the 'really', but now knew better than to press.

'I think,' said Isabel, bringing the discussion back to safer ground, 'that I may have said something about the trip as we came down here, but it was quite casual. I can easily explain that it was not for publication – if that's what I decide to do.'

'So – ?' He let the question hang in the air.

'So – will you let me make up my own mind, please?'

She turned away and walked with determination towards the door. Stephen followed, regretting his inability to control the tone of the meeting. Nothing seemed to have been settled; everything seemed to be uncertain between them. Outside, there was the sound of a door banging, a murmur of voices, approaching footsteps, and then a tentative knock. 'Come in,' Isabel called out. 'We're done in here.' It was like a cry for help.

The door swung open and Curtis came in, accompanied by a small, dark, ebullient-looking man in corduroy trousers. Peter Dobbs, brimming over with apologies for the interruption, shook hands all round. 'I was taking the evening air as usual when I saw this unfamiliar motor car sitting outside the Institute. A military car, I said to myself. I wonder if my friend Joseph is in need of some friendly assistance, I said. I didn't mean to intrude, but curiosity's my middle name, as my dear wife says. Now tell me, Dr Mallory, would you be a military man?'

Stephen was aware that behind Dobbs's cheerful smile there was the cold light of distrust. He hastened to explain that he was nothing to do with the army. The two men listened, unconvinced. Isabel came to his rescue. 'Dr Mallory is here with a heritage organisation from the mainland.'

Now it was Curtis who took up the case for the prosecution. Isabel found an unfamiliar hardness in his expression. 'Then it would appear,' he was saying, 'that the army is taking up conservation work.' His smile was challenging. There was none of his former diffidence. He was waiting for an explanation.

Throughout his recent career, Stephen had often found himself in the half-lit world between society and the state. He had imagined, coming home, that now he was returning to a more straightforward environment, there would be a compensating measure of privacy. It was annoying, shocking even – how could he have been so naïve? – to discover that here, at home, the challenge to his identity was more direct, and that there were fewer smokescreens to throw. 'I happen to have one or two friends with military connections,' he said, thinking, as he spoke, that if the general could see him now he would have an apoplectic fit. 'I needed a car at short notice to visit Miss Rome about a private matter.' He stressed 'private' fiercely.

Curtis was beginning to enjoy himself again. 'I didn't know the army was in the car hire business as well,' he said, sharing a cruel smile with Dobbs.

'It's probably highly irregular, but they simply offered me a lift.' He could not suppress the irritation in his voice. 'Just to set the record straight, and because you obviously don't believe a word I say, I'm not an art historian either,' he added, glancing ironically at Isabel. 'I do however work for an organisation that specialises in political consultancy and the evaluation of risk.'

Curtis was interested. 'Risk?'

'Electoral, business and personal. The world, as you know only too well, is full of hazards. If you are in politics, or business, you want to minimise the risk. So you come to my company for advice. We offer a consultancy on a wide range of political issues, from general elections to municipal corruption. We assess the situation. We calculate the risk. We even arrange protection.'

He pulled out his wallet and handed cards to Curtis and Dobbs. 'If I can be of service any time.' Curtis stared at the card in his hand.

Dr Stephen Mallory
FINK WAGNER ASSOCIATES
Political consultant

There was nothing else. No phone. No address. 'A nice piece of printing, Dr Mallory.' He gave a queer, chilly laugh. 'You've chosen a good place for risks alright.'

Stephen noticed that he was watching to see if he would also give a card to Isabel, and decided to keep him guessing.

'Everywhere has its dangers,' he replied pleasantly. 'Sometimes, the safer you feel, the greater the risk.' He glanced at Isabel again. 'Life is so unexpected. Things always happen when you're busy making other plans.'

'Thank goodness,' she said, meeting his eye with amusement. She seemed to have recovered herself.

The exchange of looks aroused Curtis's hostility, but Stephen sensed that this was deflected by the enigma of his unexpected arrival. Curtis was intrigued and challenged; he had to find out. Now he was suggesting that they all take 'a little something' in the administrator's office. Stephen looked at Isabel and then at his watch. 'Come on,' she said. 'The driver can wait.'

'Perhaps I should invite him to join us.'

'He's not allowed to leave the car unattended,' said Curtis.

'Especially in a place like this.' Dobbs seemed to find a special satisfaction in the hint of violence.

'Now then, Peter,' Curtis was admonishing. 'We don't want to give our visitor the wrong impression.' He attempted a smile. 'A bit of graffiti and a couple of empty houses doesn't make a ghetto.'

'It seems peaceful enough to me,' said Mallory, making conversation.

They went into a bare room with a desk and a heap of packing cases. Curtis took a bottle and some glasses out of a drawer and poured a round of whisky. 'Cheers.' Stephen felt strangely happy to be standing next to Isabel.

'So,' said Curtis equably, as if all animosity was gone. 'How are you liking it here?'

Stephen replied that he'd hardly arrived, but that he liked what he found. A memory and a curiosity met in his mind and he asked about Hickey's Mission of Hope and Salvation.

Curtis gave a brief explanation. 'They say he's not been getting the audiences he's used to,' he concluded, and refilled Stephen's glass.

Isabel said pleasantly: 'Perhaps you should come over and

take on Mr Hickey as a client. I'm sure you'd know how to boost his ratings.'

'Religion?' Stephen shook his head. 'Not if I can avoid it.' He smiled. 'I like my consultancies to be on a rational basis.'

'Then you'll take my advice and never do any business here,' said Curtis shortly. 'Will you excuse us a moment?' He drew Dobbs outside into the corridor.

Stephen wondered, with a mild flutter of alarm, what they were discussing. He looked awkwardly at Isabel. 'I should go.'

Isabel knew that she had offended Curtis's pride, but she couldn't explain this now. She found a temporary interpretation. 'Don't mind Joe,' she said. 'His bark is much worse than his bite.' Secretly, she was dismayed at the scope of his ill will; she would have to revise her hopes for his friendship. She had never imagined that a harmless joke and a few minutes with Stephen could become the basis for so much distrust and jealousy.

'In this business you get used to it,' he replied, putting down his glass. He did not want to go, but he had no choice. 'I have to get back. We have an early start tomorrow.'

In the silence, they heard Curtis's fierce undertone outside.

'I'm glad you came,' she said.

'So am I.'

'Can I have a card too?'

He knew this was only playful, but he took one out of his wallet anyway and scribbled his home number on the back. 'Do you ever come over?'

'Sometimes.' She smiled again. 'If I'm invited.' She tucked it into her pocket. 'I guess you already have my number – from your army friends.'

He nodded. 'I'm afraid so. There's not much they don't know about the people here. I didn't mean to intrude.'

'I'm glad you did,' she said again. She hesitated. 'Don't worry about the general.' It amused her to think that privately she had already rejected the broadcast.

'Thank you.'

They walked into the hallway. Curtis and Dobbs were still

deep in conversation. At the door, Stephen shook hands all round, rather formally, and went out alone. The others watched the tail-lights of his car disappear into the night.

'Now then, Isabel,' said Curtis, as the car turned the corner, 'will you tell us what that young man was up to?'

'Do you really want to know?' She had already decided that if she was going to berate Curtis for his rudeness she would do it in the privacy of her own parlour.

'I think we do,' said Curtis, self-confidently. Dobbs, at his side, nodded his agreement.

'Well, if you must know, I think he wants to sleep with me,' she said, calculating the level of frisson. 'And as a matter of fact, just for the record, Joe, I think I might let him.' She turned to go, light as ever. 'If he asks nicely.'

9

In the end, Isabel changed her mind and decided to pay tribute to Bennett's restoration work. She stood in front of her hearth, script in hand before an imaginary audience. '. . . but the millionaire who conceived this magnificent hall was a founding father of the colonial settlement here. Patriarch, gangster, landowner and entrepreneur, he was notorious in his lifetime for his sharp practice, hard bargaining and political savvy.'

Faintly, through the wall, she could hear Curtis on the telephone. She knew he would be sitting there in his dressing-gown, chewing on a cigar and leafing through the Saturday newspapers as he talked. In the summer, when the weather was good, she would see him sitting out in the back garden in his pyjamas, engaged in what he called 'keeping up'. No one, not even Mary, knew the substance of these calls.

She returned to her script. 'It's as though he made peace with himself and posterity in the execution of his grand design, a vision more splendid than many of the finest houses on the mainland from which he had come as a penniless refugee . . .'

The telephone was ringing in the kitchen. She hurried through. 'Hello,' she said, abrupt with concentration. 'Oh hello.' She carried the receiver through to her chair by the fire.

Yes, she was fine. She hoped the trip was going well. So it was over already. When was he going back? No – no, she didn't have any plans for tomorrow. Yes, she'd like that. (He was polite yet pleasantly organising.) Would he prefer to come here? 'Your military friends can direct you,' she said, and got a laugh. Now she was smiling, too. Finally, she rang off. 'Well – praise the Lord,' she said, and went involuntarily to the mirror.

How many minutes passed? She could not say, but now she was at the window, looking out, calming the expectancy in her heart. As she stood there, poised to go back to work, indecisive with excitement, a large black limousine cruised into view.

The car glided to a stop outside her front door, parking arrogantly in the middle of the street. She could see the chauffeur peering out to check the number, speaking over his shoulder to the passengers behind the glass. As the nearside door opened, Isabel stepped back from the window. There was the shortest of pauses, then a knock.

The young man in the electric-grey suit was carrying a portable telephone. His commercial smile opened on cue. 'Isabel Rome?' His accent was all-purpose American, anonymous but self-confident.

'That's right.' She noticed, as she answered, that there was another young man, advertising the same lifestyle, hovering in the background.

'Hi,' said the first. 'I'm Fred Shuster. This is Zach.'

'Hi,' said the second, also shaking hands. 'Zach Shoemaker.' He had a neat pony-tail; otherwise they might have been twins. They were both perfectly tanned, perfectly groomed, and they both had perfect, meaningless smiles. There was a moment of hesitation between them, and then Fred took the lead again. 'Tom gave us your number. He said to call.' He was laid-back, but coolly demanding. 'He sends his best,' he added.

'Tom Harris?' She tried to conceal the surprise in her voice.

'That's right,' said Zach, smiling again. 'He said he was going to call you ahead of time.'

She was about to say that he hadn't, but thought better of it. 'How can I help you?'

Fred took over; he was the senior partner. He appeared to have no interest in her marital history. From his expression, · she could imagine him saying that these days divorces were a-dime-a-dozen. 'Tom said this place might make a good location.'

'A good location?'

'We're with Troy,' Fred explained, indicating the limousine.

'It's like he hopes to shoot his next video over here. I guess you've read about the concert in the press, Isabel?' he went on, pressing the sincerity button.

She nodded. She had noted the singer's reputation in the newspapers some days ago and had consciously excluded the subject from her mind.

'So the idea is – is that we do a video.' He pointed with the telephone. 'And we've got Clive Fox very excited to do something –'

'Clive Fox?' The name was half-familiar from the old days. 'The film director?'

'Right.' Fred clicked his fingers in assent. He was like a teacher with a backward child; on the edge of exasperation, he and Zach seemed relieved she was beginning to understand their language. 'Clive's with Troy in the limo. It was Tom who suggested to Clive we got in touch. You know Clive?'

'Not really – but Tom does, of course.'

'Right.' Both Fred and Zach seemed pleased at their progress.

'Is Tom involved in this, too?'

Fred and Zach's satisfaction turned to unease, as if neither were sure what answer she would want to hear. 'Yeah.' Fred was handling this one. 'Well, maybe. I mean, probably no.'

'Perhaps,' said Zach. 'It could go either way.'

'I see.' They were so transparent they were almost charming.

Two boys, pedalling curiously up the hill, began to examine the limousine with frank expressions of amazement.

'If you parked down the street, you could all come in and talk,' said Isabel practically.

'Sure. Great idea. Thanks. It's kind of damp out. We'll just get Clive and Troy.' Fred clicked his fingers again. 'Hey, Zach, let's go.'

They almost jogged across to the car. Isabel watched as the door opened and a tall, long-haired figure in dark glasses, jeans and leather jacket climbed out. He was followed by a stouter, older man in a crumpled linen suit with a camera slung round his neck. She had only seen photos of Troy, but she recognised

Clive Fox's owlish features and tangled grey hair. She realised, with a flashbulb memory, that they had last met at her wedding.

Fred waved the chauffeur on, and the car slid off, pursued by a flotilla of curious children. The visitors, an incongruous foursome, walked over to Isabel's door, looking about them and stretching after the journey.

'What a great location,' Clive was saying. The ocean of his enthusiasm, Isabel remembered, always flooded his conversation with short-lived superlatives.

Fred made the introductions. 'Pleased to meet you, Isabel,' said Troy, gently shaking hands. His voice was surprisingly light and pleasant.

Clive said: 'Tom sends his best.'

Isabel found it all rather strange. She invited them to follow her into the tiny living-room. 'How is Tom?' she asked, realising that this was the first time since his departure she had spoken to someone who had seen him in his new life.

'He's fine,' said Clive, non-committally.

'He sure was right about this location,' said Zach to no one in particular.

Isabel tried to inject a note of normality into the situation by offering coffee.

'Decaff?' Fred asked hopefully.

'I'd prefer tea,' said Zach.

'I have Earl Grey,' she replied.

After some discussion about the stimulating properties of Earl Grey, they decided they would prefer water.

'Perrier or Badoit?' asked Zach, as if in a restaurant.

'In this establishment,' she replied, 'I'm afraid it comes from the tap.'

'The tap?' Fred was alarmed.

She nodded.

'Oh no – no thanks,' he said, sadly.

'We'll leave it,' said Clive with a smile, interpreting for the group.

Isabel asked what sort of a video they were making.

'It's a promo,' said Clive. 'At this stage it's just a five-minute promo.'

'But who knows?' said Troy, with an enigmatic smile. 'It could be a major motion picture.'

Fred and Zach exchanged significant glances.

'I like the idea of film,' the singer went on. 'With film you're in the present tense. Film is now.' He was thinking aloud. 'You get to people's dreams with film.' He strolled back towards the kitchen, inquisitive but detached, humming a tune.

Clive was training his camera on the street outside.

'There he goes again,' said Zach.

'Hey, Clive! What's got you now?' asked Fred.

'Just looking,' said Clive. 'I think this place has really got what it takes.'

'I kind of knew it would,' said Zach. 'Didn't I, Fred?'

'As a matter of interest,' said Isabel, 'what does it take?'

Clive became animated. The others listened respectfully. 'We're looking for symbols. Empty streets, burnt-out houses, soldiers with automatic weapons. We want to convey a sense of loss. You know, the waste, the pity and the shame.'

'He's good,' commented Fred, to no one in particular.

'D'you know what my album's going to be called?' said Troy, coming back into the conversation and speaking directly to Isabel.

'I'm afraid I don't.' His expression aroused her most maternal thoughts.

He was suddenly shy. ' "Going Native," ' he said.

Fred also noticed his client's anxiety. 'Great title,' he said quickly.

'Do you like it?' Troy paid no attention to his entourage. Looking at Isabel, he seemed touchingly unsure.

'Yes,' she said. 'I do like it. It sounds good. It sounds as though it's about something.'

'It does?' He seemed relieved.

'It's a great title,' said Clive definitively. He had the older man's authority. 'And this is just the place for the pictures. I mean, it's so nostalgic.' He began to speak in his own private shorthand. 'Memories of empire. The experience of pain. The desolation of bereavement. A touch of madness –'

'As it happens,' said Isabel, interrupting, 'rather more than a touch. There's a mental hospital up the road.'

'No kidding,' said Zach.

'No kidding,' said Isabel.

Fred's smile was almost genuine. 'Well, what do you know?' He turned to Troy. 'Real live crazies.'

'Now we're cooking with gas,' said Zach.

'What did I tell you?' said Clive. 'Tom always said it was the business.'

The absent spirit of Tom Harris filled the pause in the conversation. 'Were you married long?' asked Fred, with distant anthropological interest.

'Seven years.' Even now, she found it hard to admit that it was over, or to talk about it in the past tense, as if it was just a memory.

'Seven years.' Fred was impressed. 'No shit,' he said. 'This insane asylum,' he went on, focusing his attention. 'Any chance we could check it out?'

'Whatever for?' Isabel was dismayed.

'He means,' Clive explained, 'that he'd like to see round the town and perhaps have a look at the hospital on the way.'

Troy was conferring with his two managers. 'Would you mind?' For a cult singer with an international following and a name for causing trouble, he was impressively polite.

Isabel said she would ask Joseph Curtis, her neighbour, to join them. 'He really knows the town,' she said. Perhaps his sister would be at home. She found herself enjoying the prospect of introducing Fred and Zach to Mary Curtis.

They filed out into the street. The rain had lifted and there were patches of blue overhead.

Curtis's natural curiosity brought him to the door at once. Isabel introduced him all round; his eyes darted this way and that as he sized up the situation. Mary was over at the hospital, he said, catching up on her paperwork, but there would be no problem about visiting her. He was delighted to be involved. 'I've often thought this would be a good place for a film,' he said. 'Especially down by the old works.'

'That's what Tom said,' said Clive.

'Tom?' Curtis looked at Isabel in momentary confusion.

'Yes,' she said with a smile. 'We owe this pleasure to public enemy number one.'

'Don't be like that,' said Clive lightly.

Curtis drew Isabel to one side. 'Shall I bring Paul? He's here for the day. I can't really leave him.'

'You'll have to,' she murmured. 'I'll explain.'

As Curtis hurried indoors, Isabel spoke to the group, addressing herself to the singer. She broke off when Curtis reappeared with Paul, holding him by the hand. The boy was wearing his Walkman. He smiled bashfully at the group, but did not speak.

They began to walk down the street, Curtis leading the way with Paul. Troy seemed quite at ease, looking about with interest. Clive engaged Isabel in some gossip about mutual friends and skirted round the subject of her errant husband. Zach and Fred brought up the rear with the stilted gait of city-dwellers who are used to taking taxis. In a few minutes they had passed the war memorial and reached the gates of the deserted factory.

Curtis took them down the side of the main hall, along a lane with high brick walls. There was the sound of running water somewhere close underground. Thick, weedy growth was pushing up through the cracks in the concrete and choking the passages between the mill and its outhouses. They stepped through a broken door, climbed over a few fallen rafters and then they were inside, surveying an empty space scattered with industrial debris and rusty bits of machinery, spindles and shafts. As they stood there, it went suddenly bright with spring sunshine diffused through the opaque glass roof.

'Like a studio,' commented Troy. 'You know,' he said to Isabel, 'I used to be a designer.'

The others said nothing. It was quite still. The silence was broken by the sound of dripping water. 'This was once big business,' said Curtis. 'Four hundred looms when I was a boy, and now not one.'

They were all hushed, as if in a kind of church. Fred was whispering to Zach. The floor was littered with giant spools and tangled thread. Their crunching footsteps echoed under the glass. In the manager's office, there was an old coat thrown across a broken chair and a calendar on the wall.

'It took four generations to build this up,' said Curtis. 'And it went under the hammer in just two days.'

'We could use this,' said Clive, taking photographs.

'Who owns it now?' asked Fred.

Curtis explained that it belonged to Mr Hu, the restaurateur. There were vague plans to turn it into a garden centre, but nothing had been settled.

'Hey, Fred.' Troy was suddenly decisive. 'Let's get the details. This Mr Hu,' he went on, 'would he like the idea of a video?'

'If I say so,' said Curtis.

Fred was making a note. 'So that's the way it is round here.' He seemed glad to be talking to an equal.

'You can't do anything without Joe,' said Isabel, with a flattering smile in Curtis's direction. 'Can they?'

'It's best if I'm involved,' he said quietly.

They came out into the sunlight and strolled round the back of the factory. Curtis pointed out the millrace and the rotting mill-wheel. In a few minutes they were standing outside the gates again and Clive Fox was taking photographs of the violent revolutionary slogans on the wall.

Isabel stood apart, listening to the wind in the trees. Paul came up and stood next to her. 'Hello,' she said softly. He did not reply. For a moment, she thought she heard a baby crying, then realised, with a shiver, that it was only the sound of two branches squeaking against each other.

'Great graffiti,' Zach was saying to the singer. 'I mean, can we use this or what?'

'Remember that line?' Troy replied. '"Their loves and lives are written on the wall."'

'Right,' said Zach, nodding uncertainly.

Clive came over from the other side of the street. 'How far is it to the hospital?'

Curtis pointed across the fields. 'There,' he said. 'Only five minutes.'

Isabel looked at him with dismay. There was something indecent about his eagerness to please.

Glimpsed down the drive, the house had a grey quietness, a countrified distinction. As they came closer, the disrepair became more obvious. 'This is for sale, too,' said Curtis. 'There's talk of making it a hotel.'

There were some patients from 'Blue' outside on the lawn. They were playing baseball, helped by two nurses in white overalls. When they saw the visitors approaching, they abandoned their game and started to move towards them. Paul, seeing his fellow inmates, broke into a lopsided run. Another boy came towards him. 'Happy Easter,' he shouted, tugging at his hair. One of the nurses hurried after him. 'Come on, Matthew, it's not Easter yet.' Isabel watched Paul, with his Walkman in his ears, merge into the group. She waved goodbye. Paul waved back, and then turned away. Clive Fox was taking more photographs. The patients clamoured for attention with gaping smiles.

Zach was excited. 'Isn't this wild?'

Mary, hearing the noise, came out. She had her long-suffering expression. Curtis went across the gravel to meet her. Isabel could see him arguing with his sister and watched her resistance to a guided tour slowly fade. Curtis came back. 'Fine,' he said. 'She'd rather we didn't stay long, but I can give you an idea of the place.'

They followed him into the panelled hallway. There was a Victorian picture of a sailor with a fiddle and a wooden leg, a reproduction, over the fireplace. A mad child with a dog-eared book wandered past, indifferent to the visitors. They went down a foul-smelling, lime-green corridor into a dayroom with plastic toys scattered across the linoleum. Around the walls, on sheets of coloured cardboard, were Polaroid snapshots of the patients in various kinds of activity – by the seaside, at a Christmas party, lined up by a coach. A television was blaring senselessly in the corner, but the room was empty. There was a strong smell of urine and disinfectant. 'In the good old days,' Curtis was saying, 'this was the library.' Clive asked about the history of the house. Curtis gave him a short sketch as they climbed upstairs. Troy said nothing. Fred made notes.

The bedrooms had become dormitories with iron bedsteads, shiny floors, and teddy bears and dolls propped on red hospital blankets. The woodchip wallpaper was peeling where the patients had tried to tear it down. Two cleaners were mopping up. Looking out of the window, Isabel could see an empty stone fountain in the middle of the overgrown garden. Down the corridor, another patient came into view briefly, dragging a pair of trousers.

'Put your trousers on, Garry,' said one of the nurses. 'No one's impressed.'

The visitors were subdued, just looking. No one had much to say. After a while, they were back in the hallway again, standing under the picture of the sailor.

'Well, thanks Isabel,' said Troy. She had become his ally; she imagined he was lonely inside his fame.

Behind them, within, mad laughter echoed down the corridor, and then screaming. Outside, a girl of perhaps sixteen came running across the lawn, shouting senselessly. Her voice was high and disconsolate. Clive seemed to have lost his enthusiasm for taking photographs.

'Let's go,' said Troy. He nodded to Fred, who punched a number into his portable phone and began speaking to the chauffeur. 'Thanks, Joe.'

'Will we see you again?'

Isabel knew that Curtis was uneasy with the uncertainty sowed by the singer and his men. Curtis did not like loose ends.

'Why not?' said the singer airily. 'Like they said, it's a great location. The town, I mean.'

Fred interrupted with a new worry. 'What's the security situation like here? I mean, would there by any trouble?'

Curtis appeared reluctant to admit any threat of danger. 'You shouldn't believe everything you read in the newspapers,' he said with a weak smile. 'This is quiet enough. I'll guarantee that.'

Isabel felt he was misleading them. 'You'd be advised to take out some insurance.'

'No kidding,' said Zach, with a worried look at Fred.

'The ministry's on our side already,' Fox explained. He seemed anxious to allay the Americans' fears. '"Normalisation", you see.'

'You'd also be wise to organise some security,' Isabel persisted.

Curtis broke in quickly. 'Leave that to me. I can deal with security.'

'Perhaps,' Zach began doubtfully, 'perhaps we'll check with the ministry when we get back to the mainland. We don't want a screw-up.'

Isabel turned to Curtis. 'You should give them that card.'

He was deliberately obtuse. 'What card?'

'Mallory's. He's the expert here.'

Fred pulled out his notebook, sweeping aside Curtis's reluctance. 'Who's this?'

With an ill grace, Curtis explained.

Fred was already making plans. 'Sounds good. We'll check him out when we get back.'

'The last thing we want is trouble,' said Zach nervously. 'But Fred'll fix it, no problem.'

'Let's go,' said Troy, apparently unconcerned. He was already strolling towards the limousine, as it crunched over the gravel. 'See you later, guys,' he said casually.

'We're out of here,' said Zach hurriedly.

Clive Fox exchanged a private goodbye with Isabel and climbed inside.

'Want a ride?' Fred was holding the door open.

Isabel said she'd walk back. The smell in the hospital had given her a headache; she wanted some air and time to think. Curtis said he'd walk with her, and though she would have preferred the time to herself, it was hard to refuse.

'See you later.' Fred slammed the door.

They waved goodbye and the car, like a spacecraft from another galaxy, cruised away down the drive.

'A pop video,' said Curtis out loud.

Isabel knew Curtis had something else on his mind. 'What's the worry?'

'We don't want any trouble, but – ' He hesitated.

'But?'

'Think of the money.' He paused. 'On the other hand, I don't want to annoy the powers that be.'

Now she confronted him. 'Is that why you're so down on Mallory?'

He didn't react at first. Finally he said: 'If I'm against Mallory, you know why.'

'Oh, Joe,' she said, unable to suppress the sadness in her voice.

He shook his head. 'Don't say that,' he said.

IO

The turn to the main street came up round a bend before Stephen realised he had to cross the oncoming traffic. He drove on, pulled over at a bus-stop and let the cars tailing behind overtake him. There was no hurry; he was early. He could sit and listen to the radio in the dark and collect his thoughts.

It had been a relief to say goodbye to Smith and the VIPs.

When they had arrived at the airport, there had been an armed policeman on the door of the VIP lounge. Stephen, leading his party, turned to congratulate Smith on his initiative, but he admitted that it was not his doing. 'There's that rock star in there already,' he said lugubriously. 'Whatshisname.' Smith was a loser who knew his days were numbered and this was his final defeat. Stephen tried to sound encouraging. 'Well, we don't have to tell the general that, do we?'

Smith, cowed by the burden of his inadequacy, gave a bleak smile. 'Thank you, sir.'

The star was sitting in the corner of the lounge with a glass of orange juice. He was tall and loose-jointed, with off-stage vulnerability. Everything about him advertised the music business. His long brown hair was drawn into a pony tail, accentuating his pallid good looks. He was playing chess, on a travelling set, with an older man in a crumpled linen suit whom Stephen took to be his manager.

The VIPs had barely heard of Troy, and a grumble of annoyance at the infringement of their privilege ran through the group as they passed into the privacy of the lounge. One or two made small secret of their hope that there would be no unseemly scenes with fans or reporters. Stephen was amused by this demonstration of the contrast between celebrity and notability.

'Dr Mallory.'

It was Major Potter, blinking watchfully. He had come to say goodbye, he said. Stephen, diplomatic, thanked him for making the visit such a success. Potter took the compliment like a seal taking fish.

'We endeavour to give satisfaction,' he replied, with a small, corrupt smile. He became discreet. 'If you should meet Joseph Curtis again,' he murmured, 'remember that he knows more than's good for him.' Before Stephen had a chance to investigate this remark, the inscrutable major had changed the subject. 'I think we're going to have our hands full with that one,' he went on, indicating the singer.

'What's he doing here?'

'You may well ask. I'm told he's meeting some Americans. There's talk of a video. The media are going to go mad. And now that preacher's threatening to get in on the act as well.'

'Hickey?'

He nodded. 'He said on the radio last night that Troy is an emissary from the devil.' He seemed almost pleased. 'Some things we can control, some things we can't. VIPs yes, rock and religion, no.' He became confidential. 'Entre nous, Dr Mallory, the ministry has let this "normalisation" programme get out of hand.'

Stephen, puzzling over the conversation afterwards, remembered that Potter had a reputation for playing 'a deep game'. Everything was so camouflaged over here. The professional reticence of the liaison people whose responsibility it was to pass his party like a baton from hand to hand was so much their second nature that perhaps only in drink would you ever find a personality or an opinion. 'Unflappable', was the general's approving description. Here he was now, chugging across the lounge with a glass of scotch from the courtesy bar.

'Well, Mallory,' he was saying, 'at the end of the day, a pretty well faultless exercise.' He raised his glass, but kept his eyes averted. 'I hope you'll let bygones be bygones and accept my thanks.'

'Mine, too,' said the professor, overhearing the general's

little speech as he helped himself to drinks. 'An excellent trip. I'll be writing to your people. You can feel very satisfied.'

Stephen replied he was glad it had worked out. He looked around. The ex-minister was staring vacantly at a children's programme on the silent television screen in the corner. The other members of the committee were settling down with drinks and newspapers to wait for the flight. One or two were making discreet calls from the courtesy phones. He noticed Lady Lyon signalling to him across the room with a fluttering hand.

'Now, my dear,' she said, as he joined her. 'I must take your number.'

Stephen took out his business card and added his home number, wondering vaguely what he was letting himself in for.

'The professor,' Lady Lyon was probing experimentally, 'tells me that you are not travelling with us today.'

He parried her inquiry. 'I just thought I would take the opportunity of the weekend to have a longer look round.'

'Excuse me, but perhaps you will continue your acquaintance with that charming young woman from the radio station.' Her scrutiny was frank but sympathetic; he felt her coming uncomfortably close to his secrets. 'She was quite in love with you, I think.'

He gave a brush-off laugh. 'Not after I censored her story she wasn't.'

Lady Lyon seemed unconvinced. She took out her make-up compact and began quite unselfconsciously to apply her lipstick. 'Didn't you chase halfway across the country in a helicopter? The general was terribly impressed. He thought you were concerned only for his safety.' She dropped her voice to a whisper. 'Stupid man.' She popped her things back into her bag. 'Now remind me again – what was her name? – it escapes me.'

'Isabel. Isabel Rome.'

'There.' She snapped the catch on her vanity case. 'I think you are hooked.'

Stephen's denial was interrupted by a voice on the Tannoy calling the flight. With all the fuss and worry of elderly people, the party began to collect itself together. The rock star watched from his corner with ironic detachment.

Stephen made his farewells. Smith and the VIPs moved away down the tunnel to the aircraft. He had longed for the flight to be called and he had longed to regain his freedom, but now they were off, he felt almost nostalgic for their presence. He wondered what the trip had meant to them. Was it just another assignment on the heritage merry-go-round, or was it something more? He would probably never find out.

Suddenly, the hand-shaking was over and he was alone. He went back to the lounge. The rock star and the man in the linen suit had disappeared. For the first time in several days, he felt free. He went over to the bar and poured a large scotch, added ice, sat down in one of the empty armchairs and put his feet up. He half expected the general to come fussing back with a complaint about security on the plane, but his reverie remained undisturbed and in due course he heard the roar of take-off and saw the plane lift past the window and up into the low clouds.

He scanned the newspaper. Each day it published a map of the previous day's violence. Last night had been quiet. Just one killing: a father of three gunned down in front of his family as he watched the evening news. Tomorrow, or the next day, would come the inevitable retaliation from the other side. And so it went on.

He looked at his watch. It was after midday. He put his drink down, went over to the telephone and rang a familiar number. He hoped Louise would be at her gym or on her way to lunch with friends. 'I'm sorry I'm not in at the moment, but I'd love to know you called.'

'Hi,' he said. 'It's me. I'm still over here, but I expect to be back on Monday. I'll call you when I get in. Bye.'

Then he took out his wallet and found the other number he needed, divided between hope and apprehension.

★

Now Stephen shifted behind the wheel and came out of his reverie. The road was clear; it was an invitation. As he turned the car into her street, it occurred to him that he had yet to see Isabel's place in daylight.

The Peking Dragon was blazing with yellow light like an Impressionist painting. Further on, the street was darker, but there was a friendly glimmer in almost every parlour. An army Land-Rover cruised slowly towards him and he watched it out of sight in his mirror before finding number 33. Another faint glow in the window; she was home.

He parked the car and checked himself in the mirror, regretting the tiny shaving cut on his chin. He climbed out and locked up. There was no one about. The smoke of coal fires hung in the air. He walked slowly up the pavement and stopped outside Isabel's door. Then he knocked lightly, three times, and for a moment everything was held in suspense. As he stood there, alone with the thrill of imminence, he heard her turn off the radio, the sound of her casual humming and then her footsteps coming lightly down the passage towards him.

'Here you are at last,' she said, opening the door with a flourish. Her spontaneous smile of welcome dismissed his apprehensions. He said he was afraid he was a bit too early. 'No one pays any attention to time here.' She stood back to let him in. 'It used to drive me crazy when I first arrived. Now I'm as bad as the rest. Everything gets done eventually.' She offered him a drink, apologising for the absence of choice. 'This is not exactly the hub of the social universe.'

They were standing in her parlour. Under the low ceiling, he felt tall and slightly awkward. He chose scotch. 'On the rocks,' he said.

'You've spent too much time abroad,' she remarked.

'I suppose it shows,' he said. 'It's time for a change.'

'Don't tell me: Globetrotter Settles Down.' She gave him a beady look. 'Is this your own idea?'

'I don't understand,' he said, understanding perfectly.

She considered him frankly, as though he was insulting her intelligence. 'No one else in your life?'

'Well, sort of.'

'What's her name, this sort of?'

'Louise.' This was not the conversation he had anticipated, but there was something seductive about her frankness towards him. 'The deal is we both go out with other people.'

'Does she know where you are tonight?'

'She knows I'm coming home tomorrow. But that's all.' He tried to turn the conversation away from himself. 'What's it like here?'

'It's generally pretty quiet,' she smiled at him. 'But there are signs that things may be looking up.'

He smiled back with complicity. 'It does look that way.'

She affected puzzlement. 'So you've heard about it too?'

He was confused. 'Heard about what?'

'You are talking about the video?'

'The video?' Now he was lost, and he had the impression that she intended he should be.

'I thought you meant – oh, I see – ' She interrupted herself. 'There's talk of shooting a pop video here. That rock star, Troy, he was here yesterday afternoon.'

It annoyed Stephen that she had caught him out with his desires, even if she was only teasing. To recover himself, he asked about the singer, mentioning the near-encounter at the airport. He kept Major Potter's comments to himself.

She refilled his glass, and described the visit. 'They found the place nostalgic, they said.'

He said he thought it was rather an odd place to choose.

'Troy – as I've learnt to call him – is into politics. He's written this single called "Ghosts in the Colonial World". It's part of an album entitled "Going Native".'

'That sounds like the pop business.' He returned to his question. 'But why here?'

'It was Clive's idea – you know, Clive Fox, the director.'

'A friend of yours?'

'My husband's,' she said simply.

He looked at her. 'But – ?'

'My ex-husband's, I should say.'

'I see.' He paused. 'Quite risky.'

Now it was her turn to be confused. 'What?'

'Quite risky to film here,' he said quickly.

'That's what his managers think. They're petrified of kidnap and ransom, but our boy is giving them no alternative. He has his reputation to keep up.' She had her playful expression again. 'Actually, I did mention that I knew someone who might be able to help them.'

'Risk is not really my scene,' he said hurriedly, wondering why he was so defensive. 'The risk people are in another department.' He frowned. 'In fact, I'm probably about to recommend that we close it down.'

'So Joe Curtis was right.' She sounded put out. 'You were lying.'

'At the time, it seemed the best explanation. "Political consultant" sounds so vague.'

'I thought you might have enjoyed a trip here from time to time.' She stood up. 'Obviously, I was wrong.' She went into the kitchen. 'Help yourself. I have to look at the chicken.'

He poured himself another finger of scotch. He felt perplexed by his reticence, and ashamed. After a moment, to try to recover the situation, he followed her into the kitchen and sniffed with appreciation. 'Smells good.'

'Poulet à la Rome, a well-known stand-by in this household. I can't get out of old habits. Tom and I used to do this every Sunday. I hope you're hungry. It'll be ready soon.'

Stephen said it was a relief, after so many hotel meals, to have home cooking for a change. He felt formal and unintelligent, but she seemed to be recovering her temper. Once again, he saw how close under the surface her rage was lurking.

'Eating at home,' she said cheerfully. 'That's the big difference between being married and being single.' She was prodding the meat. 'Can you carve?'

'I can try.' He picked up the knife and tested the blade. 'Sharp,' he said, involuntarily.

She nodded, smiling, and offered him a glass of wine. Their fingers touched briefly. 'I must say – ' She stopped herself. 'Cheers,' she said.

'Cheers.'

She sat down and watched him pile the meat onto their plates. 'I'm glad you came,' she said. 'I hate cooking for one.'

'You seem – ' He hesitated, but her expression encouraged him. 'You seem quite relaxed about – about being as you are.'

'Probably more than I feel. I can still panic, but I'm getting used to it.' She sighed. 'Perhaps my days of mourning are over. I hope so.' There was a lull in the conversation; he was not going to get drawn again. 'This is the first time I've had someone round for a meal since Tom left.'

He asked what friends she had in the town.

She hesitated. 'I suppose there's Joe – '

'Joe Curtis?'

She nodded. 'They've been very kind, but with Joe I always know that – ' She stopped herself. 'Well, jealousy is hard to handle.'

'I see,' he said, understanding something about the meeting in the Institute. 'Are you ever lonely?'

She paused in thought. 'Not exactly lonely, but I do feel quite solitary sometimes.' She looked at him with a rather charming naturalness. 'What about you?'

'I grew up as an only child. My sister died of a fever in the tropics when she was four. I was six. Then I was sent away to boarding school. You learn to be alone with yourself in those places.'

'Tell me about your parents,' she said. 'Do you keep them in the picture?'

'Not really.' He stopped, and in his mind's eye, he saw them sitting on their shady patio, drinking gin with the neighbours, strenuously avoiding argument or controversy. 'I'd be afraid to tell my mother too much in case she started worrying.'

'What about your mother? Is she like you?'

For a moment he was almost offended; then he made a joke. 'You don't know what I'm like, so how can I answer that?'

She was quite serious. 'Perhaps I know you better than you think.'

'Oh.' Now he was getting irritated. 'Please tell me.'

'For a start, you don't like my presumption to know you.'

He smiled, unable to help himself.

'And for another thing, you don't like the intrusion. You don't like to give too much away, you like to keep your thoughts to yourself. You like to be elusive. You're annoyingly private, even secretive. You're not as icy as you can sometimes seem, and deep down, you're quite romantic. How am I doing?'

As she spoke, he realised how stupid he had become. He leant forward across the table and kissed her. She was not taken aback, even if she had not expected it. 'Close,' he said. 'Close enough.'

She put out her hand and took his. He stood up. She stood up. 'Do you want to be closer?' she asked.

He was looking into her eyes, pulling her towards him with both hands. 'Yes,' he said, kissing her again.

'Did you say yes?'

'Yes,' he said. 'Yes.' He kissed her. 'Did you?'

'Yes,' she said.

PART
TWO

I

Someone – a dark-horse candidate in a small, faraway country – had won an election against the odds and the office was in a state of whooping euphoria. The news broke at lunchtime; the champagne flowed throughout the afternoon. When the other time zones came into play, the media desk became a crossroads of political and journalistic traffic as wrong-footed diplomats and commentators came to terms with the shift in balance of power. Stephen watched from the outside, thinking: There is nothing like victory.

Once, he had been a winner in the limelight; now, in his self-imposed exile from the wider world, he felt resentful.

He watched his colleagues. They were just bright kids in their twenties having a ball, fired with the idea that they could rule the world, and sporting their yawns with pride. If they showed any interest in him, it was only because they knew he was writing this report and had the ear of the director.

At the end of the day, he sat in the press room with Wagner and two or three senior colleagues, ties loosened, jackets off, chewing over the unexpected turn of events. Images from different channels were jumping on the wall: a bank of televisions with the sound turned down. Beyond the glass, young women assistants passed up and down in bare feet. Jack, in charge of the winning account, was estimating his client's chances. No one, he said, believed that the situation would support a democracy, but it was anyone's guess how long it would be before the army stepped in. The news headlines came up. 'No dice,' said Wagner. 'Those reptiles want tanks not ballot boxes.'

As they broke up, Wagner touched Stephen's arm. 'A word in your ear,' he said.

Wagner was a few years older than Stephen, but regular

squash and swimming gave him the rough good health of an ex-commando. He had founded the company with Fink, his American partner, in the days when the Third World was, as he would put it, 'on the agenda'. Wagner had lived many lives, no one knew quite how many. He had reported small wars, done some ill-defined troubleshooting for multinationals, acted as an unofficial go-between for various agencies, and divorced two wives. He was like a teenage boy for whom the world was an amusing playground. His office was crammed with trophies – silver plaques, a golden statuette, framed diplomas, and signed portraits of forgotten political figures. His book-shelves were loaded with paperbacks and video cassettes. An elaborate music system, wired into his desk, pumped out rock and roll on compilation tapes lovingly prepared by his new wife.

Distinguished clients never saw the inside of this chaotic den, any more than they saw inside Wagner himself. He would always meet them, with a smile and a handshake, in the adjoining boardroom, a businesslike suite in satin grey, mini-mally furnished with a fine mahogany table and half a dozen antique maps in gilt frames.

Wagner closed the door and turned the music down. 'I just can't get that crazy rhythm out of my head.' He sighed. 'Twenty-five years and it still gets to me, know what I mean?'

Stephen congratulated him again on the election. It was sincerely meant, but Wagner, who had the gambler's eye for disappointment, took his opportunity. 'People always cheer the goal scorers,' he said, 'but someone has to make the pass.'

Stephen thanked him for that. He had signed up the candi-date two years before, in the days when he was still ruling the world, and had introduced him to Wagner in the boardroom next door, but in the excitement this had been forgotten. Wagner, with a smile of reminiscence, added: 'A lucky result. He still seems more Gilbert and Sullivan than Henry Kissinger.'

Wagner saw much of the world as a comic opera, and

Stephen, in temporary flight from his own seriousness, liked him for it. 'Perhaps that accounts for his popularity.'

The phone rang. 'Cuba?' Wagner zoomed into focus. 'I'll take it. Excuse me.'

But the line was bad; he stood up and began to shout. 'Tell him to film in the barrios. We need poor people looking into shops with bright lights and a voice-over saying "We don't know what to buy the kids." Okay? Ciao.'

He sat down again. 'Now,' Wagner put his feet on the desk, 'I want to talk about those fuckers in the risk department, Steve.' He swivelled in his chair. 'I could use some more champagne.'

He buzzed his assistant. She came in almost at once with an ice bucket and two glasses. Wagner put a high price on style, and his girls were always in the fast lane. Stephen gave her a welcoming smile; they had slept together in the past, but now he had Isabel on his mind.

'Back for long?'

She bent forward to ease out the cork, and her hair fell over her face in the way he remembered. He nodded, watching the champagne fizz into his glass. 'That's the plan.'

'Do you want to tell me about it?' She gave a barely perceptible wink that Stephen still found rather winning.

'I'll call you, Georgie.'

'Slag,' said Wagner affectionately, as she closed the door. Photographs of his new wife and their baby daughter were arranged like advertisements behind his desk. He glanced at them, frowned, and then raised his glass. 'Down to business, Steve.' He reached into a drawer and pulled out a legal pad and a pencil. 'What's the bottom line? Do I carpet the head of the risk department or what?'

Stephen described the dramas of his recent trip. He had not, he reminded his boss, been expected to take charge, but there had been no alternative. 'God knows what would have happened if Smith had been there on his own,' he concluded.

Wagner was in many ways a decisive man, but he liked to think aloud – as he put it, 'schmooz' – with his closest colleagues first. As he began to talk, Stephen felt his concentration veering back to Isabel. Sometimes, even with people you knew, it was hard to keep them fixed in your mind, but with Isabel he had no difficulty. Was the fact that she had made such a sharp impression on his mental retina to do with love?

'Hey, Steve, I'm talking to you?' Wagner's laid-back manner was superficial. He expected attention.

Stephen apologised. He felt ashamed. Wagner was his patron; he owed him loyalty. During his recent crisis, another boss – Wagner's American colleague for sure – would have let him go. He concentrated hard. Yes, he could have the report ready soon. Yes, he would put the risk department under the spotlight. No, it would not take him long, in Wagner's words, 'to get his shit together'.

Wagner tore off his notes and tossed the pad away, swinging his feet off the desk. 'If I'm going to fire that bastard, I'll need ammunition.'

The session was over. Wagner wanted to gossip. To himself, he was a hard man playing a hard game, but with Stephen he could become the elder brother, indulgent and occasionally bullying. He asked about Louise. Stephen looked away at the photographs behind the desk. 'I think that might be coming to an end,' he said.

'Weren't you a bit cool towards Georgie?'

'It's not like that.'

'You've met someone new?' Wagner seemed pleased. He feared failure and unhappiness like a disease, and often said he preferred his associates to be lucky in life and love.

'Alan, please.' Whatever was happening with Isabel still seemed intensely private. A word from Wagner and the whole office would be talking.

Wagner put a hand on his shoulder. 'You always were the ultimate dark horse, my friend.'

They stepped into the glass corridor. A tall, sandy-haired graduate in a forage cap, sweat-shirt and sneakers was jogging towards them, bouncing a basketball. It was company policy to promote exchanges with the American office. 'Great result, Al,' said the boy. 'Are you guys coming to play in the park?' Wagner smiled and said, regretfully, that he had to go home to his family. 'Steve will play, I'm sure.'

He shook his head. 'I've got too much to catch up with.' He made his excuses and called his assistant. There were a dozen pink message slips awaiting him. Two from Louise; he would deal with the rest in the morning.

In times past, he would have stayed late to handle the election victory, phoning congratulations to the new regime, dealing with the foreign press, and arranging diplomatic liaison. Tonight, it was someone else's baby. He could go home.

The elevator was crowded with secretarial staff lugging their shopping in carrier bags. He felt out of place here, too; he usually ate in restaurants. They reached the street level with a swoop and a bump and scattered in a shower of goodnights.

He went out into the street and felt the cold spring air on his face for the first time all day. He yawned. The tide of commuters flowed towards the steps of the subway and he flowed with it, pausing briefly at a news-stand to buy a magazine and two picture postcards. He hated the anonymity, the smell, the rush, the tangible sense of a hateful routine. The train was crowded as usual; there was barely room to unfold an evening paper. How ill and unhealthy everyone looked. He arrived home in low spirits and poured himself a drink.

Now he stood in his window and watched other people like himself hurrying through the dusk. He lived in the west of the city in a featureless block of service apartments overlooking an underground station, an arterial road, a well-known gay bar and a traffic-clogged bus route. At rush-hour, his rooms would vibrate with the railway and the road and sometimes, on waking, he felt he could taste the fumes and dust of the street in his mouth. Even the jets, cruising in towards the airport, seemed to lower the ceiling of the sky.

He had bought this place as partly a convenient bolt-hole and partly an investment. He never imagined actually having to live here from day to day. The smallness of the space in the vastness of the capital left him feeling lost and insignificant. At first, on his return, this had seemed desirable. Now he was feeling like an athlete whose broken limb is just out of plaster. He wanted to test his muscles again. In the last few days, his new life at home had seemed less appealing. On more than one occasion, he had looked out at the jumbos shuddering up into the cold air and imagined he was on his way again, ears popping, heart racing, spine pressed against his seat, flying to somewhere humid and dangerous.

The phone rang and he picked it up, hoping it was not Louise.

'Hi,' she said, in that casual but challenging manner of hers. 'Did you get my messages?'

He said he had been about to call. It had been a busy afternoon. He mentioned the shock election result, but her thoughts were elsewhere.

'I think I'll come over, okay?'

'Okay.'

'You don't sound very pleased.'

He apologised with habitual half-truths. He had only just got in; he was tired; his mind was full of problems. He put the receiver down, switched on the answerphone, topped up his drink and looked at his watch. She would be here in less than an hour.

He took out his postcards and chose a gaudy view of the city. 'Dear Isabel,' he began, and then stopped. He was not even sure how to spell her name. Isobel? He was making excuses for himself. The truth was that though he loved to read, he found writing painful. With a tape recorder in hand he could dictate almost anything; holding a pen, he was mute and intimidated, embarrassed by the parade and conflict of emotions. At every phrase he explored in his mind, he imagined her smiles at his schoolboy handwriting and callow sentiments.

There was nothing like a deadline. In a few minutes he was racing down the hall and dodging through the traffic to the postbox. Soon after, the doorbell rang and there was Louise, slightly breathless from the climb to the fourth floor.

Louise lived up to the promise of her name, at least as Stephen imagined it. She was a tall woman with short dark hair and an intimidating, even imperious, manner. She was, some said, rather foreign-looking, and Stephen was often surprised, as he watched her come into his rooms, that she should have anything to do with him, or he with her. They were not in love. They were not even close friends, but the relationship satisfied some kind of need. It had become a habit which they could take up when they wanted sex or company. In his clearer moments, Stephen felt ashamed of it, though he could not quite identify the reason. After all, the deal they had made with each other was entirely mutual, an open-plan arrangement that could still give rise to occasional furtiveness. But now, Stephen knew, the time had come to end it.

Louise had a way of invading his apartment that, when he bothered to analyse it, he found irritating. She was always complaining. Sometimes he felt trapped by the thread of scorn and bitterness that ran through her thoughts. She worked in book publishing, and her conversation was full of the vanity and greed of authors. She felt exploited and undervalued. But when he challenged her to get another job, she would reply with resignation that it was probably the best she could expect.

This evening she had a large carrier bag full of typescripts and a shopping basket with orange juice and croissants, a lifestyle manifesto. She dumped these in the hallway, came up and put her arms round him. They kissed. He held her briefly. She was warm from her walk but her face was chill with the evening air. The faint taste of garlic on her breath mingled with her familiar perfume. As he kissed her more slowly again, he felt his old affection for her rise inside him. Behind the power-dressing and the expensive hair, the resentment and the ambition was a straightforward, vulnerable woman who needed him too much and towards whom, with the passage of time, he felt oddly protective, even as he wondered in his mind how to say it was all over.

'So – ' she said. 'How was the trip?'

'It was . . . good.'

'I got your message.'

'Oh. Good. I rang two or three times.' He eased the first lie into the conversation. 'But you were out.' He began to describe what had happened, omitting what he most wanted to discuss, and then interrupted himself. 'Would you like a drink?'

So he had another scotch and she had a glass of white wine and then together they finished the bottle. He began to feel slightly drunk. He suggested they go out for a meal. There was a restaurant down the road whose waitresses reminded him of his best days in the Far East.

They walked. At each street corner they rehearsed their regular disagreement about giving money to beggars. He was for charity; Louise held Victorian opinions about self-help. The city had changed so much during his years away. In one shadowy corner, they passed a woman sitting inside a cardboard box, reading aloud to a ragamuffin child. Stephen, alongside Louise but not touching, found himself envying their closeness.

The restaurant was almost empty, as usual. The maître d' showed them to a table in the corner. Almost without thinking, Stephen ordered a bottle of white wine.

After a few minutes' conversation, Louise broke off. 'Where are you?' she asked. He looked at her as if questioning her meaning, but she said he knew what she meant.

He found a sudden candour and steeled himself to hurt her.

'I don't know where I am,' he said.

'Are you in love?'

This was the question he always feared. In the past, when there had been no one else, and to taunt her, he would say he did not know. Tonight, he was about to be truthful, and then he caught her expression and the appeasing lie came back. 'No,' he said. 'How could I be? There's no one to be in love with.'

'There's me,' she said, twisting the opal ring, his gift, on her right hand.

'I'm sorry,' he said. 'I forgot.' He knew he sounded cruel and hateful, but he did not mean to be. It was the cruelty of the situation they'd imposed on each other, a pain to which they had both grown so familiar it hardly seemed a pain. Their deal was that they were not in love, but the conventional part of Louise always wanted to be seduced before she slept with him.

He touched her hand and their eyes met briefly. He wanted to say, as in a confession, Yes, it's true, I am in love, I'm in love with a woman I met last week. But the words remained frozen inside him. Instead, he drew back still further from the crisis and said: 'It's good to see you again.'

She said: 'I've missed you too.'

When they returned to his flat, they went straight to bed. They made love but there was no playfulness in him and she wasn't satisfied. At first he was silent and miserable and she, disappointed, accused him of selfishness. He apologised again, thinking, this is the end. But the moment for truth-telling had passed.

Louise got up and made tea. He was afraid she would start to cry, but if she did she kept silent and alone. As he drifted off to sleep he heard her channel-hopping for a late-night movie. In the past he would have joined her, and then maybe the sex would have been good, but now with strong feelings of shame and self-disgust, he burrowed into the bed and was soon asleep. Once, during the night, he found himself semi-awake, caressing her body, and realised with a shock that he had been dreaming about Isabel.

He was woken by the shrill early-morning whine of her hair-dryer. She was sitting, half-dressed, on the end of the bed, her dark hair straggling over her face. When she was fully clothed she brought him a cup of tea and began to put on her make-up in front of the mirror. He sat up against the pillows, his hangover beating like a jackhammer, and apologised again for the night before. She dismissed his remorse. 'Don't apologise. It was my fault. We shouldn't sleep together when you're like this.'

Then she kissed him and left for work. He lay there, sipping his tea, unable to believe he had been so cowardly and indecisive. Once again, he stared at the wall and reviewed his life. Quite quickly, he decided he was a hopeless, no, not a hopeless, an impressive failure. Time passed. At nine, he rang the office to say he had been held up. He lay in the bath and listened to the radio. Storms, scandals and sport. The news here at home was so parochial.

The bath said 'home' too. Abroad, it was always showers. As he examined his body, squeezing himself for flab, he thought how much he wanted to share his body, all of it, with Isabel. The absurdity of sex made him smile, but then he thought, it's not absurd, it's life itself, and I want her, I want her more than anything in the world. He imagined wanting her so much he was in pain, and then he realised he was not imagining it, he was feeling it.

Through the window, he could see a rectangle of dirty brick, the back of the next-door building. It was a prisoner's view and it seemed to summarise his life at that moment. He wondered if his years abroad had made it impossible for him to be content here. When the phone rang, he rose out of the water like an animal, but it stopped inexplicably before he could reach it. He stood in the hall, with the water dripping off him, heard the radio talking to itself in the bedroom, and thought that he was the epitome of indecision, unable even to make a choice between getting back into the bath or into his clothes.

It was ten o'clock before he dragged out his office suit and made himself presentable, a business clone. Then he set off, out into the vile morning, joining the other late commuters on the long tunnel to work, passing anonymously into the press and blur of city life, his hopes, desires and frustrations lost in the lives of the millions all around.

2

Clive Fox was not in his room when Stephen arrived for their meeting, and from the way in which he was directed without question to the pool in the penthouse he supposed that the director used this hotel as his base when he was in the city. Stephen felt a little surge of envy for the freedom and anonymity. He could imagine sharing the luxury with Isabel, and wondered what she was doing at that moment. He had been back in the city nearly two weeks and was restless for her.

Fox was exercising alone. When he saw Stephen he waved and swam over to the side. 'Good morning.' He raised a wet arm. Stephen bent down and they shook hands comically. 'Two more lengths and that's my quota. Grab a seat.'

Stephen found a wicker chair under a stripy beach umbrella, took out his newspaper, and turned to the foreign pages. After a few minutes, Fox came padding across, towelling his pudgy white body. With his schoolboy glasses and almost hairless skin, he was an odd mixture of Billy Bunter and Humpty Dumpty, but though his early morning enthusiasm suggested the fat man's traditional bonhomie, Stephen detected in his behaviour a steely air of calculation.

'Fancy some breakfast?' Fox had picked up a pile of clothes and was getting dressed as he spoke. 'I'm always ravenous after my swim.'

Stephen chose a light breakfast. Fox ordered the full menu, as if defying doctor's orders. 'This hotel,' he said, his mouth full of sausage, 'has an excellent casino. Do you like to gamble, Dr Mallory?'

'I like poker,' said Stephen.

Fox was interested. 'Anything special?'

'Seven-card stud.'

Fox was intrigued. 'I see,' he said. 'A player.' He ordered more coffee. 'I suppose gambling is rather the name of the game in your line of work?'

'We try to control the odds where we can,' he replied.

'What happens when you come unstuck?'

He saw Federico's body sprawled under a pile of chairs. 'We lose our shirts.'

He could see Fox was impressed. 'You're very matter-of-fact, Dr Mallory.'

'In my business, unlike yours, the measurement of success is simple. It's win or lose when the votes are counted.'

'And you can't fool all of the people all of the time.' He glanced at Stephen. 'But I don't need to tell you that,' he said, one winner to another. 'You're a very successful guy, they say.'

Stephen laughed. He felt anything but successful. 'Of course, we don't believe everything we hear.'

'No, but I'm flattered, truly I'm flattered, that you want to come in with us on this project. It seems way outside your usual line.'

'Call it a busman's honeymoon.'

'Honeymoon?'

Stephen, annoyed with himself, said he meant holiday.

Fox began to rehearse Stephen's achievements. 'You've had a fascinating career, Stephen.'

'It always looks better in retrospect. At the time it's just a question of getting through the day without screwing up too badly.'

'Don't put yourself down. You're good.' Stephen saw that Fox was on the verge of panic. Without Fink Wagner Associates, the insurers would not let the video go ahead.

'So you'll take a gamble on me?' Stephen was enjoying himself.

'Everyone in films is always gambling,' said Fox. 'This is a jackpot business.'

'And pop videos?'

'Pop videos,' he said expansively, 'are the side bet you take while you're waiting for the cards to go your way.'

Stephen took out Fox's letter. 'Some side bet,' he said.

Fox nodded understandingly. 'I know. Visually, a great location, but in every other way it sucks.'

Stephen was surprised. He had expected Fox to be gung-ho for the assignment, ready to minimise the risks for the sake of the commission. 'Then why don't you shoot it in the studio?'

Fox sighed and shook his head. 'I know, I know. Don't tell me. You have to know Troy to understand. He's not like that. He's a political animal and always has been. Also, he's on this big authenticity kick.'

'It says here that the song you want to film is called "Ghosts in the Colonial World".' Stephen looked across at Fox. 'To me, the colonial world says jungles and safaris, gin slings and verandahs at sunset.'

Fox shrugged. 'I agree. But Troy sees it differently, surprise, surprise. He's got this thing about what he calls the Tarzan theory of colonialism. He says he wants to show another side. Hence the ghetto, the tanks and the graffiti. It turns out that his grandfather came from over there. So it's in the blood as well. This boy is obsessed. There's no talking him out of it.'

Stephen consulted his notes. 'It would appear that not for nothing is the album called "Going Native".'

'I assure you, Steve, there's no irony here that I haven't explored a dozen times. Like I said, I'll play the biggest game I can find. Just now, it's called Troy.'

A tall blonde woman in a silk blouse came over. She was carrying a briefcase. Fox greeted her affectionately and introduced Stephen. 'Have you got those contracts?' She handed him a fountain-pen and watched as he initialled the documents. As she leant forward to collect the papers, Stephen noticed that she was not wearing a bra. She caught his eye, held it briefly without embarrassment, and then returned her attention to her boss.

'My long-suffering assistant,' Fox explained, with a salacious lift to his eyebrows, as she walked away. 'I'll tell you one thing about the film business. It attracts beautiful women. Oh boy!' A new thought came into his mind. 'How do you know Isabel Rome?'

'I don't really,' he replied evasively. 'I just met her over there about a month ago, that's all.'

'Some woman,' said Fox. 'I knew her husband.'

Stephen saw the light of sexual interest flashing behind the director's glasses, but remained non-committal. 'She seemed nice,' he said.

'She likes you,' said Fox.

'How do you know?'

'She told me.'

'That's because I'm a nice chap,' Stephen parried, and they both laughed. He wondered how often Isabel and this man had spoken this way.

Fox became attentive and personal in a manner that Stephen found both calculating and untrustworthy. 'So what's your risk assessment, Stephen?'

Now they had reached the business part at last, Stephen to his surprise found himself resisting Fox's ideas.

'We're talking cars, hotels, catering, security, insurance.' The head of the risk department, fearing for his career, had briefed him well. 'This is going to cost more than you might imagine.'

'I probably shouldn't say this, Stephen, but money is not really an object with Troy.'

Stephen was disappointed. He had hoped he could dissuade Fox on cost grounds. So now he said: 'This is scary country, as you well know. I could hardly recommend it.'

'But the one person who's not scared of course is Troy. You know, Stephen, sometimes he reminds me of Peter Pan.'

Stephen nodded, and briefly a memory of going to the theatre with his mother as a child came to mind, a light dancing in the corner of a darkened stage. 'To die would be an awfully big adventure.'

Fox winced. 'Don't say things like that.'

'I have to be realistic.'

'I'm afraid Troy sees you guys as the people who can make his fantasy come true.'

Stephen frowned. 'Never-never-land,' he said, slightly abstracted.

This was another sort of poker, with Fox bidding to get him into the game. It was strange, this desire he had to keep Fox away from Isabel, indeed to conceal from the director his feelings for her, as if, unconsciously, he feared his interest.

'What do Shuster and Shoemaker say?'

'They say whatever they think their boy wants them to say. But they're scared, of course. That's why I'm here.'

The joke, thought Stephen, is that risk management is the one thing Fink Wagner is bad at, the one thing I have almost no experience of.

'Okay,' he said. 'I'll put the proposal to my boss and see what he says.' He became professional. 'I have to warn you that I'd estimate your chances with him at fifty-fifty.'

Fox laughed. 'My usual gambling odds,' he said, and signalled for the bill with a plump white hand. Now he became confidential, almost wheedling. 'This video's just the hors d'oeuvre. We could do big things together. Something's happening in the world right now and it's called "people". What do people want?' He leant closer, as though confiding state secrets. 'I'll tell you what they want. They want power. How do they get it? Through television of course. Big Brother's days are over. What do you say?'

'It sounds plausible.' Stephen disliked theories, especially when they were not his.

Fox was an enthusiast; he was not deterred. 'I know you're thinking this guy's crazy, but he's not. It's all a question of what they call linkage. It's like film. It's how you cut the pieces together. You work an international thing and a corporate thing and a privatised thing and suddenly you have freedom, the freedom quite frankly to do a lot of deals with a lot of clients.' He sat back in his chair. 'But you need television to make the connections. Especially videos. That's where I come in. Think about it, Stephen.'

He said he would think about it. Then he picked up the house phone and ordered a taxi.

Wagner was in his office, behind closed doors. He was lounging in a tracksuit, drinking a Coca-Cola after a workout in the local gym. Beads of sweat started on his suntanned features and beads of icy water ran between his fingers. He was reading a political weekly; rock music played softly in the background. As Stephen came in, he flicked the tape off abruptly, tossed the magazine aside, and waved him to a seat. 'Okay,' he said, zeroing in. 'Shoot.'

Stephen explained the idea for the video as succinctly as possible.

'God, I hate it when rock stars get political,' said Wagner. 'They should be jesters not freedom fighters.'

'Do you realise how reactionary that sounds, Alan?'

'You know I'm a democrat, Steve.' Wagner always described himself as a democrat, a word which put to rest any question of motive or higher purpose.

Stephen had half expected this. Now, for some reason, far from encouraging Wagner's objections, he found himself challenging his boss. He handed over a list of Troy's lyrics to demonstrate the singer's commitment to radical causes. 'His songs have always had a streak of protest,' he said.

Wagner studied the list, reading aloud. 'Invisible Hell, Black City, The Mean Streets of Home, The Wrong Place at the Wrong Time, The Imperial Hotel, A Molotov Cocktail . . .' He put the paper down. 'Jesus Christ, Steve. A protest song is one thing. But this is crazy. This is asking for it. This is like throwing shit at the fan. Why can't he shoot the sodding thing over here on the mainland? In the studio? Anywhere, in fact, anywhere but that place?'

'That's what I said. According to Fox, it's a question of authenticity.'

'Oh my God. Authenticity. I forgot.' He rolled his eyes. 'We're talking about art here.' Wagner liked to ham it up as much as he liked to switch accents. 'Correct me if I'm wrong,

Steve, but weren't you the one who was telling me last month that the risk department was a bunch of incompetent arseholes? Now here you are suggesting we provide security – '

'I'm not suggesting anything. I'm giving you the opportunity to make a decision.' Even now, he was thinking, This thing is fifty-fifty, and in a funny way I don't give a damn.

Wagner tipped his head back and drained his Coke. Then he threw the empty expertly into the bin. 'Hey, Steve, what's happening here? You're writing a report for the board. You used to be the house Marxist. It's not like you to be star-struck.'

'Think of it as my holiday,' said Stephen. He pointed to the company's brochure on Wagner's desk. 'You yourself say we want to replace the concept of class antagonism with the concept of political consumerism. Think of this as the soft end of politics and the hard end of consumerism.' He paused. 'This could be worth a lot of money, Alan.'

'But that place is dodgy, Steve. People get killed over there. Blown up. Kidnapped. This whatshisname, he could get kneecapped, or turned into hamburger meat, for fuck's sake. And then we'd look . . .' He left his sentence unfinished. He stood up. He was a big man and there were big damp patches on his tracksuit. He picked up a golf club and began practising chip shots. 'But I suppose . . . I suppose it would be a coup if we pulled it off. Do us a bit of good in the business. Broaden our base and show people we aren't as up ourselves as they think.'

Stephen said: 'You're always saying we're weak on the domestic side of the business.'

'This is helluva domestic, Steve.' Wagner leaned the club against the desk. 'This would have to be your project. You'd have to take personal charge. It still makes me nervous. We're supposed to be dealing with governments, presidents, ministers, ambassadors, and you're our resident intellectual. I mean, for Christ's sake, a rock star?'

'We did that circus last year.'

'That was a favour for the minister of tourism. One day,

when he's in charge of finance or foreign affairs, those lions and tigers will come home to roost.'

Stephen smiled. His boss was renowned for the mixture of his metaphors.

Wagner stood in front of him. 'This guy Troy is something else. He could have us in the cemetery, or at least the madhouse. Do you realise that?'

Stephen agreed that it would have to be a one-off. He suggested, seeing that Wagner was not totally opposed, that the project could be used to develop new attitudes in the risk department.

'You confuse me, Steve. You're a political consultant, an analyst, a pollster, a friend of those in power. When we acquired that security company you laughed at me. I remember it well. You said it was a rest-home for bent policemen and superannuated mercenaries.'

Stephen became enigmatic; he knew Wagner would not bully. 'Things change.'

'What's going on, Steve?' Wagner's intuition was usually good, and he was appraising his colleague's reaction, but Stephen was giving nothing away. It was hardly the moment to mention his planned weekend with Isabel, but he was amused at Wagner's instincts.

'What you see, Alan, is what you get.'

Wagner laughed. 'With you, my friend, what you see is what you most certainly never get.' He got up to change the tape in the machine. 'Okay, let's take a gamble and give it a whirl, but before we press the button why don't we do a feasibility estimate on it?'

'Sure.' Now that the decision had been taken for him Stephen was relieved and excited. A 'feasibility estimate' was standard stuff; you could always make it say what you wanted.

'Jesus Christ.' Wagner pressed the play button. 'A pop video.'

3

On the day of his lecture, Stephen did not go into work. His deal with Wagner was that his boss could sit at the back and ask awkward questions in exchange for the time off. Just then, it seemed to him, Wagner's potential criticisms were the least of his worries. What on earth was he going to say? He sat at home and tried to pull his notes together. In the next-door building an out-of-work soprano was practising her doh-re-mi and screeching the top notes. In his distraction, he found himself wondering what kind of satisfaction the singer was getting from this. If you loved such music, surely you would know what you were doing to it. Then it occurred to him that it was often the undaunted efforts of talentless or mediocre people that kept culture going.

At lunchtime, still unfinished, he took his papers to the cocktail bar across the road. The place was half empty; after the coloratura, the undifferentiated murmur of sound from the scattered lunchtime regulars was a relief.

He had planned to order a Coke, but when the bartender offered a Manhattan on the house, he caved in.

'Writing a book, then?'

'A lecture.'

'Oh, very nice.'

Stephen excused himself, picked up his papers and went over to a table by the window, overlooking the street.

A waitress in a cowgirl costume came up and he ordered a cheeseburger and a beer. He looked at his notes. Perhaps, at last, they were beginning to take shape.

Outside, people in mackintoshes struggled by, the wind and rain buffeting their umbrellas. It was early summer, but everyone said the weather was upside-down. Last week had been a heatwave; today it was a tropical downpour. An ambulance wailed past, a fire engine following in its wake. Stephen caught the eye of one of the firemen as he climbed into his protective clothing and for a moment the worlds of commentary and action were joined. It was odd, the thought that everyone is always the most important person alive. Considering the egocentricity of life and the ferocity of belief, it was amazing that the world worked at all.

The cheeseburger arrived and he concentrated on his food. The truth was, it seemed to him, people did not like the country they were living in any more. They felt ashamed. Even the old distinction between the regime and the society did not seem to hold water. The regime had been around so long it was the society. Everyone who battled through the weather in the street was a sort of collaborator, everyone except the beggars and homeless. Yet at the same time there was a profound love of the country that was not really patriotism in the old-fashioned sense.

He turned back to his lecture. The waitress asked if he would like another beer. He looked at his watch. His talk was still hours away. 'One for the road,' he said. He considered his argument: he was going to be provocative tonight. This would be his swansong, his belated farewell to the groves of academe. 'The resident intellectual,' Wagner had said. Stephen knew he had lost touch with the literature, but he wanted to show off one last time. He found himself hoping that Wagner would turn up after all.

He walked home the long way, via the park, revolving sentences in his head. He passed a row of houses he had always fancied. There was a For Sale sign outside the one on the end, number Seven, his lucky number. Some of the houses had been subdivided; others were intact. He loitered briefly, but the estate agency's only clue was 'superb leasehold'. His mind went back to Isabel again. Perhaps he should sell up and move here. He could afford it. His lotus years of tax-free living abroad had been good for his bank balance.

With enough well-being in him to clinch a deal sight unseen, he called the agency. 'You're selling some property next to the park,' he said. 'Is it a flat or a house?'

The telephonist sounded as if she had been crying. 'Just hold on, please,' she said thickly. Lute music intervened. 'Hello, sir. It's a two-bedroom maisonette.'

'I want to live in a house,' he said, and rang off.

Back at his desk he revised his middle section, adding a couple of recent case-studies, and then turned his attention to the conclusion. He would quote Shakespeare. Why not? He found what he was looking for, copied it out, and then, mildly exhilarated; poured himself a large, celebratory scotch.

He sat in the chair by the fireplace and ran through his argument again. He had left enough room for improvisation: experience told him that it was a mistake to have things over-prepared. He checked the time and venue in his diary. His eye was drawn to the following weekend. He had spaced the letters of Isabel's name across three days, and for a moment the lecture went out of his head. He poured himself another drink, feeling good. There was horse-racing on television, then a children's programme. He knew he was drifting to sleep, but reassured himself that he would be fresher that way.

He was woken by Louise insistently buzzing on the bell. He could not disguise the flush of his sleepiness. 'Do you know what time it is?' she said, as he pulled open the door.

'Well, obviously I don't,' he said. She had disturbed a pleasant dream. He felt headachy and bad-tempered.

'It's five-thirty. You must be depressed,' she said.

'I wouldn't be surprised if I was,' he snapped.

'Have you finished it?' Louise was adept at ignoring him.

'What does it look like?' He felt astonishingly resentful of her presence. 'Why are you all dressed up? It's only a stupid lecture.'

'Don't tell me you've forgotten. There's that party after-wards. At Lady Lyon's.'

'Oh.' His annoyance at her intrusion into his life, at her catching him asleep, made him doubly cold and offhand. He said he would take a quick bath, and then they would go. 'Would you like a drink?'

'Do you think you should, before – ?'

'I'll do what I bloody well like,' he replied, and poured a large glass of red wine. 'Help yourself.' He went into the bathroom and flung on the taps.

When he re-emerged, he was wearing a clean white shirt, a newish tie, and his best suit. He was glowing with his bath and with the wine, slightly keyed up, but confident. 'I'm sorry,' he said, and kissed her.

'You're just tense,' she said. 'You'll be fine once we get there. I've ordered a taxi.'

Stephen poured himself another scotch, thinking, I'll be better if I take the edge off my nerves. Then the buzzer went, he knocked back his drink, and they hastened out to the street.

The driver said that in this weather the traffic would be diabolical but he knew a back route to the university. Stephen looked at his watch. There was still plenty of time. He checked the papers in the pocket of his coat, and wondered vaguely how many people would be showing up to hear him.

'Would you rather I didn't come?'

He hated it when Louise became self-effacing. 'I don't mind,' he said.

She changed the subject. 'What's Lady Lyon like?'

'Posh,' he said. 'Very elegant and very rich.'

The taxi hit traffic briefly, but the driver was as good as his word and soon they were coasting down an empty mews, crossing a one-way street, and weaving round the back of some mansion blocks, a small black beetle at the foot of stucco cliffs.

'When we get to the hall,' said Stephen, 'would you mind sitting to one side, or at the back? I don't want to be distracted.'

Louise nodded mutely. They sat in silence for the rest of the journey. When they arrived at the university, the driver pointed out their destination, a brutal building of totalitarian design, only slightly softened in aspect by a massive bronze peace symbol at the foot of the steps. At a distance, the hall seemed forbidding, as they drew nearer it seemed dark and empty and closed up. 'Are you sure?' said Stephen.

'Listen,' said the driver, 'my son got a degree here. I know what I'm talking about.'

'We are a bit early,' said Stephen, mentally cursing Louise. 'Any place we can get a drink?'

The driver pointed at another building across the quadrangle, indicating a dimly lit door. 'You could try the students' union,' he said.

Stephen paid off the taxi and they began to walk through the twilight. Students on bicycles whizzed past; one or two joggers hammered by. He felt out of place and overdressed, and he badly wanted another drink.

'Don't they look young?' said Louise. 'Do you think we looked that young?'

'Must have done,' he said, morosely.

They approached the building. It was seedy and damp-looking. ENTS' UNION flickered uncertainly over the entrance. Next to a row of foul-smelling dustbins was a stockpile of aluminium beer barrels, thrown anyhow.

Inside, Stephen's sense of personal incongruity deepened. There was a long bar, with two solitary drinkers, both in their forties, he guessed. It was not clear if they were members of faculty, or lonely alcoholics, or both. A few students had collected at the far end by the pool table and the juke-box. The music was turned up loud and, even to Stephen's ears, it seemed astonishingly tuneless. The floor was tiled in brown linoleum squares and furnished with clusters of red bar stools, most of which had been vandalised. Halfway down one wall was a bulletin board smothered in scraps of paper, posters and flyers, next to it a large picture of a naked couple kissing, and beneath it the words: AIDS Kills. It was more like a hospital waiting-room than a place of recreation.

No one showed any interest in their presence. Stephen went up to the bar and ordered a double gin and tonic for himself, and a white wine for Louise.

When he joined her, she pressed close to his ear. 'Don't you think we should go?' she shouted, looking at her watch.

It was true. The walk had taken longer than he had expected. 'They can't exactly start without me.'

They drank without further conversation and then hurried back towards the lecture hall. Now they could see there were lights on and Stephen felt a premonitory fluttering inside. He fingered his pages.

Louise squeezed his arm. 'It's going to be fine,' she said.

As they went up the steps, and pushed through the heavy institutional door, Stephen became aware that others were pressing through the dusk behind him. Inside, on an easel, was a simple poster: 'Terrorism, the Army and the State by Dr Stephen Mallory. The Queen's Hall. Tonight at 7.00 pm.'

An elongated man in a suit was coming towards them. 'Dr Mallory?' He was immensely tall and thin and his most prominent feature was his beaky nose and Chamberlain moustache. Looking down on Stephen, he resembled a bird of prey.

'I hope I'm not late,' said Stephen, with the nervousness of a miscreant before a headmaster. 'We were held up in the traffic.' He introduced Louise. 'This is my friend, Louise Parry.'

The bird of prey smiled bleakly. 'Miss Parry, a pleasure.' He put out his hand, an elderly claw. 'Mortimer Warren.' Louise responded gracefully, more like an ambassador's wife than a girlfriend.

'I'm sorry we have no refreshments, but there will be coffee and biscuits afterwards for those – ' he gave Stephen a frosty smile ' – who wish to carry on the discussion.'

Stephen experienced a sudden paranoid fear that Warren suspected him of drinking. He could do with another glass of something now, but all he could see through the door into the hall was a lectern with a flask of water and two glasses. Various latecomers hurried past to take their seats. He estimated, his view blocked by two burly security guards, that there were about a hundred people in the hall.

He felt a wave of nausea. Perhaps he was going to faint. He

found himself clutching Professor Warren's arm. 'Excuse me, where's the men's room?'

Warren looked puzzled. He was of another generation. 'The men's room?'

'The gents, the loo, the toilet.'

'Oh, of course, I beg your pardon.' He pointed. 'Third door on the right.'

Stephen hurried, almost ran, down the gloomy corridor. The lavatory was deserted. He found a stall and stood there fighting his nausea. Then it hit him; he leant over the bowl, retching violently. At first it was a relief, but then, when he was empty, the spasms gripping his stomach were simply painful and tears came into his eyes, and his nose filled with snot, and he wondered, panicking slightly, when he was going to be able to return to the outside world. Finally, it was over and he stood up, realising with shame that there was sick on his sleeve. He wiped it away with toilet paper. Then he splashed cold water on his face, straightened his tie, and walked out into the corridor.

Warren was very stiff-upper-lip. He behaved as though nothing had happened. 'I was just telling Miss Parry that the most important person – saving your presence, of course – has yet to arrive.' He smiled as though his mouth was a painful wound. 'I'm glad to say that General Windermere will be here tonight. I believe you are acquainted with the general, Dr Mallory?'

Before Stephen could answer there was the sound of a car pulling up quite fast outside. A door banged, and shortly afterwards Windermere swept into the draughty antechamber, accompanied by two staff officers in uniform.

'Ah, there you are, Mallory.' He shook hands all round. 'Professor Warren.'

'Shall we go in?' said Mortimer Warren. A spasm of irony passed across his face. 'I expect you'd like to engage with the enemy, Dr Mallory.'

Louise kissed him good luck and took a seat by the door. Stephen, following the others to the front, noticed that Wagner was there, with Georgie from the office. His anxiety was well under control now, but he hoped they were not in his line of vision.

Mortimer Warren's introductory remarks were almost all aimed in the general's direction. When he came to say what a pleasure it was to have Dr Stephen Mallory, the author of *The Conflicts of Peace*, to talk to the society there was an unmistakable air of routine to his words. Stephen studied his audience. A scattering of faculty types was easy to identify; otherwise, the majority were students, mainly postgraduates, he imagined. He hoped they weren't the usual seminar bores with obscure points based on the latest articles, articles he was sure not to have read. Not for the first time that day, he wondered why on earth he had agreed to give this lecture in the first place.

Finally, Warren finished. There was a patter of applause and then Stephen got to his feet and went to the lectern.

'Good evening.' The faces before him swam in a pointillist abstract and recomposed themselves as his audience. 'I should say, before I start, that the advertised title, as so often with titles, is misleading.' He paused, and a new thought struck him so forcibly that he was compelled to utter it regardless. 'You could say, informally, that a more accurate description of what I want to say tonight would be The Empire Strikes Back.'

There was a ripple of laughter among the student section.

'Speaking more formally, as such an occasion demands, tonight I would like to examine the nature of terror and counter-terror in the post-colonial world, and to suggest that it is not the colonised but the colonisers whose societies are ultimately the losers. To put it another way, I want to argue that it is at home not abroad that we must look for the real consequences of such conflict, consequences we often strenuously deny.'

He looked up, and thought for a dreadful second that he saw the general about to interrupt. The rest of his audience seemed to be listening with interest. He felt it was time to put down his first challenge.

'I should like to make it clear, before going any further, that what I have to say tonight is of course based on my work in Conflict Studies, but it is, more importantly, the product of actual first-hand experience in the field.' He directed a hard look at Mortimer Warren. 'Our discipline – if that's the word – is dominated by so-called experts whose hands-on knowledge of their subject is, at best, twenty years out of date, and at worst non-existent, and whose world view is shaped by what they have read in common rooms and libraries. I want to make it clear that I have small patience for such expertise. When I contradict prevailing orthodoxies I am doing so not out of a desire to advance my career, or indeed, sheer perversity, but because – ' here he emphasised his words on the edge of the lectern ' – I know what I'm talking about.'

This seemed to go down well with some of the students, but Mortimer Warren's wintry expression took on a new austerity. Stephen noticed him whispering something to the general, who nodded and took out a small pocket notebook.

'If I may speak personally for a moment, I should like to suggest that many of the assumptions on which the relations between the state and the people have traditionally rested no longer obtain.' He saw Clive Fox cleaving the blue waters of the hotel pool. 'The world has changed. The diplomatic bag has gone the way of the gunboat. We live in an age of the satellite image, the spin-doctor, and the ten-second sound bite. Today, the speed of information exchange has given people the ability to form perceptions and have opinions about anything, almost simultaneously, worldwide. This unlocks them from the prisons of ideology and tradition in which, in some cases, they have been incarcerated for generations.'

His headache told him he was dehydrated; he paused for a gulp of water, a Lazarus in hell. 'This is the age of electronic democracy. If, through research, you can discover what people's expectations are, then you can help a government to satisfy them. Once, in the days of Big Brother, television was seen as a medium of control. Now, with people power,' he smiled to himself, 'it is still a medium of control. It's just that the levers are different. It's our job to find those levers. To put it another way, first you learn what the local reality is, then you find out how your product – your campaign, your policy, your candidate – can relate to that reality. So the voter becomes a consumer and the consumer becomes a voter.'

At the back of the hall, he saw Wagner stretch back in his chair and whisper to Georgie and he guessed he was saying 'What the fuck has this got to do with Terror and the State?' Stephen held his ground, rolled on impromptu for a few more lines and concluded his opening remarks with a flourish. 'So, the battlefield is communications. Information is the disputed territory, and control of it is the prize, the currency of power. And let us not forget: information comes in many forms. Newspapers, books, radio bulletins, television interviews, even pop videos.'

He looked down at his papers. He had spent the morning laboriously collating statistics. Now, in the presence of the general, and slightly reckless with irritation and drink, he decided to go for broke. 'All that, of course, is a kind of prologue, a necessary aside.' For a wild moment, he saw the phrase, 'Think, when we talk of horses,' dancing in his mind, but he recovered himself. 'I had intended,' he went on, 'to illustrate my main thesis with many different examples, but the more I think about it, the more it seems to me that we have, on our doorstep as it were, the locus classicus of such conflicts, and I propose, tonight, to base my remarks on that.'

Stephen could tell, from the movement among his audience, that they were aware of the controversial nature of this statement. He could see that Professor Warren was worried. He pressed on, mildly exhilarated.

'The truth is that in conflicts like this – and it's interesting, en passant, to note that in situations of this kind we have no agreed vocabulary: I mean to say, are we discussing a war, an emergency, a guerrilla action, an insurrection, or merely civil disobedience? – in situations, as I say, such as this, we find many departments of the state drawn into the fray: the law, the economy, the army and police, and of course, the media, the right to free speech.' He hesitated, and then decided to nail it home. 'Drawn into it and corrupted by it. Technically, as many of you will be aware, under the latest Emergency Powers legislation, it is actually an offence to discuss certain aspects of the situation in public. So my words tonight come to you with, perhaps, more than their usual freight.'

The hall was very still. He felt pleased. So far so good. He looked down at his notes. For the occasion that was now taking shape, they seemed too mild, too measured. He dug himself in deeper, extemporising recklessly. 'I'm not saying this is a unique situation. Far from it. All the great powers, I should say former great powers, have it. There's always one place – a province, or an island or a territory – that is full of shame and darkness. And the more the politicians and the generals try to wish it away, the more it takes charge. This is where laws get bent, freedoms curtailed, deals are struck, and nothing is quite as it seems. The theory is always that it's limited to one place – the province, the island, the demilitarised zone – but of course it's not. It seeps into the organs of the state like a poison. It's like an evil deed in the life of a man, a moment of immorality that ends up corrupting it beyond recognition. In the old days, the name given to this deed was "colonialism".'

The hall was quiet. His headache had come back. Just now he would have loved a pint of ice-cold lager, or a glass of champagne. He continued, turning to the details before him.

'In this context, let me consider the example of the police. Traditionally, the role of the police has been to uphold and defend the values of a free society. For better or worse, they are the guardians of the civil state. And yet, as all of us here tonight are only too well aware, there have been a number of recent cases in which, it would not be too strong to say, the police have behaved in ways that go far beyond the reach of the law. It's here we find that falsification of evidence, interference with witnesses, vetting of juries and even judicial murder are commonplace. And it's now, of course, that our difficulty with definition starts to bite. Apologists for the behaviour of the police will say that the ends justify the means, that such actions are necessary in the fighting of a counter-terrorist war. And yet, in the same breath, when asked to comment on their actions, the police, far from admitting the indefensible nature of their actions, affect, with puzzled expressions on their collective public faces, not to understand what all the fuss is about. Thus we find, at the highest levels of the organisation, senior officers claiming that lies are truth, that right is wrong, and that, no doubt, the earth is flat and the sun goes round the moon.'

He looked at his papers, glanced up briefly at Windermere, wedged in the front row, and plunged on. 'In the same connection, I now want to consider the experience of the army.' Out of the corner of his eye, he saw the general stiffen, and it was an incentive.

'We are told,' he continued, 'that the army has handed over almost all its functions and powers to the local agencies. This is called "normalisation". We are further told that the army is now well adjusted to fighting the terrorists or – as they would call themselves – freedom fighters. I want to read to you a description of army life there which will, I think, demonstrate that not only is the army unable to beat the terrorists, except in the most literal sense, it is also increasingly unable to stop its troops becoming an undisciplined rabble.'

He was relieved to discover that his audience was still with him. He found the article he was looking for, an extract from a radical pamphlet published by a small left-wing press.

'One soldier describes life in his regiment. I quote. "At first it was relatively peaceful. Everyone was fearful and did not even dare to say anything much. The violence followed fairly soon. Those who had served there before began to give orders. The degradation does not begin with a bang. Everything starts slowly, then becomes stronger and stronger. Eventually you forget that you are a human being altogether."'

Someone – the general? – he did not dare look up – spoke

out loud, a single word, and though lost in the hall, it had the effect of disturbing the audience. Stephen pressed on.

'Another soldier writes as follows. I quote. "Over there, all situations are extreme. You learn to be cruel and brutal in the army and to suppress humanity as much as possible. Only then is it possible to keep afloat. For example, the night after New Year, the boys in the next platoon started to drink. They woke me up and made me do pushups. I did a few as I was told and tried to go back to sleep. But they wouldn't let me. A fight started, and I started to bleed. Eventually, I had to go into the washroom for a wash. The platoon commander followed me. He was a veteran. He came and told me to go into the drying room. First he beat me again, then he demanded that he sexually satisfy himself through my anus. I resisted, but that was not much good because I was already dazed from the beating. And then he satisfied himself through my mouth – "'

There was an explosion at the front of the hall. General Windermere was on his feet. 'May I ask Dr Mallory,' he said, looking round at the rest of the audience, 'what exactly this absurd pornography has to do with the advertised lecture?' From the middle of the hall, one of the students shouted: 'Sit down, fascist.' Two elderly ladies towards the back of the hall got up, collected their bags and bundled out into the night.

Stephen said: 'If you'll bear with me, general, I hope my point will become clear.' He closed the pamphlet hurriedly. 'I now turn to the way in which the judiciary has become so implicated in its support of the army that here, too, we find the colonial conflict wreaking a terrible revenge at home.'

Emboldened, perhaps, by the general's intervention, someone towards the back was standing up, not to leave but to ask a question. Stephen knew that if he gave way now all would be lost. He studied the notes on the lectern with extra thoroughness and when he looked up the questioner had sat down. It was touch and go, but he was holding his own. He rattled on for a few more pages and then made another summary, feeling like a lonely traveller who has reached a remote staging post on an arduous journey.

'The fact is, ladies and gentlemen, that when you total the sum of our behaviour over there – the cost to the exchequer, the human cost, the loss of free speech and so on and so forth – and when you throw in the impact of all this on the mainland, you have a victory that looks extraordinarily like a defeat. A campaign, if you like, that the terrorists are winning. So, the question we must now examine – and it is the fundamental question – is: Why? Why does the state in these circumstances feel compelled to intervene at such a cost?'

'I'll tell you why,' said an American voice.

Stephen had noticed the young man at the side fidgeting during his latest remarks, and this time there was no ignoring his audience. He stopped. The student was wearing Clark Kent glasses, a tweed jacket and grey trousers. Stephen had already pegged him as hostile. Some of the other students groaned, and a girl in a beret shouted across: 'Shut up, Lowell.'

The American student smirked self-righteously, and held his ground.

'Very well, then,' said Stephen, reaching for the water. 'Tell us.' He looked at his watch. Twenty-five minutes gone. With a bit of luck, he could wrap it up in forty, forty-five, and then take cover in questions. 'Tell us.' He sipped his water, as if suggesting that such an intervention was part of his strategy.

'There is a moral imperative to the conduct of foreign policy, Dr Mallory . . .' The American student was reading from a yellow legal pad. Christ, thought Stephen, he's making a speech. He appealed to Professor Warren. With some reluctance, the angular professor rose to his feet. 'Mr Stone – ' The American stopped. 'I'm afraid I must cut you off. We are here to listen to Dr Mallory. Your views, though doubtless valuable, will have to wait. I am sure Dr Mallory will take questions at the end.'

The American student sat down. Stephen returned to his audience, but it was no good. Whatever hold he had taken initially was broken. His best material was largely used up. He had thrown away his comparative literature and now he was regretting that moment of impetuosity. The truth was that he had barely enough to sustain another twenty minutes. He ploughed on, waffling gamely, aware, as he spoke, that the faculty types were losing patience. Wagner was slumped in his seat, head in hands. Louise remained loyally attentive.

'In conclusion,' he said, returning gratefully to the last page of his text, 'when we analyse the imperial theme, the imperial tragedy, we find, in the last act, moments of madness and bloodshed undreamt of, so to speak, by the players who so cheerfully stepped onto the stage in the opening scenes. In this tragedy, we find the unassailable grandeur of kings and emperors brought low by the common people. We see power corrupting, we see an expenditure of money and resources that is often literally insane. There are times,' he went on, 'when it seems to me that the experience of empire can be likened to the building and upkeep of a fine country house. In the early days, the house and its spacious grounds will be an agreeable home for the ruling elite. Time passes. The family declines and falls into bankruptcy. The silver is sold, the servants dismissed, the house becomes a school, a hotel, or worse. Finally, it is pulled down. It is my contention that we are living in the ruins of a great house, but pretending that we still have to dress for dinner. This is our tragedy and, at the end, only Shakespeare's words will serve: "The weight of this sad time we must obey; speak what we feel, not what we ought to say."'

There was no applause, just a general sense of relief, in which Stephen was now sharing, that it was all over.

Mortimer Warren was on his feet, and with barely a nod in Stephen's direction, he was asking for questions. Already, quite a number in the audience were voting with their feet.

A dark, straggly-haired woman in a poncho stood up. 'I would like to ask you, sir, whether you believe it is language not territory that is the prime cause of aggression in situations such as the one you have just described?'

In the unpredictable way of recollection, an old memory of

a first-year anthropology lecture came back to him. 'I think you are saying,' he replied, 'that once language has the power to express abstract concepts, it provides society with sophisticated totems to defend, a basis in fact on which to go to war.'

The woman in the poncho nodded uncertainly.

'You can support this theory, I recall, with reference to two tribes of African monkeys who lived next door to each other in some woods near a stream. Perhaps you are familiar with this example?'

She was not.

'Both of these two tribes subsisted on a diet of bananas. One of the tribes, however, had developed the habit of washing its bananas in the stream before eating, while the other monkeys were, so to speak, non-banana-washers. And yet, both tribes lived side by side without quarrelling, perfectly happy. Now this, the anthropologists say, was because the monkeys lacked language to give abstract meaning to the act of washing, or not washing, the bananas. With language, both wet and dry bananas would have become sacred objects, the basis of a religion, perhaps even the origin of a war.'

Stephen felt that these were borrowed ideas, and it gave him no surprise to see a number of students – so far his most loyal supporters – leave during this rash excursus into unfamiliar territory. Now another student stood up to say that perhaps the monkeys did not fight because there were simply enough bananas to go round. Ah ha! thought Stephen, at last a Marxist! He was almost thrilled.

Mortimer Warren had heard enough about monkeys and bananas. Before Stephen could answer, he was up at the lectern, with surprising agility, bringing the proceedings to a close. Stephen could not decide if he was offended or relieved.

'Most stimulating and unusual,' Warren was saying. He was so grateful to Dr Mallory for interrupting his crowded schedule, adding that owing to unforeseen administrative difficulties it would not, after all, be possible to have coffee in the senior common room as usual.

Stephen made his way to the back of the hall. His shirt was

wet with perspiration, but he felt weirdly exhilarated. He passed down without interruption, though one or two of the remaining students looked at him with curiosity. Louise was waiting for him with Wagner and Georgie. No one was speaking.

'Well done,' said Louise, loyal as usual.

'Thanks, Steve,' said Wagner. 'I'm glad I witnessed the end of your academic career. It was fun.'

'See you tomorrow,' said Georgie, exchanging an unfriendly look with Louise.

'See you.' Stephen watched them go and turned to Louise. 'Where's the general got to?'

'I don't know.' She seemed irritated. 'Have you said good-bye to whatshisname?'

He nodded. 'Let's get out of here. I don't want to be late for the party as well.'

They hurried into the darkened quadrangle. It was not raining, but there was a strong, damp wind. Stephen wanted a drink, but Louise was concerned to find a taxi and her anxieties prevailed.

When they were on their way to Lady Lyon's, Stephen said: 'Tell me the truth. Was it that terrible?'

'Actually, it was quite funny. But yes, it was terrible.'

'Thanks.'

'You asked me.'

'It wasn't that bad, surely?'

Louise refused to be drawn now, and they both sulked in silence. In a few minutes, they were pulling up outside an eighteenth-century mansion by the river. They were not late; taxis and limousines were lined up three-deep in the street.

These parties were so well known they were almost as familiar to those who were not invited as to those who were. At some time or other most of the prominent people in the capital – that kaleidoscope of media celebrities, politicians, personalities, hangers-on, civil servants and lawyers – had received the call, an engraved invitation to join Sir Edward and Lady Lyon 'At Home'. Some had even described the experience in print.

Stephen had not expected the summons so soon. Part of him so distrusted it that he put the card – 'Dr Stephen Mallory and Guest' – in his pocket as evidence. Remembering the conversation at the airport a few weeks earlier, he had decided to ask Louise, correctly predicting that she would be thrilled by the occasion. Curiosity was the magnet that drew most people to these events.

Here they were now, trooping into the draughty vestibule to deposit their coats, umbrellas and briefcases before taking the noisy baronial staircase to the drawing-room on the first floor. Tonight the guests included government ministers and the security was tight. Stephen half-wondered, as he watched the crush of arrivals filter slowly through the electronic screening device, whether he had been invited to give professional advice.

He looked around, gradually becoming calmer after the lecture. Lady Lyon's guests might have been a theatre audience, focused on the forthcoming drama. Even the grandest seemed to accept the indignity of being searched without complaint. His first thought was that no one knew anyone else. But then, as the butler announced their names, and they stepped forward to greet their host and hostess, he realised that of course there was a sense in which everyone knew everyone.

'Doctor Mallory.' She seemed so pleased to see him. 'And this is Louise. My dear, I've heard so much about you.'

Before either Stephen or Louise could answer properly, her attention was distracted by the arrival of a famous conductor who threw himself on Lady Lyon in a blizzard of lavish kisses. They found themselves forlorn and adrift in the crowd, wondering whether they should introduce themselves to the faces they recognised from the newspapers and television.

Their predicament seemed quite general. No one seemed very much at ease. Stephen and Louise made a half-hearted attempt to admire the pictures on the walls, a mixture of affordable old masters and expensive contemporaries. They listened to the guests who knew other guests greet each other. The most common phrase seemed to be: 'What on earth are *you* doing here?'

Stephen's temptation to catch up with his drinking returned the moment the waiter offered him a second glass of whisky. Louise now became censorious. She told him he was drinking too much and was in danger of making a fool of himself. He became sarcastic. 'I thought you said I'd already done that.'

'But this is a party,' she said, rather unnecessarily.

'Quite so,' he replied, working off his frustration. He told her that, in case she hadn't noticed, as a general rule parties were occasions at which people enjoyed themselves, often with a drink. 'We can't be miserable all the time,' he said. She told him to fuck off under her breath. Stephen made a determined move to cross the room. As he did so, a familiar voice said: 'Mallory.' He turned. It was the general, without his staff officers.

Stephen's first thought was to make a run for it. In a less crowded room, he could have made an excuse, but here there was no choice. He could not move in the crush.

'That was a most unorthodox little talk, Mallory.' The general was strangely amiable. 'If you have a moment,' he added, taking Stephen firmly by the arm, 'I'd like to introduce you to an old friend from the ministry of the interior.'

4

The moment he glimpsed her at the airport, standing apart at the back, beyond the small waiting crowd, he knew that it was going to be fine, after all.

'Here you are at last,' she said, stepping forward with that smile of welcome he remembered from before. She was wearing jeans, a man's white shirt, and a loose crumpled jacket of midnight-blue cotton, and managed to seem both casual and elegant. He kissed her briefly, and then, forgetting everything, dropped his bag and kissed her again. 'Isabel,' he whispered, as though they were alone.

'Thank God you've come,' she murmured, as they began to collect themselves together. 'I've been going crazy.'

'Being here,' he said. 'It's the best idea I've had for a long time.'

They walked out to the car-park; Stephen had forgotten her shortness beside him. He was trying to find a mode of normality, but there was no escaping the strangeness of coming back again. He half expected to turn and find a crocodile of VIPs.

They had exchanged jokey postcards, and spoken on the phone, but in that insubstantial contact there were opportunities for evasion. Now there was nowhere to hide their feelings, except within, and Stephen knew that Isabel would not allow that. To his surprise, he found it joyous, the sensation of being alone with her, and free.

'I think this is rather brave of you,' she said, as the car passed the final security barrier and they reached the junction with the main road. She had put on a pair of glasses to drive and was peering forward, like a character in a cartoon, from behind the wheel. He replied that there were some things that could not remain unexplored. He was as light and airy as an overture; he felt confident and excited. Sometimes you threw the dice and whoever it was up there rolled you a double six. That was how he felt: on a winning streak. He added that it was quite brave of her to invite him over in the first place.

'I don't think I had much choice either.'

'Anyway, if we can't think of a thing to say to each other,' he teased, 'I can always pretend I'm over here on a recce for Clive Fox.'

She glanced sideways. 'Are you never without an alibi?'

He stared ahead. 'Oh – never,' he joked, but feeling hollow and found out.

How many weekends had he known? How many had she? Isabel had been married, so he supposed that he was more accustomed to the excitement of the unknown and the unfamiliar. For an instant, he saw himself in previous lives, some of them quite recently discarded, with various girlfriends in different parts of the world. He saw airport taxi queues, art galleries on Sunday afternoons, and fashionable restaurants with conversations going on under water, and then he remembered the killing loneliness of the hotel bedroom and the temptations of the 'adult' cable. He rationalised to himself that sex without intimacy was just another aspect of a life for hire. Now he was home, or sort of home at last, and his discontent was melting. Sitting next to Isabel, he felt quite different; he felt happy and complete.

Here was the turn into her street, and now she was parking the car. 'I hate reversing,' she said, grasping the gear-stick with both hands.

'I can always walk to the kerb.'

'Oh, very amusing.' She was smiling as she forced the gear back with an effort, but he recognised the Beware of the Dog notice in her voice, her instinctive vigilance.

He stood waiting on the pavement. It was quiet, as usual. Clive Fox was right: it was a perfect location. The sun had set, but the evening was clear and the sky at the end of the street was as hard and still as a cyclorama.

'Go on in,' she said.

The door was indeed open. He pushed inside, his bag thumping against his leg. The house smelt warm and lived-in. She followed, and he noticed with half a beat of excitement that as she closed the front door she dropped the latch. 'Now, since I'm your hostess here,' she said, evidently nervous for the first time since he had arrived, 'I'll take your case upstairs.'

She was decisive; he was awkward. He stood there wondering if it was an invitation to follow. Instead, stooping, he went into the little book-lined parlour. There was a newspaper on the sofa in front of the fire. He picked it up but he couldn't take it in. He heard Isabel moving about upstairs and the sound of curtains being drawn. He had enjoyed making the commitment to come here, but now he was hesitating. Finally, still wondering at his own unusual reticence, he threw the paper down and went to find her.

'I'm here for the guided tour,' he said, as he reached the head of the stairs.

At the sound of his steps she had come to meet him and was standing in the doorway to the bedroom, half in shadow, so that he could not exactly determine her expression. 'There's not much to see, I'm afraid,' she said.

'I'm sure there's plenty, if you're interested,' he replied, walking slowly to the back room and putting his head round the door. There was an elderly sewing machine, a heap of clothes on a couch, and a trestle table stacked with periodicals and newspapers. The half-empty bookshelves in the alcoves either side of the chimney breast had a pillaged look.

'This was Tom's study. I'm still tidying it out. For some reason, I don't seem to have the energy.' She stood next to him. 'Would it be very wrong of me to throw away those papers?'

He said he was surprised she hadn't been more ruthless already.

'Do you think I'm ruthless?' she asked, flirtatious.

'I think . . . What do I think?'

He paused, and she interrupted him quite sharply. 'Sometimes you don't know what you think. It's as though you're making it up as you go along.' The cat came onto the landing; she pushed it away downstairs.

'Aren't we all like that?' He strolled past the bathroom, like a prospective house-buyer, and crossed the threshold into her bedroom. No longer confident, he added: 'I don't apologise. I've always preferred to improvise.'

It was cosily elegant, almost a picture, a low-ceilinged room with black wooden crossbeams at one end and a bow window overlooking the street. The curtains, a pretty pattern in blue and white, were drawn, and she had lit two candles. There were flowers in a white vase on the dressing table and the bed was made up. He was charmed by the composition, and turned to say so. She was standing right behind him. They kissed, drew back for a moment, as if knowing they were about to be lost, and then kissed again. She pulled away and held him, at arm's length, and looked at him. 'Don't you think we should wait?'

He shook his head and kissed her, and she laughed, knowing as she did so that she had answered her own question. Suddenly they were neither shy nor hesitant, and found an exhilarating directness towards each other that took them, first undressing and then naked, into each other's arms.

They lay between the sheets, not moving, holding each other, perfectly still. He could feel her heartbeat thumping contrapuntally with his own. 'Read to me,' she said, and leaned over and kissed him softly on the lips. 'But I want to fuck you,' he said, kissing her back, touching her teeth with his tongue.

'I want to fuck you too,' she whispered, 'but read to me first,' she insisted. Read what? he wondered as he climbed out into the cold. There was a shelf of paperbacks against the wall. He chose three collections of poetry, playfully hiding the covers from her, and began to read, finding his own favourites. Isabel sighed with contentment and he felt her wrap her body close to his. He heard himself read easily and evenly, letting the words find their emphasis. 'You read nicely,' she murmured. 'I like the way you read. Go on.' He finished one poem and chose another. 'What's that?' she asked when he had finished. And he told her. 'I liked that. "A ship of gold under a silver mast." Read it again.' He said he was surprised she did not know it. There was a note of regret in her voice: 'As Tom never stopped telling me, I'm very badly read.' It annoyed him to think of another man lowering her self-esteem, and he turned the page, looking for something harder. Her body was warm now and her eyes were closed. He put the book down and ran his hands over her, very gently. 'Don't stop,' she said. 'Stop what?' His lips were very close to her. 'Don't stop anything,' she whispered. He found a simple love poem, but as he read it he felt tears come into his eyes, unexpected tears of such joy and happiness that he was glad to let them fall onto the page and fall onto her skin, and he was unashamed. 'I'm wet,' she said, opening her eyes quite round. He felt opened up by her look, fully exposed, with no secrets or alibis. He bent down to kiss her, putting the book aside, and coming into her without difficulty. 'Don't stop,' she whispered.

It was getting light when he woke finally. The burnt-out candles had become icicles of wax. Isabel was still asleep, lying on her side, curled into the sheet, with a hand next to her face, almost babyish. He watched her as she slept, the fine hairs on her neck, the tiny freckles on her nose, and the faint blush of colour on her lips. Her breathing was shallow and even, and as he looked at her she opened her eyes, focused briefly, and smiled. 'So there you are again,' she said, and stretched up for a kiss. 'What time is it?'

'Too early,' he replied. He put himself round her and they whispered together about their dreams. 'You had a sort of nightmare,' she said. He had feared this, and asked what had happened. 'It was almost comical,' she said. 'You sat up and said something like No, no, I can't do it. Then you went back to sleep again.'

'You weren't frightened?'

'Don't forget that I spent seven years with a heavy drinker.'

'When I'm like this with you, I could forget anything,' he said.

'We are like two spoons,' she murmured, holding him.

They began to make love, as if in a dream. The closeness scared him. He had not imagined feeling so happy to be possessed in the way she seemed to possess him.

He found he was dozing. He was woken by a mutter of sound through the wall. Stephen said: 'Is that a radio?'

'No – it's Joe. Joe Curtis. He likes to lie in bed and make phone calls.'

'Who to?'

'I've no idea. Contacts. He's quite a weird guy. Nothing goes on here without him knowing.'

Stephen felt a momentary panic. 'There's something between you two,' he said. 'But I don't know what it is.'

She lay very still. 'He can't work me out, that's all,' she said. 'And that annoys him. He can't bear secrets that he doesn't share. All that matters to him is power.' She touched the wall. 'These phone calls are the sound of the spider in his web.'

'Can he hear us?' The thought made him feel suddenly exposed.

She shook her head. 'I don't think so.' She smiled. 'That's why I have the bed away from the wall.' She looked into his eyes. 'Do you mind being overheard?'

Their faces were almost touching and they kissed. 'I think the mystery of what happens between two people should remain a mystery,' he said seriously.

'Mystery man,' she said, teasing.

They lay there, listening to Curtis's indistinct murmur and to scuttering sounds in the roof. 'Birds,' she said. 'Or mice. I'm not sure. I like to hear them there. They tell me I'm not alone. You have no idea: there have been times when that has almost saved my life.'

She described the other sounds that reached her bedroom – the early morning voices in the street, the rattle of the milk float, the melody of wood pigeons resting on the chimney stacks, the boots of the foot patrols passing down the street.

She confessed that she did a lot of reading in bed. 'And writing too.'

'I think you like it here.'

'Sometimes I miss my friends, but when Tom went I had to lie low and find myself again. It's been a good place to put myself together, among people I didn't really know.' There were, she said, several benefits to keeping house in the country. 'People keep an eye on you here.' The women of the town, gossiping in Curtis's store or the Chinese takeaway, would see that she was all right with a certain unabashed nosiness. 'It's funny. The thing I couldn't stand about this place when I arrived with Tom was that there was no privacy. Now that I'm on my own, it's the one thing that keeps me sane.'

He was curious. 'What do they know about my visit?'

She laughed. 'Well, I didn't exactly broadcast it on the radio, but it won't remain a secret for long.' She hugged him for encouragement. 'So what? They'll only be pleased. They keep on saying they hope I won't grieve about Tom forever, which is just their way of saying, Go out and get laid.'

She got up, pulling on a creamy silk dressing-gown, and for a moment the Jazz Age filled his inner eye, an incongruous vision of cocktail parties, crackly gramophone records and bitter-sweet conversation.

'Don't worry,' she added. 'They'll have plenty to think about once the news of the video is out. Our little drama will soon be quite insignificant.'

There was still the muttering through the wall.

'What about Curtis?'

'What about him?' She was standing in the window, almost imperious. Perhaps she should have a cigarette holder and a highball.

'Didn't you say he was crazy about you?'

'That's his problem.' She was unexpectedly dismissive. 'It's just a pathetic fantasy.'

'I shouldn't say this,' he remarked lazily, as he watched her pull back the curtains, 'but that man disturbs me. There's something strange about his eyes.'

'Don't be silly,' she said, and went downstairs.

They were having coffee together and browsing through the papers when there was a knock outside. 'Oh, I forgot. The door.' Isabel darted into the hall. Stephen admired her nimble movements. He heard her say, 'Come in, Joe, come in,' and the part of him that admired her gift for society fought with the part that wanted to be left alone with her all day. She was leading the way. He braced himself for a moment of awkwardness. 'You remember Joe,' she was saying, rather deliberately.

Stephen stood up, defensive. 'Good morning, Joe.'

'Oh, hello there.' There was no disguising the conflict of disappointment and surprise on Curtis's face. 'Back so soon?' He shuffled uneasily by the stove.

Stephen decided not to give an inch. 'It should have been sooner.' He sat down again. Isabel offered Curtis a cup of tea, which he accepted, though he was clearly in two minds. He had wanted to know who was staying with Isabel, but once his curiosity was satisfied, there was only resentment, even bitterness.

The boiling kettle provided a distraction. Isabel poured the hot water into the teapot. 'It seems we shall be seeing quite a bit of Stephen,' she said.

'Oh indeed.' His cold look betrayed nothing. 'Why's that?'

Stephen explained that the plans for the video were almost finalised.

Curtis's attention hardened. This was his territory and he had not been consulted. He tried to affect unconcern, but without success. Whenever Curtis's curiosity broke through the surface of the conversation, Stephen, deliberately casual, refused to co-operate. He would not even confirm the ministry's involvement in the project. Eventually Curtis said: 'Well, I must be on my rounds. Glad to see you again, Dr Mallory. Interesting news, interesting news indeed.'

'See you later,' said Stephen, not getting up.

Isabel walked with Curtis to the door, and then returned to the kitchen with a worried smile. 'The real Inspector Curtis at work,' she said. 'The news will be all over the place by lunchtime.' She came over and sat on his knee, kissing him affectionately.

'He doesn't like me,' said Stephen.

'He's okay.' She smiled. 'He'll come round.'

'I wonder,' he said. 'He's fascinated with you, I'm afraid.'

'As I said before, that's his problem.' They were quiet for a moment. She looked at her watch. 'Now what?'

'I feel so lazy,' he said, running his finger down the bridge of her nose, 'I can hardly stand up.'

'I may tell you, Dr Mallory, that it's a glorious day and we should be outside. We'll make a picnic and go up into the hills.'

She jumped up and began to clear the table. In no time at all, it seemed, they were heading down the road and into the hills. As they drove down the avenue of beech trees that signalled the town boundary, he asked if it was safe to make such a journey.

'Everyone round here knows my car. You're only at risk if they don't know where you're coming from.'

The country was opening up and the road – now little more than a lane – ran alongside a stream. Stephen imagined it full of fish and saw himself as a boy lying in wait for a trout or a pike. In the water meadows to left and right there were long-horned cattle grazing among tussocks of marsh grass. The lane began to climb and then, after a series of hairpin bends, they were on top of a hill with a fine view of the country all round. Isabel pulled the car over onto some open ground, and they got out.

The land in front of them was a patchwork of smallholdings, seamed with stone walls and broken up with clumps of trees or clusters of white farm buildings. To the left, they could see the church spires of the town. It was a deceptive landscape, a pastoral camouflage: in the distance, if they looked hard, and Isabel knew where to look, they could see army helicopters buzzing in and out of a military base.

'It's hard to imagine all the killing,' he said, speaking his thoughts.

The sun was up high now, warm on their faces, and somewhere far above them, floating on a dizzy thermal, there was a singing lark.

As they stood there, taking in the scene, hardly speaking, they heard the sound of a vehicle braking behind them. Stephen turned. A small, grey van, appearing out of nowhere it seemed, was pulling up next to Isabel's car. 'I know that van,' she said, walking across.

Stephen watched from a distance. He could not see the driver, but from the movement of Isabel's body, he knew instinctively that she was answering questions. Finally, she was waving the van on its way. 'Inquisitive old so-and-so,' she said, coming back.

'Who was that?'

'Mr Birch. He owns a garage, out of town. He and Joe don't get on.' She laughed. 'They always want to know what the other is up to.'

Stephen dreaded such complications. 'Does Birch have power, too?'

'I shouldn't worry. Let Joe take care of everything.' Stephen knew that a look of anxiety must have come into his eyes because she put her arms round him and kissed him.

They drove on, winding through sun-dappled lanes, past meadows and apple orchards, towards the hills. There was hawthorn in the hedges, clouds of frail white flowers. At midday, they found a shady rowan tree by a stream, spread out Isabel's tartan travelling rug, and drank a bottle of white wine with her picnic.

After they had eaten, and the bottle had been emptied, Stephen lay on his back looking up at the blueness of the sky, and Isabel put her head on his chest, and they talked. Later, when he was back in the office, he was asked about their time together, but found he was at a loss to answer without seeming to betray the moment.

They had talked about things in a way that felt new to him. They had talked of their childhoods and their parents and the story of their lives so far, their hopes and fears. As they spoke, he could feel his frozen, apprehensive heart melting in the warmth of her laughter and her fun. There was always a part of him that seemed absent and elusive, a part that felt missing, but still he told her she made him feel relaxed; she told him he made her feel warm and wanted.

He confessed that in his work he had never seemed to find space for a relationship that lasted.

'I'm not surprised,' she said, quite serious. 'Public and private lives don't mix.'

'My work is full of cheap thrills. It's hard to suppress the same instincts in love.'

'I suppose it's hard for you to risk being vulnerable.'

'All my risks are professional.' He frowned. 'I think I've been afraid of private life.'

'You probably thought it was boring.'

How exactly she seemed to know his thoughts. 'Yes,' he said. 'Boring, or perhaps restricting.'

'Do you imagine you will ever change?'

'With you I can.'

She had laughed at that. 'You hardly know me, you silly boy. Let's wait and see.'

Again, later, when he tried to explain it to his friends, he said that being with Isabel was like hearing a tune in your head, a good simple tune, and having it magically orchestrated by a great composer.

When they finished talking, they slept, or dozed. When he woke again, the sun was sinking and there was a chill in the air. Isabel was down by the stream, drinking the ice-clear water. It was time to go back. He could feel they both wanted to go to bed again, and he said this. Isabel just smiled and nodded her head, shyly, cupping her hand in the water.

Much later that evening, they ordered one of Mr Hu's takeaway specials and sat talking over the events of the day in the kitchen.

A familiar knock interrupted the conversation and Curtis came shambling through the shadows beyond the kitchen glow, mumbling an apology for the intrusion.

'I don't believe this,' Isabel murmured with exasperation, but she rose to make him welcome and offer him a drink.

Curtis sat down at the end of the kitchen table in a chair that seemed habitual to him, refused all offers of food, and took out his pipe.

He seemed weighed down with a burden of worry. Isabel put his drink beside him, but he hardly seemed to notice. 'You won't mind if we finish eating?' Isabel's politeness was unfailing, a counterpart to her directness. He did not reply. 'What's the matter, Joe?'

He considered this question for a while, staring into his glass. Stephen had a secret fear that Curtis would suddenly rise up and denounce him with violence. There was something cramped and inarticulate about his posture that suggested a deep, unacknowledged rage. Finally, he spoke, dragging the words from deep inside him, breaking out of his habitual code. 'It's this film,' he said. 'This video.'

'What about it?' Isabel could be quite abrupt when she chose.

'I'm afraid,' he replied, enigmatic again. He took a sip of his drink and the fire of it sent a tremor across his features. Stephen noted that he had not shaved and that his beardline accentuated the mushroom pallor of his skin.

'Afraid of what?'

'There are people here who are against it.'

Isabel knew his weak points. 'What does Mr Birch think?'

His face darkened. 'Don't talk to me about Birch,' he said.

Isabel was dismissive. 'Welcome to the real world, Joe. You can't always expect everyone to agree with you.'

Stephen intervened, doing Curtis the courtesy of taking him at his word. 'How serious is this?'

Curtis seemed glad to have drawn his rival onto his own ground, and to have some power over him. 'It depends.'

His silence invited further questions. Stephen said: 'Depends on what?'

'They are good, straightforward people here, Dr Mallory,

who love their families and mind their own business and believe in the old virtues.'

Stephen said he did not understand.

'Well, perhaps, coming as you do from the mainland, you're used to its ways, but the people here are not so ready to accept what you accept. The singer's reputation is a cause for concern here.'

'You mean because he's gay?'

'There are rumours,' said Curtis, unspecifically. 'I have heard,' he went on, 'that the preacher Hickey is also denouncing him.'

'Is this a problem?'

'The people listen to Hickey, but there's another fear,' he went on quickly. 'People say he's taking a stand on an issue that doesn't belong to him.'

'His family came from these parts.'

'One grandparent does not give him the right to write a song called "Going Native" and they're laughing at the idea.'

Stephen was surprised. 'Do they know that?'

'They'll know everything,' said Isabel, breaking in. She seemed almost embarrassed. 'That's the point about this town.'

Curtis smiled, proudly. 'People tell me things,' he said.

Isabel looked away.

Stephen realised then that he had to put himself in Curtis's power. He saw that this was what Curtis wanted more than anything else, and he also saw that he had to show Isabel that he was not afraid to do it. He was not sure why Curtis had withdrawn his enthusiasm for the video, but he knew he had to win him back. 'Well, then, you must help us,' he said, making a direct appeal. 'We could put you on a retainer,' he added, 'as our special consultant.'

'Special consultant.' Curtis's satisfaction was tangible. He put out his hand, as though clinching a contract. 'So we have a deal.'

Stephen shook hands, exchanging looks with Isabel and wondering at the odd intensity of Curtis's manner. 'You must trust me,' he said.

'Why did you say that?' she asked, later, when they were in bed again.

'It was like an instruction to myself.' He kissed her. 'When Curtis is around I realise I love you too much.'

5

The minister of the interior was tired. He was short and wiry, like a jockey; he appeared almost to crouch behind his desk. Without the greyness of exhaustion in his face, he might have seemed sporting, even jaunty. His tight, inquisitive manner contrasted strongly with the bland, big-bottomed officials who hovered nearby like a bevy of butlers, anonymous, discreet and bored. One of them was speaking now, addressing his remarks to Stephen, but with a cautious eye on the minister. 'I hope, Dr Mallory, that it is not necessary to over-enunciate the point, but this meeting is not taking place and indeed never will have taken place.'

Stephen nodded. He was familiar with the conventions. A certain deferential muteness seemed appropriate to the occasion. There was no mistaking the atmosphere of power and authority: a fine, high-ceilinged room, tall windows with a view of plane trees, a pervasive air of quiet elegance. The word 'chancelleries' came to mind.

The minister was sitting with his back to the window; his face was in shadow and his voice was weary; he punctuated his sentences with stifled yawns. It was as though every aspect of his responsibility was wearing him out.

'I gather from my officials,' he said, looking at his visitor, 'that you have recently returned to this country after many years abroad.'

Stephen was not surprised they had a file on him, though he was curious to know how extensive it might be. He knew that etiquette dictated he should briefly explain his work as a political consultant. He began to outline some of the places to which his time with Fink Wagner Associates had taken him, but omitting all reference to Federico. It was simply a ritual. The minister was shuffling through the papers in front of him, hardly listening. Stephen, relaxing slightly, noticed that there was a ghetto-blaster and a pile of classical tapes on the floor beside the desk. He yielded at the first hint of interruption.

'What I'm most intrigued to know,' the minister remarked, with the air of an expert considering a nice academic question, 'is how, as an outsider, you think we're doing.' He waved expansively at the world beyond the grey blinds. 'Things are better out there, wouldn't you say?'

'Doesn't it depend where you look?'

'Well, maybe.' The minister yawned again. He seemed to have lost interest in his party's record. He pointed at the huge operations map on the wall to his left. 'Now then, tell me something Dr Mallory, how did you find it over there?'

'I'd say you were doing surprisingly well,' Stephen replied diplomatically.

The minister's interest quickened. 'Surprisingly well? You mean, given the intractable nature of the problem?'

Stephen agreed.

The minister looked round at his officials, as if to say 'I told you so', and involuntarily straightened his tie. 'Everything's relative over there, of course, as my staff never stop telling me, but yes, I think we are on the right lines. I won't make any bones about it, Dr Mallory, but I've staked my political career on this policy of "normalisation". I'm determined to see it through and make it work, come hell or high water. That's why I asked to see you today, as a matter of some urgency.' He paused, and became businesslike. 'Now tell me about this video.' He seemed to pride himself on working without notes, extempore. 'A well-known rock star with an alleged taste for sado-masochism. Two dubious American promoters. An ex-whiz-kid director with some debts to settle and a reputation to retrieve. This is quite a proposition, wouldn't you say?'

One of the butlers leant forward. 'There is that additional problem, minister,' he prompted.

'What's that?' The minister interrupted himself. 'Yes, of course. This preacher.' Now he consulted his briefing paper.

'Hickey. Stirring up trouble, apparently. What do you say to all that, Dr Mallory?'

Outside in the street, faintly, like a thread of sound in the larger tapestry of city noise, Stephen heard a racing police siren. 'Your intelligence is pretty good,' he said.

The minister was pleased. 'There's not much we don't know, is there, Simon?' He directed a satisfied smile at one of the butlers, who murmured discreetly that no, there was not much that was missed these days.

'It is, of course, a small country,' observed the minister.

'Is there a problem?' Stephen asked.

'That's what we are here to discuss,' said the minister. 'You see, my prejudice is in favour of normality, as I say, and I'm hoping that your plans will enable me to show my sceptical colleagues that, under the umbrella of a military presence – let's face it, we're committed to that for the foreseeable future – it is possible to achieve some semblance of ordinary life there.' He stood up, warming to his theme, and began to pace up and down, an intense, slightly hunched silhouette in front of the shrouded window light. 'And what could be more normal, more absolutely contemporary, than the shooting of a rock video on location?' He pointed outside. 'Every suburb in this city would love to have that chance. If we can show the world that we can do it over there – ' he pointed at the wall to emphasise his words ' – over there – then we've got something, wouldn't you say?'

Stephen agreed; he had to. The butlers had already made it clear to him that the video was quite impossible without full government approval.

The minister was standing like a general in front of the operations map. 'What I say is that if Mrs Smith and Mrs Jones can take their children to school in the morning, and then go shopping in the local supermarket, perhaps play bingo or go swimming in the local sports centre in the afternoon, and then take their husbands out for a drink in the evening, and do all this without fear of random killing, shooting, hijack or explosion, then we may say, and we may say this without fear of contradiction, that these people are living a normal life. We're not there yet, but we're getting close.' He took his seat again, plainly invigorated by his little speech. '"A normal life" – that's what I stand for. What do you say to that, Dr Mallory?'

'In the circumstances, minister, you could hardly hope for more.'

'We shall of course continue to provincialise the military presence, though we have our limits.' He turned to one of the butlers. 'Remind me, James, what's the percentage of adult males in the security forces and their ancillaries now?'

'Thirty-six per cent, minister.' It was the prize pupil's answer but the voice was grey and uninterested. He might have been reporting the weather.

'Thirty-six per cent,' the minister repeated, with his own, rather appealing, animation. 'You see, Dr Mallory, that at least one-third of all the available males is tied up in the peacekeeping programme. Actually, it's become a way of life. Our private surveys show – don't they, Simon? – that these people actually like it. The truth is, peace is boring. There, the crisis gives them something extra. They have comradeship, a sense of purpose and a job. They get overtime. If they survive, they're well off. The odds aren't bad, either. Quite bizarre, isn't it?'

Stephen agreed it was an unusual situation, but one he'd seen in other parts of the world.

The minister was quick to react, almost with rivalry. 'Well then – how do we compare? How are we doing?'

Stephen repeated his earlier view that they were doing quite well. 'After all,' he said, 'there's no doubt that it does have a special history.'

'Ah, history.' The minister yawned again without apology and rubbed his eyes. 'I've been in politics twenty-five years, Dr Mallory, and a minister for ten. I've been in departments of health, farming and trade, and now here I am in charge of this nightmare, but I have to tell you in all candour that throughout my years at the centre of things I have never, until now, felt brushed by the wings of history.' There was a weird pride in his voice. He got up and went over to an antique bookcase at the back of the room. The butlers stood aside to let him pass. 'Come over here, Dr Mallory, and look at these.' Stephen followed obediently. 'I collect first editions and have done for years.' He took one of the volumes off the shelf with care. 'Whenever I travel around the country I make a point of asking my officials to arrange at least one visit to a decent antiquarian bookshop, don't I, gentlemen?'

A murmur of schoolboy agreement ran through the group.

'Now for years I've specialised in new verse. Let me tell you there's not much poetry in hospitals or cowsheds. But here,' he went on, running his hand possessively down two long shelves, 'in just one generation, there is a whole library of poets. Now that I find exciting.'

'Do you know the work of Tom Harris?'

The minister looked at him with renewed interest. 'I do indeed, Dr Mallory. One of our brightest hopes.' He might have been describing a promising sportsman. 'Very difficult of course, but very rewarding.' He passed down the bookcase. 'Harris, Harris, Harris. Here.' He pulled out a thin, maroon volume. They admired it together; Stephen silently took in the dedication to Isabel. Then the minister closed the glass door of the cabinet again and they returned to their seats. 'That's history for you.'

'Nothing like the inspiration of oppression, minister,' Stephen volunteered cheekily. For an irreverent, happy moment he saw himself walking arm-in-arm with Isabel. He supposed they knew about her too.

'Remember the Borgias, Dr Mallory.' As the minister warmed to the conversation, his tiredness seemed to fall away. 'There's something stimulating about crisis. You get hooked, don't you? Now I have a theory about this. Let me try it out on you.'

The officials stirred amongst themselves. They had heard it many times before. The minister paid no attention: he had the politician's capacity to find inspiration in cliché.

'My theory is that although we have more control over our

planet than ever, we have never felt so helpless, perhaps because we know so much. Was there, indeed, ever a moment to have more cause to fear for the world because of our dominion over it?'

Stephen did not interrupt. The minister plainly enjoyed his right as a spokesman to hold forth. He pointed at the operations map again.

'Over there, it's different. Over there, we are in a medieval world. Everything is black and white, right or wrong, good or bad. Every day, lives are at stake in the most literal sense. The place is full of certainties, the kind of certainties that everyone can understand. It's not like – what shall we say? – global warming or nuclear pollution. Those are threats we simply cannot comprehend. But there, we know the enemy. We know where he lives, and what he looks like. We meet him on the street and even say good morning to him. He uses weapons we can understand. We can smell blood and fear. It's a bad, old-fashioned war, and we – or rather, they – like that. The only frustration, *entre nous*, is that we cannot kill him as easily as we would like. Hence "normalisation".' He paused, looking at Stephen for comment. 'What do you say?'

'It sounds good,' said Stephen tentatively. 'I hadn't thought about it like that before.'

'To pick up your earlier point, Dr Mallory, we have to go into these deep places and analyse them and cast light and take the risk that what we find is extremely unattractive.' The minister drew him to one side, a courtier with a confidence. 'That's why I like being called "Minister". The noun has medical connotations and in my better moments I believe I am ministering to people. I suppose that's why I want power, why power has its own morality, why politics for me comes before family, friendship, even literature – because it's all those things – a way of life – and if that way of life is sound and healthy then perhaps the state will be too.'

The telephone on the desk was purring. The minister broke off to pick it up. Stephen looked round at the butlers. They remained impassive but watchful. He wondered how often

175

they had listened to their master speaking in this vein. The minister rang off quickly and returned to the discussion.

'Well now, perhaps we should get down to the nitty-gritty.' He had enjoyed holding forth. 'Would you care for a glass of something, Dr Mallory?' He checked his watch. 'The sun is definitely over the yardarm, and I have a rather agreeable white wine in the refrigerator.'

One of the senior officials signalled to a junior, who hurried out of the room.

'Frankly,' the minister went on, 'after last night, I could do with a pick-me-up.' He became confidential. 'We were up into the small hours going over the fine print of my "normalisation" bill.' He accepted a glass of wine. 'Thank you, William. Cheers.'

'Cheers.' The wine was dry, with a faint taste of wood. The minister was obviously as keen on his cellar as his library. Stephen said this.

'One should never neglect the little pleasures of life, Dr Mallory.'

They both savoured their drink for a moment. Stephen was wondering if it was up to him to bring the conversation back to the video when the minister took the initiative again. 'Speaking of "normalisation", tell me about this character,' he consulted his notes, 'this Troy – so to speak, a nom de guerre, I take it.' He glanced up at Stephen. 'What kind of risk is he? Does he fit into my profile of normality? What d'you say?'

Stephen wondered exactly how much the minister knew about the singer and his reputation, but guessed that he was well briefed.

'I think you've already referred, minister, to his sexual preferences – '

'No problem. Actually, we rather enjoyed – ' he looked at his brief – ' "Spanking the Maid", didn't we, James?'

One of the butlers coloured deeply and muttered something inaudible.

'You also have to recognise, minister,' Stephen went on, 'that he's on the other side of the political spectrum – '

'No harm in that.'

Another official, older and greyer, intervened. 'As you are aware, minister, the report we have had from military intelligence is extremely discouraging.'

The minister dismissed the report with a wave of his hand. 'We all know the military loathe my plans,' he said. 'They want a full-scale war over there. Anyone who tries to lower the temperature is anathema to those people.' He studied his notes again. 'I gather that our rock star friend has just recorded a new song called "Ghosts in the Colonial World".'

Stephen said: 'That's the inspiration of the video. It's part of what he calls a trilogy.'

'A trilogy?'

'He recorded two others last year. "An Area of Occupation" and "Invisible Hate".'

'"Invisible Hate".' The minister challenged his team. 'Do we know about that one?'

A very junior official, a pallid young man in his twenties, said after some hesitation that he was familiar with the song in question.

'Any good?' The minister's curiosity was spontaneous and enthusiastic.

'It was rather good, minister,' said the young civil servant, blushing.

'Excellent, excellent,' said the minister. 'We'll listen to it tomorrow.' He turned back to Stephen. 'Nothing like research, Dr Mallory.' He smiled. 'I must say I'm intrigued by this Troy fellow. Let's hope he's not too extreme, eh?' He made it sound like an instruction, and Stephen admired his lightness of touch.

'I think he'll be okay,' he said, encouragingly.

The minister looked across at his book collection. 'Perhaps he's a poet, too. It makes a change when these pop stars have something between the ears.' He looked at his watch again and then drained his glass. 'Well, I think I'll take a flyer on this one. I've enjoyed our meeting. Good luck, Dr Mallory.' He stood up, adroit and effortless and evidently powerful. 'Don't do anything that will upset the apple-cart and we'll get along fine. Now, I must be on my way. Nice talking to you.'

He pushed his papers together, dropped them into his ministerial briefcase and swept from the room, followed by his entourage, a jockey surrounded by stable boys. Stephen found himself alone with the junior civil servant who was now clearing away the glasses. 'Busy schedule, I suppose.'

'Actually,' said the young man with a smile. 'It's time for the minister's swim.'

6

The promise of spring was over, and now the road to the west was bursting with the signs of early summer: white blossom in the hedgerows, a carpet of green on the slopes of hills, and newness everywhere. Isabel felt happy. There was hope in the air, and optimism and joy. Was this the pathetic fallacy? Tom would have said so. She did not care. She stopped at a roadblock for a routine identity check. One of the soldiers had a buttercup in his cap, but no one seemed to mind. She drove on, singing aloud, while the sun rose high in the sky like a golden coin. Sooner than she remembered, she was turning off down the lane to the great house.

Christopher Bennett was waiting to greet her. In his mysterious way, he seemed to know the moment of her arrival. He was standing patiently on the steps, not moving, a benign presence watching while she parked and collected her things. He held a paint-brush in his left hand, as if just summoned from work, and was wearing fawn corduroy trousers and a checked shirt. Close to, his clothes were speckled with paint and frayed from washing. To Isabel, he seemed clean and warm and elderly and full of trust. 'Welcome,' he said, accepting her impulsive kiss with a deep smile.

'I have something for you,' she said, holding out the rolled-up portrait.

'Something special, I hope.' She was reminded, as he looked at her now, how in his presence she felt as if there was all the time in the world.

They went inside, straight to the private part of the house, and Isabel felt the balm of the place close round her. It was quiet and cool, and there was the smell of baking in the air. In the distance, she could hear music, Haydn or Mozart. A familiar voice spoke her name and she turned. Sarabeth was there, floating over the flagstones like an enchantress in a Victorian storybook. She was wearing a loose, rather faded, blue smock and some silver jewellery, and her long grey hair was fastened with a blue velvet bow. As before, there was sympathy and amusement in her eyes and a sense of other-worldly knowingness.

'Did you come alone?' she asked.

In her heart, Isabel had wanted to return here with Stephen; she was not surprised that her fantasy was anticipated. 'Not quite,' she replied, indicating the canvas. 'You could say I brought the friends of a friend,' she added, feeling strangely light-hearted.

Bennett and his wife exchanged a smiling look and escorted their visitor down the corridor to their studio, a converted conservatory. The smell of paint and turpentine met them as Bennett pushed open the rickety glass door.

Canvases were stacked around the walls, in various stages of restoration. In the middle, under a bright overhead light with an oblong shade, was what Bennett called 'my operating table'. Today, there was no treatment in progress. Isabel laid out Curtis's canvas for inspection.

Bennett's curatorial instincts were quickly aroused. He bent over the table, his scrutiny accompanied by a mumbled commentary. He was like a doctor with an unusual medical condition to diagnose, pointing out the stains and scratches and shaking his head over the rip in the canvas. When Isabel asked if it was beyond repair, he looked up at her sweetly. 'Nothing is beyond repair,' he said.

He began to ask her about the portrait's history, but she had to confess ignorance. 'I want it restored for a friend. My neighbour,' she added, to make herself clear. 'He takes a special interest in the locality.'

Isabel had supposed that Curtis's canvas was badly damaged, but Bennett showed her many worse cases, patients apparently beyond the reach of help. Then Sarabeth explained her remedies. How she would place tissue paper across the face of the picture for protection; how later the canvas was lifted off its stretcher and how, with cotton wool and warm water, she gradually swabbed away the dirt of the centuries. 'Our golden rule,' she said, 'is reversibility.'

'Reversibility?'

It was Bennett's turn to speak. 'We believe that pictures have their own lives. We aim to do nothing to them that is irrevocable. So often you see the worst kind of plastic surgery, where all that was needed was simply a bit of love and attention.'

'So you don't add colour?'

'As little as possible.'

Isabel, thinking aloud, said that it sounded like a good subject for one of her broadcasts. Bennett and his wife looked at each other uneasily. 'If you don't mind,' he said, 'we'd much rather not.'

'We love to listen to what you say,' added Sarabeth, 'but . . .'

Isabel regretted the intrusion of her work into an occasion that was otherwise so free from calculation. 'Of course,' she said quickly. 'I quite understand.'

She walked over to a fine seventeenth-century seascape with a bad gash in the sky, and asked if landscapes were different from portraits.

'With portraits,' said Bennett, 'you come to know the people.'

'It's always the same with us,' said Sarabeth. 'It starts as a job and ends up as a labour of love.'

Bennett ran his finger over Curtis's canvas. They would be delighted to do the work, and confident they could make something of it. They would need about three months. 'We are so glad to see you here again,' he said.

This was the cue for Sarabeth to invite Isabel to stay to lunch. She accepted gratefully and they walked back to the kitchen. It was cluttered and cosy, with no hint of the great house beyond the servants' door. A flower-patterned table-cloth and three places were already laid at the table.

'We thought you might stay,' said Sarabeth, and they all laughed.

'It's certainly more relaxed than our last lunch together,' said Isabel.

'That was some affair,' said Bennett, hesitating to say more.

Isabel came to the point. 'I'm afraid I ran away.' She laughed. 'It didn't do me any good.'

Sarabeth glanced at her husband. 'We're not surprised, are we, darling?'

'No,' said Bennett. 'Not at all.'

Isabel took up the invitation to talk about Stephen. Her hosts listened with interest, prompting her with occasional questions. She did not mind the warmth and force of Sarabeth's inquiries, but eventually she managed to change the subject. 'I envy you living here.' She looked about her. 'It feels so peaceful.'

'It is now,' said Bennett. 'Remember, we had builders for about five years.'

'Did you always have the studio?'

'Always,' said Sarabeth. 'It was one of the attractions of coming here.'

Isabel asked if it was something they had always wanted.

She looked thoughtfully into her glass. 'Chris and I met at art school. I was going to be a painter. Once I had come to terms with the limitations of my talent, restoration work was easy. I still draw and paint a bit, but now I prefer to use my time differently.'

Bennett anticipated Isabel's question. 'She loves to write. She sits in her study, surrounded by books and papers. Whenever I go away, she has a field day, don't you, darling?'

Sarabeth smiled faintly.

Isabel was intrigued. 'What are you writing?'

'What am I not writing?' she replied rhetorically. 'Sometimes it's a novel, sometimes an autobiography. I call it my scrapbook. He – ' she nodded at her husband ' – likes to go to conferences and meetings, but I prefer to stay here.'

'Don't you ever get bored?'

'There's something quite exciting about routine. You discover things you never discover if you're always on the run.'

Isabel was making a mental note to repeat this to Stephen when she found Sarabeth's next question shadowing her thoughts. 'Now your – your Stephen. What does he do?'

'He calls himself a political consultant.' She smiled. 'I still don't exactly know what that means, but I suppose you could say he's a kind of hired gun.'

'Well,' said Bennett, coming back into the conversation, 'we're all for hire.'

When lunch was over, they went out into the garden and gave Isabel a tour, explaining their plans. Isabel felt envious of their belief in the future, and wondered at the confidence that planted trees for a hundred years ahead. Finally, with promises to return echoing round the façade, she set off down the long gravel driveway. In the mirror, she could see Sarabeth and her husband on the steps, still waving, dwarfed by the old house.

It was dusk when she reached home. She stopped in for an evening meal at Mr Hu's, as she often did, her mind still buzzing with the journey. In her bag was a half-written letter to Stephen and she fancied the idea of finishing it in the hubbub of the restaurant. By chance, one of the tables was free. She sat down gratefully and spread her things. Michelle, the younger of the Hu girls, neat and dimpled, brought her the menu, though she knew in advance that 'Miss Rome' would almost certainly choose spring rolls, sea spice aubergine, and chicken with cashew nuts.

The other table was taken by a group of teenage girls from the town whom Isabel vaguely recognised. They were discussing the video.

'Mr Curtis says I can be an extra,' reported one of the girls.

'What's he got to do with it?'

'He says he's been hired by the producer.'

'My mum says that Troy worships the devil,' said another.

'She heard that on the radio,' said the fourth. 'That's what Hickey says.'

'Just because he's gay.'

'If you didn't know that you'd think he was gorgeous.'

'He is gorgeous.'

'He looks like a poof to me.'

'I think he's lovely. He gives all his money to his mother. I read it in the paper.'

'That proves he's gay.'

'It does not.'

'It does so.'

'He can sleep with his great-grandmother for all I care. I still want to be in the picture.'

As she put Isabel's spring rolls on the table, Michelle whispered: 'Dad's going to do all the meals. Mr Curtis is going to get him a contract with the film company.'

Isabel shared her pleasure. 'Isn't it exciting?' She looked up into Michelle's smiling face. 'Perhaps you can be in it, too.'

'Oh – I do hope so.' Michelle was hugging herself with anticipation. The other girls had fallen silent and were listening to their conversation with belligerent expressions. Two police-men in flak jackets came in and Michelle hurried away to take their order. Isabel pushed her letter to Stephen aside and turned to her meal.

When the policemen went out, one of the girls at the other table came and stood over Isabel. 'We know all about you,' she said. She was wearing heavy jewellery and too much make-up.

'I beg your pardon.'

'You and your boyfriend.'

Isabel felt the pounding of anxiety in her heart, but tried to stay calm. 'I'm afraid I don't understand.'

The others sat at their table, watching, as a second girl got up and joined her friend. They were large and blonde with hard, unforgiving faces, and they were incredibly young. 'What's he doing over here, your boyfriend? That's what we want to know.'

'He's not here at the moment.'

'He's from the mainland, isn't he?'

'He's – ' Isabel hesitated, slightly flustered. 'He'll be over here as a consultant on this film – you know, the video.'

'We know all about the video,' said the first.

All four girls were on their feet now, standing in a semi-circle round Isabel's table. There was a strong smell of cheap perfume and they were wearing almost identical clothes. Isabel did not know whether to stand up or carry on with her meal. She could see Mr Hu, behind the counter, but he was talking earnestly on the phone, and she could not catch his eye.

One of the girls snatched up her letter. 'Dr Stephen Mallory. Oh, very posh – '

'Give that back!' Isabel heard the panic in her voice. The girls laughed.

'"Dearest Stephen, When I heard your voice – "'

Isabel snatched at the page, but the girl danced away.

'Excuse me, Miss Rome – ' Mr Hu was hurrying round the counter. 'What is the matter, please?'

The blonde girl threw the letter back onto the table. 'We know all about Stephen Mallory.'

Perhaps she would have said more, but at that moment the door of the Peking Dragon opened and Joe Curtis hurried in. The four girls fell back from the table, wrapping away the hostility in their faces. The first girl, the leader, said, very coolly: 'Evening, Mr Curtis.'

Glancing at Mr Hu, he came over to Isabel. 'Is everything okay?'

The girls were already scattering through the door.

Isabel was shaking. 'It was nothing – just a stupid incident.' She put her letter to Stephen away. 'A bit of silly intimidation. I'm lucky not to have had it already. I think they were trying to tell me something about – about Stephen.' She was relieved but unsmiling. 'It was a good thing you turned up.'

'Mr Hu called me.'

She nodded at Mr Hu, now back behind his counter. 'Thank you.' She was collecting her things. 'Just for a moment, I didn't know what to do.'

Mr Hu was sympathetic. He escorted her outside with

anxious ceremony. He reminded her of an elderly schoolmaster.

Curtis said: 'I'll walk you.'

Outside in the street, she said: 'You've been spreading rumours.'

'I don't know what you mean.'

They were standing in front of her door, and they were alone. 'Oh yes you do, Joe.' Her fear was turning to anger, and she could not stop herself. 'As you never stop reminding me, all the information in this place comes from one source. If four know-nothing girls are making comments about Stephen Mallory it's because Joe Curtis has put the word out. I don't know who you talk to, and what they tell you, but perhaps you should remember who put you on Mallory's payroll in the first place.' She felt the tears rising inside her, but she was not going to be put off; she could feel the conventions dissolving before her anger. 'Now of course you and I know very well what it's really all about, but I'm not in a position, even if I wanted to be, to dish the dirt on you. All I will say is that Stephen has done you nothing but favours and if you're so screwed up with a jealousy you can't handle then you're sicker than anyone in your sister's hospital.'

He was so calm it was eerie. 'I don't know what you're talking about, Isabel,' he said.

She looked at him; her hand was on the latch. 'Sometimes I think you're trying to drive me crazy,' she said, and went indoors.

7

In the city, Stephen waited alone. Louise left messages which he did not return. His thoughts were with Isabel and he called her often, but the telephone which had at first enhanced the romantic fantasy between them now seemed to frustrate it. The video contract was still not signed. Such delays were normal, Fox said. Stephen lost himself in other work; his report for Wagner became the antidote to inactivity. He set himself a weekend deadline and revelled in the prospect of a clear desk.

On that Friday evening, he switched on his answerphone, stocked the refrigerator with TV dinners and settled down in front of the word-processor to prepare the final draft. The aluminium trays piled up in the bin; his heart pounded with caffeine; he hardly slept. He was reminded of his final examinations. Occasionally, the answerphone would click into action and a disembodied voice would sound in the next room, sometimes near, sometimes far, a message from elsewhere.

At first, with all his notes and data spread around, he sat and daydreamed, lulled by the music on the radio. He had seen Fink Wagner Associates grow from a suite on a rented floor to a full-scale office complex, complete with dining-room and screening facilities. Compiling an assessment of its problems and prospects was like writing a chapter of autobiography. Leafing through the cuttings, he noted the lies and the hype. Wagner was a 'pinstripe imperialist', while Fink, across the ocean, was a 'global spin doctor'. Together, they were the 'networker's networkers' and once, in a memorable counterblast, the 'fairweather friends of banana republics'. He smiled as he remembered some of the early dramas and deals. How naïve he had been in those days, he with his freshly minted doctorate in international affairs, and his so-called specialist knowledge of international terror! Wagner's gambling instincts always gave him a taste for conflict; he had created his own war, forcing his staff into action. Wives, children, girlfriends and colleagues had all been expended in the course of the company's relentless upward mobility. In retrospect, it seemed to Stephen that they had been in combat and not known it. Perhaps only now were the wounds beginning to show.

Federico's handsome, smiling face came back to Stephen again and again as he remembered those last hours, backstage in that downtown hotel, before the fateful rally. The candidate's aides had booked a suite on the nineteenth floor, and throughout the afternoon a succession of generals, air marshals and their bodyguards had gone clanking down the corridor to pay their respects to the man everyone knew would win. How many had known what was to come? It was impossible to estimate, but suspicion fell on several. Could he have prevented the risks Federico had taken? Could he, with greater vigilance, have saved him? He had rehearsed these questions a thousand times. Wagner had been sympathetic but philosophical. 'I'm sorry, Steve, but it happens. We're talking Third World here.'

He pictured the plaza again, the floodlit podium, the sea of red-and-white flags, the chanting, 'Fed-er-i-co! Fed-er-i-co!', the faces and the fireworks. At first he had thought it was just fireworks. It was only when the screaming began and the sound of Federico's voice was no longer vibrating through the speakers banked high as a house that he realised it was gunfire. The image of the hooded gunmen, aiming down, was splashed round the world: front page news that Stephen would never forget.

He closed his eyes with a shudder and got up to make more coffee. Then he returned to a careful consideration of what he had to do: the report.

He began with an overview, numbering the paragraphs in the approved management style. First, he considered their various corporate accounts. Wagner called these his 'cash cows'. There seemed to be no limit to the money some organisations would spend on expert reassurance. Then, there was his old stamping ground, the flashy, headline-grabbing international division in which he had cut such a dash. He knew his colleagues would be out for blood here, but however hard he tried, he was forced to conclude that, with some small adjustments, it managed 'to wash its face' (as Wagner would put it). Moving to the domestic accounts, he reached the most vulnerable part of the company. Here, their business was being stolen by their rivals. As Wagner often said, standing still was a kind of failure. The truth was that they were becoming over-dependent on foreign clients. Bitter experience had shown that overseas accounts were most likely to default on their debts. Finally, there was the risk department. Before the takeover it was just a two-bit company they turned to, from time to time, for help with security. There was no doubt that the merger was a failure. None of the political consultants in the other divisions took it seriously, and its staff were despised as a bunch of misfits with a taste for safe-blowing and dangerous driving.

He organised this analysis and then turned to his proposals, knowing that Wagner liked bold, broad initiatives. 'I don't want you rearranging the deckchairs on the *Titanic*,' he had said, almost his only instruction. With this in mind, Stephen made sure his report was provocative. So he abolished the distinction between fieldwork and research. Accountability would be disseminated throughout the organisation. There would be a new press office to co-ordinate the company's public relations. The risk department would be broken up and reassigned to each of the other three main divisions, effectively incorporated within the body of the consultancy.

There was a certain elegance to his scheme and he amused himself, when the writing was done, with drawing a flow chart of management responsibility. He knew this would appeal to Wagner. By now it was late on Sunday evening. He poured himself another drink, stood up and went to the window, tired but satisfied. Sometimes, but not often, he regretted the move he had made from the library to the transit lounge, and tonight was such an occasion. Then someone from the other side of the world would speak to his answer-phone about news of an impending election and he knew that this, the sphere of action, was where he was really meant to be.

From time to time, he looked absently about his apartment. It was a kind of monument to his life: a desk covered in bills and circulars; duty-free bottles racked by the empty refriger-ator; shelves piled with half-read hardbacks; a bulletin board with holiday snaps (mainly Louise's); and a scattering of mementoes from abroad, a Buddha, a lacquer tray, one or two primitive carvings, a witch doctor's mask and a spear.

After a few hours of restless sleep, he went into the office early on Monday morning. There was summer light on the wet city pavements and the first commuters were arriving for work. Only the caretaker was up and about. Stephen stood by the Xerox machine, watching it thump and flash into action, and gossiped about sport and office politics. The caretaker knew all about the video. 'Hey, man,' he said, when Troy's name came up. 'That boy – he's crucial.'

'Perhaps you'd like to put in a good word with Mr Wagner.'

Stephen took the copy to his office and typed a memo to go with it. Here was his report. Now he proposed to turn his attention to the video project. The 'feasibility estimate' had gone well, as anticipated. He was expecting written confirma-tion of the deal any day, and assumed, he said, that he was authorised to proceed. He signed the memo with a flourish, put the document on Wagner's desk, and went to make coffee.

He sat in his office, with his feet up, and let his thoughts turn to Isabel. Where are you? she had demanded. I want you here. Her voice was hovering on the edge of tears. Her unexpected vulnerability disturbed him. He would be with her soon, he replied. What had she been doing? This and that. She had gone back to that house. The Bennetts. They chatted about the portrait and about Sarabeth. Have you told me everything? she asked. He was confused. Everything? Mystery man, she said, trying to find a laugh. Meaning? You will always want to keep things back. He became annoyed and wanted to know what she was suggesting, and she apologised.

'Joe Curtis has been bugging me,' she said.

Now it was his turn to speak about mystery men. Curtis had sent him a strange report about the town, more of a threat than a briefing. 'He was full of cryptic warnings about this preacher,' he said.

She explained that Hickey had been denouncing Troy to the local media. 'He's only trying to attract attention.'

'Curtis seemed to think we should take it seriously.'

There were many other bizarre innuendoes and threats in Curtis's notes. It was as though he could not decide whether he wanted the video to happen or not. The idea of Curtis distressing Isabel stirred Stephen's anger. What did she mean? he asked again. Would she like him to speak to Curtis? She panicked. No, no. She was okay; she could look after herself. He would be with her soon, he said; they were in the final planning stages now. As he rang off, it scared him to notice how strongly he missed her, but also how much her anxiety disturbed him.

He looked up. Wagner was standing in the doorway. He was wearing a well-cut dark suit. 'You son of a bitch,' he said. He was holding the report, smiling. 'Just one thing.'

'What's that?' Stephen smiled back, admiring Wagner's knack of making his colleagues feel on top of the world.

'I couldn't find the paragraph proposing we take on rock stars.'

He yawned. 'Look under Miscellaneous.'

'I meant to tell you, I had a phone call from someone in army public relations.' He swung the report through the air in a mock tennis serve. 'He didn't sound very keen. He had this line about giving no guarantees for anyone's safety.'

'They were just trying to spook you. The minister's given the go-ahead, but the truth is that the army and the minister don't see eye-to-eye.'

'The forked tongue of authority? That sounds familiar.' He

threw the report on the desk. 'Go for it, Steve. And mind you don't fuck up,' he added in a characteristic coda.

'Thanks, Alan. I won't.' Stephen always said, when asked about Wagner by curious outsiders, that his two qualities were toughness and generosity. So long as you performed, he let you do what you wanted. But you had to perform.

Wagner went back to his room, and Stephen called his secretary to say that he was going out for the day. At the present moment, the other dimension to solitude was elusiveness. Just for a few hours, he wanted to be free, and out of reach. He went down in the elevator and out into the city.

Home again, nothing could beat the sheer pleasure of walking in the streets. In the foreign towns and cities where his work had sent him, there was usually hassle, watchfulness, even fear. Here, the biggest anxiety was crossing the road. Just to stroll and window-shop and browse in bookshops was like a holiday.

At lunchtime he rang in for his messages, and found there was nothing urgent. 'Don't forget your meeting tonight,' said his secretary.

It was nearly five o'clock when he turned the key in his door. The telephone was ringing. He ran to answer, hoping it would be Isabel.

It was Louise.

'Hi,' she said. 'Where have you been?'

'I thought we weren't speaking to each other.'

'Oh, that.' He could see the expression of disdain on her face. 'You were drunk and so was I. Who cares? Are you free for supper tonight?'

He said he was sorry, but he had to see some clients.

'Tomorrow?'

'I probably won't be here tomorrow.' It was a lie, but when he explained about the video it didn't seem like one.

She sounded alarmed. 'Haven't you heard?'

'Heard what?'

'There was another bombing this afternoon. Here. At least ten people killed.' She sounded anxious. 'You will be careful.'

He affected unconcern. 'They're only after what they call legitimate targets.'

'You are legitimate.'

'That's your fantasy,' he said coldly.

There was disappointment in her voice. 'Well, call me when you're back.'

'Okay.' He paused. 'Bye.' He put the phone down and flicked on the television. The evening news was just coming on. As he listened to the reports, he changed out of his suit, and into something suitably casual for Clive Fox.

The bomb had been planted at a barracks. Twelve soldiers had been killed, seven of them married with children. The reporter gave the death toll for the year, adding grimly that 'One thing is certain: there will be more army widows before the summer is over.' The month of June, he said, was traditionally the start of the terrorist season. He made it sound like a sport. Stephen wondered what effect this latest atrocity would have on Troy's enthusiasm for the video. The news camera panned across a mountain of splinters and rubble. The police had no leads, no suspects. Nothing, or so they said.

The on-screen reporter noted that this was a blow to the government's plan for 'normalisation', and Stephen found himself wondering what the minister was saying and doing at that moment. Was his policy in ruins like the barracks, or would this attack stiffen his resolve? Was this the time to throw everything into reverse and put a ban on the project? The minister had the power.

He was about to ring Isabel when the buzzer went. 'Hi, Steve,' said an American voice. 'We're downstairs in the limo.'

The man in the pearl-grey suit was admiring himself in the hall mirror. He was holding a portable telephone in one hand and smoothing his moustache with the other. As Stephen reached the foot of the stairs, he gave himself one last approving glance in the glass and turned, extending his hand in welcome. 'Hi,' he said. 'I'm Fred – Fred Shuster.'

They shook hands. 'Where's Clive?'

'He's held up. He'll join us later, maybe.'

Stephen followed him outside. A peppermint-white stretch limousine was drawn up in the space reserved for disabled drivers. Shuster opened the door and Stephen climbed in. There was another American, with a pony-tail, lounging inside, watching a small portable television. 'Hi,' he said. 'Zach Shoemaker.' He pointed at the barracks and the screaming sirens and the pall of smoke. 'Troy is just going to love that,' he observed grimly, and switched it off.

'It's kind of where he's at right now,' commented Fred, looking worried. 'And there's not a thing we can do about it.' He leant forward and tapped on the glass. 'Okay, let's roll.' He turned to Stephen, brightening. 'There's this great little place down on the river. Just now it's a cocktail lounge, but later on it gets kind of funky.'

'Great dancing,' said Zach.

'He loves to dance.' Fred was prodding him playfully. 'Don't you?'

'Who says this country's boring?' Zach looked straight at Stephen. 'I'm having a great time.'

The limousine stole through the traffic. Soon they could see the river, a ribbon of gold in the evening light. The chauffeur dropped them by a discreet, unmarked door, which opened to reveal a riverside garden, beautifully watered, and a conservatory bar with ferns and statues. The clientele was hushed, smart and, from the discreet waves and smiles with which Fred and Zach made their arrival known, habitual. The maître d' showed them to a secluded corner with the air of a prince bestowing a favour on fortunate subjects. A young man in a white tuxedo came to take their order.

'Is Les here tonight?' asked Zach.

The waiter exchanged admiring looks. 'He should be, later.'

They ordered drinks. Fred wanted a kir royale, Zach a crème de menthe cocktail, and Stephen settled for lager.

Zach broke in. 'Say hello to Les for me when you see him.'

'Oh, sure, Mr Shoemaker,' said the waiter. He turned, almost pirouetting, on his heel.

'That,' said Zach, 'is a dancer.'

'He's so cute,' growled Fred, 'he gives me a pain in the ass.'

When the drinks arrived, Stephen was relieved to find that the conversation became serious again. Fred explained that Clive Fox had requested the meeting to ensure that the advance preparations for the shoot were going smoothly.

'Then perhaps I should warn you it's not going to be straightforward,' Stephen began.

'Listen, Steve.' Fred put a hand on his arm. 'Zach and I, we pride ourselves on zigging when everyone else is zagging, okay?'

Stephen nodded, fighting himself inside. 'I have a briefing paper for you,' he said, taking out a brown envelope.

He watched the two men study the document. He knew, from experience, that they would be impressed. Fink Wagner's clients always were impressed.

'Heavy,' remarked Fred, after a while.

Zach nodded in agreement. 'Molto heavy.'

'You approve?'

Fred looked up. 'What's the bottom line, Steve?'

'I was told you didn't care about the bottom line.'

'We're not talking money, Steve,' Fred explained. 'We just want to know your assessment.'

Zach was pressing as well. 'Is it crazy?' He lowered his voice. 'You see, the thing about Troy is . . .' He appealed to his partner.

'The thing about Troy is that he tends to groove on the wild side.'

'You mean – ?'

'We're talking wild, Steve,' Fred emphasised, with a significant glance at Zach, who nodded back.

Stephen looked at the two promoters. He saw their dilemma exactly. The singer was their top earner, their boy, their pension, their guarantee of a place in the sun, their star. Troy meant that people returned their calls, bought them lunch, called them up at all hours of the day and night, and made them feel like big shots. They couldn't go against Troy, however crazy he got, however wild. No way! At the same time, despite their talk, they didn't want to commit professional suicide, and Stephen could see that, once their initial euphoria had passed, they could understand the risks involved in shooting the video only too clearly. He realised now that Fox's call was a blind. They wanted to get him on their own and find out the true story, 'the bottom line'.

He hesitated. Then he said: 'I think it'll be okay.'

Fred was tougher than he seemed at first. 'You "think"? Hey, Steve, you guys are being paid a fuck of a lot of money to do more than think, I want "know", I want "certain", I want "sure". I'm not paying for "think" here.'

Stephen saw that Fred was the bulldog to Zach's pussycat. He corrected himself hastily. 'Of course it will be fine. You can have every confidence.'

'That's better.' Fred stroked his moustache with the air of one who has enjoyed asserting himself.

Now it was Zach's turn. He looked carefully at Stephen. 'What about this dingbat preacher?'

'What about him?'

'You've seen the reports in the paper.' Fred was pressing again. 'I don't like it when flakes like Hickey say those kinds of things about Troy.' He became threatening, sincere. 'What are you going to do about it, Steve?'

'I've already got someone working on it,' he replied.

'Who's that?'

'A good man who knows the ropes. You've met him, I believe. Joseph Curtis.'

Zach looked doubtful. 'Well,' he said, 'I guess he knows where the bodies are buried.'

Fred joined in. 'You won't screw up, will you, Steve?'

Stephen found a certainty the better part of him distrusted. 'Fred, Zach,' he said, phoney as hell, but convincing nonetheless. 'We're the best. Trust me.'

The two Americans understood this language. They smiled at each other as if to say, Our boy is in safe hands, our investment is secure, we made a good decision here.

'Let's get that waiter over here,' said Zach, 'and do some champagne. I want to celebrate.'

8

It was the morning of what Zach liked to call 'shoot minus three'. Stephen was up and gone. Isabel buried herself under the duvet, full and warm with a drowsy happiness that she could almost taste and smell. When you slept alone, you longed for a partner. Now that Stephen was here and she was sleeping with him most nights, these moments of solitude in bed were precious, a chance to ponder the mysterious force of what was happening to her.

She pressed her face to the sheets and took in all over again the sex of the night that was past. As morning came up, the light strengthened and the shadows went from the room, Stephen had left to supervise the security arrangements. She felt his part of the bed grow cold, and she curled herself tighter into her own nest, not wanting to let go but knowing that, with consciousness, the responsibilities and irritations of the day would inexorably return.

Through the wall she could hear Curtis's insistent muttering on the telephone. She imagined him lying there, a few feet away, on his own, cradling the receiver. There was a time, she reflected, when the voice beyond the wall had been a comfort to her. In the beginning with Stephen, it had been a kind of joke. Now it had become an annoying reminder of a tension in her life with Stephen that seemed to worsen every day.

The more she thought about Curtis, the angrier she became. She could not lie idly in bed. Her determination to confront the issue made her restless. She found herself getting up, almost without thinking. It was ridiculous that it should have gone this far. She would go round and talk to him. She would be calm, but firm, and unambiguous. She would make it her responsibility. She would admit her misjudgement, her error even. Why did women always have to volunteer the blame?

No matter: she would close – no, slam – the door on the past. All she wanted at that moment was to draw a line under the account in the ledger of her old life.

She ran the bath and while the water thundered in the pipes, she stared at herself in the mirror. It was true that sex did something for you, though looking at the evidence, not enough. The other morning she had been thinking, as she performed this daily ritual, the visit to the altar of her vanity, that she looked every second of thirty-two. She had confessed this thought aloud to Stephen. 'No, you don't,' he said. 'You look fine.' He had said this with such confidence and ease that she had felt good about herself all day.

Lying in the water, watching the steam rise over her body and feeling the heat seep into her, she was with him again. He was slowly rubbing her with a bar of white soap and they were splashing around in the water like children, lost in each other.

The censoring thought of Curtis came back into her mind, his inscrutable duplicity and scheming. There was something unbalanced about his self-control, and some of his actions no longer made sense. There was, for instance, the recent episode in the church.

A few days after the incident at Mr Hu's, she had joined the crowd that turned out to hear Hickey preach the Sunday sermon he had been promising in the press and on the air, the latest salvo in his campaign against Troy and the controversial video.

For a while it had seemed as though Hickey's mission would be starved to death by indifference, but now he was the focus of attention, and Isabel had witnessed an evangelist reborn. She had sat in the hastily organised press section with several correspondents from the local newspapers, and even one or two nationals, together with a scattering of pop writers covering the story from the music angle. Behind, in the main aisle, television lights flared high above the congregation. 'They'll only broadcast this if someone tries to off him,' said one of the reporters with a cynical laugh.

The measure of Hickey's triumph was the number of rival ministers who were now scrambling onto his bandwagon. Before the long-awaited moment of Hickey's address, a variety of village preachers took the microphone to denounce the manifold sins and wickednesses of the modern world and the church echoed to Revelation and Saint Paul.

Isabel noticed, looking round during this ecclesiastical warm-up, that the congregation was different too. Before, the aisles had been filled with a benign hum of rural people and their families, soft-eyed believers for whom the word of God was the mysterious accompaniment to the rhythm of nature. Now she recognised, in the blur of the crowd, the faces of prominent businessmen and politicians. The pews were crowded with city types, men and women who might have come here only for the entertainment. There were, indeed, some people who were obviously drunk.

The church itself had been sealed off by the army and the faithful had to walk the last few hundred yards on foot. Beyond the military barricades, local pressure-groups chanted in the dusk. Mobs of teenage boys had thrown stones and tried to start a riot, but they had been dispersed with CS gas and water cannon. At the church door, more controls were in force. Isabel had been intrigued to note that Hickey's protest was becoming political. Grim-faced ushers checked coats and bags for weapons. In the side aisles, uniformed officials with radio-mikes were reporting back to a hidden operations room. A police officer with a dog was sniffing for explosives.

The last speaker stepped off the podium and a godless buzz of conversation spread through the church, now full to overflowing.

There was a drumroll. The congregation came to its feet. A small, vicious-looking pipe band was marching down the nave. It wheeled in formation and drew up by the altar, Hickey's honour guard. The pipes were lowered, the drumbeat faded and the silence was filled with a crushing chord from the organ. The congregation opened their throats in a savage bellow.

Would you be free from your burden of sin?
There's power in the blood, power in the blood.
Would you o'er evil a victory win?
There's wonderful power in the blood.

As they reached the last chorus, Hickey stepped out from behind a curtain and stood at the lectern in a theatrical shaft of light, his arms raised high.

Isabel, who was sitting quite near him, to one side, could see in his eyes the trapped, vengeful look of a man who must kill or die himself. When she thought of Troy and his spaced-out entourage, it alarmed her to see it. Hickey was playing for keeps. Once, he had been humble, diffident and winning; now his voice was racing towards a mad scream. 'Brothers and sisters in Christ!'

Isabel decided that it was not just in her imagination that Hickey's voice was colder and harder. There was none of his former homely, fireside simplicity. He had his armour on and he was crusading. Red-eyed with stress and at times on the edge of hoarseness, he was gripping the microphone for comfort. In becoming a fighter, he had also, in some strange way, ceased to be a foreigner. He was one of them now. She noticed that he spoke of 'we', not 'you'.

Hickey was warming up. 'My friends,' he was saying, 'it is my custom, in times of trouble, to ask our Lord for his comforting words. I take my bible in my hand – ' he held up a small, battered volume ' – I open it at random, and I let the Lord speak to me.'

Someone at the back of the church shouted something indistinct, and Isabel saw a flurry of ushers move towards the disturbance.

Hickey was not distracted. 'Tonight, as I was praying alone on my knees, asking for God's guidance and courage to say what I have to say to you tonight, I opened this bible, the bible I have carried through every adversity, the one my mother gave me, God rest her soul, and this is what I found.' He turned to a marked page and began to read.

'"Now is the end come upon thee . . ."' Hickey's words echoed down the nave. When he had finished reading, he closed the bible with a flourish and let his words work their way into the minds of his audience, silent and rapt before him. '"An evil, an only evil, behold, is come." The words of the prophet Ezekiel. A vision of the final desolation. A glimpse of the apocalypse. A moment of truth. That, friends, is the word of God to us here tonight.'

Again, from the darkened recesses of the church, there was a cry, but it was a stifled 'Hallelujah' and the stewards made no move.

'The ways of Satan, my friends, take many guises and forms. For instance, there are high-up people, I'm telling you, high-up people on the mainland who talk with the forked tongue of Lucifer about "normalisation" for this precious world of ours. We read about it in the newspapers and we see it discussed on our television screens – ' he pointed accusingly at the cameras ' – but we are not consulted, not by the higher-ups who want to tell us how to live. What does it mean, this "normalisation"? I'll tell you what it means.' He paused for effect. 'It means sodomy and perversion, it means drug addiction and corruption. This ugly, evil little word is a synonym for Satan, it is the language of Beelzebub and Apollyon, it is the vocabulary of viciousness and all the abominations of the corrupted mainland. We are blind, my friends, blind to the evil that is come into our midst, this standard bearer for the Prince of Darkness. Now we must stand up and be counted. We must tell the atheists and unbelievers and godless hypocrites who live over there what we think of their "normalisation", we – '

Suddenly, the microphone went dead and all the lights went out.

For a moment there was silence, then panic and confusion, and Hickey's voice, strangely weak and remote, struggling to rise above the hubbub. 'This is the work of my enemies, this is the hand of the devil himself . . .'

'Round one to Satan,' said the cynical journalist next to Isabel.

In the dim light of the church candles, Isabel could make out Hickey in a huddle with his assistants. After some minutes, he banged on the lectern for silence. 'My friends, there has been sabotage.' His words were faint and unimpressive. 'The electrical system of this fine church has been attacked by my enemies. I have no choice but to save my words for next Sunday. Loudspeakers or no, I shall be in good voice for you. Let us meet again then. Good-night and God bless you all.'

The congregation began to file out into the night. When the church was deserted, apart from the technicians rolling up electrical cables, Isabel made her way behind the altar. She was stopped by a pointy-faced evangelical minder in a black suit. She flashed her press card. 'I would like to speak to Mr Hickey,' she said.

The man studied her credentials suspiciously. Finally, after some deliberation, he asked her to wait and disappeared through the darkness towards a small door. As she stood quietly waiting, she could hear raised voices inside.

There was no one around. She edged closer. Hickey's voice was tense and hard with anger. 'I told you to keep an eye on those television people,' he was saying. 'They can damn well arrange their own goddamn power system. You've ruined the whole goddamn show. What is it, Jesse?'

Isabel could hear her emissary interrupting the argument. But Hickey was raging. 'The press? I ain't speaking to no shitty press. All those sons of bitches want is to tell their readers how bad we blew it tonight. Tell her to go screw herself, I'll see her next week.'

Another American voice intervened. 'Hey, Russ, hold on now. You should talk to the press. We need the coverage. You know that.'

The discussion became hushed and calmer. Isabel moved back out of earshot, pretending to examine a family tomb. She stood in the dark, quite alone, pondering the situation. It was then that she heard a familiar step on the stone flagging and,

looking up, was surprised to see Joe Curtis slipping through
the shadows of the aisle and disappearing through the door,
unchallenged and unannounced.

She had puzzled over this for some days. Curtis was
working for Hickey's declared enemies. What was he doing
visiting the evangelist after hours? When, finally, she had
confessed her anxiety to Stephen, he had pursed his lips and
said he would have Curtis vetted again.

Now she stepped out of the bath, dried herself and dressed
quickly, pulling on whatever came to hand. Then she blasted
her hair impatiently with the dryer and hurried downstairs.

She watched the coffee drip through the percolator and
wondered what Stephen was doing. At least he seemed unconcerned by Curtis's activities, or so he said. It was sometimes
hard to tell what he was thinking. At first, she had teased him
about his elusiveness, finding it attractive; now, there were
times when his absence in her company was an irritation.

Life was annoying. She had imagined that the video would
be a way for Stephen to be with her, and for them to be happy
together. Why was it that the things you looked forward to so
often turned out to be more complicated than you imagined?
The filming threatened to put the town into a state of siege,
and simultaneously her relationship with Stephen had become
beleaguered as well. She knew that if she told herself they
would be happy when this was all over, she would be making
a mistake.

She heard Curtis's front door open and shut. He would be
taking Mary to the hospital. She would catch him on his
return. The phone rang. It was her producer checking some
details about the next broadcast. Finally, her business done,
she went outside.

The arrival of the video crew had brought chaos. The place
was being turned upside-down. Today they were starting to
dress the main street, removing television aerials and adding
fake shopfronts to private houses. Clive Fox had spoken of his
plans for the contemporary brutalism of the video, but it
seemed he also wanted to intercut some soft-focus nostalgia.

She hurried over to Curtis's store, which was still closed. She looked at her watch: nine-thirty. Two members of the film crew in identical blue parkas were also hanging about, waiting. They recognised her and nodded good morning.

'He never opens on time,' she explained. 'It's like that round here.' She crossed the road to Mr Hu's. The restaurant was locked and deserted. She peered inside; it was gloomy, with a greenish light coming from the tropical fish tank. In the garden at the back, Mrs Hu was doing her t'ai chi, her eyes closed, twisting and stretching in a private world of meditation.

Isabel came back to the main street. A unit van was cruising towards her, blocking the view. As it passed, she gazed intently towards the school and the factory and beyond at the film unit trailers. Then she spotted the familiar red anorak. She began to hurry and then to run. Her steps echoed on the pavement. He heard her, turned, and stopped, as still as she was animated.

'What's the matter?' He was distant, but he could not be cold.

'I have to – ' She was out of breath. 'I have to talk to you.'

'Now?'

'Now.' She pushed open the door of one of the trailers. 'In private.' The space was full of theatrical props, but it was deserted. 'This will do fine.' He followed her reluctantly. She closed the door and sat down on a giant plastic coconut. He chose a medieval throne.

She could not suppress a smile. 'King Curtis.'

He was defensive. 'What do you want?'

'What's going on, Joe?'

'I don't understand.'

She had resolved to stay calm and patient. 'Joe, I'm terribly fond of you, and you've been good to me, but I'm not in love with you.' She saw the hurt pass across his face like a shadow. 'You must accept that what happened was a mistake – my mistake.'

She knew well that he was unskilled in the interpretation of feelings and was not surprised by his answer. 'What on earth are you saying?' he asked.

'I'm saying what I've said before, ad nauseam. You have no quarrel with Stephen. There's no reason to persecute him.' She stopped, hoping he would admit something.

He replied, quite calmly: 'What do you really know about Stephen Mallory?'

'Not much.' She allowed herself a taunting smile, and lit a cigarette. 'I'm finding out.'

'I suppose you know that the minister himself gave special permission for this video.'

'So what? Everything here is monitored from the mainland.'

'Exactly.' He was triumphant, as though he had proved something.

Isabel felt a sadness come over her. 'Your mind is full of paranoid nonsense, Joe.'

He flinched. 'Isabel, if you knew what I knew – '

When he used her name she felt her annoyance stirring again. 'What do you know?'

'I'm sorry, Isabel.' His look of regret was infuriatingly self-important. 'It's confidential.'

Her anger broke the surface briefly. 'You're not in love with me. You're in love with yourself, with your so-called power over people, and I think it's driving you crazy,' she said.

Her words threw him further back on the defensive, a boxer on the ropes. 'Things are very complicated at the moment.'

'You bet they are. Mostly, it seems to me, thanks to you.' He looked quite crushed by her anger, and she recovered herself. 'There's no need to mistrust him,' she said, gentle at last. 'He's only doing a job.' She smiled. 'It's not even a job he's especially qualified for. Believe it or not, this is supposed to be a bit of light relief, a holiday.' She put out her hand and took his in hers. 'Don't be weird, Joe. There's no need.' She tried to offer some hope. 'After this is over, I want to be friends with you.'

'After what is over?'

'The filming.'

'It will never be the same.' There was bitterness in his face. 'Mary's right. We've ruined this place.'

'We?'

'You, me, all of us. Everyone's to blame. I should never have had those stupid ideas about the Institute.' His eyes were full of private sadness. 'That place is costing me nothing but trouble.'

'Don't listen to Mary.' She stubbed her cigarette impatiently into the floor. 'She wants you to live in the past.'

'I like the past. I always have. I'm happier there.'

'The past is a prison. It's full of pain. You have to move on. Take a risk, Joe. You'll feel better.'

'I did.' He was almost crying, and again she feared for his state of mind. 'I took a risk with you.'

'I'm sorry.' She took his hand again. He was like a boy. 'There. I've apologised. Is that better?'

'I wish – I wish I could get you out of my mind.'

'Don't be silly. Of course you will.'

There was a pause. Outside, echoing between the walls of the houses, there was the sound of hammering.

'Do you love him?'

She looked away; this was the question she feared. 'I don't think we should have this conversation,' she replied. In her thoughts, she saw him holding her that winter Sunday afternoon, and felt saddened by the distance that had opened up between them. She was like an exile who had discovered that home no longer had any meaning. 'I'm sorry,' she said again.

'I understand,' he said. 'It's probably best to forget the old days.'

Why did things always have to be so exclusive? This was not the moment to argue that one. It was enough that they had spoken. She had one last item on her mind and, since he would not volunteer it, she had no choice. She looked at him steadily. 'You went to see Hickey, didn't you?'

He held her gaze. 'He's the last person I'd want to see just now. He's making life impossible here.' He could not stop himself. 'Where did you hear that?'

She wanted to hide her disappointment, but could not stop herself. 'You're lying to me. Why can you never speak the truth?'

He panicked. 'What do you mean?'

'I saw you. In the church. On Sunday. Don't lie to me, Joe.'

There was no escape. His eyes darted away from hers. 'He asked to see me.'

She was quick to spot the flaw. 'But you don't know him.'

'I mean, I was asked to see him.'

'Is that all you're going to say?'

'There's nothing to add. He wanted to know what was happening. I told him the facts. He told me what he was doing. An exchange of information.' He managed a smile. 'It is my forte.'

She opened the door of the trailer and summer sunshine flooded in. For a moment of clarity she thought she had broken the code of Curtis's conversation and understood what he was really saying, but then obscurity returned. She stepped out into the morning and went to look for Stephen.

Stephen sat in the production headquarters, another chaotic trailer parked on a patch of waste ground. He was flying high with the adrenalin of command. Various schedules, timetables and rosters were spread out before him. Out of the window he could see the other trailers drawn up in a battle line and it amused him to imagine them as his divisions, ready for action.

Next door, the technicians, florists and interior decorators were still fussing over Troy's personal suite. Beyond, there was the wardrobe and make-up unit, the accounts, publicity, music, technical, properties and catering. Stephen knew from the meticulous schedule in front of him that Mr Hu was, at that very moment, having his first meeting with the imported galley staff, flown in from the mainland the night before. The air of urgency and expectation was enhanced by the comings and goings on the impromptu helipad next to the deserted factory.

The military atmosphere was not just in Stephen's imagination. The authorities were taking Hickey's threats of protest and disruption seriously and the army had closed the location to the outside world. The townspeople had been issued with special passes, the members of the film unit wore plastic identity badges and Stephen's team was grappling with the media invasion – television news crews, reporters and rock journalists. There had been a preliminary briefing at a press conference in the Institute the night before, and now everyone was awaiting the arrival of the star, an unpredictable event. Fred Shuster, relying on years of experience, believed he would show up some time during the next twenty-four hours, but, as he said, 'With Troy, all bets are off.'

It occurred to Stephen, as he surveyed the schedule on the table in front of him, and watched the preparations outside, that if the minister could see what 'normalisation' meant in practice, he might have had second thoughts.

Clive Fox came into the trailer. He seemed bulkier and louder with each day that passed, and appeared to be starring in a private movie of his own. Today he was wearing a flak jacket, heavy military boots, a baseball cap, a white silk scarf and aviator glasses. He was brandishing a video cassette.

'Got it,' he announced, a note of triumph in his voice.

'Got what?' Stephen looked up coolly from the table. There was something about Fox he did not like, but he had not yet been able to formulate his antipathy.

'Hickey's last sermon.' Fox switched on the television and video recorder as he spoke. 'One of the news people got it for me. A delicious little PA with wonderful breasts.' He kissed the tape to her memory and slotted it into the machine.

'I thought there was a power failure.'

'Apparently he spoke for a minute or two first. I want to get a look at this creep in action.' He pressed the play button. The picture jumped into view. A minister in a black suit was making the sign of the cross.

'That's not him,' said Stephen.

Fox was fast-forwarding. 'Here we are.' He pressed the

pause button and an image of Hickey froze on the screen. 'Let us pray, right?'

Hickey was screaming, in close-up, his face twisted with fear and hatred. 'Brothers and sisters in Christ . . .'

Fox turned to Stephen with a look of surprise. 'Nice.'

'It will probably get worse – or better – depending on your point of view.'

'. . . the bible I have carried through every adversity, the one my mother gave me, God rest her soul . . .'

The camera cut away to the congregation briefly and Stephen scanned the screen for faces he might recognise. Hickey was still speaking. 'An end is come, the end is come: it watcheth for thee.'

Fox held the frame for a moment. 'This guy is actually saying the end of the world is nigh.'

'Isabel says that when he starts talking about hellfire and Satan he gets quite frightening.'

Fox looked at him curiously. 'You didn't waste much time there, did you?'

'Excuse me,' said Stephen coldly.

'Aren't you two what they call an item?'

Stephen knew the director's reputation with the opposite sex, and he could see that being here on location was like an aphrodisiac for him. Fox's self-confidence had ballooned and he had already slept with at least one of the production assistants. The pleasure he took in seduction was known throughout the crew and tolerated as an amusing foible. Stephen said: 'I'm surprised it's taken you so long to find out, Clive.'

'Just checking. I don't want to make a fool of myself with Isabel. She's very attractive.'

'All's fair in love and war, Clive, but I'm serious about her.'

'In my book, Steve, with women nothing is ever serious. If you think that you're in for some big disappointments.'

Stephen was annoyed by Fox's cynicism, but found some detachment. 'Perhaps we're in love. Sorry about that, Clive.'

Fox looked uneasy, almost embarrassed, and turned back to the video. Hickey was now pointing at the camera. 'This ugly, evil little word is a synonym for Satan, it is the language of Beelzebub and Apollyon, it is the vocabulary of viciousness and all the abominations of the corrupted mainland . . .'

'Jesus Christ,' murmured Fox.

Then the screen went blank. 'That was when the power went down,' Stephen explained. 'Hickey accused his enemies of sabotage. Apparently what really happened . . .' Stephen was glad to introduce Isabel into the conversation again, re-establishing his claim. 'Isabel overheard Hickey shouting at his staff for overloading the mains circuit. From what she told me, he sounds anything but godly.'

He would not, he decided, repeat Isabel's doubts and anxieties about Curtis. In their many late-night discussions of Curtis's motives and methods, they had agreed that a success-ful investigation of his activities could only be done in secret. Fox was not to be trusted; he was as discreet as a megaphone. If Curtis's finely-tuned network of informants and eavesdrop-pers picked up even a whisper of his intentions, Stephen would get nowhere. Increasingly, too, he was coming to fear Curtis's irrational behaviour, and the threat of violence in his manner.

Fox was winding the tape back for a second look. 'Are you staying with Isabel?'

Stephen felt annoyance creeping in. 'Listen, Clive, you're getting on my nerves. Leave it alone, will you?'

Fox shrugged. 'For Christ's sake, Steve.'

The door of the trailer opened and Isabel came in. 'Hi,' she said.

'We were just talking about you,' said Fox provocatively.

'Naturally,' she said, with a reassuring smile. She was wearing jeans, sneakers and a woolly sweater several sizes too big. She came over to Stephen and kissed him. He put his arm round her briefly. Clive watched them frankly, almost voyeur-istically. Isabel went and sat on the couch next to the television. 'I see you managed to get a tape.'

'A friendly mole,' said Clive, with a knowing look in Stephen's direction. 'I've not seen Hickey in action before. It's wild stuff.'

'I was there.'

'So your boyfriend was telling me,' said Fox.

Isabel frowned with distaste. 'I hate that word,' she said.

Stephen wondered if she had come to dislike Fox as much as he did. They had spent so much time analysing Curtis and his motives, they had overlooked the director. He dragged the conversation back to the issue in hand. 'When you look at that tape you can see why we have to seal off the location.'

'I think you're making trouble for yourselves,' said Isabel. 'People don't like it.'

Before Stephen could react, Fred Shuster came in. He was wearing a sky-blue tracksuit and he was on the phone, walking and talking in the way he liked best. 'Yeah – bye-bye now!'

He switched moods, jumping into the conversation, sharp and aggressive. 'Who doesn't like what?' He was looking at Stephen. 'I need to know about this.' Stephen noticed that Fred was becoming like Fox, a character in an imaginary movie. He supposed this was inevitable.

'Apparently,' he said, glancing across at Isabel, 'the locals don't like the security restrictions.'

'I don't give a flying fuck for the locals. I don't want that flakey evangelical dingbat fucking up the shoot.' He glared at Stephen. 'Who was it who assured me, assured me on the bones of his fucking forefathers, that Hickey was no problem?'

Stephen said nothing.

Fred was pointing to the schedule on the bulletin board. 'Look, we're shoot minus three.' He began to count the days on his fingers. 'We're out of here in ten. What the fuck do they think this is – a babyfood commercial?' He kicked an empty Coca-Cola can the length of the trailer.

There was an awkward pause. Stephen found himself appealing to Isabel. 'Can't you talk to Curtis?'

'I can try.' She kept her recent conversation to herself. 'You know how quirky he is,' she added.

'Actually,' Stephen replied, with an ironic smile, and speaking mainly to Isabel, 'I don't think any of us have fathomed exactly how weird he can be.'

'What is this?' Fred broke in. 'I thought Curtis was the guy you hired. The guy who runs this place. What does he think he's getting paid for?' He was getting angry and exasperated. 'It's his job to get these people to shut the fuck up. Tell him it's time to shit or get off the pot.'

He stopped. Curtis was standing in the doorway. He had a cunning, superior expression on his face, as though he had overheard everything.

'May I come in?' He seemed to be addressing himself to Fred.

Stephen looked at Isabel.

'Sure, Joe.' Fred put out his hand.

'Actually,' said Fox, dangerously, 'we were about to call you for some help.'

'Oh, I see.' Now Curtis seemed unsure about how to respond. 'What can I do?'

Fred took charge again. 'It's your people, Joe. We understand they don't like the security arrangements.'

Curtis looked across at Isabel and then at Stephen, savouring his position between them. Isabel met his eye briefly and then turned away. Curtis's expression was cold and indifferent. 'No,' he said deliberately. 'They don't.'

'Well, then, Joe.' Fred was casual but unmistakably firm. 'As our consultant, what are you going to do about it?'

For a moment, no one said anything. Then the portable phone began buzzing. Fred picked it up. 'Hi,' he said abruptly. His manner changed into smiles. 'Oh, hi . . .' He mouthed 'Troy' at the group. He began to pace up and down. 'Yeah – no shit – we'll be there – great – sure thing – yeah – see you – going well – bye-bye now!'

Fred put the phone down with a sigh. 'He's chartered a yacht,' he said. 'He's landing at some stupid fucking harbour on the high tide tomorrow morning. First thing. We have to be there to meet him.' He put the phone down. 'He's decided he's afraid of flying.' He yawned. 'Oy veh.' He looked round. 'Where's Zach?'

PART

THREE

I

The singer's yacht was moored at a wharf that had once seen battle fleets, ocean liners, tramp steamers and banana boats. Now the docks were lucky to service the occasional deep-sea trawler, and the haunting gantries were still. Fred's chauffeur bumped the limousine across a waste of abandoned tram tracks. A chain of lights, faint in the dawn, traced the distant outline of the harbour mole to the river's mouth and the open sea beyond.

Troy was already on deck. His cries of welcome floated across in the crisp early morning air. The visitors stepped carefully down the gangplank. The star embraced his manager. Fred considered his client. 'Very . . . nautical,' he said, admiring his navy-blue bell-bottoms and matelot jersey.

'Where's Zach?'

'Keeping the natives happy.'

Stephen hung back, watching. The singer seemed older than before, perhaps because his hair was now cropped in a new style. He seemed fitter and more relaxed; he had been in the sun. Standing, he was taller than his publicity photos suggested. In the music press, he was 'wild-man Troy', or 'the singer who likes to think too much', but face to face, he seemed reassuringly easygoing.

Fred turned. 'Troy,' he said. 'This is Dr Stephen Mallory. He's our insurance policy here. He's also quite a bit of an intellectual, aren't you, doctor?'

Stephen flashed his enigmatic smile and put out his hand.

'Pleased to meet you,' said the singer. His eyes were very blue and intent, but passionate not cold. 'Welcome aboard.' He spoke in a way that hinted at his sense of the yacht's absurdity.

Fred was looking about, obviously impressed. 'This is some vessel.'

'When it was commissioned,' said Troy, leading the way, 'it was state-of-the-art, so the crew say. But that was a few years back.' He began an impromptu tour, pointing out the luxury features with a mixture of irony and pride. The boat had belonged to a notorious arms dealer who had fallen on hard times. The liquidators were leasing it short-term, though actually it was for sale. 'We're talking seven figures,' he said.

Fred's boastful laugh was ripe with American poolside arrogance. 'No problem.'

The yacht was a miniature fantasy. They inspected the gym, the pool, the cinema and the staterooms. Wherever they turned, there were uniformed staff, suntanned and watchful. Finally, they returned to the bridge.

'Fred tells me you dislike flying,' Stephen ventured.

'I'll fly if I have to, but this makes a change. We had a great crossing.' He looked out beyond the salt-streaked glass. 'I love the sea. The smell of it, the danger, the power. I can look at the movement of the water all day and not be bored. You know, I like to write and compose by the sea. I also love to swim.'

'I've got it, Troy.' Fred's chameleon mind was adapting fast. 'It must be the womb.'

The singer lifted a guitar propped against the bulkhead. 'I'm hungry. Let's have some breakfast.'

They went into the panelled dining-room, followed by two silent crew members. Fred began fussing over the menu. He looked up suspiciously. 'How is the chef with the eggs?'

The waiter was puzzled. 'Yes sir?'

'How is he with the eggs?' Fred's patience was paper-thin.

'The chef was trained in France, Fred,' said Troy, smiling away his exasperation.

'You can die from eggs.' Shuster made a querulous gesture.

'Fred!'

'Okay – now listen.' Fred began to give precise instructions

216

for the cooking of his eggs. The waiter listened politely; he did not appear to understand.

'Hey – Fred!' His client cut him short with an impatient gesture to the waiter. 'We haven't got all day.'

'Sorry.' Fred seemed chastened. 'It's just I have this thing about eggs.'

'It must be the womb,' said Stephen, slightly reckless.

Fred seemed dismayed, but the singer was laughing. 'Hey!' he said. 'I like that. "It must be the womb." That's funny.' He considered Stephen with new interest. 'I hope you're not taking the piss out of my manager, Dr Mallory.'

Stephen shook his head, betraying nothing. 'I wouldn't dream of it.'

Fred looked irritated and doubtful.

Troy got up and began to pace up and down, humming to himself in thought. He picked up the guitar but thought better of it. 'Let's get serious for a moment. This video. How's it going, Fred? Everything in place? No threats, no trouble? Is this guy Hickey as bent out of shape as they say?'

Fred passed the question across to Stephen, the light of mild vengeance in his eyes. 'This is your baby, Steve. What would you reckon?'

Stephen wondered how candid he could afford to be. Troy seemed to prefer frankness, but he didn't want to make a mess of things on their first meeting. Experience told him that, so long as they trusted you to protect their interests, clients preferred to have the full story.

'I underestimated Hickey,' he said, testing the water.

Fred was still wounded. 'You sure did,' he muttered.

'But,' he went on, ignoring him, 'we're doing our best.' He went into his Mr Smooth routine. The location had been sealed off. The publicity people were dealing with the press. He regretted he could not provide a more encouraging report at this stage but he felt confident about achieving an appropriate environment in which Clive Fox could shoot the video.

'An appropriate environment?' Fred broke in. 'Are you kidding?'

Troy shrugged. 'Something was going to happen here.' He laughed. 'At least we know it's only God we have to worry about.' He lit a cigarette. 'I'm thinking of writing a song about it,' he said. 'About the hypocrisy,' he added, with a wry smile.

'Great idea.' Fred's enthusiasm was automatic.

The singer paid no attention to his manager. 'The fact is that him and me, we're kind of the same. We're performers and entertainers, really. I'm not that bothered by him. He's just after a bigger audience.'

Stephen was relieved that the star was rather better informed than he had been led to expect. So now he described the failure of Hickey's mission and his need for a dramatic revival. He explained Hickey's absurd 'crusade' and the pressures mounting on the townspeople. He elaborated on the sense in which a lot of Hickey's support was political, part of the wider campaign against 'normalisation'. He said that in his opinion Hickey was being used by some powerful people.

'Just as I'm being used,' said the singer. His penetrating blue eyes stared thoughtfully into the distance. He seemed quite philosophical, and Stephen wondered if he had been contacted directly by the ministry of the interior.

There was a small silence. Fred looked surprised at the idea. Stephen hesitated; there was no mileage in dissembling. 'That's right,' he said.

Fred was obviously out of his depth. 'I don't understand.'

Stephen saw the American difficulty with the devious ways of the Old World. 'This video suits some people very well,' he said. 'It proves there is normality here after all.'

Fred shook his head. 'It doesn't seem very normal to me,' he remarked, with a puzzled face.

Troy was intrigued. 'What do the authorities say?'

'Here or there?' Stephen replied.

'Either.'

'It depends who you talk to. That's the point, really. The authorities don't agree about what to do, and according to where they sit have different ideas. Some of them want to declare a curfew and fight an all-out war. Others, like the minister, just want to pretend that the problem's been exaggerated and say this is a peaceful place with a bit of killing and the occasional riot. And then there's a range of opinions in between.'

'It's all good for me,' said the singer. 'If they want to try to use me, I'll use them. The album's about various kinds of colonial mentality – it couldn't be better.'

Shuster looked baffled again. 'I don't get it, Troy,' he said.

'No reason why you should, Fred.' He came over and put his hand in a brotherly way on his manager's shoulder. Stephen noticed that he liked to express a physical control over his staff. 'This isn't your country.' He looked across at Stephen. 'He knows what I mean.'

Fred scowled with irritation. He was the manager here, and he disliked sharing his relationship with the singer.

At this moment, there was a diversion. The waiter came in, pushing a trolley. There was an arrangement of roses in the middle of the food. Troy snatched one of the blooms and danced theatrically across the room, studying it as he went, and throwing out scraps of Shakespeare. He stopped in front of the waiter. 'Where do you get roses at this hour?'

'The deep-freeze, sir.'

He turned to Mallory. 'You see.'

They watched the waiter arrange things. 'Why don't I put it this way,' said the singer as they settled down at the table. 'I'm thirty-five years old. I have a worldwide reputation.' He smiled knowingly. 'And not just for smashing up hotel rooms.'

'That was a long time ago,' Fred interrupted.

'Exactly. I have an international following. I need never work again. You could say, I'd made it.'

Fred was tapping his egg with a silver spoon, and he spoke without listening. 'You have, Troy, you have.'

The singer caught Stephen's eye and smiled. 'Yet not a day passes without a painful memory of my childhood, a little flash of sadness and pain.'

'I still don't get it.' Shuster had his worried look. In his lexicon, Stephen saw, to be puzzled in this world was a kind of failure. 'What's that got to do with colonialism?'

'Countries are like children, Fred, like people. They suffer experiences they can't shake off. That's what we call History.' He was helping himself to yoghurt. 'I love this stuff,' he said. 'My doctor says it's the best there is. What's that you're having, Stephen?'

'Kippers.'

'Fish is good.' Troy nodded his approval. 'Good for the brain.' He seemed happy to see his guests eating well, and turned with appreciation to his manager. 'Dr Mallory's a pretty clever kind of fellow, Fred. Well done.'

'Are you kidding?' Fred's sourness was slowly turning into jocularity. 'I think he's the only one who understands what you say, Troy.'

'You'll get it, Fred. Just give me time.'

'I ain't got all day. What's this stuff about countries being like children?'

'It's like this.' He sat back in his chair. 'I grew up on a city housing estate.'

Fred shot a boastful smile at Stephen. 'I've been there.'

'Yeah,' said the singer. 'So you know what I'm talking about now. Good. Fifty years ago,' he went on, 'it was model dwellings for the working class. Now it's a slum. Drugs, unemployment, violence, the whole schmeer. When I was a boy the only exits were crime, music and sport. All the other doors were closed. It was a vicious circle. The girls got pregnant, their boyfriends and husbands got local jobs, if they were lucky, and their kids were born into the world of their fathers. We were like a colony, you see, kept under by the system. It was an ecology all of its own.'

The light was dawning with Fred. 'Ghosts in the colonial world,' he quoted.

'That's how I put it in the song. We were invisible really, within our own society. No one cared, so long as we didn't make trouble. We swept the floors and washed the linen of the upper class and we remained invisible. But we remembered everything of course. We remembered what our parents and grandparents told us. We remembered the slights, the grievances, the discrimination and the indifference – everything. And we resented it like hell. That's the way the colonised always feel, wouldn't you agree, doctor?'

Stephen saw with his inner eye the experiences of the Third World, the combination of gratitude, shame and fury in almost every transaction. 'Yes,' he said. 'That's right.'

The singer was staring out of the window, looking across at the low-lying land beyond the harbour. There was a small city airport there, and from time to time as he talked private jets and commuter planes cruised in low over the water to land. 'But here – ' he went on, 'what we have here is a much deeper kind of colonialism. That's also in the song.' He smiled teasingly at Fred. 'Isn't it?'

'Is it?'

The star began to hum. 'A thousand years, a hundred thousand deaths . . .' He stopped. 'Here, those childhood memories go back a lot further, and so does the pain. But the principle's the same. Everything that happens here is stored up, and in the end a price is paid. Nothing changes much.'

'That sounds very . . . final,' said Shuster, exhibiting the American dislike of fate. 'You don't believe that, surely?' He wanted a world that was getting better all the time.

'I do,' Stephen interrupted. 'I believe that.' The singer's own candour made him feel almost confessional. 'I describe myself as a "political consultant", and yet in many ways I'm – ' He searched for the words. 'Well, put it this way, the company I work for is still in the business of ruling the world, one way or another.'

Troy was interested. 'Is that right?'

'The names change, but the habits remain the same.'

'The thing about history,' said Troy, 'is that it gives the human race its unconscious. It's something you can read like you can read a person – the psyche of mankind. Hey! That's not bad.' He took a pen and a hand-made notebook out of his breast pocket. When he had finished making the note he wagged the pen at the shore. 'There's a fuck of a lot of history out there,' he added.

'Does that make you feel insignificant?' asked Stephen.

He did not answer for a moment or two. He seemed lost in thought. 'Insignificance – that's something a star knows more about than anyone alive.' He turned to Fred Shuster. 'We've talked about this, haven't we?'

'Sure have.' Almost as an aside to Stephen, Fred remarked that this was one of the star's 'little obsessions'.

Troy picked up a guitar and strummed a few chords. He began to improvise. 'I'm going to trade this old guitar for a harp with golden strings . . . I'll have a harp with golden strings to play with the angel band . . .'

'He loves country,' Fred commented.

'There's nothing like being up there in the firmament, twinkling away, ha-ha, to make you feel insignificant. You think to yourself, What have I done? And you say, I'm nothing. When you're up there in the universe, even if you know there's a million people out there looking at you with their telescopes, you really appreciate the immensity, the infinity, of things, and your own unimportance.'

'Don't say that, Troy,' Fred broke in. 'You've gone platinum three times.'

The singer winked at Stephen. 'See what I mean?' He plucked at the strings of the guitar. 'I suppose I just can't stop badgering myself. It's my problem. People say I'm intense, but what does that mean? A tense is a word we use about time – present tense, future tense. So, sure, I'm in-tense, because I'm in time. If I pull back on that, who am I cheating? Myself, of course.' He yawned. 'You've got to keep on going, boats against the stream and all that. This album, the one we're doing here, is about losing yourself to find yourself.'

'Great title,' said Shuster, back on automatic pilot, '"Going Native".'

'Thanks, Fred.' Troy looked round at the debris. 'Nice breakfast. I guess we've got to hit the road.' He turned to

Fred. 'Talking of insignificance,' he said. 'We've got a problem with Hanif. He's bottled out at the last minute.'

'I'll kill him,' said Shuster, becoming the manager again. 'Why?'

'He read something about racial discrimination over here and said he was scared to come.' Troy smiled at Stephen. 'My masseur,' he explained. 'I can't work without him. I know it sounds gross, but it's true.'

Stephen was pleased to discover he shared a personal foible with the star.

'That girl of his,' Troy was saying, 'she's always putting the frighteners on him.'

'I'll kill her too,' added Fred. 'Silly bitch.' He seemed perplexed. He turned reluctantly to Stephen. 'I don't suppose there's a masseur in the town?'

'It's not exactly that kind of place,' said Stephen. He could see that Fred was beginning to panic. 'Funnily enough, I think I may be able to fix something up.' It was a risk, but the golden rule was always to use people you knew. He turned to the singer. 'You'll accept my personal recommendation?'

'Sure.' Troy was impressed. He went over and put his arm round Shuster. 'Hey, Fred, you should have told me sooner. This guy's okay. He's bright, he's cool. Where did you find him?'

Shuster preened himself. 'You know me, Troy. I have my contacts.'

'Well, for once, baby, you didn't screw up.'

Fred was relaxed now. 'Don't be like that.'

'I'll be any way I please, as you well know.'

'Yeah, that's true.'

They were still bantering like an old married couple when they climbed into the limousine for the drive to the location. Stephen, watching them go, found himself wondering if they had been lovers, and then, more urgently, where he could find Skylark. 'Don't you trust me?' the boy had said. Now he would have to.

One of the crew interrupted his thoughts to say that there

was no problem about car rental. They would have someone here in about half an hour. Stephen knew he should call Isabel while he waited and put her in the picture but, for no good reason he could think of, he didn't.

2

When, after a day of silence, Isabel realised that Stephen was not going to call her and that she had no idea where he was, she felt betrayed. They had begun something together that seemed special and different. She had loved him for the claim he had made, his directness and commitment. Now he seemed careless and selfish like everyone else. In her better moments, analysing the irrational anger in her heart, she knew this was not true, or at least ungenerous, but she had lived long enough with disappointment and neglect to have become an extremist in such matters. She had listened to him regret his past failure to police the demands of his working life, yet here he was offering a master class in all that she most feared. Her thoughts strayed hopelessly back to her missing husband.

She had dreamed of Tom again last night, and had come to with tears wet on her cheeks. Then, floating in the dozy empyrean between sleep and waking, the faces of Tom and Stephen had become muddled in her mind. She had risen in a state of confusion, and at midday found herself calling trans-atlantic, slamming the phone down at the first connection. Perhaps she was going a bit loopy.

A shadow passed across the window onto the street and she heard footsteps. Probably it would be Curtis. She did not want to see him. Perhaps it would be Stephen, but she was startled to find that she did not care if he was back or not. She went to the kitchen window and composed herself in the reflection, dabbing her tears with a dishcloth.

'Joe,' she said, not turning round. There was no reply. 'Stephen.' She could hear someone shuffling in the hallway and she felt a pulse of fear. 'Hello there,' she called, turning. 'Is that you, Joe?'

There was a long pause, and then a head, close-cropped and

comically nervous, appeared round the door of her parlour.
Isabel was relieved to recognise Paul from the hospital. She
stood very still, as you might stand in a wood with a frightened
deer, and said softly: 'Come in. Don't be afraid.'

Paul had the Walkman round his neck, and as she spoke she
remembered his neurosis and wondered if he had mistaken her
door for Curtis's. Ever since the arrival of the film crew, the
day-release patients in the hospital had taken a special interest
in the location. None had been given passes, of course, but it
was proving difficult to prevent them from penetrating the
security, as Stephen had already complained. Their strange,
disconcerting presence among the exotic creatures from the
pop world had stimulated the idea with the press that somehow
they were also to be involved in the filming.

The boy looked at her hard, assessing the sincerity of the
invitation, then pushed the door open. He was limping slightly
and he wore a blue anorak. He had bad skin and was, she
guessed, looking for Curtis.

'Come and sit down,' she said. 'Make yourself at home.'
She took a step forward. 'You know me. I'm Isabel.' She did
not know what more to say, and she was afraid to arouse his
anxiety with speech.

The boy came up. His large brown eyes were fixed intently
on her, as though he feared she might vanish if he looked
away. He carried with him the smell of the hospital and his
hand, when she took it, was deathly cold.

There was a long, stuttering pause. Then the boy said:
'Isabel.' He smiled fiercely and pointed to a badge on his
anorak she had not noticed before. 'I'm Paul,' he said, speaking
with difficulty.

'Yes,' she said gently. 'I know.' Perhaps her foreignness to
him excused her language. 'Would you like some tea, Paul?'

He gave an exaggerated nod, like someone miming gratitude. She sat him down on the sofa and went back into the
kitchen. When she came in with the tray, he was hunched
forward on the sofa, staring at the cat.

She gave the boy his tea and sat down next to him on the

sofa in front of the empty hearth. In her desolate mood, she found his presence a comfort, and his distraction took her out of herself. After a moment or two, Paul put his mug down and fiddled with another badge on his anorak. He detached it without too much difficulty and held it up. 'Do you like my smile?' he asked.

She held out her hand and he passed her the badge, as though it was a fragile or precious ornament. It was, in fact, a souvenir from an amusement park, a cartoon face with a childish grin. 'Yes,' she said. 'I like your smile. I expect he cheers you up when you feel down.'

He did not seem to hear her. He was back in his own world, fumbling with his anorak. Isabel could not stop herself offering to help him with the zipper, but he drew back proudly. 'I can manage,' he said, reddening with the effort. She felt annoyed with herself for her insensitivity. Underneath, he was wearing a shapeless grey institutional jersey covered with badges. 'Look.' He began to point. 'This is my house. This is my dog. This is my holiday. This is my gun.' Isabel came closer. She saw he was wearing one of Hickey's badges.

'What's that?' she asked, pointing.

'Hope and salvation,' he replied, without hesitation. 'That man came,' he added. 'We sang songs.'

She was surprised to hear that Hickey had visited the hospital, and wondered at the significance of this news.

'Miss Curtis has promised me another badge for my birthday,' said the boy.

'When's your birthday?'

'Tomorrow.'

'Well,' she said. 'Happy birthday for tomorrow.' A thought came to her and she went to her desk. For months she had kept a promotional badge advertising the radio channel for which she worked, a simple white '2' on a red background. 'Happy birthday,' she said.

He seemed offended. 'I'm not two,' he said. 'I'll be twenty.'

'It's for you and me,' she replied, thinking quickly. 'The two of us. With love.'

'Smile,' he said, apparently won over, and pinned it next to the cartoon face. 'Thank you, miss.' He was blushing furiously.

'Thank you for visiting me,' she said, and meant it.

Now Paul took a wallet out of his anorak. The wallet was empty but in the back there was a single Polaroid photograph, a woman with dark Mediterranean features standing in front of a view of the sea. 'That's my mum,' he said, handing it over. 'She's dead.' She felt him watch her study the picture. 'Do you have a mum, miss?'

'Yes, I do.'

'Is she alive?'

'Yes.' She felt almost ashamed of her luck.

'My mum's in heaven,' said Paul definitively. 'That's where people go when they die. That's what Miss Curtis says.'

She handed the photograph back and watched him put it carefully away. He stood up, quite at ease. 'I'm going now.'

'Come and see me again,' she said. This time she did not offer to help with his anorak.

'Goodbye,' he said, putting his hand out.

She took it, and then impulsively pulled him towards her and kissed him, as his mother might have kissed him, on the forehead. 'Goodbye, Paul.'

He limped towards the door. At the step, he turned and gave a funny kind of salute. 'Goodbye, miss, goodbye. See you again soon.'

She watched him go with a sad smile and then turned indoors. She was just taking the teacups into the kitchen when Curtis came in, unannounced as usual.

'What are you doing here?' she demanded. 'He's just gone.' She saw that his eyes were bruised with tiredness and he had not shaved. 'Or perhaps you have come to apologise?'

He shook his head defiantly. He seemed harder than usual, and more decisive. 'You don't believe what I said about Hickey, do you?' he said, speaking quietly. It sounded like a rehearsed question.

'No,' she said. 'I don't.' She was calculatingly offhand. 'Especially now that I've heard he was up at the hospital.'

'I can explain that, too,' he replied, not hiding his surprise.

Something about him reawoke her anger. 'Don't bother,' she said. 'It's easier that way.' She stood there, challenging.

He became awkward and distant and, to reassert himself, asked if he could borrow the phone.

'Sure,' she said coldly, leaving him alone in the parlour.

She reflected, as she did the washing-up, that her sudden vulnerability was making her dangerous, but she could not stop herself. She supposed she should be forgiving, but somehow Curtis stirred up her most vengeful feelings.

She heard him put the phone down next door and wished he would now go away. She sensed that the film people made him feel defensive; they were as self-confident and foreign as an invading, victorious army. To them, no doubt, Curtis was just the local fixer, a familiar figure on any shoot. She guessed that deep down he wanted reassurance, but today she did not feel like offering counsel, and besides he would never admit his need.

'Shouldn't you be down at the location?' she said.

He was about to reply when there was a knock at the door. Curtis turned awkwardly, as if he feared to be found alone here with Isabel.

She called out: 'Who is it?'

Clive Fox came in. He said he was looking for Stephen and she answered, casually, that he was 'away'. Clive was wearing khaki fatigues and was bursting with energy and power. At another time, she might have been irritated by him, too. Today, with Curtis here, and with so much disappointment and tension in the air, she felt suddenly reckless. She went up to Fox and kissed him. 'Would you like a cup of tea?' she asked, smiling warmly. It was not her normal behaviour but she knew the effect it would have on Curtis and she found the cruelty oddly enjoyable.

The director was surprised, but he soon recovered his poise.

He would be delighted. He followed her into the kitchen. She heard his boots clicking on the tiles.

'Is he away long?'

She did not want to admit she didn't know exactly. She said: 'I expect he'll phone in soon.'

'I wish I was like him,' said Clive. 'I get too emotional about things. He's so . . . organised and simple-minded.'

If he was really organised, she thought, he would have phoned. To Clive, she said: 'He can be emotional too. He just doesn't always show it.' She handed him his tea and he thanked her, looking straight into her eyes. Curtis, a helpless spectator, said something strangulated about Isabel's hospitality being well known. Clive made a joking comment about tea and sympathy.

'You should see the walking wounded in this place,' she said, rolling her eyes in Curtis's direction.

The director laughed, and grew bolder. 'It must be a relief to have Stephen around.'

She hesitated wickedly. 'I suppose.'

'I thought you were in love.'

She looked across at Curtis, and wondered how else she could hurt him. She laughed and said that she no longer knew what that meant.

Clive put his cup down. 'If he doesn't come back tonight, perhaps I can take you to dinner?'

She found herself pleasantly challenged by his daring, but took refuge in teasing. 'You're supposed to be shooting a film, Clive. You haven't got time for that sort of thing.'

'The only movies I shoot at night are home videos,' he said.

He was so absurd and sleazy she found him almost appealing. 'Let's do it anyway,' she said, with a quick glance at Curtis. 'You can take me somewhere special and tell me about your deepest desires.' For a wild moment, she saw herself ascending a wide dark staircase, leaving a trail of evening clothes on the silent carpet. Suddenly, a part of her wanted so badly to be caught in flagrante delicto with this man that she was shocked at herself. The part of her that was not hypnotised by her relationship with Stephen told her that she wanted to do something so wilful and assertive and stupid that she knew she was free and independent.

Clive knew none of this. He was astonished at the shift in his fortunes, but covered up well. 'I'll see you later, then,' he said, coolly nodding at Curtis. Isabel escorted him to the door.

'See you,' she murmured, and kissed him again.

Isabel felt light-headed, outrageous and calm. Her heart skipped as she closed the door and she found herself humming Troy's melody. That was the thing about the video, it encouraged you to play truant from your ordinary life, to take risks and become a little bit crazy.

'There was something else I wanted to tell you,' Curtis was saying as she came back into the parlour.

'Going native, going native,' murmured Isabel, still private. She felt thrilled and appalled by her own risky bad behaviour. 'What's that?' she asked, hardly listening.

'I'm thinking of emigrating.' With his words, he killed her mood of expectation, and annoyed her even more. He explained that he had been talking to the cameraman about America.

'What about your sister?'

Curtis said that once the hospital was closed there would be nothing to keep her here, either.

There was something about the madness in the air that day that made Isabel suddenly clear and unforgiving and almost brutal. 'You're kidding yourself, Joe. You'll never leave. You'll live and die here and you know that.'

He was startled. 'I'm nearly forty. If I don't go soon, I'll never go.'

'What about all your plans?'

'Oh.' He sounded quite detached. 'I'd sell the Institute without a second thought.'

'I can't imagine who'd want to buy it.'

A strange expression passed across his face. 'I know I could always do a deal with Mr Hu.'

'You're lying to yourself. You haven't got the courage to

go, or the stupidity.' Her scorn seemed to have no limit; she heard it with dismay. 'You know this is your home and you know you wouldn't last five minutes away from here. It's sick, but it's true.' She paused. 'If anyone's leaving it's me.'

He was stunned by her vehemence. 'Well, good luck to you,' he said. 'I've had enough of your lectures, Isabel. Why don't you fuck off back to the mainland where you belong?'

As he went out, he slammed the door behind him. He had never done this before.

3

The city was on fire. As Stephen came over the hill, speeding down the motorway, the glow of rebellious bonfires added the darker hue of insurrection to the familiar orange of the urban night. From time to time, a firework, a tiny scratch of light, would shoot up into the outer darkness, but it was a silent picture and only the noise of the car intruded on his thoughts. He heard Hickey say that on judgement day the wickedness of the city would be purged by the blood and fire, the vanity of man revealed at the final apocalypse. Perhaps this moment had arrived. Perhaps Hickey's followers were even now awaiting the end of the world with sackcloth and ashes.

There was a military checkpoint where the three-lane carriageway merged into one. The commanding officer had taken charge, flanked by two soldiers with automatic weapons and flak jackets. The rest of his platoon crouched in the dark, covering lines of fire. Stephen watched the officer's eye take in the tell-tale evidence of the rental car, the eye of a sportsman hunting game. Now he was being asked the purpose of his trip. The filming seemed reason enough. He noticed the soldiers' relief at his mainland speech, but there was also a hint of curiosity at the video. 'Save a part for me,' joked the officer, involuntarily adjusting his natty khaki cravat as he waved him through. Perhaps he knew that on such a night the real drama was elsewhere, down in the heart of the city where the flaming effigies and beaten drums would incite the spirits of the demonstrators into the annual riots.

For the moment, there was no hint of trouble. Stephen's route took him through the inner suburbs, featureless rows of semi-detached houses with identical garages and aprons of identical garden. Small groups, mostly teenagers, some with flags, were making their way towards the city centre. They might have been going to a football match.

He found the hotel without difficulty. The security guard on the gate came over. 'Full up,' he said, bending down. There was a fume of drink on his breath and he was leaning against the car window for support.

Stephen gave him a calculated stare. 'You have to let me in. I'm looking for Skylark.'

'Skylark?' The guard's expression registered his meaning, despite the drink. He walked over and unlocked the gate, waving Stephen through with mock courtesy.

Inside, the hotel was as busy as ever. People with drinks were spilling out of the bar. Others were watching television in the foyer. Through the buzz, there was the sound of ragged singing from deep inside the dining-room. Stephen went up to the desk. There was no sign of the manager and he did not recognise the receptionist.

'Is Skylark around?' he asked, silkily complicit.

The woman looked up from her comic book, polite but puzzled. 'There's no one of that name here, sir.'

'You must know Skylark. The manager's son?'

She looked blank. She was temporary; she didn't know the manager had a son. She was obviously not lying. 'He has a daughter,' she added brightly.

'Is she about?'

'I'm afraid I wouldn't know, sir. But I suppose I can ask. Who shall I say is calling?'

Stephen gave his name and stood by. He felt surprisingly tense.

'The manager will be with you shortly,' said the receptionist, putting the phone down and returning to her reading.

He took a seat in the window, keeping an eye on his car. A young man with a can of beer was leaning against the wing, talking to a friend. Stephen turned back to the foyer, suddenly placing his sense of ironic déjà vu. Waiting in hotels for people he did not know was typical of his years abroad. It occurred to him that he would need some kind of story for the manager, but how much would he know about his son's activities? Experience suggested it would be as well to lie as close to the truth as possible.

'Dr Mallory?' The manager had an out-of-hours look, spongebag trousers and a woollen waistcoat, and the irritated manner of one who has been disturbed in the middle of supper. If he recognised Stephen from before, he did not show it. 'How can I help you?'

'I'm looking for a young man known as Skylark. Your son, I believe?'

The manager's expression hardened. 'When that boy was my son,' he replied, 'his name was Andrew.' The memory seemed painful. 'I'm afraid,' he went on, 'that we don't speak any more. May I ask you, sir, what is your business?'

Stephen's reply seemed to confirm the manager's worst fears. 'Just the kind of bad business he would be mixed up in,' he murmured, putting a plump white finger in his mouth and dislodging a piece of food. He shook his head. 'He is not to be relied upon, sir, not to be relied upon in any way.' He looked at Stephen as though suggesting he was also out of place in such activities. 'Would you mind telling me why it is that he is wanted for this film?'

Stephen heard himself speak about the special advantages of using local people. 'The producer felt he could be useful,' he replied non-committally.

'That boy will promise anything if there's profit to be had,' said the manager.

'I expect you know where I might find him.'

The manager refused to respond to this suggestion in the way Stephen had hoped. He shook his head. 'On a night like this he could be anywhere. If I was you, sir, I would look elsewhere for assistance with your film, I would.'

They shook hands and Stephen watched him disappear back into the private part of the hotel. He was about to go and look for a telephone booth to confer with Fred and Zach about his next move when he felt a touch on his arm, and he turned. It was the waitress.

'Harriet,' he said, smiling. He found his involuntary relief met with annoyance and he corrected himself. 'I mean Mouse.'

She nodded suspiciously in the direction of her father. 'What did he want?'

'As a matter of fact, I was asking about your brother.'

'What about him?'

'I need his help.'

'Why?'

He said he would prefer to explain outside. She put her hands behind her back, feeling for the buttons of her pinafore as she spoke. 'I'll find him for you.'

'What – now?'

'Sure. It's nearly the end of my shift, and anyway no one stays in on a night like this.' She darted away and was back at his side before he had time to consider the wisdom of her offer. 'Okay,' she said. 'Let's hurry.' She glanced quickly at the receptionist. 'I don't want my dad to find out.'

With her uniform off, she looked older and more self-possessed, less like a schoolgirl. She had her brother's determination, leading the way to his car. 'I saw you arrive,' she said. 'It's funny, but I had a premonition you'd come.' He opened the passenger door and she dived in. His spirits lifted; he was enjoying himself again.

As they headed towards the security gate, Stephen noticed that Mouse had ducked down below the dashboard. He waved at the guard, who looked up from his television and waved back. The boom jerked up automatically. 'Okay,' he said. 'No one saw you.'

Mouse sat up. 'You have no idea,' she said. He knew she was right and felt absurdly naïve.

Suddenly there were headlights dazzling the driving mirror. The interior filled with light. They both turned. Another car, up close behind them, had appeared as if from nowhere. He put up a hand in protest and the unseen driver dipped the beam. Then they swung out onto the main road and, glancing in his mirror again, Stephen noticed that the other car had turned with him.

'You see,' she said, not looking back.

'Are you sure?'

'No.' She laughed. 'That's the point.'

'Well then?' he said, coasting down the hill towards the city centre. 'Where do we start?' He felt pleased to have found her and was glad to place himself in her hands.

'We'll try down by the docks,' said Mouse. 'There's a club there he goes to a lot.'

'Is it safe to drive?'

'Safer than walking,' she replied. 'I'll take you a back way. Go left at the lights.'

The signal was against them. As they waited, they heard first one and then a second siren. Two fire engines, lights flashing, thundered past in a blare of emergency.

'I love fires,' said Mouse.

'Then you'll be happy tonight.' He looked at her sideways. She was smiling inwardly, and in the light of the oncoming cars there was a fierce, excited gleam in her eye that was even a little frightening. It occurred to him that she must have grown up with the occupation, its arson and violence, and known nothing else.

'Turn right,' she said. He followed her directions with obedience. The road was quiet and dark and they were, apparently, no longer being followed.

'Are you close to your brother?' he asked, a few moments later.

'I'm the only one who wants to understand him.' He saw the same inward smile come back. 'He's only a little bit crazy.'

'Are you crazy?'

'We all are, don't you think?'

'Your father seems conventional enough.'

'He's not been the same since the last bombing.' She explained how the hotel, always a target for terrorist attacks, had been reduced almost to rubble by a well-aimed mortar attack two years ago. There had been many casualties. Her father, unhurt, had been traumatised by the experience. 'You know,' she said, 'he never sleeps in the dark now.' It was after this that her brother Andrew had taken to the streets.

'And became Skylark?'

'That's one name,' she said. 'It depends who he's working for.' She pointed up ahead. 'Look.'

They had reached a busy intersection. A boy in a Joker mask was directing traffic. A huge bonfire of used tyres was burning on a vacant lot. Dark shapes in silhouette were standing round it. Volcanic black smoke-devils twisted upwards, and occasionally a plume of sparks would fly into the night. Mouse was staring in fascination. Stephen let her watch for a moment or two, then asked for more directions.

She came to, as if from a trance. 'Down there.' The road led onto a long wharf. They coasted slowly past the shells of warehouses. There were long Marxist slogans on the walls, and faded posters. 'There,' said Mouse, pointing. In the distance, he could see a pool of light and tiny figures coming in and out of a door.

Stephen parked the car by a wrecked phone box and they got out.

Inside, the music was deafening. The club was a converted abattoir with raw concrete floors and sweating brick. The interior darkness was broken by a strobe light show that threw jagged beams across a mass of dancers, mostly dressed in black leather. The disco sent a heavy, sado-masochistic beat reverberating through the cavernous, shadowy chambers that opened off the entranceway. Stephen stood by the door, feeling extraordinarily alien. Mouse shouted in his ear that she would be back, and plunged into the crowd. He watched her crossing towards the disc-jockey's podium on the far side. Then a new track started, the lights changed to purple and orange, and he lost her.

A young man with cropped, bleached hair and fluorescent streaks on his face came up. 'Hey, mister. You a dealer or a cop or what?'

Stephen shook his head. 'Just looking for a friend.'

'You want friends, mister?' He waved at the crowd. 'All my

238

friends. Be my guest.' He came closer. His pupils were like buttons. 'You got any acid, mister?'

Stephen shook his head again.

'Fuck you,' said the boy, and staggered away.

Alone once more, he scanned the faces for Skylark, but realised he was unlikely to recognise him in this crowd. He wondered where Mouse was and began hoping she would reappear soon. Suddenly she was at his side, slightly breathless from the crush.

'Any luck?'

She shook her head and pressed her face to his. 'Let's get out of here.'

'Don't you want to dance?' he shouted back.

He saw her laugh but could not hear it, and followed her outside. On the quay, it was refreshingly cool and quiet, with sea in the wind. They stood still for a moment and drew breath. 'He was there earlier,' she said. 'Someone saw him having a drink at a bar down the road. I know the landlord. Perhaps he can help.'

When they reached his car, she examined it methodically.

'Do you always do that?'

'Always.'

When he switched on the ignition he wondered what it would be like to have a bomb explode at your feet, and his thoughts strayed back to the blast in the capital the week before Federico died. With hindsight, it had been such an obvious warning . . . Mouse interrupted his thoughts with new directions. The search for Skylark was becoming her quest, too. Perhaps she knew less about her brother than she pretended. He smiled at her determination. 'Well, I'm certainly seeing another side of the city.'

She gave him an odd look. 'You like that, don't you?'

He asked what she meant, hoping for an observation that might flatter his self-image.

'Seeing the darker side of things.'

'I think it's called troubleshooting. I prefer it.'

'If you're looking for trouble,' she said, 'Skylark's your man.'

'He said I should trust him.'

'You should.' She sounded knowing and sisterly. 'He's not as tough as he comes on.'

'What about you?'

She laughed. 'Quiet as a mouse, of course.'

He was intrigued. 'How old are you?'

She was suddenly shy. 'Sixteen.' He looked at her and she saw the look. 'I know. I look younger, and anyway I think I'm too funny-looking for most boys I know.'

'You're very attractive,' he said. 'I don't think I was in love until,' he paused in thought, 'until I was eighteen.'

'Did you marry her?'

He smiled. 'No.' He sighed. 'No, I didn't marry her.'

'Are you in love now?'

He did not reply at once, and then said, with a candour that startled him: 'I think so.'

'My mum says if you can't say yes at once you're not.'

They were cruising, locked away from the weirdness of the city inside the car. He felt strangely relaxed. He switched on the radio and fiddled with the frequency. He caught a snatch of a familiar tune and turned up the volume.

She was curious, looking for clues. 'What's that?'

He realised the record had been made before she was even born. 'Just an old song,' he said, and she did not ask more. In his heart he thanked her for respecting the privacy of his nostalgia.

They were quiet for a moment. The music filled the car. 'This is the end, beautiful friend, this is the end . . .'

A military helicopter with thumping rotors came house-hopping towards them and hovered in the night a few streets away, its searchlight probing the smoky darkness.

'Bastards,' she said. It was the first time she'd expressed her political feelings.

'. . . wilderness of pain, and all the children are insane . . .'

As they turned the corner, they found the bar. There were

sandbags round the entrance and heavy wire grilles on the blacked-out windows. 'Andrew used to work here,' she explained. 'They know me well.'

As they got out, a car cruised past, almost at walking speed. The two men inside glanced casually at Stephen, and drove on. A nagging, suspicious part of him wondered about their identity, but he said nothing to Mouse. She was already at the door, making contact. Her forecast was correct. The security nodded them through without question.

Inside, Stephen felt the scrutiny of many eyes and was glad to have her with him. Alone, he would have been unwelcome and he knew it. In the past, in dozens of awkward situations abroad, he had experienced the irresponsible confidence of the stranger. Here, so close to home, and identified with the mainland, he felt vulnerable and ill-at-ease.

It seemed to be a traditional venue. At the far end, there was a singer with a guitar, a young man with a blond beard, leaning towards the microphone. Some of the drinkers, working men enjoying a night out, stood around clapping in a ragged rhythm. Stephen recognised the tune but not the words. There were hardly any women. In his anxiety, Stephen felt grateful for the music.

Mouse made her way to the counter, squeezing through the crowd, pulling Stephen with her. Here, among the men, she seemed suddenly much younger, a runaway schoolgirl again. The bartender had a neat moustache. He blew her a kiss.

She cut through his indulgence. 'Have you seen Skylark?'

'Who wants him?' He considered Stephen carefully.

Mouse nodded. 'He's okay.'

'Wait on.' He went to consult a group at the end of the bar.

Mouse whispered: 'Andrew used to sleep with that guy for money.' She seemed, from her expression, unsure of her feelings about this, and Stephen wondered why she had mentioned it.

The song ended and a patter of applause passed through the place like a shower of light rain. The barman came sauntering back. 'He was here earlier,' he said, 'but he went out. They think he's probably over at the house.' He looked at Stephen. 'If he's not throwing bricks at the pigs.'

Mouse thanked him, but she seemed subdued. When they came out into the street again she seemed to have lost her enthusiasm. They stood indecisively by the car. Stephen asked: 'What house?'

She looked away. 'Phil's place,' she said in a small voice, as though embarrassed and disappointed. 'You've been there.' Then she seemed to make up her mind. 'Come on,' she said, taking him by the arm.

He drove faster now, sensing a resolution to their search, but then suddenly the road was jammed. Mouse suggested a detour, but the traffic was backed up in all directions and he could not turn. Boys with drums and sticks were hurrying past, shouting and singing. Someone banged the side of the car. He felt cornered, foreign, and on the edge of panic. There was a crowd ahead, and a blue light flashing. 'Stop,' said Mouse. 'I want to see what's going on.'

He pulled over and they both got out. Oddly, it was a relief to be away from the car.

At the junction of three roads, there was a patch of scrubby grass covered with litter, and a few dried-out municipal saplings. People who had been marching had been distracted from the demonstration and gathered in a circle. The blue light was an ambulance. Mouse stopped a woman with a small boy. 'What's happening?'

'Animals,' said the woman, and dragged the boy off into the night.

Mouse and Stephen slowly edged towards the front. 'Can you see anything?' she asked, standing on tiptoe.

'Not much,' he replied.

Two medics in Dayglo tunics were loading a stretcher. The siren began to wail. As the ambulance nosed forwards, the crowd parted and broke up. Mouse stopped another passer-by with her question.

'They crucified him,' he said.

'I don't understand.'

242

'Nailed him to the turf. Half a dozen kids. Ran off when the march came. It's going to be a bad night.' The man hurried away.

They looked down. There was hardly a mark on the ground, barely the imprint of a man's body. Stephen thought, This is the insignificance of violence. Mouse had something in her hand.

'What's that?'

She held it up. 'A nail.' She gave a little squeamish shrug and threw it away. 'Let's find Andrew,' she said.

Without warning, they found two youths, with sticks, standing in their path. 'Having fun are you?' said one, looking to his friend for support. 'It must be nice to be a tourist.'

Stephen saw the spikes in their weapons and felt the rush of fear. When he heard Mouse's disdainful laugh he almost panicked.

'Go and pick on someone your own size,' she replied, advancing fearlessly.

The boys, almost sheepish, stood aside to let them by. Stephen wondered if they would be followed, but the moment of intimidation passed.

The traffic was dispersing. They walked back to the car, not speaking, and set off again into the back streets.

'There,' said Mouse, breaking the silence at last. 'Beyond the No Entry sign.'

A light was shining over the porch and the sound of music filtered out through the curtained windows. After the darkness and violence of the city, it was oddly welcoming. With a start of surprise, Stephen noticed a policeman in a flak jacket standing in the shadows. Mouse had seen him too. 'Evening,' she said.

'Evening, miss,' said the officer, quite normally.

They went up to the front door. 'What's he doing here?' Stephen asked.

'No idea,' she replied. 'Perhaps he's with a government minister. They run it, you know.' Mouse, who had been so free on her territory, seemed momentarily nervous. She pressed the bell, shifting uneasily on her feet as though wanting to turn and run. Then the door opened with a flourish and light flooded into their faces.

'Well now, here's Miss Harriet,' said a familiar voice. It was Philip, the master of ceremonies. Tonight he was wearing a suit of hunting tartan and in his arms he cradled a small Pekinese.

'Now this is a welcome surprise,' he went on, in his actorish voice. 'I wonder to what we owe the pleasure – ' Then he recognised Stephen. 'But good evening, sir. The mystery explained. I'm glad to see that our little establishment appears to give satisfaction.' He smiled judiciously. 'And how can I help you this time?' he asked, ushering them into the hallway.

'We're looking for Skylark,' said Mouse. 'I mean – ' She nodded at Stephen. 'He's looking for Skylark.'

There was a queerness in his answering smile. 'He's not available at the moment.'

Mouse glanced down, as if ashamed. 'It's not like that. He just wants to talk to him.' She appealed to Stephen. 'Isn't that right?'

'Well now,' said Philip, cutting in. 'Talk is free, free as air, but walls have ears.'

Stephen found his laugh hard and unpleasing and he changed the subject. 'Tonight's a big night for you, I imagine,' he observed.

'A big night?' Philip played with the idea. 'In this house it's always a big night. We're larger than life here. We're your richest fantasy, your wildest dreams, your – ' He stopped, and then lifted his voice. 'Mister Speed.'

There was an obscure reply from within.

'You've been here before,' Philip went on. 'You know how special we are.'

Stephen remembered Monica, and said nothing. Speed came in. He nodded at Stephen. When he greeted Mouse she almost flinched, and Stephen wondered if this was the source of her reluctance to come here.

Philip was graciousness itself. 'You will take some refresh-ment while you wait?'

Mouse shook her head, but Stephen gladly accepted a scotch on the rocks. Speed disappeared, leaving a strong trace of aftershave. Philip paced up and down. Occasionally, he would go across and peer through the blue velvet curtain screening the half-lit corridor to the back of the house. He appeared to have much on his mind and his conversation was detached. 'So what brings you back to these parts?' he asked, during one of his turns.

Stephen explained that he was here with a film crew. Philip seemed to know at once that it was to do with the controversial video. 'Now I would put that Hickey on the first plane home. At a stroke, your problems solved. At a stroke! Surely you can buy him off? Everyone has their price.'

Speed came back with Stephen's whisky. Philip held him briefly and affectionately by the arm. 'There's nothing like a man of God for corruptibility, is there, Mister Speed?'

'I hate the Church,' said Speed, without emotion.

'Mister Speed,' said Philip in his most pedagogical manner, 'is an orphan. He was thrown on the tender mercies of the Church at an early age. Fortunately, I rescued him before he became completely spoilt.' He patted his protégé playfully on the backside. 'Off you go, dearie. Don't forget you have your duties. Is all well?'

Speed nodded and disappeared through the blue velvet. There was a burst of music from the corridor, a door slammed and the house was quiet again. In a little while, the curtain was fumbled aside and an elderly gentleman in a pinstripe suit came into the hall, a bit unsteady. He seemed surprised to see Mouse and Stephen sitting there.

'Good-night, sir,' said Philip reassuringly.

'Good-night, Philip.' A deep avuncular voice suggesting port and cigars. 'See you next week.'

They watched him move slowly through the door. As he reached the top of the steps, the officer in the flak jacket came forward to escort him to his car.

'One of my oldest clients in every sense of the word,' said Philip, sotto voce.

Mouse turned to Stephen. 'Andrew says the judges pay the best.' She sighed. 'Come on, Andrew.'

The grandfather clock by the stairs chimed the quarter, and Stephen remembered a childhood fear of clocks in the night.

Skylark came in. He was like an athlete after a race, freshly showered and so light and poised on his feet that he was in their midst, instinctively coming over to Mouse, almost before any of them realised it. Stephen watched him bend down to kiss his sister, and the striking normality of the gesture made him wonder about the fantasies the boy had been fulfilling behind the blue velvet.

'You remember Dr Mallory?' said Mouse. Stephen was touched to see that she loved her brother. Whatever her doubts, now that she had found him she was glowing with pride and admiration and pleasure.

'Sure.' He looked frankly at Stephen with an after-work cheerfulness. 'So what's the story?'

'Can I have a word with you – alone?'

Philip stood up, parodying a sense of outrage. 'So it's like that, is it? Well, and I thought there were no secrets among friends.' He took Mouse by the hand. 'Come on, my dear, we're not wanted. We'll go and have tea and cakes in my parlour.' He wagged a finger at Skylark. 'Don't be long, dear boy. Time is money and all that jazz.'

'You're telling me, you stupid fairy. You owe me a month already.' He gave him a hard, passionless stare.

'Don't be like that,' said Philip, drawing the curtain behind him.

Skylark watched them go and turned to Stephen. 'You're back soon.' He cracked his knuckles and grinned. 'So – did I pass the audition?' He was appealingly boyish.

Speaking softly, Stephen described the preparations for the video and his meeting with Troy.

Skylark was impressed. 'They say he's wild,' he said.

'You'd like him,' Stephen replied.

246

'Jesus,' murmured Skylark, miming a couple of chords on a guitar. 'Troy.'

Stephen described the conversation on the yacht. 'D'you think you could make him feel at home while he's here?' He indicated money. 'I need someone reliable.'

Skylark listened, occasionally jogging a couple of loose-limbed paces across the hall like a boxer exercising for the ring. 'Why don't you ask Phil?'

Stephen explained the need for discretion. He needed some-one he could trust. He lowered his voice further. Philip was too close to his paymasters; he didn't know whom he might talk to. Besides, he guessed Philip wasn't the singer's type. 'You asked me to trust you before, and now I'm doing just that.'

Mouse was right. For all his Love/Hate toughness, Skylark seemed flattered. 'Yeah,' he said. 'You can trust me. Give me a job with Troy and that's me happy for a week.' A thought came to him. 'Assuming the price is right.' He jutted his head forward with pride and fingered his crotch. 'I'm not cheap,' he said.

'The money will be good.'

'Come on, how much?'

Stephen thought quickly. 'You'll have to negotiate with his manager.' He became collaborative. 'You should ask for a substantial daily rate plus expenses.'

Skylark kicked an imaginary ball. 'Sounds okay to me. When do I start?'

'Tomorrow.' Stephen looked at his watch. 'I mean, now. We start shooting tomorrow.' The singer had insisted on having everything set up before the cameras began to roll. 'Is there a problem?'

'No problem,' said Skylark. He put his fingers in his mouth and made a low whistle.

Speed put his head round the curtain. 'Wotcha,' he said.

'Gotcha.' Skylark was grinning. 'It's Troy,' he said.

'Troy!' Speed replied. 'There – you – go!' He gave out a whoop.

Philip came back, trailing Mouse behind him. 'All set then, boys?'

Skylark went deadpan. 'Yes thanks.'

Philip waited, slightly ridiculous in his tartan. 'Well,' he said, after an awkward silence, 'just remember who made you and who pays your bills, that's all.' He turned to Stephen. 'One for the road, sir, while his royal highness adjusts his tiara?'

'Thanks.'

Skylark scowled and went over to Mouse. 'Silly old queen,' he said.

'Mister Speed,' Philip was recovering fast, 'if you will be so good as to do the honours.'

Speed, obedient as ever, went out. Stephen looked at his watch. He asked Philip if he could make a quick call and was handed a portable phone in the shape of a frog prince. He rang Isabel's number, but there was no answer.

'No one at home?' said Philip, very camp. 'Ah, the old, old story.'

'Why don't you shut up, you old fart?' said Skylark furiously from the far side of the room.

When the drinks arrived, the tension began to go down. Philip came over and whispered that Monica was 'in tonight'.

Stephen shook his head. He was tired. Soon they would have to start back.

Philip seemed disappointed. He sat down at the piano and began to sing music hall songs to himself in a melancholy operatic baritone. Gradually, the others joined in. From time to time, clients would pass through the blue velvet curtain, nodded in and out by Speed. Mouse curled up on the sofa and fell asleep.

Philip seemed happy to have his boys round him. His eyes became misty with drink. He leant across to Stephen. 'No one appreciates how much I love my boys. If it wasn't for me, that cunt Potter would screw them five ways to Sunday.' He nodded at Skylark. 'He's special, that one.' He was at once proud and pathetic. 'Look after him for me, won't you?'

4

Isabel woke alone. It was early; outside in the street the crew were preparing for the first day of the shoot. Through the wall, she could hear Curtis murmuring on the telephone and she saw how accustomed to this sound she had become. He was perhaps more of a companion than he knew. She lay in bed and let the events of the previous day recompose themselves in her mind for analysis.

Her dinner with Clive had been rather more sober than either of them expected, as though the allure of sexual danger had been satisfied by her acceptance of his invitation. In retrospect, the evening was decorous and conventional, almost a disappointment. Far from sharing his deepest desires, the director had wanted only to reminisce about his old friend, Tom Harris. At first Isabel was intrigued to hear things she had never known, and encouraged the memories. It was like discovering some lost correspondence lying open on a desk. When Clive seemed unable to change the conversation, she felt herself quite quickly losing patience. Surely he could see that she was trying, perhaps unsuccessfully, to put Tom out of her mind? She realised that Clive wanted to establish common ground, but his strategy was inept and the more she disliked him for it, the more she began to imagine it was malice that prompted his harping references to Tom. He would make her feel doubly unwanted, then pounce.

Her own thoughts, as Clive was speaking, turned again to Stephen, and here too there was a growing sense of regret. She had wondered whether he had left any message at the production headquarters, but when she called there at the end of the day neither Fred nor Zach had anything for her but silly banter about 'dream dates' and 'a night out on the town'. She was annoyed to find that they seemed to be laughing at her, but her pride prevented her from inquiring further. Troy was there, as relaxed and polite as ever, but distracted by details of the approaching shoot. Outside in the evening sunshine, a troupe of dancers was rehearsing a routine with the choreographer on an improvised stage.

She walked back home imagining a conversation in which, if Stephen phoned now, she would say she was going out with Clive, no explanation offered, to test his jealousy. But he had not called of course, and then all she had was the frustration of his absence and across the table the unlikely, shallow, loquacious object of her hopes for the evening.

These had remained fantasies. Clive had every opportunity to speak freely, but in the event he risked nothing. The restaurant was almost deserted. They could have been dining alone. Plates of delicious food came and went, but the nearest he ventured to an expression of his feelings was to tell Isabel that his pal Tom had been 'an idiot' to leave her. She demurred at this, as she always did. 'I am not what I seem,' she replied, and he did not inquire further. Instead, he began to talk enthusiastically about a subject dear to his heart, himself. He was, Isabel decided, one of those men who seemed emotionally self-confident, even overbearing, in public, most at ease when speaking – in his case, literally – through a megaphone. In private, the sound of his feelings never rose above a whisper, and in the exploration of sentiment he could only risk scratching the surface. He was actually rather boring and self-obsessed, and all the more so because he almost knew it. Disappointment gathered over the table like a cloud, and it was finally a relief to be stepping, alone, through the doorway to her house while Clive shot off into the night with a perfunctory wave.

There was no sign of Stephen then, either, and she had gone to bed fighting in her mind with the instability of her feelings.

Now, fully awake, with the realisation of his absence growing, she became concerned, and with her concern came that rebellious pulse of anger at the intrusion of difficulty into a relationship she had so recently celebrated for its absence of complication. Perhaps it was, after all, what she had half feared, just a brief encounter.

She pulled on her dressing-gown and went downstairs, calling out Stephen's name. The house was empty. She went to the front door and collected the newspapers, pausing on the step. It was light, but there was a slight chill in the air and no sign of the sun. The newspaper boy, an orange blob and a pair of legs, was making his way from house to house, his whistle the only sound in the stillness of dawn.

She glanced at the headlines. The annual tide of violence was receding. Hickey was still one of the top news items with his 'crusade' against Troy's video. Inside, a long editorial about the preacher's finances, entitled 'Who Pays for God's Word?', contained a coded suggestion that Hickey's campaign might have received some kind of official sanction.

She made coffee, dawdled indecisively for a while, then dressed casually in blue jeans and a loose shirt and went out into the street. By now the technicians were hard at work with last-minute adjustments. Thick ropes of electrical cable snaked along the pavement. The cameraman was testing the dolly-tracks for the umpteenth time, squatting down like a golfer with a difficult putt. His electricians and gaffers, a medieval siege-army, were scaling up and down towers of scaffolding. After the noise and chaos of the last few days, there was now a pre-curtain expectancy in the air. Today, they would start shooting.

Isabel looked up, assessing the prospect. The sky was lead-grey and full of rain. She watched one of the scene-painters putting the final touches to a false shopfront. Two soldiers from the military detail assigned to the town for the duration of the shoot strolled past. Perhaps Hickey was right. This was an odd kind of normality. Where was the fiction? What was more real? She saw the scratches on the soldiers' guns, the Elastoplast on their fingers, and the grenades in their belts as they passed, and thought that only the killing and the hatred she had seen round the bonfires was real. In that harsh, atavistic light the face of the country seemed old, scarred and bloodstained.

Isabel made her way to the production headquarters. There was no one about outside. She pushed the door open. Stephen was lying on the couch, wrapped in a blanket. He stirred as she came in, grunting something she couldn't understand.

She heard her anger spiralling out of control. 'What on earth are you doing here?'

He looked at her, cold and distant and unshaven. 'I should have thought that was my question.' He sat up, rubbing his face. He was half dressed under the blanket and his hair was tousled with sleep. She saw he had been reading *Nostromo*, a battered paperback.

'Why didn't you come home?'

'I didn't want to cramp your style.'

'What are you talking about?'

'Nice evening with Clive?'

She recalled Curtis's vengeful expression as she had flirted in front of him and realised that it was pointless to dissemble further. 'So what did Joe tell you?'

'He's not speaking to me, as you well know, but he made sure that Fred and Zach heard all about your little outing, and funnily enough I just happened to bump into them when I got back from the city.'

She found herself annoyed by his calculated insouciance, and felt her own anger rise. She took a step forward, an imaginary ballet step. 'I'm interested to discover that you listen to Curtis's word not mine.'

'If only I had such an exquisite choice.'

She hated sarcasm. 'What do you mean?'

'I mean,' he replied evenly, 'that I never had your word for it. I mean,' he went on, 'that you never told me.'

'You never asked.'

A nasty sardonic light came into his eye, a light she had never seen before. 'Well, I suppose I'm glad to have discovered that you have to be clairvoyant to have a relationship with Isabel Rome.'

'Do you always speak in riddles when you're angry?'

'How can I ask about something I know nothing about?'

'You never called me. I had no idea where you were.'

'I was on the road. You knew that.'

'All day? You could have telephoned.'

'I was busy.'

'So I see.'

'And when I did call, you were – ' he shrugged ' – out.'

'Don't be ridiculous.'

'I think that's my line. Do I have to remind you that Clive Fox is probably the most sexually rapacious person in this neighbourhood?'

'I had no idea your self-esteem was so low.'

'I had no idea your indifference to my feelings was so high.'

'Indifference!' Now she was upset. 'What about your indifference to me?'

He replied that he didn't know what she was talking about, and spoke in a weary tone of voice that said, Go away and leave me alone.

She came over and sat on the couch. 'Look. You were away. You didn't ring. I became upset.' She felt tears in her eyes, and wished she didn't. 'I'm sorry – I thought – ' How could she begin to explain about Tom, about her dreams? 'I was annoyed – I was angry with Joe really – his endless prying – I wanted so badly to talk to you – I warned you I can get angry – that's when I get crazy – all I did was try to provoke Joe – we had dinner – it was boring – Clive talked about his problems – nothing happened – I came home – I can't imagine where he gets his reputation.' She smiled at last, and took his hand. 'I think this is our first row.'

He pulled her towards him and they kissed.

'You look tired,' she said, touching his face.

'I haven't slept much these last two nights.'

'Did you really think that Clive . . .?' She could not finish the sentence.

'I didn't know.' He became calm and serious. 'I suddenly realised how little I know you.'

They were silent together for a moment, acknowledging their separateness. Then Isabel said: 'When this is over, we'll go away.'

'We just need time.' He saw how badly they both wanted it to work and how much they feared it failing. 'Perhaps we found each other too quickly.'

'After Tom, part of me is still afraid to come out of hiding,' she said. 'That's when I get angry.'

He tried to lighten her mood. 'So where would we go?'

She smiled. They had played this game before. 'The sky's the limit and the world is our oyster.' She had a faraway look in her eyes. 'Under the bamboo tree.'

So they played the game, swapping fantasies. Stephen boasted his knowledge of fabulous hotels in exotic locations, and they planned holidays they both knew they would never take.

'Are you happy?'

She looked at him oddly. 'Why do you ask?'

'Why do you think?' He became reflective and sad. 'Perhaps we are lost.'

She kissed him lightly and stood up. 'Not forever,' she said, stepping quickly outside. She wanted to be alone.

Now it was raining. Isabel hurried back to the house for her anorak before heading out to look for Hickey.

By ten o'clock the rain was falling hard, but the faithful, undeterred, were assembling by the 'Hope and Salvation' van beyond the location. Nearby, the Stars and Stripes flapped damply in the wind. Hickey himself was sheltering inside. News crews were taking up camera positions. The conflict between the evangelist and the rock star had become a regular television item. The crowd gathered round, waiting.

Isabel watched from a distance, turning over in her mind the conversation with Stephen. The rain trickled down the back of her neck. It seemed like a good place to feel repentance. Beyond the umbrellas, Hickey's van was surrounded by placards, quotations from the bible and attacks on Troy. Time passed. The evangelist remained inside, unseen. One of his assistants began to read extracts from the Old Testament over the loudspeaker, but the rain had got into the amplifier and his words were broken up by bursts of static. Crackling phrases – 'thus saith the Lord of Hosts' – added a disjointed biblical commentary to the rotor-beat of the helicopter hovering overhead and the growing murmur of the crowd.

As the wait stretched out, and more marchers arrived, Isabel edged closer to Hickey's headquarters. Eventually she had a clear view of the evangelist. He was holding a mug of something and consulting a map. The authorities would not let him penetrate the town but, like Joshua at the walls of Jericho, he could march round the perimeter, trumpeting against the wickedness within.

Amongst the faithful, Isabel detected groups of curious local people braving the weather to watch. How strange it must be for them. They were a forgotten community who generally sustained a fathomless indifference to the outside world, a place they would read about in the newspapers or watch on television, but which had almost nothing to do with them. Now, in the space of a few weeks, their isolation and tranquillity had been shattered. A few were pleased to be the centre of so much attention, some were bewildered and others simply angry at the disturbance, though they would never show it. It was Isabel's fear – though she could not know for sure – that the townspeople secretly blamed her for this turn of events. When she had tried to ask Joe Curtis he had been unhelpful.

'These things happen.' His coldness and remoteness was complete.

When she wondered where Curtis was now she realised that she reciprocated his anger, and the knowledge of this made her slightly fearful for the future.

At last Hickey was leaving his mission headquarters. He cut a jaunty figure in an electric-blue anorak. Those in the crowd nearest the van gave a cheer and waved their slogans. Hickey, followed by his acolytes, made his way to the front of the crowd, dispensing blessings. Then he turned towards the cameras, climbing up on a box put there for the purpose. 'Let us march for the Lord,' he shouted.

At the answering roar, he jumped down and they set off, Hickey striding out in front, followed by a gaggle of cameramen, reporters and technicians. His supporters snaked behind him over several hundred yards. Isabel chose to bury herself in the crowd, as anonymous as she could be, trudging along in the rain. She was reminded of school walks and decided that if it had not been for the rain it might have been a pleasant excursion. As her feet found a walking pace, her thoughts drifted back to her vindictiveness towards Stephen, her uncontrollable sense of panic and injury.

She found herself haunted by her first words to him in the spring. It was true he was a romantic – nothing in their relationship had caused her to revise her judgement – and it was true that he hated to be threatened. He would store away this crisis and it would work on his imagination. Something would die between them. He would become secretive where he had been open. He would be private where he had been sharing. He would be hesitant where he had been trusting. She wondered if his need for romantic perfection and hers for attention would survive what they would both interpret as an obscure kind of betrayal. And then she herself began to wonder about her own interest in someone who seemed, she now regretted to admit, emotionally naïve.

Hickey's route was taking them to the south, into low-lying pasture away from the hill roads, over a little stone bridge across the river and then, in a flanking move, down a footpath through the fields behind the deserted factory. Across the damp, poppy-strewn meadows and through the distant beech trees, Isabel could occasionally glimpse the backs of the houses, or the factory chimney, or the gaunt outline of Curtis's abandoned Institute. Whenever the marchers reached an intersection that offered a turn to the town they were met by a cluster of army Land-Rovers and soldiers in flak jackets.

Hickey was never dismayed. He seemed to thrive on adversity. He would remonstrate with each cordon. The troops would listen, some unmoved, some with embarrassed smiles. Then the preacher would rejoin the head of his forces and the column would struggle on through the rain. Isabel, looking round, estimated that there must be at least a thousand on the march.

Now they were climbing. Taking her bearings, Isabel realised they were approaching the hill overlooking the town from an unfamiliar angle. Perhaps Hickey intended to preach on the iniquities of the video from literal as well as moral high ground. But when he reached the crest of the hill, there was no sermon on the mount. The evangelist paused only long enough to admire the misty rain-washed view before plunging down the other side.

His people, his crusaders, followed him obediently, though some were getting weary and slow. A warning was passed up to the front that the crowd was in danger of losing heart and the word came back that rest was in sight. Now they were on the road that ran alongside the football pitch. There was no road-block, but when the way straightened out, offering a clear view into the main street, they could see the army and police Land-Rovers waiting in the distance.

Hickey had other plans. From the back of the crocodile, Isabel saw the leaders veer sharply into the grounds of the hospital.

Amazingly, almost eerily, there was no security and no resistance. The crowd followed their leader down the drive into the ragged garden. They clustered round the empty stone fountain and spread across the roughly mown lawn with the molehills and dandelions. Hickey took up a preacher's position on the terrace overlooking the grounds, standing in the centre of an almost natural amphitheatre. The camera crews planted their tripods while the crowd murmured curiously to itself and became subdued. The rain had stopped and the sun was breaking out. Through the windows, Isabel could see the white faces of the inmates.

Hickey's short speech was the usual mixture of apocalypse and bravado. He spoke of 'a moral crusade', of 'the powers of

Satan' and of 'Sodom and Gomorrah'. Without naming him, he accused Troy of sexual perversion, corrupting the minds of the young, ruining the peace of the land and provoking civil strife. He attacked 'normalisation' and 'the lies of the mainland'.

'There are, indeed, no depths to which this fiend will not sink,' he bellowed. His words echoed against the stonework ' – ink, ink.' He went on: 'I have a witness here, a witness to our faith, who will tell us more than I ever could.' He turned his gaze to the front of the crowd. 'Please welcome Miss Mary Curtis.' He put out his hand. 'Step forward, sister.'

Isabel watched Mary climb hesitantly up the three steps to the terrace. She was nervous, but there was the proud light of battle in her eyes. The mystery of Curtis's visit to the church was explained.

Hickey addressed the crowd. 'Miss Mary Curtis, the administrator of this fine hospital.' Prompted by his assistants, the crowd applauded. Hickey signalled for quiet. 'Is it true, Miss Curtis,' he boomed, 'is it true that this devil actually proposed to use the helpless people of this home in his depraved video?' He paused to let the crowd appreciate the significance of the accusation before thrusting the microphone into her face.

Mary looked frightened. In a very small voice she replied: 'It is true, yes.'

Hickey's expression was triumphant. 'Did you hear that?' he demanded, scanning his audience. 'Did you hear what this good woman has just told us?'

There was an affirmative murmur from the crowd.

'Mary Curtis has just told us that this man was planning to use these defenceless people for his wicked purposes. Who knows what degradation they might have been subjected to? For a man who is no stranger to sodomy, there is clearly no limit. Thanks to this good woman his plans were thwarted.'

One or two people shouted 'Hallelujah' and the assistants led a burst of applause. Hickey turned back to Mary. 'Will you allow us to meet some of the good, simple people this man was proposing to humiliate and degrade?'

Isabel saw Mary nod mutely. Hickey spun round and signalled to the attendants watching from the side door. Four nurses in starched uniforms, shyly self-conscious in front of the cameras and the crowd, escorted about a dozen patients from 'Blue'. They shuffled out, limping and smiling, and lined up in front of Hickey, staring at the people in front of them. Isabel noticed with a shock that Paul was among them.

The crusaders in the garden were still.

Hickey faced the cameras again. 'These good, simple people live here, at peace, in their own way. They are well cared for. Some of them may, through God's grace, in the end find a useful life in the community outside. Is it not a scandal and a crime to exploit their disabilities? Let us show them that we welcome them to our crusade!' At a prearranged signal, Hickey's acolytes began to sing 'Onward, Christian Soldiers!' and the crowd joined in.

During the hymn, Hickey went down the line, blessing each in turn. They stared back at him with distracted, grateful stares. He was unmoved. Finally, victorious, he returned to face the crowd. 'This crusade, brothers and sisters in Christ, is for all of you. It is for the rich and poor, it is for the sick and the well, high and low, black and white. Let us now march forward and deliver our message of hope and salvation to the powers that be.'

Hickey strode off the terrace and out into the driveway of the old house. The patients, shepherded by their nurses, followed behind. The marchers on the lawn formed a queue through the rusty gate and trailed after. The camera crews, sensing the climax to the story, raced ahead, closing in on Hickey and his demented entourage. As he walked at the head of his army, he gave impromptu interviews to the reporters, expanding his claim that Troy intended to use Mary's patients as extras.

Isabel hurried to the front as well. The march was now approaching the main street, forming a crowd by the war memorial. Beyond, behind the military Land-Rovers, she

could see Stephen watching the approaching army with Fred
Shuster beside him. He seemed small and far away.

At the road-block, the crowd watched their leader negotiate
with the local commander. It was all rather civilised. Isabel
could not hear the conversation, but it was clear that Hickey
was being told he could go no further. In the distance, under
the hot lights angled from the scaffolding, she could see the
huddle of the video production around Troy and his dancers.

Hickey turned to his crusade. 'Brothers and sisters in Christ,
let us sing a hymn to the power of the Lord.' Someone handed
him a guitar. He struck the opening chords. The girl with the
tambourine took up the rhythm. The acolytes knew the words
and the crowd could hum the tune. Hickey began to sing:
'Would you be free from your burden of sin?'

As the soldiers watched in silence, Isabel caught Paul's eye.
He grinned and waved; she smiled back. Crazy, she thought.
Then something made her glance up towards the Institute, and
as she did so she saw, behind a dusty window on the first
floor, the pallid faces of Dobbs and Curtis, looking down on
the scene like snipers.

On the second day of the shoot, Isabel realised she had to get out. Hickey's accusations, screaming across the front pages of the local press, were now echoed in the sober columns of mainland newspapers as well. The issue had become increasingly political. An army spokesman had made a statement, and the minister of the interior had been quoted, too. Isabel told Stephen she had the sense of a power struggle behind the scenes. 'The army loathes the minister,' he explained. 'He's putting them out of work. They'll do all they can to block him. I wouldn't be at all surprised to find out that someone was running Hickey.'

They were sitting in the location headquarters watching Fred and Zach play backgammon. It was Fred's contention that the game calmed his nerves, but the atmosphere was tense. Troy had secluded himself in his trailer. The two producers, who had ordered a thousand white carnations to create, as Zach put it, 'a simpatico mood ambience', were dismayed to discover that Troy had sent the flowers up to the hospital with his compliments.

'The stupid fuck,' said Shuster.

'Oh boy, I can't wait for tomorrow's headlines,' added his partner, rolling the dice, 'Six and four.'

Clive Fox came in. He was wearing a safari suit and carried a green and white golf umbrella. Retrospectively, his failure with Isabel was making him hesitant in her presence, and awkward with Stephen. With this latest crisis he was almost able to ignore them. He was holding a video cassette. He went over to the table where Fred and Zach were sitting. 'Listen guys, at this rate, we're going to need ten days,' he said.

'Ten days?' Fred looked up. 'Am I hearing you correctly, Clive? What kind of bullshit is this?'

'Listen, Fred, we've had some considerable delays – '

'You mean you've had some considerable fucking delays.' Fred put down the dice. The others went very still. 'If this schedule goes down the toilet, Clive, that's your fucking responsibility.'

'There's no need to get so aggressive, Fred.'

'Aggressive?' Fred looked at the director in outrage. 'I'm just doing my fucking job, and you call me aggressive?' He turned to Zach. 'What is this crap?'

'Calm down, Fred.' Zach threw the dice, affecting nonchalance, a pocket Drake playing bowls before battle.

'No – I have to talk this one through.' Fred stood up. 'The fact is, Clive, you're the one who's being aggressive, storming in here with the rushes like a fucking Nazi and carrying on with all this fucking delay talk.'

Fox remained calm. 'Troy won't leave his trailer, Fred.'

'He's depressed.' He sat down again and picked up the dice. 'You've depressed him.'

'I think Hickey's depressed him,' said Zach, conciliatory.

Fox threw the cassette on the table, gesturing at Stephen and Isabel. 'Look, they're probably depressed as well. We're all depressed, but we've got a fucking job to do.'

'Hey, Clive!' Fred jumped up again. 'Give me a break, will you? You do your fucking job and I'll do mine. You shut the fuck up right now, get out there and get set up and I'll have Troy ready for you in half an hour.'

'Okay, Fred.' Clive was suddenly sweet. 'You are being aggressive now, and I'll accept that. But when we get on set, I'll be aggressive.' He stopped in the doorway. 'I get very aggressive on set. And you'll have to accept that.'

'Fucking directors,' said Zach to Fred, as the door closed. 'Fucking prima donnas.'

'I hate them,' murmured Fred, calming down. 'Time for one more game and then I'll talk to Troy. See if I can't speed things up.' He looked across at Stephen. 'Did he have his massage?'

'He did. And liked it, according to Skylark.'

'That boy's a real weirdo,' said Zach, setting the pieces. 'Where did you find him?'

'In the city.'

'You're not telling me something, Steve.'

'Hey, Zach.' Stephen was grateful for Fred's interruption. 'We've got a game to play. You owe me a hundred.'

'Not after this game I won't.'

'Double or nothing.'

'You got it,' said Zach. 'I always wanted to be rich.'

'Eat shit and die.'

Stephen, who liked to believe that he remained cool when others were hysterical, found himself becoming quiet and overwrought. The whole business seemed less and less like a vacation. He had passed the night, sleepless into the dawn, worrying about the schedule, the costs and the crisis in general. Now, mid-morning, with delay piling up on delay, he was feeling weary and he had a sore throat coming on.

After Fox had gone, Isabel took him outside, leaving the Americans to finish their game. They stood together watching the dancers posing for the unit photographer. 'Once they get Troy in front of the camera again, you'll be fine,' she said. The warmth and directness of her sympathy touched him. He felt secure and happy in their reconciliation, and he apologised for his poor temper and low spirits. 'Am I unbearable when I'm like this?'

She smiled. 'You're all unbearable, and I'm going to leave you to it.'

He held her for a moment. 'Is Clive right? Are you depressed?'

She kissed him sweetly. 'Not any more.'

He asked her what she planned to do. She said she would drive to work. She had still not written this week's broadcast. He asked what her subject would be.

'I'm afraid it has to be Hickey.'

'Don't even mention that name.'

Isabel saw he was only half joking. It was time to go.

★

Back at her desk at the radio station, it was as though she was returning from holiday. She realised, from her colleagues' solicitous greetings, how absorbed she had become in Stephen and the video.

Charlie, her producer, dropped by. 'Are you still in love?' he joked. 'Didn't they tell you I was dying of a broken heart?'

She smiled enigmatically. Inside, she was panicking. Am I still in love? She did not know any more. He sat on the desk and asked about the video. She was glad to put her anxieties into temporary cold storage and gave an amusing account of the goings-on at the location.

'What about Hickey?'

'That's a whole other story.'

He suggested she tell him over a drink. She was happy to accept. As they left the newsroom, the time signal for the lunchtime bulletin reminded her of the world beyond.

Charlie was a gossip who wanted to share Isabel's story with his colleagues. When she first joined the station, their visits to the bar had been a weekly ritual in which he had made an obscure public claim on her that everyone knew was unequal. Lately, of course, she had lost touch, but the bar itself was always open, a crossroads of rumour and speculation. They passed through the swing doors into the crowded basement, and were welcomed by the regulars.

The two folk singers, Young and Carpenter, were at the bar as usual. They turned to greet Isabel like a pair of comedians, with flushed wet faces and appealing mops of silvery hair.

'If it's not Miss Rome,' said Young, putting his glass down and giving her a kiss.

'Mr C and Mr Y.' She smiled with pleasure. 'What a nice – and unexpected – surprise.'

They laughed at her familiar irony.

'What will you take?' asked Carpenter, signalling to the barman. The drinks came quickly and they raised their glasses. 'Good to see you back,' said Young.

'First things first,' said Carpenter. 'They say you're in love.'

'Who is this simpleton?' asked Young with a sly wink.

Isabel gave a light-hearted account of Stephen's appearance in her life. She was surprised to discover that, while she was happy to talk about him, it was only in the most flippant and self-mocking terms, as if she was protecting herself from her true feelings. In her heart, which she would not show, she feared to risk the serious version.

'Is this the real thing, then?' Charlie's face betrayed his anxiety. 'Are we about to lose you?'

She laughed, but only at the hidden irony of the question. If she went to the mainland, it would not be to follow Stephen. 'Don't be silly. I'm too old for that.' She found no echo of her laughter inside, only sadness.

Isabel noticed, as the others joined in the conversation, that their voluble little circle was attracting the attention of an anonymous-looking, middle-aged man with a shaving-brush moustache, sitting alone at the bar. During a lull in the conversation, while Charlie was holding forth as usual, Isabel leaned across to Young. 'Who's that?' she asked, nodding surreptitiously.

He glanced sideways. 'That's Potter,' he replied confidentially. 'He's a major with military intelligence but he pretends to be attached to their PR department. He hangs about here trying to plant stories, and probably picks up a few as well. No one knows quite how seriously to take him.'

Now the others were pressing for her account of Hickey's crusade. She told them, teasingly, to listen to her broadcast. Young protested that he was always drunk by the time she came on the air.

'You're always drunk, period,' said Carpenter, getting up to call for another round. 'Give us a sneak preview, Isabel.'

Young wanted to know who had informed Hickey about the hospital. Isabel expressed her opinion that it was her neighbour, Joseph Curtis. She noticed, as she explained her reasons, that Major Potter was listening in.

'Curtis? The one who fancies you?'

'Charlie!' She had forgotten she had once shared so much of her life with him. Why is it, she thought, as she reproached him, that, as a woman among men, I always end up being discussed like anthropology?

Carpenter came back with the drinks. He too wanted to know who had told Hickey about the singer's plans for the patients. Isabel repeated her view that it was Curtis's doing. 'His sister runs the place. She was the one who confirmed the story.'

'Is it true?'

She explained that it was a clever half-truth. 'Clive, the director, has talked about it, and there were one or two stories in the press, but it was never a serious option.'

'Hickey certainly knows how to make a good headline,' said Charlie.

'So who is this Joseph Curtis?' asked Young. 'And what's his game?'

Isabel admitted that she did not know. 'It's all the more confusing because he's supposed to be working for the film company as a local fixer.'

'Perhaps, like me, he has been driven mad with unrequited love!'

'Charlie – please!'

'Another man has stolen the woman of his dreams . . .'

'You're as crazy as Hickey,' said Young, picking up his guitar case. 'Come on, Mr C, we're going to be late.'

The two singers had a lunchtime gig. As they made their farewells, Charlie excused himself to go to the men's room and Isabel found herself sitting alone.

As she feared, Major Potter took advantage of the situation to introduce himself. 'Excuse me, Miss Rome. We haven't met. Eric Potter.' He put his arm out with the comical stiffness of a wind-up toy. 'I'm a great admirer of your programme.' They shook hands. 'I couldn't help overhearing your conversation.'

'So I noticed.'

Potter was professionally inured to hostility. He ploughed on. 'As I expect you appreciate, the army has a rather special interest in the activities of the Reverend Russell Hickey.'

'I can't see why.'

'Oh, well.' He recovered quickly. 'You see, anyone who disrupts the equilibrium here is of concern to our people.'

'I should have thought you would be rather glad to have someone to justify your existence.'

Potter played carefully with his moustache. 'There you have a point, Miss Rome, a point indeed.'

He broke off. Charlie was coming towards them. Isabel saw with dismay that he was carrying another round of drinks.

'So you've met.' Charlie handed out the glasses. 'What lies are you spreading today, Potter?'

The major thought this was rather amusing. He had the unblinking persistence of the stooge. He chortled happily into his beer; a rim of foam formed on his moustache; seeming almost benign, he succeeded in saying nothing.

'So what's the story about Hickey?' Charlie pressed on, addressing Potter. 'Are you going to tell us that he walks on water?'

Major Potter shrugged. 'Of course.'

Something occurred to Isabel. 'What do you know about Joseph Curtis?'

Potter's performance was so good it was almost convincing. 'Joseph Curtis? Joseph Curtis?' He pursed his lips thoughtfully. 'That name does ring a distant, a very distant, bell.'

'We were talking about him ten minutes ago,' she said sharply. 'Don't pretend you didn't overhear.'

'Curiosity killed the cat.' He wiped the froth from his moustache, smiling watchfully and challenging her to go on.

She stared at him hard, deciding that she might as well go for the jackpot. 'You see, it occurred to me that you might have some informal connection to this Joseph Curtis. He's very much in with the powers that be, or so he claims.'

Potter's eyes were rock-steady. 'I cannot imagine where you got that idea, Miss Rome.' He became thoughtful. 'But perhaps you can help me.' He looked at her. 'How well would you say you knew Mr Troy?'

She wondered what was behind the question and how much

Potter knew about her, too. 'Slightly,' she replied cautiously.

'He's gay, of course.'

'I don't know what that has to do with anything. '

'If I may say so, Miss Rome, I think that's rather naïve. There's a story going round that he has a preference for under-age boys.'

'So?'

'People don't like that sort of thing,' he murmured, almost to himself. 'They don't like it at all.'

'I suppose you could say it makes a change from mental patients.'

Potter gave a cold, detached laugh.

'Come on, major,' Charlie interrupted. 'Give us the full version, for old times' sake.'

Potter lowered his voice and leant towards them both. 'The story, as I've heard it, is that Troy is hiring boys from a well-known vice ring here in the city.' He started to scribble on a scrap of paper. 'Here. Perhaps you'd care to check it out with the proprietor.'

Isabel looked at him in astonishment. She wanted to say: 'Why on earth should I want to do that?' All at once Stephen's reticence about his trip to the city and the appearance of Skylark on the set acquired a kind of bizarre logic, and she heard her hesitant reply underlining her doubts. 'Why should I accept that there's even a grain of truth in this?'

Potter retreated. 'I'm sorry, Miss Rome.' He became feline. 'I forgot that you are a rather special kind of journalist. One gets so coarsened always dealing with hacks.'

Isabel looked at him severely. 'How many so-called hacks have been exposed to this disgusting little slur so far?'

'As a matter of fact, you are the first.' She felt he was telling the truth. 'It's a very new story.'

'Well,' she said, putting her glass down. 'With rumours of this kind, I prefer to go to the source. I'm expecting to see the singer this evening. I'll ask him. Troy, there are some people in the army who are suggesting that you're into rent boys. Can you confirm or deny? Perhaps, Major Potter, you can give me a number where I can reach you for an on-the-record comment.'

'Look,' said Potter, 'I only said it was a rumour.'

But he scribbled a number in her notebook anyway. 'Any time,' he said. 'Day or night.'

6

Mr Hu was precise and old-fashioned, and his entrances were rarely noticed. He was there, or he was not there; but when he was with you the intensity of his presence demanded your complete attention. He had been educated by missionaries and used words like 'beseech', 'abundance' and 'manifestation'. He always referred to Fred and Zach as 'the American gentlemen'. He did not converse easily, except with his family, to whom he habitually spoke Mandarin Chinese. With outsiders, he made little formal speeches and listened intently to the replies he received. If he was satisfied, he would merely nod and disappear. If not, he would make another speech, until he had achieved what he wanted.

Stephen was sitting alone in the production headquarters, doodling on a legal pad, when Mr Hu materialised before him. The shoot was in full swing two streets away; here, backstage, it was pleasantly deserted. He looked up from his paperwork and found Mr Hu standing in the middle of the trailer, holding a catering-size bottle of Coca-Cola.

In the beginning, before the rows started, Stephen had been intrigued to be down at the location. He had found the slow accumulation of footage, the 'Running', 'Action' and 'Cut', the anxious scrutiny of the video playback and the many other rituals of film-making a source of fascination. As the problems mounted, the long delays between each take and the interminable negotiations among the main players became intensely frustrating. Clive Fox was as good as his word: on the set, he became unbearably aggressive, and refused even to speak to Fred or Zach. The director was a perfectionist. Nothing was being left to chance. Yesterday, he had, apparently, made the crew wait for an hour to get the fading light he wanted.

Now, thankfully, the process was nearing completion. To

keep things in perspective, Stephen was working on his expenses. He pushed aside a pile of receipts. 'What's the problem?'

Mr Hu told Stephen what was on his mind.

First of all, there was the matter of 'my beloved daughters'. They had been promised parts, simple walk-on parts, in this film, and the promise had been broken. They had set their hearts on this, and now they were distraught. Tomorrow, he understood from his schedule, was the last day of filming, and still no word from the producers. This, he felt, was a serious injustice. He was not nobody here, he was Mr Hu. Keeping his indignation in check, he went on to say that he felt this humiliation was typical. 'The production is not shipshape,' he remarked, 'not shipshape at all.'

Stephen nodded in sympathy. 'Who made this promise?'

Mr Hu set down the Coca-Cola and, becoming confidential, took a step nearer. 'I have to tell you that it was Joseph Curtis,' he said.

'Curtis?' Stephen could not conceal his surprise.

'Quite so.' Mr Hu was now standing very close. There was garlic on his breath and his skin was the colour of old butter. In his opinion, Curtis was behaving oddly, very oddly indeed. Only the night before, he explained, he had gone down to check the factory premises, his property, after the day's work was over, and had seen torchlight inside the Institute. 'Burglars, I decide.' But, as he approached the building in the dark, he found Curtis, alone in the auditorium, wandering about in a kind of distraction.

'Curtis is not himself,' he said, shaking his head.

Stephen said he was inclined to agree and asked what he meant.

Mr Hu hesitated. The truth was he no longer trusted Curtis. He would not, he added, trust Joseph Curtis any more than he would trust Judas Iscariot. He stood there, sizing up Stephen's response with an impressive oriental stare.

Stephen, startled by this strong language and fierce scrutiny, asked why this should be.

Mr Curtis was friends to everyone, said Mr Hu, but he was friends with too many people. He was 'Mr Facing-Both-Ways'. Before the film, perhaps, that was okay. Now he was in with the wrong people. He paused and then added, without preamble: 'Mr Hickey is an evil man.' Yes, he went on, he could see that Dr Mallory was surprised, but the truth had to be told. 'He is not a man of God. He is a false prophet who is leading people astray.' Mr Hu had seen what had been done with the mad boys at the hospital and he had been shocked. 'Hickey has transgressed,' he said, and the verb hissed on his lips like a drop of water in hellfire.

Sounding more casual than he felt, Stephen wondered what Hickey had got to do with Curtis.

Mr Hu glowed with certainty. 'Everything,' he said. 'Me,' he went on, 'I am invisible. Me, they do not see. They think I do not understand.' He shook his head fiercely. 'They are wrong.' People in his restaurant always talked too much. They had no discretion, he said with contempt. This was how he knew that Hickey and Curtis were 'like a pair of chopsticks'.

Stephen, puzzling over the implications of Hu's words, observed that Curtis was supposed to be his partner and friend. Did they not share plans for the redevelopment of the town?

'That will not be possible,' Mr Hu replied. 'Curtis is full of wickedness.'

Stephen was intrigued. 'What wickedness?'

Mr Hu seemed embarrassed. 'He says bad things about that poor boy.'

'Who?' Stephen was curious. 'Troy?'

Mr Hu shook his head. 'That new boy.'

'Skylark?'

He nodded.

'Curtis is spreading stories?'

He nodded again.

On another occasion, Stephen might have been inclined to ignore Mr Hu, to dismiss his tale and to temporise. Yet here, in a vicious new guise, was the story Isabel had been given by

Major Potter. The only mystery was Mr Hu himself. Stephen looked at him hard. 'What has Curtis done to you?'

Mr Hu returned to the injury done to his daughters, but Stephen cut him off cold. 'There's something else you're not telling me. What's happened?'

Outside in the street, the bass rhythm of the soundtrack went thump, thump, thump.

'Please,' said Mr Hu. 'Confidential?'

'Very confidential.'

Another pause.

'He lied to me,' said Mr Hu at last. 'He owes me money.'

Quickly, as if confessing to a matter of great shame, he explained that he had helped finance Curtis's acquisition of the Institute on the basis of a fixed-term loan. When the time came for repayment, Curtis had lied, prevaricated, and finally threatened Mr Hu with closure. 'What could I do?' he asked. 'He is number one here.' The debt had been rescheduled. When the talk of the video began, Mr Hu made a proposal. Curtis should strike a deal with the producers, and put his fee towards the deficit. This had been their agreement. Now, even this was in doubt. Curtis was claiming he had honoured the spirit of the deal by fixing up Mr Hu's catering contract. 'I have had enough,' said Mr Hu. 'We are no longer friends.'

'You mean you are enemies.'

Mr Hu shook his head. 'I am in business. Contract is contract. No question of personal feelings, no sentiment, please!'

He paused impressively and proceeded to explain how Curtis should be removed from any involvement with the production. 'If something offends me,' Mr Hu went on, 'I follow the wisdom of Scripture and cut it out.'

Stephen listened carefully. 'I agree with you,' he said.

Mr Hu smiled. He picked up his Coca-Cola bottle.

'I will see what I can do about your daughters, and I will take your advice about Curtis.'

'Thank you, Dr Mallory,' said Mr Hu, and was gone.

Stephen was left alone with his reflections. His thoughts

went involuntarily to the previous night. Isabel had described her encounter with Potter. At first, he had been grateful for the information. and had urged her to keep it to herself. Then, without meaning to, he had made Isabel angry again. He had insisted on analysing Curtis's position, even though he knew this was a dangerous subject. Isabel accused him of being vindictive and paranoid. He said her accusations didn't add up: she had always been the one who was most anti Curtis. She said there was no reason to hound him, especially as the man was obviously becoming unbalanced. He said Curtis was in danger of ruining the entire project. She said she didn't believe him. He said Curtis was playing a double game. She said it was his nature, he couldn't help being everyone's friend. When Stephen said: 'He's not my friend,' she had rounded on him. 'Who is your friend? You have no friends. You use people and then you throw them away.'

But it was when he suggested she was still secretly in love with Curtis that they had a real screaming row.

He had stayed in the house, but slept in the little room, Tom's old study. In the morning they had made it up, and she had gone to the city to research her next broadcast. He was glad she was not around now to argue with what had to be done.

He went and stood on the step. The weather was fine. It was the lunch break. Some of the crew were standing with paper plates by the mobile canteen, queuing for food. Others were sunbathing on the grass. Two or three sequin-covered dancers with exotic headgear were exercising silently in front of the set. Troy was presumably in his trailer.

Stephen called Fred and Zach on the radio. He watched them through Clive's binoculars, a pair of frowns hurrying towards him.

He came straight to the point. 'We have to fire Curtis.' He paused. 'I was wrong about him and Hickey.'

'When are you going to be right about something for a fucking change?' Fred's belligerence was predictable. 'That's what I want to know.'

Zach joined in, serious now. 'This guy's no ordinary fixer, he's a big wheel with all kinds of weird connections. You don't get rid of guys like this unless you know what you're doing.'

Stephen could see fear in their eyes, the fear of people at risk in territory they did not trust. He felt strangely confident. 'Then you haven't heard what Curtis is saying about Troy?'

Fred looked puzzled. He gave his partner a 'what's-he-talking-about?' look.

Stephen explained, choosing his words carefully, not wishing to give inadvertent offence.

'Holy cow,' said Zach. 'Are you kidding?'

'Why should I be kidding?'

'Stephen.' Zach was standing over him. 'If you're telling me what I think you're telling me – I simply can't believe it – I mean – Jesus Christ!'

Stephen was unrepentant. 'You wanted a masseur.'

Zach had subsided back onto the couch. 'It's – it's un-fucking-believable.'

Fred stood his ground, very much the senior partner. 'I always knew this shit-hole place was a mistake,' he said. 'We should have insisted on a studio. In future, what I say goes.' He went over and kicked the door with frustration. The trailer shook slightly. Stephen noticed that he was wearing cowboy boots with little silver caps studded into the leather at the toe and heel. He seemed willowy thin and vulnerable and foreign. For a moment, Stephen felt sorry for him and found he almost liked him.

Zach was plaintive. 'What are we going to do?'

'That's what we have to figure out,' Fred snapped.

'Perhaps we could hold a press conference.'

'Great idea.' Zach cowered before Fred's sarcasm. 'Ladies and gentlemen, the story that our client Troy sleeps with under-age boys isn't true. Questions, please.' He glared at his partner. 'Are you out of your mind?'

Zach looked crestfallen. 'Do we tell him?'

Fred continued to pace up and down in his beautiful boots

as though he was secretly admiring himself in the role. During the silence, they could hear the music from the playback, the familiar chords of 'Ghosts in the Colonial World', drifting across the set.

'Troy's no fool.' Fred was brooding. 'He will find out.' He was standing next to Zach. Now he reached out and placed a forgiving hand on his shoulder. His voice softened. 'We've never lied to him before.'

'Much,' said his partner, with a weak smile of relief.

'Only white lies,' Fred corrected. 'Those I can live with.' He resumed his caged walk. 'You were right, Steve,' he said, suddenly generous. 'In your first briefing, you said there was always a risk that a political gesture like this video would become politicised and we'd lose control. Troy said he could handle it. We went along with him, supported him as a matter of fact. But you were right and we were wrong.' Before, he had been inclined towards the hysterical. Now, confronted with a genuine crisis, he was becoming calmer. He was still pacing. 'This guy Skylark. Is he a plant?'

Stephen had worried about this all morning. 'There's no guessing,' he replied. 'And there's only guessing.' He told himself he had taken him on knowing the risks, but trusting him all the same. That was the problem with working here. The place was finally a hall of mirrors in which all reflections were distortions. He could question Skylark a dozen times and still not find out who was running him.

He had seen Skylark only a few hours ago. The boy seemed happy on the location, and had spoken eagerly of wanting to work in films. He'd been offered a job on the mainland, he said, something in a horror movie. Stephen had urged him to take it. Skylark nodded. 'I love horror movies,' he said. There was a light in his eyes Stephen had not seen before, an awakening. When questioned further, it was clear that he and the singer had struck up a touching rapport.

Fred was questioning again. 'So you're suggesting that Troy's just a pawn in a bigger game?'

Stephen nodded. He was glad to find Fred so cool and sensible. 'It's probably best to work on that assumption.'

'What about the minister of the interior? Can we talk to him?'

'I think we should.'

'Let's do it.' Fred's mind was working. He was beginning, as he would put it later, to 'hack it'. Decisiveness was stealing over him. Finally, after some more pacing, he said: 'What else, Steve?'

Stephen was glad to be challenged. Crisis-management was supposed to be his forte. 'We have to come up with a story that's bigger than their story.'

Zach was out of his depth. 'Like what, for instance?'

Stephen was thinking aloud, making it up as he went along. 'We have to get him out of here.'

'Who?' Zach had that left-behind look again. 'Curtis? Skylark?'

'I know!' Fred was pleased with himself. He was making connections; he was making order out of chaos. He was about to do what he liked doing best, play God. 'Hickey.'

'Hickey!'

'Yes, Hickey.' Zach's astonishment was obviously gratifying to Fred. 'We've got to bust his ass once and for all.' He turned to Mallory. 'Isn't that what you're saying?'

Stephen smiled enigmatically. 'It is indeed.'

Fred was smiling too. 'Hey, baby,' he said to Zach. 'I think I feel a plan coming on.' He turned to Stephen. 'How good is your network, would you say?'

7

Peter Dobbs hurried into Curtis's store in the late morning, swinging an empty plastic bottle in a supermarket carrier-bag. The bell over the door clanged as it had for Curtis's father and grandfather. The round-faced girl behind the counter seemed to be expecting his visit. 'He's out the back,' she said, with a bashful smile. Dobbs made his way down the aisles of tinned food and household supplies to Curtis's office, a windowless, overheated cubbyhole full of invoices, old calendars and commercial samples.

Curtis was sitting alone watching a black and white movie on his portable television. He had been drinking. There was a plastic beaker on the table, and something spilt on the cover of the colour magazine beside it. He looked up indifferently when Dobbs appeared and indicated a broken chair. It was very hot. A two-bar fire glowed at his feet. Dobbs, already warm from his walk, sat down on the cool side of the table. 'Help yourself,' Curtis murmured thickly, pointing at the bottle. He turned back to the screen, absorbed in the flickering drama.

When Dobbs asked him for the second time what he was watching, he looked round with a scowl. 'American trash,' he said. 'Sometimes I think I'm losing my mind.'

'We all have to relax,' said Dobbs amiably.

'Entertainment,' said Curtis, as if pronouncing a curse. 'Why is nothing serious any more?'

The credits began to roll. Curtis leaned forward and switched off the television. Then, without a word, he stood up and took his visitor's carrier-bag into the corner. Buried under a heap of old newspapers, part of the neglectful chaos of the office, was a small metal cask. Curtis held the bottle to the tap. As Dobbs in grateful fascination watched the ice-clear liquid rise to the neck, he absently took out his wallet and began counting banknotes. Curtis screwed the top on the bottle and handed it back. He hardly looked at the money, putting it without comment into the breast pocket of his jacket. 'Hickey,' he said with a sigh. He seemed distracted.

'What happened?' Dobbs asked. 'Where did he go?'

'I don't know,' said Curtis bitterly. 'For once, I have no idea.'

He told his story and Dobbs listened. He had been woken early by the silence, he said. The moment he came out into the street he realised something had changed. It was incredibly quiet, as it always used to be. The road-blocks had gone. There were neither soldiers nor helicopters. The brilliant blue summer sky, cloudless and bright, added to the air of unreality. In the eerie calm, the technicians preparing for the final day's shooting seemed cheerful and relaxed, a mood he had not witnessed before. When he asked the crew what had happened, all they could say was: 'Hickey's gone,' as though further elaboration would jeopardise their new-found freedom.

Curtis had not had to go far for confirmation of this remarkable news. The common land at the top of the main street, beyond Mr Hu's, the site of Hickey's encampment, was deserted. Overnight, the Mission of Hope and Salvation had disappeared. He had stood alone and baffled on the muddy ground. The only evidence of the evangelist's campaign was a pile of litter and a few placards.

'Didn't Mr Hu see anything?' Dobbs asked.

'Mr Hu and I are not speaking,' said Curtis shortly. He had heard himself narrate these experiences calmly, but underneath he was feeling angry and humiliated. For Hickey to vanish like this without a word of explanation, especially after all he had done for him, was a bad betrayal. He wondered how much this showed, but funny little nervous Peter Dobbs was not a mirror to rely on.

'Why don't you ask the Americans what has happened?' Dobbs asked.

Curtis poured himself another drink. 'I can't do that.'

'Why ever not?'

Curtis, frowning, forced himself to answer. 'I don't have the same access to those people any more.'

Dobbs said he didn't understand.

The man was so guileless and naïve it made Curtis almost cry out with frustration. 'In the charming way they put these things,' he said grimly, 'they let me go.' The more he thought about it, the more rejection seemed not only unbearable, it was also extremely disturbing.

Dobbs, hesitating, asked why they should do this.

'A very good question, Peter,' said Curtis approvingly. 'There is more to this than meets the eye.' He did not elaborate. Just then he did not want to admit to himself that Mallory and his people had found the nerve to fire him. Perhaps his fears about their connections were better founded than he realised.

Dobbs pondered the mystery in silence, staring at his drink.

Beyond, in the shop, they heard the tramp of boots. A foot patrol had come in for refreshment, chocolate bars and soft drinks. There was the sound of laughter and conversation and then the bell clanged again and the soldiers trooped out. In the stillness that followed they heard Curtis's assistant singing to herself, a traditional ballad. They both listened, sentimental with drink, momentarily distracted from their various worries and anxieties.

'She'll be married soon,' said Dobbs. 'She's that age now, and ready for it.'

Curtis was not listening. 'I have to do something,' he said, speaking his thoughts. 'I have to show who I am.' Dobbs looked at him with uncertainty and Curtis said he would explain what he meant.

This was his town, he said. Everyone acknowledged that he organised it and kept it peaceful. The soldiers outside reminded him that the authorities never caused any trouble here. He could never explain how that was exactly, but it was a case of the ends justifying the means and he had no reason to apologise for anything. Before Troy and his people came, he said, there was this understanding with the powers that be, as Peter Dobbs knew well, and it was this that kept things regular.

The video had changed all that. He blamed himself. He could have stopped it. He had made a bad mistake with Troy, perhaps because he had been influenced in his decision by matters he should not have been influenced by, matters that had nothing to do with the welfare of the place. But he did not want to go into that. He glanced across at Dobbs and, seeing that he had no idea what he meant, pressed on, grateful for his simple loyalty.

No, the damage had been done. He had allowed the wrong sort of people to take control, arrogantly thinking he was strong enough to control them. How misguided he had been! Hickey had persuaded him that he had committed the sin of pride, and in his hour of repentance he had surrendered the town to the preacher by way of atonement.

He heard himself say this and wondered – checking again with Dobbs – am I going mad? But the faithful mirror across the table gave no hint of that: he was being heard with serious, dutiful attention and it was this that convinced him now to confess perhaps more freely than he might have done with someone he respected. The truth was, he said, that he was faced with the terrible realisation, the terrible truth, that Hickey too had failed, that Hickey had not saved the town from the wickednesses of the mainland. Indeed, far from strengthening his position he had actually weakened it. 'What we have here now is a mess,' said Curtis, 'and it is all my fault.' He was, he admitted, facing a tremendous personal crisis, a crisis almost of faith.

Peter Dobbs, slightly bewildered, said he should not judge himself too harshly. He added that his influence in the town was none the worse for the trouble with the video. 'People don't blame you, Joe.'

'Don't you believe it. Our friend Mr Birch will soon have something to say about this.'

Dobbs said he could not accept that.

'I would – in his position,' Curtis replied, filling their cups again. He felt his anger and his sense of humiliation surging again, and fought to contain them. He could not forget his duty. He had, he said, been brought up to believe in the exercise of responsibility and he had failed. He had to take the initiative again. 'We have to make our own video,' he said, his anger finally translating itself into a kind of weird idealism.

Dobbs was confused. 'Make our own video?'

That was, said Curtis, just a manner of speaking. He was going to create an opportunity which would bring everyone back to the tradition of life here, remind people of their heritage. He was, he said, proposing a celebration that no one would ever forget. He was now feeling light-headed and optimistic. 'Come and see my video,' he said, getting to his feet.

Dobbs followed him into the store-room, a large blind shed tacked on to the back of the shop. Among the careful inventory of canned food and the bulk supplies of window cleaner, floor polish, light bulbs and matchboxes, there were a number of wicker laundry baskets in the middle of the floor. Curtis went over to one of these, fiddled with the strap and threw it open with a flourish. 'Look there,' he said. 'I don't expect you've seen those in a few years.'

Dobbs was at first amazed, almost frightened. Curtis watched him hold the musty-smelling tunic in his hand, feeling the coarse weave of the cloth, gazing in silence at the colours. Finally he said: 'Joe, where on earth did you get these?'

Curtis smiled with quiet pride. 'There are people I know,' he said, fingering the distinctive braid. 'And these have been lying around the Institute for ages.' He threw open one of the baskets. 'Go on – ' He pressed a jacket on his visitor. 'Try it.'

Dobbs hesitated. Then, not daring to contradict him, he slipped out of his coat. Cautiously, he pulled on the military jacket. He looked at Curtis, smiling nervously.

'Feels good, I expect,' said Curtis.

Dobbs nodded uncertainly.

'Fits you like a glove, Peter. Suits you, too.'

'But – ' Dobbs faltered, and then stripped it off in a hurry, as if it were stolen property. 'We can't wear these. They were banned years ago.'

'Why not?' There was excitement in Curtis's eye. 'They can't arrest the whole town.'

Dobbs stared at him, repeating slowly. 'The whole town.'

'Exactly.' He threw open another basket, and pulled out a string of flags, in the outlawed colours. 'This is our birthright and we should not let the authorities take it away from us. That's what I say.' He faced Dobbs. 'Hickey was right about many things. He said we should be ready to fight for what we believe. We are not mainlanders. We have seen with our own eyes what the mainland means. We have to assert ourselves and our identity.'

'But if Hickey couldn't do it, how – ?'

Curtis cut him off. 'Hickey was an outsider. That made him weak, finally. This is our land. We are strong here.' He went to the side of the store. 'Listen.' There was an old gramophone plugged into the wall and a pile of 78s. The needle crackled briefly and then they heard the first notes of a familiar anthem.

'Joe,' said Dobbs. 'Are you crazy?'

Curtis stared at him across the floor, and heard his own question reverberate boomingly in his mind. For a wild moment, anything could have happened. He could have killed him, or kissed him perhaps, or laughed out loud, but then the madness passed and he found his answer coming reasonably.

'If I am crazy,' said Curtis grandly, 'then so are my ancestors, and so are yours. They had a vision of a society here, and over the years we have let them down. We have allowed the occupation to get the better of our independence, and to become a way of life.'

He put his arm in a comradely way round Dobbs and steered him back towards the main part of the shop. 'You and I,' he went on, 'we shall show the authorities what we are made of. We shall, quite literally, reveal our true colours. I am planning a parade,' he explained, 'and I cannot do it without your enthusiastic support.'

Dobbs nodded weakly. He had no choice.

'Mary-Joan here,' said Curtis, smiling at his freckled assistant, 'is going to sing for us.'

283

Mary-Joan, blushing, admitted this was so.

'You have a fine voice,' said Dobbs.

'We all have fine voices,' said Curtis, 'but we have not used them. We have to find our voices again, or remain forever mute.'

They went to the door. The fresh air was welcome. Curtis the proprietor stood on the step, looking down the road. 'There will be so many flags here,' he said, 'that the old people will rub their eyes and think they are children again. And we shall give the new generation a glorious reminder of what has been, and what can come again.'

'Quite a video,' said Dobbs.

In the distance, at the end of the street, but out of sight, they could hear the sound of cheers and clapping.

'Bloody mainlanders,' said Curtis scornfully, and took Dobbs inside for another drink.

Clive Fox had just called the final wrap. There was spontaneous hooting and applause from all over the set. The cameraman crossed himself in gratitude, and Clive, coming forward to throw his arms around Troy as he stepped out of the scene, said: 'We made it.' Stephen, watching from behind the camera, saw the singer's eyes close briefly and sensed the pressure he had been under and now his extraordinary relief that it was all over. Already, some of the technicians were beginning to dismantle their equipment. Others, mainly local boys under the supervision of the floor manager, were standing by to strike the set.

Behind them, doors open, air-conditioner purring, a black limousine with a boomerang aerial was blocking the street, exuding power. Fred had swept up during the last scene, commanding and triumphant, sending a frisson of energy through the exhausted crew. He had not been seen for two days but everyone knew that the extraordinary transformation wrought in the town was Fred's work, and in his absence all kinds of magic had been attributed to him, chiefly by Zach.

Fred had watched the final takes lounging in the back with

his partner, gossiping in whispers and drinking champagne. He looked tired and unshaven (Zach was telling everyone he had not slept for two nights), but he had the satisfied expression of one who has done well, and knows it. Here, in victory, it was obvious that he had enjoyed executing his coup, saving his star client. Besides, his own contract was safe, too. There was plenty to celebrate.

Now Troy was breaking away from the director. 'Steve,' he said, touching him on the arm. 'Could you come to my trailer?' He looked at his watch. 'Give me ten minutes.'

When Stephen knocked on the door twenty minutes later, there was a pause and then a weary voice said: 'Yes.' Troy was just out of the shower, wrapped in a scarlet bathrobe, towelling his hair. 'Come in, Steve,' he said. 'Sit where you can.' The trailer was in chaos. The singer threw off the robe and began to pull on a fresh pair of jeans. Undressed, his body was painfully thin and white, like a medieval Christ. His power was in his voice, in his eyes, and in the guitar-playing magic of his fingers. Stephen imagined a shy, pallid weakling who had been bullied at school. Perhaps he had taught himself to talk to his guitar because he could talk to no one else. He'd already confessed that the wild behaviour of his early years had been an inarticulate celebration of a freedom he'd never had while growing up.

There were clothes everywhere and half-finished sketches. 'I love to draw,' said Troy. 'It's how I relax.' He picked up a sheet of cartridge paper with a pencil study of Skylark, a nude. 'What do you think?'

'Not bad,' said Stephen. He wondered if this was an invitation to make a comment about Skylark but decided to remain discreet. 'Not bad at all.' He picked up another drawing, a charcoal portrait of Fred, talking on his portable phone. 'That's good.'

Troy finished buttoning his shirt and began combing his hair. 'You and Fred did well.'

'It was Fred, really.' Stephen, who preferred to cover his

tracks, enjoyed the secret pleasure of putting Fred in the frame with his boss.

'Fred's a player.'

The comb snagged as he spoke. 'But – that's his job – that's what managers are paid for.' He examined himself in the mirror. 'That guy Hickey was getting on my nerves.'

'I feel a bit responsible,' Stephen confessed, looking at the picture of Skylark.

Troy rounded on him warmly. 'Don't,' he said. 'You did well. Everyone did well.' He came back to the sofa and began to pull on a pair of soft leather boots. 'Besides, Fred's an American. They love doing things like that.'

If the singer inquired more closely, Stephen had his answer rehearsed. There was little else to say: he had left the details, the legwork, to Fred. What else?

He had seen American influence at work all over the world, and it was always the same. The call from the ambassador; the appeal to the State Department; the application of the dollar; the suggestion of patriotic duty mixed with coded references to forgotten secrets and buried shames; the persuasive power of the files. Stephen did not believe in conspiracies, but he felt sure that Hickey was an American before he was a Christian and worshipped the flag before the cross. In the end, the video was being financed and distributed by an American multinational. He would have been told to go, and he would have gone because it was in American interests that he went. The stability of these parts was of profound strategic importance to the exercise of American power. There were sea-lanes at stake and listening posts to be protected. Finally, they were on the side of 'normalisation' and that was that. There would have been late-night phone conversations, meetings on both sides of the ocean, a conference call, a faxed instruction, and in a twinkling Hickey was gone, spirited away – a mite, a speck, blown away in the wind of history. Stephen had seen a dozen variations of this in the past, and when Fred had asked him about his network he had simply advised him that the power was there, all he had to do was exercise it. If there was a surprise it was only that Fred had proved so decisive.

'So, Steve.' Troy had finished dressing. 'Tell me, what happens now?' He picked up his sketch pad and a scrap of charcoal and began to draw.

'I become a pumpkin again and go back to the office.'

'Won't there be another assignment waiting for you?'

'With luck.' Already he was dreading his return to the city.

'Any ideas?'

'All I know is that it won't be another pop video.'

The singer laughed. 'Was it that bad?'

'It was supposed to be a holiday, but it turned out to be a crash course.'

'Sorry you did it?'

'Of course not.' He heard himself protest too much. 'I wouldn't have missed it for anything.' Now that it was over this was easy enough to say. 'It's just not my normal line of work.'

Troy stopped drawing for a moment. 'You have reservations. Tell me about them, Steve. I'm interested.'

He realised that it was rare for this man to be alone with someone who did not hold up a mirror to his vanity.

'I suppose it's human nature to wish you could have done better. Looking back, I can see mistakes I'd never make again.'

'There's always a first time.' Troy's face was set in concentration. 'Fred's theory is that you took the assignment because of that girl, Isabel.' He held up his drawing hand to gauge perspective. 'Is that true?'

'Yes and no.' In the circumstances, Stephen thought this was an honest answer.

'Are you still seeing her?' He was chatting as he worked. It was the appeal of his manner that he never seemed inquisitive.

'Yes and no.'

They both laughed and then Troy said: 'So – what about Skylark?'

'That's what I mean about mistakes.' He did not know what else to say; it was against his principles to apologise too much.

287

'I liked him,' said the singer. 'A free spirit.' He smiled in memory. 'A very free spirit.' He looked concerned. 'Where is he now?'

'He's gone back to the city.' Stephen saw the overheated hallway, the blue velvet curtain, and Philip with his Pekinese. 'Home.'

Troy nodded, still working. 'You had to get him out of here, right?'

'Right.'

'Well,' he said, looking up. 'I'm grateful.' He shook his head. 'Sex and religion. Some nightmare.' He seemed to be enjoying a private joke. 'Will you come back?'

'I expect I'll come back to see Isabel.'

'That sounds –' He glanced up briefly, ' – fairly provisional.'

'It is.'

Troy said nothing for a moment. He was putting the detail into his picture. 'Look at me,' he commanded. Stephen faced into his eyes. The singer held up his pad, comparing subject and likeness. It was not quite done; he bent over his drawing again. 'When we first met you were in love, weren't you? And now you're not.'

Stephen began to protest.

'I can see. That's the worst,' he added sympathetically.

Stephen shrugged. 'It happens.'

'Don't deny it,' said Troy sharply. 'You have to face the pain. You can't pretend it doesn't exist.' He smiled at Stephen. 'I'm sure you have a lot of girlfriends.'

'Have had,' he replied. He hesitated and felt a slight pricking in his eyes. 'This time it was different.'

'So what went wrong?'

Stephen did not answer at once. He looked out of the window. The last few months whirled past in his imagination. 'I don't know. Just at the moment, I honestly don't know.'

Troy said nothing; he could be extraordinarily tactful. He hummed as he worked. 'Afterwards, it always takes longer than you think to figure these things out.'

Stephen looked at him curiously and took a chance. 'When were you last in love?'

'I can't remember,' he said sadly. 'In this business, you're always talking about love and never knowing it.' It was clear he was telling the truth. 'There.' He tore the sheet off the drawing block. He was done.

'Thank you,' said Stephen.

'Don't thank me.' Troy was scribbling a signature and a date. 'You're a good guy. I like talking to you. I hope you'll stay in touch.' He passed over the sketch. 'Portrait of the consultant as a young dog.'

It was quite a good likeness, done in bold, black strokes. Stephen decided it was always a shock to see yourself as others did. He wished he had a more interesting face.

Troy was watching him. 'You don't like the limelight, do you?'

Stephen smiled. 'As a consultant, I'm always half in the shadows.'

The door opened and Fred and Zach came in, full of high spirits. Zach was mouthing one of the songs from the album. 'In – the – asphalt – jungle, in the human – zoo – '

Shuster was triumphant. 'We did it.'

'You did it,' replied Troy, a sincere light of gratitude in his eyes. He went up to his manager and kissed him on the cheek.

Fred was touched, and proud. 'Now and then I suppose I earn my fee,' he murmured modestly.

'No shit,' said Zach, happily hero-worshipping. 'It's going to be a great video.'

'And a great album,' added Fred.

'You betcha!' Euphoria always seemed to go to Zach's head. 'Listen,' he said, turning to Stephen for want of an audience. 'He actually spoke to the president.'

'Which president?'

'Of the record company. On the coast.' He shook his head at the impressiveness of it all. 'No one speaks to the president.'

Stephen exchanged a quizzical look with Troy. 'Then who does the president speak to?'

'God,' said the singer.

Zach gave an uneasy laugh; he was unsure who was sending up whom. 'You got it,' he said.

'It's called imperialism,' said Stephen, thinking: America, America!

'It's called winning,' said Zach, with a little defensive thrust of aggression.

'Well thank God the game's over.' Fred brought them down to earth. 'Will I be glad to be out of here, or what?'

They began to discuss their departure plans. After much toing and froing Fred and Zach decided they would fly over to the mainland at once. There was a problem. Troy wanted to sail back in the yacht. Zach called to alert the captain. Fred paced up and down. The Americans were in a quandary they could not quite express. The truth was that their client wanted company for the long ride to the sea, and their duty lay with him. Stephen, who wanted to give Isabel time to herself, saw his chance to escape too, and volunteered his services. Troy seemed pleased. Fred and Zach were delighted to be off the hook. Stephen explained he would need a lift back in the morning to say goodbye to various people in the town. He caught Fred winking at Zach, but ignored him.

'I don't expect you'll be saying goodbye to Curtis,' said Zach. 'I saw him last night. He looked pretty crazy.'

Stephen said rather seriously that they had been right to fire him. 'I was very polite,' he said. 'I simply explained in the nicest possible way that his services were no longer needed.'

'I said there'd be trouble,' Fred chipped in. 'Didn't I say there'd be trouble?'

'Listen to this,' said Zach. He described visiting Curtis's store to buy cigarettes. The place was open, but there was no one on the checkout. As he waited, he heard martial music coming from the back of the store and went to have a look. Curtis was alone in the packing room listening to the Mars theme from *The Planets* on a portable gramophone. He was wearing a military tunic. He stood up when Zach appeared, stopped the music abruptly, and asked what he wanted. He seemed slightly drunk. Zach apologised for the interruption. He only wanted to buy some cigarettes.

'Buy what you like, you've bought everything else here.'

Zach had tried to conciliate him, but was ignored. Curtis, he said, seemed resentful about his dismissal, saying that he imagined it was 'Mallory's doing', and something Zach didn't follow about the Institute. Then he said: 'You can make your video and I'll make mine and we'll see who has the bigger audience.' Zach had not known what to make of this, and when he admitted that, Curtis replied: 'You'll understand soon enough. This is my town.'

As he told the story now, Zach still seemed mystified. 'What do you think he was talking about?'

'God knows,' said Stephen. He was saddened by the growing evidence of Curtis's breakdown.

'He spoke as though he owned the place.'

'Before you came, in a funny way, he did.'

They all looked out of the window. It was raining again, hard grey rain, driving down. 'Will I be glad to be out of here, or what?' Fred repeated.

Zach was talking to the chauffeur on his phone. The car would take them to the airport in an hour. They could catch the last flight to the mainland. The limousine would get Troy to his yacht by mid-evening. Stephen could stay overnight and the chauffeur would bring him back the following morning. 'For your goodbyes,' said Zach, with an ironic smile.

Soon Troy was holding court in his trailer, making his farewells and his thank-yous to the crew, the make-up artists, the choreographer, the dancers, and the various technicians, gaffers, grips, best boys and runners. They had been brought together by the filming and become a unit. Now they were scattering again, and a hundred provisional connections were being broken – 'until next time'. The little phrase tumbled into every conversation, the imp of optimism that sustained their freelance lives. Yes, they would all meet again on the mainland. Yes, there would be a special screening, 'the cast and crew'. Yes, it had been quite an experience. Etc., etc.

Finally, they were ready to go.

They stood by the car looking down the street towards the factory and the Institute. Already, much of the make-believe they had introduced was gone. Bits of scenery were piled up on the waste ground for burning. It was late afternoon. The light was fading, and with the rain the landscape seemed dark and strong and incredibly close, almost oppressive, as though they were about to be swallowed by it. Troy gave an involuntary shudder and got into the car. Stephen followed.

Curious groups of townspeople had gathered to watch the singer's departure. As they drove away, some waved, others shouted obscure comments. Stephen, looking out from behind the privacy of the reflecting glass, wondered if he could see Curtis standing in the doorway of his store, but as they reached the top of the street he saw that the place was shut for the day, and secretly he was relieved.

For a while, they did not speak. Then Troy began to reminisce about leaving home for the first time. 'And then the road itself becomes second nature,' he said, 'and you find you cannot settle anywhere.'

Stephen decided that perhaps this was why they liked each other. He said: 'Until recently, I was worried about that, too.'

'And now?'

'Now I think that home is an illusion. You make it where and when you find it.'

'Living like refugees,' said Troy definitively.

They talked on, and the limousine swept through the evening. When the approaching city became a hint of orange in the distance, Troy asked the chauffeur to pull off the road.

He got out and walked over to the fence. Stephen waited for a few moments and then got out himself to stretch his legs. Troy finished and came back towards him. They stood together for a moment, absorbed by the silence of the fields and the hush that comes with the approach of night. The wind had dropped and the light was held briefly on the horizon, accentuating the presence of the earth. It seemed to Stephen that everything around them was being drawn into this great stillness.

'Spooky place,' said Troy, and climbed back into the limousine.

8

Leaving the harbour with Troy's yacht riding high on the tide behind him, Stephen was stopped by the port authority police. Two outriders in black leather, with radio-mikes and automatic pistols, escorted the limousine into the customs area and some men in blazers came forward to examine the car, inside and out. There was no sense of menace. The investigating officers were polite, and one of them, half apologising, actually used the phrase, 'standard operating procedure'. Stephen sat in the back and watched the pale-fingered clerk behind the glass punching his details into the computer. A gust of salty wind distracted his attention from the surveillance and brought back childhood memories of a holiday by the sea, that last summer before he had been sent away to school. Making another connection, he decided there was something about these officials that was reminiscent of his teachers then, the inherent suspicion perhaps, or the routine enforcement of regulations. Finally they were satisfied, and now the car was accelerating over the forgotten railway tracks towards the exit.

As they found the highway, the driver tried to make conversation but Stephen did not respond. The journey to the town was becoming familiar, but his thoughts were not at ease. He felt lonely and nostalgic, remembering the lighter mood of recent times past. Now there was only anxiety about Isabel and a growing sense of departure. After a short break here, he would go back to the mainland, and when would he ever make this trip again? Before, with the video, there had been an element of uncertainty; today he was just a visitor and it shocked him how little he was able to enjoy the experience. Isabel's accusations came back into his mind and he wondered fearfully if it was true, as she had said, that he was unable to live without public risk.

Now he was here, in the town again, marvelling at its speedy return to normality. The driver pulled up outside Isabel's, wished him well, and cruised away down the street. There was that strange, almost pleasurable, moment of panic as he knocked on the door. But then, as she opened up to greet him, it passed, and they were together again, mutually apologetic.

He gave his account of the last twenty-four hours and felt the tension going from his head. Regretting the memory of his recent doubts and relieved at the uncomplicated pleasure he found in her company, he acknowledged to himself how glad he was to be here. She prepared food and they had a bottle of wine and then they went to bed.

It was very late, quite still and dark, when Stephen was woken by the telephone ringing downstairs. 'Let it ring,' he said, half asleep. But Isabel was already up to answer it. He heard her voice, then a pause. She came back upstairs. 'It's for you,' she said. He could not see her expression, but the tone of her voice was enough to tell him she was concerned.

He wrapped a towel round himself and went downstairs, shivering in the cold.

'Dr Mallory?' The voice at the other end was civilised and discreet. 'Eric Potter here. I'm sorry to bother you – '

'What on earth – ?' He stopped himself.

The voice was inexorable. ' – but I wonder if we could meet tomorrow for a quiet chat.'

'Tomorrow?'

'As a matter of fact, I mean today. It is, I'm afraid, a matter of some urgency, as I'll explain when we meet.' There was no avoiding Potter's claim. He named the bar of a local hotel. He would be there 'at noon'. It was his 'hope', he said, that Stephen would 'feel able' to join him. It would not take long. As he listened to his instructions, he heard the command in Potter's voice and realised that this, not the deferential neutrality of their first meeting, betrayed the man's true nature. Stephen put the phone down and went back to bed.

'Who was that?'

'I'm afraid – ' He hesitated, wondering whether to lie. If he mentioned Potter's name she would be alarmed. 'I'm afraid it was one of those army people,' he said vaguely.

She sat up. 'What's going on?'

'Nothing.' He climbed back under the duvet. 'I mean, I don't know.'

'How do I know if you're telling the truth?'

'Do you think I could lie to you?'

She did not hesitate. 'Shall we put it this way – I know from experience that you leave things out.'

'We all do that.'

'With you, it's an art form.'

He felt a complicated sense of grievance, but feared to spoil things. 'It's common enough. It's called need-to-know.'

'Whatever happened to trust?'

He tried to stay light. 'Perhaps you could say it ran into corporate paranoia.'

They lay in silence for a while, and then he said: 'In this business we're always on the edge of a rather dodgy world, but I keep as far away as possible.'

'You must have some idea what it's about.'

He shook his head. 'I can't imagine why they want to see me, really I can't.'

She said nothing more and they went back to sleep.

In the morning, she did not refer to the phone call. At first he was grateful for her discretion, but when he saw she was brooding he felt a stab of disappointment.

'You're annoyed,' he said. He could not help himself.

'No. It's just – ' She stopped, and shook her head, as though erasing the thought from her mind.

He pressed her.

'It's just that you seem so elusive sometimes.'

He looked at her, and a spark of candour flashed between them. 'Perhaps I'm elusive to myself.'

She smiled. 'The enigma of Stephen Mallory.'

'Look.' He tried to be matter-of-fact. 'There's no mystery here. Those guys have to justify their jobs.' He was running away with himself. 'It's probably a bit of routine checking by the ministry before – '

A chasm opened up in the conversation and he felt himself falling.

Isabel seemed disoriented. Finally, in a small hard voice she said: 'Before?'

He said that all he meant was that he had to go back to the office soon, and he imagined that Wagner would have plans for him.

'There's still something you're not telling me.'

There wasn't, there was only his inner knowledge that he would soon be on the road again. He said: 'There's bound to be another assignment waiting. There always is.'

Now it was her turn to experience disappointment. 'I thought you said those days were over.'

He sighed. 'I know. I suppose – ' He could not go on. He had betrayed his account of himself to her, and he knew it. It was not meant to be a treachery, but that was how it would seem, whatever he said by way of self-justification.

'Thanks for telling me.' She was hurt, and also bemused.

'I have told you.' He became defensive and then conciliatory. 'Anyway, I have a proposal.'

She stood up and went into the kitchen. 'The answer's no.' She sounded knowledgeable and self-possessed.

He followed her, wishing he didn't have to. 'You don't even know what I'm going to say.'

'I can guess.'

'Well?'

'You want me to give up my house here and come and live with you on the mainland. You are anxious to say that it's not a proposal or anything of that kind. You don't want to invade my space, but you'd like me to share what you have over there. And the terrible truth is you're about to say all this at the moment when we both know in our heart of hearts that it's over.' She paused, seeing the dismay on his face. 'I'm sorry,' she said, and came over to him.

'Is that what you feel?'

'I don't know what I feel any more.' She sat down at the table, and when she motioned to him to join her he remembered their first meeting. 'I used to think I could never be alone. A year or two ago I would have jumped at any suggestion of companionship. Now I'm not so sure. I'm used to myself and my solitude. I like being alone. It's not so hard. I don't know that I can handle the pressure of a constant relationship. You're almost the only man I've known, apart from Tom.' She smiled. 'Does all that make us equal?'

He said nothing. He did not really know. There was silence between them. Stephen brought his cup to his lips and tasted a mouthful of cold coffee. He looked at his watch. Soon he would have to go to meet Major Potter.

'Will you ever leave here?' he asked.

'One day. In my own time. Who knows? I'm just not ready yet.'

'Would you come back to the mainland?'

'Probably.'

He put his arm round her, and looked into her eyes. 'Where are we, Isabel?'

'I don't know. I honestly don't know. When we met I fell for you at once. I thought I was in love with you, but now I don't know any more. I wish I did.'

'What's happened?'

'Nothing's happened, really. That's just it.'

He said he didn't understand.

'We haven't shared enough. There's something that stops you from giving in. You might want to, but you can't. You're lost in your own world, and no one can get through. That's why you are always on the move. You have to be.' She passed a hand over his cheek. 'The great escape artist.'

He felt depressed. 'You make it sound terrible.'

'I don't mean to. I'm so fond of you. But – but you can't connect, and perhaps neither can I.'

Stephen was thoughtful for a moment. 'Is that it, then?'

Isabel seemed amused, but also exasperated. 'Why are you so impatient? Why is it always all or nothing, now or never?

Why can't you take things as they come? Okay. You'll go on your next assignment. I'll stay here. Maybe we'll see each other. Why can't we see where that takes us? What's that line? You have to have a little faith in people.'

He looked at her and the thought came to him that with the opposite sex men only really wanted peace and quiet, a kind of deliverance. Women were different. They wanted movement in their lives, and the cross-currents of emotion. Anger, love, joy, jealousy, all these were essential to a woman's existence, her vindication really and in some profound way this made them tougher. Women, even women who had not had children, had an instinctive knowledge of birth and rebirth, they knew about the potential newness of life and could place a trust in it. 'A little faith.' The truth was they were endlessly provisional in their attitude to things that seemed vitally important to them because nature had given them a finger on the only pulse-beat that mattered, the future of life itself. They would always adapt themselves to the rhythm of that pulse-beat with an apparently effortless changeability. Men weren't like that. As they grew older they became more and more like their image of themselves, as black and white and stiff as the cards they handed each other at the end of meetings and conferences. Everything in that world was active and testing, a trial of strength in which you were either victor or vanquished. A man's life was so self-important. Moments always seemed so decisive; matters were often so extreme. He could express it to himself as a proposition that women, who were content to be, because in being they were fulfilled, were always growing. Men, for whom life was doing, not being, simply became fossils in their own lives. Once again, he saw the jet soaring into the air.

'Hello?' Isabel was looking at him in that disarming, quizzical way of hers. He had no idea if he was being conned or seduced or cheated or re-educated, but knew there was still some love here and that he should listen to what this told him. She put her arms round him and they kissed.

'A little faith,' he repeated, with a hopeless shrug. 'I'll try.'
'It will be good for you,' she said.

Major Potter was sitting with his back to the wall, a sporting newspaper open in front of him and a full glass easily to hand. With his lugubrious moustache and his small, pig eyes he reminded Stephen of a safari hunter, pathetic and laughable and almost brave. He brightened as he caught sight of Stephen making his way through the maze of empty tables, folded his newspaper, and stood up to shake hands.

'I trust you'll join me,' he said, motioning to the barman for another round. He seemed less sombre than usual, and Stephen was encouraged to comment that he seemed quite at home here. 'So I should be, Dr Mallory,' he said, savouring his reply. 'The landlord has been on our payroll for donkey's years.'

Stephen expressed only the faintest surprise. He wanted to keep the encounter low-key, to fulfil his obligation to attend, and depart as quickly as possible. Now he realised, as the drinks arrived, that the two men staring dully at the television screen above the bar were police minders.

'Cheers,' said Potter, raising his glass. He thanked Stephen for answering his summons at such short notice. He wondered, he said, whether he had any idea of the reason for his call. Stephen, who was now in a holiday mood, shook his head casually. He had speculated to himself of course, but had found no obvious explanation. It seemed better to appear unconcerned.

Major Potter became serious. Although they were alone, he lowered his voice. 'I need to talk to you about this man Curtis,' he said.

'You mean your man Curtis,' Stephen challenged.

Potter was unflappable. Any wild beast could charge at him out of the bushes and he would only pull the trigger when he was sure of putting a bullet in its heart. Stephen guessed from the thoughtful silence that he was trying to decide how far to take his visitor into his confidence.

'Well then,' he said at length, 'perhaps you can help me. What's your assessment?' It was a question straight from an interrogator's textbook.

Stephen looked away. Through the hotel window, he could see a lake and two swans. There was nothing to be gained from holding back; he would only be caught out in the end. So he described what he knew, leaving out the complications with Isabel, trying to keep his account matter-of-fact and economical. Potter listened, blinking slowly from time to time, a hunter waiting for his quarry.

When Stephen had finished, Potter looked at him carefully for a moment. 'I agree,' he said, concentrating, 'that in his present mood Curtis is extremely dangerous.' He seemed nostalgic for a time when Curtis had been a different person. 'You are right, Dr Mallory. He is supposed to be answerable to me and my colleagues.'

Stephen refused to let himself express satisfaction. 'It was never possible to explain his influence in any other way,' he said, clarifying a number of things to himself. 'I imagine he is not the only one,' he added.

'You seem to understand this place better than you used to,' Potter commented with a wintry smile.

'Only because I want to,' he replied. 'When I first came here it was under duress. Now I'm beginning to feel almost at home.'

'A dangerous delusion,' said Potter. 'I've seen it often enough in the past, and it can prove fatal. The more you think you know, the more you are known. Then you are no longer anonymous and the stories start.'

'Are you warning me?'

Potter's dead-shot look did not waver. 'Curtis is increasingly unpredictable, Dr Mallory.' He cleared his throat like a prompter. 'He is under the impression that he was given certain undertakings about your presence here that have not been honoured.'

'Undertakings?'

Now it was Potter's turn to sound detached, even theoretical. 'It was based on the stupidest of misunderstandings, but that is so often the way.' He bent even closer to Stephen. 'Curtis is convinced – wrongly, as we both know – that your operation is in some way linked to ours. I'm afraid to say that the unfortunate business with that boy did nothing to eradicate the impression.' Potter was choosing his words carefully. 'Now, because of his relationship with us, he believed that he had influence with my office to have you reassigned or transferred.'

'Couldn't you put him straight?'

'Surely, Dr Mallory,' Potter's smile hovered briefly, 'with your understanding of our work here, you can appreciate why that was not possible?'

Stephen felt his control going. 'Actually, I don't.' He heard his pomposity booming hopelessly. 'As a matter of fact, I think you owe me an explanation.'

Potter began to speak with the clinical detachment of an instructor. This was simply one case among many, neither more nor less interesting, it seemed. 'You have spent enough time here, I believe, to appreciate that in the work we do it is extremely disadvantageous to allow any sense of weakness or deficiency in our operation to be communicated to the local population.'

'I've heard a few things about this operation of yours.'

'Really?' Potter seemed intrigued. 'What sort of things?'

'Well – pretty unflattering, frankly.'

'Perhaps it has not occurred to you that in my line of business a certain amount of confusing disinformation is prudent, Dr Mallory.'

Stephen found he had no answer to this.

'You see,' Potter went on calmly, 'it is important to foster a sense of – how shall I put it? – mysterious omnipotence here, a certain godlike power. This is by no means just an illusion, as the sudden departure of the Reverend Mister Hickey illustrates – ' He held up a hand, forestalling further inquiry. 'These are, by and large, a simple people. It isn't difficult to exercise a restraining hold on their imaginations. In these circumstances it would not be possible to deny the common local belief in your connection with us.'

'I suspect,' Stephen broke in angrily, 'that you actually encouraged it.' He felt suddenly alone in open ground, without protection and intensely vulnerable.

Potter did not reply. Instead he took out his pipe and a tobacco pouch and began to fill the bowl with maddening deliberation. 'Our advice – my advice to you – is that Curtis's unreliability puts you at considerable risk now.'

Stephen could not stop himself. 'What have you heard?'

'The usual rumours.' Potter lit a match. 'Curtis is out of control and his ideas are getting wilder by the day.' He drew on his pipe. 'Your presence here is increasingly provocative to him, I think.'

'I only came to say goodbye.'

'We are aware of that, Dr Mallory, but it doesn't lessen the provocation.'

'This is crazy,' said Stephen, mainly to himself.

'It is very sad.' A look of regret came into Potter's face. 'For years we relied on Curtis. He kept these parts exceptionally quiet. But now – ' He shrugged and gestured uncertainly with his pipe. 'One for the road?' He signalled to the barman. Stephen looked at the newspaper.

'Are you interested in the turf, Dr Mallory?'

Stephen remembered going to the races in the Far East, the oriental obsession with gambling, the sticky heat and the sweet stench of horses in the enclosure. 'I have been,' he said.

'There's a horse running today in the two-thirty. Brigadier Jones.' Potter smiled. 'It may interest you to know that we own this animal. His trainer, Mr Birch, is one of our most reliable sources. It's amazing what you can pick up at the races. I'm a great believer in the secrets of the loose-box and the hayloft.' The drinks arrived. Potter lifted his glass. 'Cheers.'

'Is there anything you haven't got your hooks into here?'

Potter considered the question carefully. 'To be honest, no. Our philosophy is that if we have knowledge we have the power to control the situation.'

'So the ends do justify the means?'

'But of course.' Potter was quite calm. 'They always have.'

'Does that policy apply to Curtis as well?'

'Naturally.'

'So what are you proposing?'

Potter's métier was unattributable suggestion. He disliked direct questions as much as he disliked straight answers. He said: 'Would you care to come for a little walk? It's a beautiful day.'

They came out of the hotel into the sunshine and strolled by the lake, lulled by the flux and reflux of the tiny waves on the shore. The bodyguards followed at a discreet distance. Outside, in the open, Major Potter seemed smaller, less imposing. After a while, he resumed. 'The truth is, Dr Mallory, that Curtis has gone too far. He has crossed the line between the acceptable and the unacceptable.' He kicked a piece of driftwood irritably with his shoe. 'In fact, you could say he has gone mad.' He stopped and looked at Stephen. 'You've heard about his plans for the parade?'

'I've heard stories.'

'He's playing with fire,' said Potter. 'Those ideas have been kept on ice for years, and we don't like it. We don't like it one little bit.'

Stephen said it was only petty nationalism.

'Only?' Potter seemed shocked. 'That petty nationalism has killed thousands of good people over the years.'

Stephen said they always had trouble at this time of the year.

Potter shook his head. 'It's not so much the trouble, it's the example. Those parades are illegal. If we let Curtis get away with it, who knows where it will end?'

Stephen tried to tease him. 'I thought you guys were against "normalisation".'

'That's just press gossip,' Potter replied dismissively. 'I'll tell you what we are against,' he went on warmly. 'We are against chaos and anarchy.' He paused authoritatively. 'Sometimes there is no avoiding military solutions.'

They walked on for a few yards. Stephen bent down and

chose a flat stone. With a flick of the wrist, he watched it skim across the water and sink out of sight.

'Not bad,' said Potter, bending down competitively.

Stephen counted Potter's stone jumping seven times and saw the boy-scout satisfaction in his eyes. He remembered his mother telling him that he was not the only pebble on the beach, and reflected how little he had attended to that wisdom. 'Do you always operate like this?' he asked.

'When we have to,' said Potter summarily. He picked up a larger stone and tossed it with a dead splash into the lake. 'You will be wise to return to the mainland as soon as possible.'

Stephen was mystified. 'I don't understand,' he said. 'Why are you telling me this?'

'I was ordered to,' said Potter shortly. 'You appear to have friends in high places, Dr Mallory. That's all I can say.' He turned and walked back towards the hotel.

Stephen watched him go, but could not follow. The sky was like beaten tin and the sun was hurting his eyes. The little waves grated repetitively on the shore and he felt extraordinarily alone.

9

On that still summer morning the sky was as bright as a mirror and every sound in the street was as sharp and clear as breaking glass.

Stephen lay next to Isabel, his body touching hers, feeling warm and safe but lonely again. She had spoken of the need for trust in each other, 'a little faith', but his meeting with Major Potter had come between them like an infidelity, and their mutual reluctance to acknowledge this seemed to have grown stronger since his return. The moment he had described his lakeside encounter she wanted to know why he had dissembled, at first, brushing aside his assertion that he wanted to spare her anxieties. 'What did he want?' she demanded.

'He wanted the latest news about Curtis.' He could not bring himself to mention Potter's warning, perhaps because he could not bear its implications, and Isabel, seeing his immovable reticence, had drawn back as well, defeated inside. All at once, their respect for each other's privacy had created a monster of uncertainty between them.

As well as a sense of guilt and failure he could not quite define to himself, there was his own resentment at Potter's words. Three days had passed and he still felt as much the victim of an alien, dark, clandestine process as the woman lying asleep beside him, and this disturbed him. He had said it was his golden rule never to be pinned down, but he had to acknowledge he had broken this rule with Isabel and its consequences left him feeling stupid and vulnerable and depressed. To admit this was shocking, but he found he was now looking forward to his imminent departure.

He listened to Isabel's soft breathing. She had been the first to admit there was something wrong. For all her tact, there was no doubting her emotional candour: it emphasised a fragility in her feelings that was at times almost painful. When he wondered about the future pain they might be facing, he recognised that, for him, it was part of a pattern. He might tell himself that he longed for the ordinary, but the truth was that his life found more meaning in its opposite. He had always been fascinated by the workings of politics and, if he was honest, he had chosen to look for himself in the whirlwind of public affairs. Now, more than ever, he could feel the quiet and stillness of his relationship with Isabel threatened by the unrelenting force of events.

Stephen lay alone with his thoughts, wondering if he could find gratitude for what there had been or regret for what he was losing. If he looked on the bright side, there was always the thrill of a new start, a focus for hope and optimism perhaps. Now, at least, compared with a year ago, he could face the world.

When Isabel opened her eyes, she looked at him and smiled sadly, as though she knew what he had been thinking. She moved closer towards him and he felt her warmth and her nakedness. 'I had this dream,' she said.

'How was it?'

She made a wistful face. 'It was nice to have a happy dream for a change.' Recently, she had been having bad dreams, nightmarishly confusing the faces of Tom and Stephen. In her worst moments, she was beginning to fear that she could not differentiate between her sleeping and her waking life.

As she described her dream, Stephen admired the deft way she had with detail, her choice of words, and her sense of a story. But, try as he might to be detached, he found this sharing poignant, even unbearable. Lovers shared dreams to find clues to the intimacy of their hearts, and they had done this. Now, those moments were lost. There was only the habit, not the feeling, and her version was too composed. There was no hint of sexual danger between them, no implicit invitation, only the fact of the dream, almost as neutral as a newspaper article.

'It was so vivid,' she concluded. 'It was like a movie.'

'I used to love dreams like that,' said Stephen. 'Now I'm not so sure.' He remembered the dreams he had after the death of Federico, the crying, the sleep-walking, and the incomprehensible dreads that came back night after night like an unappeasable demon. He thought of Major Potter and he thought of Curtis. 'At the moment, I'd rather not have any dreams. I'd rather not know what my unconscious is saying.'

'Sometimes you have these conversations in your sleep.'

He felt a stab of fear that he might have said something he would regret. 'Like what?' He did not conceal his anxiety well, and she smiled. 'Relax. You don't make sense.' A thoughtful note came into her voice. 'Your secrets are always in code. The interior is safe.'

'I imagine you'd say that was appropriate.'

She smiled regretfully and an awkward silence intervened. He wished he could break the spell, but he could not. Sometimes, and increasingly, he found it disturbingly easy to see in himself the man Isabel seemed to believe him to be. They dozed again, and then, a few minutes later, Isabel got up and went downstairs to make coffee.

Stephen watched her small, lithe body disappear through the door, then he too forced himself out of bed, dressing carefully for the journey he expected to be making later that day. He joined Isabel in the kitchen. 'What time does it start?'

'Ten forty-five.' She looked at her watch. 'Soon.' She sighed. 'Joe's big day,' she said. 'I hope – ' She paused, and changed direction. 'For someone who's been used to working in the shadows, this is very public.'

He was about to say that she knew he enjoyed taking risks, and then realised his misunderstanding. 'He's crazy,' he said, remembering his conversation with Potter. 'Perhaps the army will have to intervene.'

She looked at him, as though he were giving her a clue. He shook his head. 'I have no more idea than you do,' he said.

Outside, as they stood behind the excited ranks of the spectators, Stephen saw how easily the occasion could get out of hand. Almost all the town had turned out to watch the ceremony, and the atmosphere was charged with extraordinary expectation and drama. The older people, who could just remember the events they were no longer allowed to commemorate, waved paper flags. Young mothers held up babies. Children in Sunday best watched the adult excitement in mystification.

The main street had been closed to traffic. Now, over the rise, they could see the gilded tips of banners, and behind these the harlequin colours of forgotten units, magenta and emerald, canary yellow and sky-blue sapphire, the richly embroidered symbols of independence. The marching column breasted the slope and came into view with a rattle of drums.

Stephen was impressed at the show Curtis had mounted. As well as the militiamen in the old battle uniforms, there were veterans with sticks in their hands, young men in combat gear carrying automatic weapons, and then, behind, the victims of bombings and shootings in wheelchairs, the men and women of the ambulance services, local dignitaries with municipal honours flashing in the sun, charity workers and councillors in pinstripe. Among the many faces that he recognised in the procession, Mary's proud stare stood out, an expression of sisterly loyalty. She was wearing her administrator's uniform, and had the forbidden colours in her hat. Stephen saw that it was Curtis's bizarre inspiration to have found a way to bring together all the elements of the town, uniting them in a display of local solidarity. This was Curtis's plea, on behalf of himself and the people, for a place in the world, for recognition. The cleverness of his strategy struck Stephen all the more forcibly now that it was taking shape before his eyes. By making this an occasion for defying the authorities, Curtis was reminding the town of its heritage and celebrating its right to exist on its own terms, apart from the occupation.

The parade streamed past the spectators in a thunderous military crescendo and marched down the road towards the memorial in front of the Institute. As the column passed, the spectators closed in and joined the procession. Stephen and Isabel found themselves walking next to Mr and Mrs Hu and their daughters. It seemed right that the outsiders should be sticking together.

Mr Hu, animated and smiling, was sharing something with his family. Next to them, Isabel seemed tall and slender. Ghosts, thought Stephen, remembering the Chinese word for Westerners. He was a ghost here, too. He would never have any substance among these people; he was right to leave.

Michelle Hu, holding her father's hand, translated. 'He used to play the drums.'

Mr Hu beamed with nostalgia.

'He was a big deal in the Sixties,' said Mrs Hu, joining in, shy but proud. 'We still have his album.'

'Number one Hong Kong band,' said Mr Hu enthusiastically. As they walked, he pulled Stephen to one side. 'Today,' he said, 'I am over the moon.'

'So I see.'

'You are my friend, Dr Mallory, so I will tell you why.'

Stephen leant towards him. 'Please.'

'He is selling out.' Mr Hu nodded at the front of the procession. In his eagerness, the composure of his sentences became disturbed. 'Curtis. He's leaving.' He brushed aside Stephen's surprise. 'Yes, yes, it is all mine. Will be. Factory. Institute. Perhaps even shop. Lock, stock and barrel.' He was almost clowning happiness. He put his finger to his lips. 'Big secret, you understand.'

The procession was drawing to a halt, gathering in a ragged circle around the memorial to the fallen, facing the drawn-up ranks of Curtis's militia. Stephen could see him conferring with Dobbs and two other men in black suits. They were checking their watches. Then the officer commanding the parade stepped forward and began to give orders. His shouts reverberated against the brick walls of the Institute and were lost in the thick green canopy of the nearby beech trees. The lettering on the memorial stood out black in the hard white sun. The parade lowered arms. A drumroll began. Mr Hu watched with shining eyes. As the tattoo faded there was a cannon shot in the distance, a single report. The priest standing next to Curtis lowered his head and, after a moment's uncertain hesitation, the circle of townspeople followed his example. Stephen, watching, saw that Curtis did not bow. He was savouring the act of obeisance as if it was for him. He simply stared ahead, arrogant, wilful and victorious. He seemed to be standing straighter and fiercer, more commanding and vigorous than ever. What strange fantasy was running through his mind? A chief, or a king, surrounded by his people? Once, briefly, Stephen caught his eye – or so he thought – and a look of the purest hatred and triumph blazed from Curtis's eyes. It was an extraordinary moment, held, forever it seemed, in silence. Then a second gun went off, sending a flock of crows caw-cawing into the air, as though disturbed in their enjoyment of the solitude and tranquillity by an imperialising power from another world.

As the echo of the second cannon died away, Stephen saw Curtis give an almost imperceptible nod. A young militiaman stepped forward and raised a trumpet to his lips. The clarion call sounded across the square, bringing back memories so distant they had almost been forgotten. The trumpeter's face, contorted with effort, was stark white in the sunshine; his instrument was flashing gold; his tunic was scarlet and green.

Beyond the militia and the officials in their black suits, Stephen could see Curtis's car, parked at the side of the Institute, a mundane reminder of his importance in these parts. Everyone knew Curtis's car; everyone smiled at his solicitous ubiquity.

Mr Hu was wrong. Curtis might sell up, but he would never leave. He might hand over the balance-sheet of his everyday life to a foreigner, but only to strengthen his unseen influence in other ways. The sale was a stratagem, a ploy. If he was selling, it was only to transfer an impossible debt. Perhaps, secretly, he was trying to ruin Mr Hu.

The trumpet's call echoed round, and now it was joined by the clear sweet voice of Mary-Joan. In his mind, Stephen saw the charging armies of Curtis's ancestors, and heard the roar of their cries in battle. It was as though Curtis had decided to listen to his ancestors and take a stand, to step out of the shadowy world of fixes and deals and make a declaration. It was, Stephen recognised, a statement fuelled by rage. If Curtis could not have Isabel, and if he had lost the confidence of his erstwhile masters, then he would show them that he was master of a family, a community, an inheritance that had roots, a society with a tradition that the authorities could never begin to understand.

The notes of the trumpet sounded higher and higher. Stephen watched the tears streaming down the face of a veteran in front. The old man did not flinch. He remained at ramrod attention. Who could say what terrible moment of loss or shame or betrayal he was remembering? In a vain attempt to cool the martial spirits of the place, the authorities had not allowed him to have these thoughts in public for most of his adult life. Stephen could see that when it was over, he and the others here today would be grateful to Curtis for giving them their moment of catharsis. They would return to their homes purged by the fanfare of the trumpet, the fire and thunder of the drums, and the surge of blood in the march past.

Now, as the last notes of the trumpet died away across the fields, Curtis was stepping forward, the first to lay his wreath at the memorial. He moved with great dignity, as though the eyes of the world were on him. He bent down, straightened up and saluted, then stood for several seconds staring at the names on the plinth.

Stephen had heard Isabel say she thought Curtis capable of losing his sense of reality, and now here were her fears made actual. He seemed to have become crazy with the delusion of power and control, with the desperate urge to govern and rule and have significance. This was the price of isolation. It seemed to Stephen that Curtis was becoming like the inmates of the hospital, out of touch with the world.

Curtis walked back to his place. Perhaps it was in his imagination, but Stephen thought he seemed to glance across at Isabel with a look of defiance. The local dignitaries and senior militiamen followed his lead, and a pile of wreaths grew at the foot of the memorial. The crowd murmured, noting the names of the participants. Finally, the ceremony was over. The parade came to attention and the marchers wheeled through the gates of the Institute, past Curtis's car to the waste ground at the side. While the militia was dismissed, the people began to disperse back to their houses. Stephen paused for a moment to watch Curtis moving among the parade, shaking hands, exchanging greetings and receiving congratulations, sharing his delight.

Stephen and Isabel walked slowly back up the slope. They did not speak. Something had happened; something was over.

They stood inside her house, and he felt as though he hardly knew the place.

'Well,' she said, 'at least it passed off without incident.' She looked at him, with the hint of a challenge. 'Were you surprised the army stayed away?'

He knew what she was getting at, but refused to meet the accusation. 'I suppose they decided to play it cool,' he said casually, 'as you suggested they would.'

'You suppose?'

He mastered his annoyance with an effort. Curtis's first accusation had never finally been laid to rest, an accusation that was all the more ironic in the light of Potter's admissions. It angered him to think that she still did not quite trust him, she who had spoken of faith, but since he would be off soon, he smiled and said simply: 'What else can I say?'

It was time to be on his way, time to go. He did not want to linger and risk the awkwardness of bumping into Curtis. He had received enough odd looks during the parade to know that he would always be someone they did not trust and never would. Major Potter's warning nagged in the back of his mind, and he wished he could bring it into the conversation, confess it and hear her interpretation.

Suddenly, there was a kind of thud, a muffled thump, and then a shock wave, close at hand, and the sound of glass shattering. Stephen looked at Isabel. He felt his stomach go weak. A moment of silence followed the blast, and then he heard screams and voices shouting outside, and the sound of running feet.

They hurried back into the street.

People who, only a few minutes before, had been standing in dignified silence contemplating the anniversary of the revolution and the memory of the dead, were now heading in a panic towards the Institute. Looking down there, Stephen could see a column of black smoke.

He began to run. Isabel followed.

Now they were meeting people running back up the hill towards them. Someone was screaming hysterically.

'Call an ambulance, call an ambulance.'

Stephen ran harder, then stopped. Already, a helpless semi-circle had formed. The car was in flames and the heat of the fire was blackening the red paint. The force of the blast had thrown it against the railings of the Institute. A couple of men were trying to get near the car door, but without hope. Someone was shouting for an extinguisher.

Inside the car, through the smoke and heat, there was a thing, a black shape slumped against the dashboard.

Stephen saw this, stared briefly in horror, and turned to meet Isabel running behind him. 'No,' he said, still catching his breath. 'Go back.' He tried to block her path.

'What's happened?' She was almost fighting him.

'It's a bomb, a car bomb.'

She seemed confused. Her resistance went. 'Who is it?'

When she saw his hesitation and his eyes darting away, she realised. 'No,' she said, almost in a whisper. He held her firmly in his arms and began to help her up the street. People were standing outside their houses, not daring to move, watching curiously. Already the sirens were sounding in the distance. When they reached her door, an ambulance was racing into the street.

She broke away from his grip and looked at him. 'You bastard,' she said simply.

He felt numbed and hollow and silenced. 'You'll never believe me, will you?'

'No,' she said. 'I won't.' She turned away. 'Not ever.'

10

After the funeral, Isabel found herself, hardly knowing why, driving west. She wanted to get away from the town and its sorrow. The road lulled her grief and the solitude of the car gave her time to herself, the kind of seclusion she had not had since the death of Joe Curtis.

The nightmare of it all. The unbelievable pain; the inertia; the anger; and then the senseless buzz of the world: the inquiries, the speculations and the intrusions of the authorities and the media. Part of her seemed so detached from her own world. Even now, she was still too much in shock to remember precisely the order of events. Her only decisive gesture had been to insist on Stephen's immediate departure, for everyone's good. In her grief, this second loss passed off almost casually. He was saying goodbye almost before she realised it, standing in the hallway, holding his bag, as he had at the beginning. He was serious-faced and defensive, as anxious as she to get it over with. He kissed her lightly, as though they would meet again that evening. She was fond of him, but he was such a boy. At that moment, she imagined, even hoped, she would never see him again.

For hours after, she could not be sure of herself. She sat, defeated, at the kitchen table with the unread newspapers before her. She felt her mortality and her fear and the madness of the situation in which she was living. She felt almost hysterical with the conflict of emotion inside her, unable to trust her instincts. In a little while, she made tea and tried to be calm.

She realised, staring about her now, that the dramas and excitement of the video had temporarily disguised the truth about this place. Despite their quest for what they called 'reality', the film people had, in fact, created an absurd, even reassuring, fiction. They could not begin to convey what it was like here. People were being killed every day, but only now was she experiencing the force and meaning of that. 'In the midst of life we are in death.' She had heard this phrase often enough in the past, but it had not registered. Now, with an illustration she could understand, the idea of a life taken violently away was something her imagination refused to explain. Her mind swam with the chanciness of things.

She saw Curtis again in her mind. He had pushed himself beyond his own limits. He had seemed at home among the enigmas and ambiguities of the life he had made for himself; in retrospect, his obsession with the power of knowledge had driven him mad. Some, like Mr Birch, were openly saying that there was a kind of justice in his fate, but Isabel could never believe that. For her, Curtis's bear-like presence and darting looks, an incongruous mixture of animal and bird, only brought back memories of his sympathy and understanding, and she would always be grateful. She remembered, with distress, their last real conversation. She imagined him in these last few days looking forward to the end of the video, to the parade, dreaming about the things he would do next week, next year. He was always scheming.

And then, suddenly, no future. Nothing. What was the end? Was it an unendurable noise or a bright flash of light? Was there pain, or surprise, or nothing? This was the mystery of death: it was impossible to know. Her own imagined death was certainly different. In that fantasy, there was usually a long illness with time to say goodbye, time to make amends, time to deal with her anger. And when the moment came at last her idea was of something intensely private, cosy and almost sexual, an imperceptible crossing from one state to another, a drifting to sleep. This was not such a death. This, she had to assume, was what the terrorists would call an 'execution'.

She found herself flicking the pages of her notebook. There was the number and the unfamiliar hand. 'Day or night,' he had said. She hurried to the telephone. 'Yes.' A mainland accent, slightly abrupt, as though disturbed in the middle of something important. Could she speak to Major Potter? 'I'm sorry. You must have the wrong number.'

It was then, when the line went dead, that she thought her crying would not stop, as all her feelings of dread and fury and betrayal welled up into a grief that would, it seemed, never leave her. Only next day, when she saw Curtis's coffin being shouldered from his house into the street, did she know that the first, immediate, shocking phase of her sorrow was coming to an end.

He had been buried well, in a fine cortège, with many mourners, led by Mary. There were press people and television crews; throughout the ceremony a military helicopter hovered overhead, a reminder of the double life Curtis had left behind. At the graveside, the tributes praised his vision, his dedication and his patriotism. The cemetery was on the hill overlooking the town, new white headstones dotted among the grey like shells on a seashore. Isabel thought it was appropriate that Curtis should lie here looking down on his own place, history and people.

At the moment of interment, Mary's grief overpowered her, and she had to be helped by the priest and Peter Dobbs, who was at her side. Isabel, standing well apart from the main body of mourners, felt the general anger and resentment at the incomprehensible ways of God. The splendid family tombs scattered across the hillside said that Curtis should have been buried with his forefathers at the end of a fine, rich life, laden with honours, ripe with prosperity, and lamented by his children and grandchildren. More than one speaker made the point that the murderous madness of their land had finally reached their town. But you cannot choose your death, Isabel thought, and especially you cannot choose it here.

Afterwards, Mary had thrown open the doors of her home, and many neighbours had gone in to pay their respects, exchange subdued gossip, and take tea. Isabel felt foreign to that and went home alone, afraid to encounter Mary's cold, unforgiving stare. The noise of the wake through the wall

317

reminded her that she was both of the town and yet isolated from it where it mattered most, at moments of life and death. Who knew what they were saying about her at that very moment? What vindictive accusations against Stephen might not imminently ignite some cruel retaliation against her? To soothe her nerves, she listened to Bach's unaccompanied cello suites, but it was no good. Feeling hopeless and lonely and a little afraid, she had hurried out to the car with no clear view of what she might do next, just a determination to escape the claustrophobic atmosphere of recrimination and woe.

It was only after some miles that she remembered the portrait, and a plan came to her, an idea that made sense of her flight. At the first pay-phone, she pulled over and made her call. Sarabeth answered almost at once, sounding pleased to hear Isabel's voice. Christopher was away on heritage business. She would be delighted to see her. 'Good timing,' she said. 'We've just about finished your restoration.'

Isabel was so relieved that she found she was crying as she came away from the telephone, though she could not exactly say what she was crying for. She drove on, the road swimming with her tears, until gradually she took control of herself again.

In a little while, she reached the monument, standing out on the moorland like a massive tombstone. Before, she had driven past. Today, in no special hurry, and with her thoughts whirling in odd directions, she stopped, parking next to the garage and the solitary roadside café. No one was about. She walked over the brown grass, feeling the wind on her cheeks. The monument was set in a paved surround littered with fast-food cartons. Close to, the plinth was covered in graffiti. She circled round, looking up at the towering featureless slab. On the moorland side, out of view from the road, there was a door. She went inside. The interior was a windowless bunker, shaped like a church without an altar, and the darkness was broken by a few rusty lights. Her feet echoed on stone and, putting out her hand, she found the concrete white and powdery to the touch. It was as though she could feel decay under her fingers. In a generation it would be crumbling; in two or three it would be a ruin, and the people who drove past would look on its broken grandeur with mystification.

Isabel walked slowly back to the car and drove on. Up ahead, there was a sign. The house, now advertised to the public, was forty miles off. As she turned into the drive, she was pleased and surprised to see a notice, 'House Closed Today'.

Sarabeth was waiting on the steps to greet her. She was wearing a long black skirt and a loose matching blouse, and she had a sombre elegance that seemed completely uncontrived. 'Isabel, my dear,' she said, in her whispering grey voice. 'I'm so glad you decided to come.' She seemed to know that Isabel's visit had nothing to do with the portrait. 'You have had a terrible time,' she went on definitively, 'but here you can be yourself.'

Sarabeth's clasp was strong and invigorating, and Isabel felt the sinews of her embrace with a weird, slightly scary, thrill. Sarabeth gave her a penetrating look, as if from the brink of some great inner starvation, and invited her to follow. She was welcoming, but her manner was disconcerting, and Isabel, who had been looking forward to the moment of arrival, found herself feeling surprisingly nervous.

'I hope I haven't disturbed you,' she said, realising that her recent tears must still show.

'Come and see what we've done to your picture.'

They walked together to the studio. After the heat of the road it was cool there, and bright, sharp with the smell of paint. Waiting for them on an easel, draped in a dusty white cloth, was the portrait, shrouded like a ghost in a child's story. Sarabeth was explaining their choice of frame as she went over to it and Isabel, hanging back, appreciated that this must always be a moment of theatre between artist and client. Then, with a flourish, she pulled the sheet away, and stepped back.

The transformation was astonishing. A dirty, torn, dun-coloured shadow of a thing had become a man and a woman in the prime of life, framed in gilt splendour. Isabel came

319

closer, studying the woman. There was colour in her cheeks and fullness in her breasts, and she was standing proudly, a mother of children, presumably, a creature of intelligence, even sensuality. The man next to her, whose arm she was holding, was not smiling exactly, but he transmitted a benign authority, as if, with a nod, he could command the universe. Who were they? What were their thoughts, their hopes, their fates? There was charm in the absence of an answer, a fascination in the mystery. Isabel studied the restoration. The paint was glowing again and the tear in the canvas had been invisibly repaired. She found herself looking and looking, but saying nothing. Finally, she found her voice. 'You've brought them back from the dead.'

'It's just cleaning. It's amazing what you find when you get below the surface.'

'It's marvellous.' She frowned. 'I'm only sorry that – ' She stopped, and Sarabeth seemed to understand her regret without further questions.

'Come,' she said, taking her arm, and she led the way back into the interior dimness of the house. The Bennetts' wing was curtained and shuttered up against the light, and faintly in the distance there was the sound of Gregorian chanting. Isabel found herself in a tiny parlour, a room she had not seen before. A low lamp was burning by an armchair in the corner; it was warm and mysterious with shadow and the scent of herbal tea. The floor was covered with papers and books in a semicircle round the chair. Sarabeth lifted a heap of documents off the chaise-longue, and stretched herself out with a sigh, as if preparing for psychoanalysis.

'You can sit in my chair,' she said, pointing. 'I'm tired of it.' Across the room, her face was as clear and pale as wax, and her greying hair, framing her oval features and high clear forehead, gave her a medieval serenity.

Isabel, taking the chair, realised she was to be scrutinised and felt again that flutter of apprehension. She settled herself and folded her hands, miming a calm she did not feel. Then she began to talk about Stephen and Curtis. 'I suppose I want to know,' she said, after some minutes, 'what you can tell me about loss and grief, what help you can give.'

'When I listen to you,' Sarabeth replied, 'I do not hear what you say, but I hear the anger in your voice. I think there is a rage within you that you have not fully understood.'

Isabel admitted that this might be so, and now more than ever. 'I'd say I have plenty to be angry about.'

'Tell me about it.'

Gradually, she found a focus to her thoughts; slowly, and more calmly as the minutes passed, she began to explain herself. Finally, after she had lost track of how long she had been speaking, she said: 'I'm sorry, this is crazy, isn't it? I mean, does it make any sense to you at all?'

If she was expecting an immediate answer, Isabel was mistaken. Sarabeth was silent for a long while, so long that Isabel was afraid she might have fallen asleep. Finally, out of the shadows, there was a hushed inquiry.

'What is your understanding of the word "love"?'

This was not what Isabel expected, but as she answered, she found her mind returning to the first days with Stephen. At one point she began to cry, but she felt unabashed and comforted by the silence of her mysterious companion. After she had spoken for a while, there was another long silence.

In due course, she was being challenged again. 'Can you say what is in the most secret corner of your heart? Can you confess your sins?'

'I think I can try.' She paused. 'I didn't realise until today how lonely I could be.'

'You are lonely because you thought the world could take away your loneliness.' She shook her head. 'That was a mistake. The world is something you can do without just now.' She gave a little private laugh and Isabel heard her stir on the couch, making herself comfortable. One of the images that came to her was of an audience settling itself for a performance, and she wished she had a greater mastery of her lines.

'When you lose someone close, you have to learn patience.'

Isabel found herself protesting. 'Joe was just a friend, but – '
She could not go on. She heard her words about truth mocking
her. 'I mean, our friendship – ' She stopped again.

'Did you sleep with him?'

'Once. After my husband left.' She felt her tears coming to
the surface of the conversation. 'It was a mistake.' Now she
was crying. 'A terrible mistake.'

'No.' Sarabeth's contradiction was decisive and final. 'It
wasn't.' As Isabel composed herself, she saw Sarabeth's
shadow disappear through the door. She sat very still until
Sarabeth reappeared with two steaming mugs of tea on a tray.
'There are no mistakes, my dear. Only explorations.'

Isabel replied that she must feel guilty.

Sarabeth seemed intrigued. 'Why?'

'I have these terrible dreams.' She explained that the night
before she had dreamed her own death. She was walking
through this empty house. 'I opened a door into a large white
room with sunshine coming in through tall french windows.
There was a coffin on the floor. Nothing else, just this coffin.
My first thought was that it was Joe's. But when I walked
up to it and looked in I found that it was me. But I wasn't
shocked; I was glad.' Tears came back into her eyes. 'When
I'm awake it's different. It's as though a light has been
switched out.'

'No.' Sarabeth was contradicting again. 'You must think of
him as music.'

'I don't understand.'

'It's the difference between having and being. Light is an
absolute state. You can only have it, or degrees of it, or none
at all. Music – a tune, a theme – has a life that no one can take
away. Think of Joseph as a melody in your head, the notes of
a favourite quartet, and he is always there. He has being.
That's what I mean.' She took a sip of her tea. 'Perhaps that
idea will help you one day. For the moment, you have anger,
and I think you also have shame.'

Isabel felt her words strike deep. How did she know? But
she did know. That was the quality of her strength. 'He saved

me – at a certain moment, he saved me. I could have saved him, perhaps, but I didn't. I let him go. Worse, I humiliated him. That is part of my confession.'

'But you found Stephen, perhaps.'

Isabel hesitated. 'Perhaps.' She saw him back on the mainland, preparing to be on the move again, immersing himself in the world she found so painful, and realised why they were no longer together.

'I remember that young man so well,' said Sarabeth, speaking as though it was Stephen who was deceased. 'He was – ' She thought for a moment. 'He was looking for himself.'

'He's still looking, I think,' said Isabel.

'Did you find him?'

'There was a moment, I believe, when we touched somewhere deep.' Tears came into her eyes again. 'It was very brief and did not last.'

'But nothing lasts, Isabel. Nothing.' She sounded almost angry. 'Surely you know that – or have you forgotten?' She bent down and picked up a book from the floor, turned the pages, searching rapidly and, holding it up to catch the light from the lamp, began to read.

Isabel interrupted with a murmur of recognition. '"The nest is rifled and the bird mourns . . ."'

She stopped. 'You know that?'

'I was in it,' said Isabel, brushing away her tears with a smile. 'At school.'

'That should have taught you that it's only the temporary things that have any chance of permanence.' Sarabeth put the book down, and picked up another. 'Do you believe in God?' she asked.

'I don't know.'

'I think you are afraid to admit that the answer may be Yes. Can there be a dimension to life without God? I think not. We have to honour the majesty and wonder of the world, but understand that it is absurd and irrational too. At least, that's what the bible says to me.'

Isabel remembered Hickey's words echoing through the church. 'Saved through the blood of the lamb,' she said.

'There is no salvation,' said Sarabeth. 'There is only consciousness.'

'You mean self-knowledge?'

'If you like.' She looked away. 'I like the idea of life as a conundrum. It makes the human race seem more interesting. I don't want answers. Faith is a fascinating concept.'

Isabel asked about the books and papers scattered across the floor. 'It's your scrapbook, isn't it?'

'I always turn to it when Christopher is away.' It was, she added, the story of their life here. 'We really have been out on the frontier. There is so much material. It won't be a conventional book.' She laughed ironically. 'A patchwork not a seamless web. I'm more of an old gossip than a serious historian.'

She picked up a piece of closely typed paper. 'May I read you something I wrote last night?'

Isabel put her head back, closed her eyes and listened. But she found it hard to concentrate. She wanted Sarabeth's words to come unscripted; she wanted her inspiration to remain in the air.

After three or four minutes, Sarabeth put the paper down, suddenly diffident. 'Do you like it?'

'It's very unusual. I'd like to see it written down. I like the mood of it, and the way you read.'

'Please don't be polite.' There was that warning note again. 'Remember, you are here to speak the truth.'

'I'm not sure I have the strength,' said Isabel.

'You must find it – and you will.' She was delivering a verdict. 'Then you will be yourself again.' She stood up optimistically, looking at her watch. 'Can I offer you a drink?'

'Perhaps I should be getting back.'

They were walking back towards the kitchen.

'Stay with me for a while. It's nice having you here. I've never really got used to having Christopher away.'

Isabel said: 'It's odd, isn't it, sleeping alone?'

Sarabeth smiled sadly, and went to the sideboard. She uncorked a bottle of red wine, and poured two glasses. Now she laughed. 'To the opposite sex.' They clinked glasses. Sarabeth put her drink down. 'What about Stephen?'

'If only there was an answer to that question!' She sighed. 'What can I say – that the timing was wrong? That we weren't ready for each other?'

'You must say what you feel.'

'If only I knew.' She opened her eyes wide in thought. 'All I know is what I don't feel.'

'Then you have somewhere to start.'

'I also know that just now I prefer my own company. It feels safer, though I expect you would say that it could be even more dangerous.' She smiled. 'Perhaps I would welcome that.'

'Then you are not afraid of what you will find within.'

And so they talked on, Isabel in a circle of light, Sarabeth in a cave of shadows, while night fell and the silence of the great house crowded closer and closer.

In their seclusion, the conversation had the intensity of words whispered in the crypt of a cathedral, a faint and vital thread of dialogue linking two women whose need for each other, half glimpsed before, was not properly acknowledged, and Isabel understood at last why Sarabeth had challenged her to intimacy when she arrived. More and more, they began to laugh together, and to find in laughter another dimension of their friendship, like seeing another angle in a mirror.

Later, after the clocks in the hallway had raggedly chimed nine, they made a simple meal of salad and pasta, and ate it, sitting at the table, by the light of a single candle. Sarabeth opened another bottle of wine, and Isabel began to feel drunk and happy, at ease with herself. The darkness poured round them, growing warm and friendly.

It was nearly midnight when Sarabeth showed Isabel upstairs, unsteadily lighting the way with the candle, laughing at the shadows thrown on the wall, laughing without knowing the reason why. Isabel had her arm in Sarabeth's for guidance, and again she felt in the strong sinews of her body an electric charge of sexuality. She could hear the alcohol roaring in her ears and she knew she was lacking control. In her weariness and relief, she wanted simply to roll up under a blanket in the warm. She had an overpowering longing for peace and oblivion. It had been a long day.

She was aware, as a child half asleep is aware, that she was being helped, still half dressed, into bed. The comfort of the pillow and the freshness of the sheets greeted her like absolution. Then she realised, uncomplaining and not at all surprised, that Sarabeth was next to her. She was putting her arms round her and, like sisters not lovers, they were drifting together into sleep itself and – was she dreaming now? – she heard Sarabeth's voice murmuring next to her.

II

Coming back to the mainland was always strange, a moment of readjustment that was instinctive and yet unwelcome. Stephen sat in the back of the taxi from the airport, watching the grey city materialise beyond the hard shoulder of the motorway, and fought in his mind with the ugly familiarity and comfort of the place. Was there nowhere else to return? Inventing himself, he was free to answer the question as he liked, but this, for better or worse, would always be 'home', even though he knew he could never settle here for long.

He tried not to think about Curtis.

The taxi driver was smoking a cigarette and half-listening to the radio. Occasionally he shouted something down-to-earth and intolerant through the gap in the glass. Stephen, resting his chin on his hand, lost in the noise and blur of the road, answered non-committally, wondering, in the numbness of his spirits, how he was going to handle the speedy chatter of the office. In the past, he had imagined becoming nostalgic for these voices, even while another part of him wished it were otherwise.

At this moment, there was nothing that thought could make better.

The taxi left the motorway and rattled through sleepy back streets, a roll-call of names evoking far-flung colonial wars. His grandparents had lived in this neighbourhood and he had often stayed here, visiting from overseas. As the geography of childhood memories came back, he was a boy again, skipping over the cracks in the pavement, holding his grandfather's hand. The suburb was no longer as he would reconstruct it to himself – some buildings had been torn down, others thrown up in their place – but it answered well enough, just as an experience, once vivid or painful, becomes altered with time and forgetfulness.

He tried not to think about Isabel.

Now the driver took a short-cut and they were nosing down through a street market with stalls and barrows on wobbly iron wheels. In this noisy theatre, some of these raw, working faces seemed not to have changed in thirty years, but now there were new players in the crowd as well, refugees from abroad whose children were mixing the songs and myths of many scattered lives and traditions into the repertoire of the new generation. Stephen always found himself noting this change with satisfaction, recognising how little he liked his own people and his own country. Being at home was best for him when it had a touch of the foreign about it.

If he went away soon, he would probably never see her again.

The taxi slowed in a traffic jam, and he gazed out at the passers-by. Once, these alleys and cornerways had hosted a traditional pageant of city life – street traders, small businesses, local residents. Then the speculators moved in and rents began to rise. Money washed through the streets and suddenly everything was up for grabs. Everywhere, it seemed, was becoming either a restaurant or a smart new office. This was when Wagner had relocated his company. Change followed swiftly. The old inhabitants left. The greengrocer with the hook hand sold up while the going was good; his shop was now a wine bar. The pet shop became a brasserie; so did the stationer. The cobbler became a high-class delicatessen. In the space of half a mile you could eat out in five continents.

Isabel would always believe he had lied about Curtis.

Here was the office, a converted warehouse. He settled with the taxi, dumped his suitcase with security and, health-conscious, took the stairs to the second floor. The office was like all offices, a world of its own, a botanical hothouse whose temperature and inner activity were artificially controlled. Although Wagner's business was affected by the ebb and flow of events, his headquarters had their own rhythm, chiefly directed by the whim of Wagner himself.

Stephen, who had a headache coming on, negotiated the solicitous inquiries of the receptionist and made his way unobtrusively to his room, hoping to have a few minutes to himself before Wagner's inevitable summons. He found his desk piled with foreign-language newspapers and videotapes, and he had just begun to realise that this referred to the possibility of a new assignment when the internal phone rang. It was Georgie telling him that 'the boss' wanted to see him at once.

'Stephen.' Wagner was unusually formal; they shook hands. It could have been the preliminary to a job interview. 'So you're back,' he said, closing the door.

Inside, it was silent and tidy. 'Yes,' said Stephen, taking a seat. 'I'm back.'

'You okay?' Wagner was sombre, concerned.

He yawned. 'No.'

A frown passed across Wagner's features. 'Promise me one thing?'

'Whatever.' This was the unavoidable post-mortem and he knew he was going to have to endure it.

Wagner shook his head. 'Never again, okay? *Nunca mas.*'

'Whatever you say. You're the boss.' Stephen didn't feel casual but knew it sounded that way.

'Have you any idea what we've been through here these last few days?'

Stephen could not stop his annoyance in time. 'What do you think I've been through, Alan?' He glared at him through his headache. 'Perhaps it's slipped your mind, but I was there, remember?'

When Wagner was angry he could be very loud or very quiet. Generally, with his staff, he was very quiet. 'I've had every agency in town on my back about you, Mallory, so I'd be grateful if you'd stuff your sarcasm up your arse and listen to me.'

He began to speak, in an urgent, weary monotone, and

Stephen could see that he had indeed been given the once-over by the authorities. The overseas part of their business, he said, was always on the edge of politics, they all knew that well enough, but on this assignment they had, inadvertently no doubt, gone too far. The video was one thing, but the entanglement with Curtis and the authorities was something else. The conflicts between the ministry of the interior and the military were things they could probably only guess at. The fact was that they – he – had stumbled into a minefield and it was lucky, in Wagner's opinion, that only one person had been killed. It was the deceptively routine nature of the occupation that made it so lethal.

As Stephen listened, he realised that Wagner was angry because he had been afraid for him, and that once he had said his piece, they could be friends again. He blamed himself, he was saying, for taking his eye off the ball. He had been asleep at the wheel when Stephen had proposed taking on the video project. Catastrophe had been waiting around the corner. If only they had read the signs.

Wagner was calming down. He was beginning to seem almost himself again. 'Go on.' He looked at his colleague in a way that was almost paternal. 'Tell me what happened.'

Stephen, slowly relaxing, explained as well as he could, admitting that finally he had been out of his depth. It was difficult to concede to Wagner that he had failed, and he feared Wagner's retribution. For all their closeness, Stephen knew that if Wagner thought he was finished he would – while putting it ever so nicely – fire him. In the event, his boss seemed happy to share the responsibility.

'It always was a weird place,' he said, becoming conversational. 'I covered it for the paper once. I found it fascinating, but – ' He shrugged. 'I could never make sense of it. There was always a story behind the story, and you never really knew who to trust.'

Stephen saw that, after his outburst, Wagner only wanted to chat and build bridges. 'I'm sorry, Alan,' he said. 'I've had a hard time.'

Wagner always responded well to a white flag. 'Listen, Steve, it wasn't all your fault.' A reflective note came into his voice. 'I should have known better.'

'But you told me not to fuck up, and I fucked up. That's the bottom line.'

'We all fucked up.' He sounded impatient, as if he too disliked admitting defeat. 'It's over now. Caput. Finis. The End.'

'After Federico,' Stephen could not stop himself opening up old wounds.' 'I thought – I thought it could never happen to me again.'

Wagner did not like to dwell on death. 'It's a war zone. Kind of. It was always on the cards.'

'He was supposed to be our man.'

'It sounds as though he was everyone's man.' He leant towards him earnestly. 'Come on, Steve. You mustn't take it so hard. Look on the bright side.' When he was encouraging, he could be like an uncle or an elder brother. 'You completed the video, didn't you?'

'That's true enough.'

'Exactly! At least I can invoice those bastards with a clear conscience.' He shook his head. 'That guy, Fred whatshisname – Christ!'

'What about him?'

'Drove me crazy. Phone calls day and night.'

'Why didn't you call me?' Stephen found himself feeling almost offended again.

'There was nothing you could have done. Nothing. Fred Thing was handling it his own way and you know how glad I am to leave those diplomatic back-channels to the Americans.' He frowned. 'It's our people who give me the creeps.'

Stephen saw Major Potter sitting in the corner of the bar with his deadpan smile and his store of innuendo. 'They have loyalties we'll never understand,' he said, almost to himself.

Now Wagner smiled for the first time. 'I told you risk control was a no-no.'

Stephen protested.

331

'Don't give me that look, Mallory.' He was finally in good spirits. 'It was a nightmare, and we might as well admit it. None of your college kid tricks will persuade anyone otherwise. At least we can make some money for a change.' He zeroed in again. 'How's your girl?'

He yawned; all these questions. 'Isabel?'

'I don't think I know her name, do I?'

'I never told you.'

'I mean the one you – '

Stephen cut in. 'She's fine.'

'You mean it's over?'

He sighed. 'We'll see.'

Wagner nodded wisely. 'It's over.' He stood up. Stephen was always struck by his ruthless way with anything that was, as he put it, 'ancient history'. To Wagner, such matters simply ceased to exist. He was only interested in the intriguing dimensions of the present. 'Let's talk about your next move.'

'Do I have one?'

'That's up to you.'

'Is it sitting on my desk?'

'It could be. If you're free for lunch today, we could discuss it in a more congenial atmosphere.'

Even in his present mood, Stephen could not suppress a wan smile. The boss's eating habits were more or less the office joke. Wagner saw the smile and told him cheerfully to go to hell, he would see him at one o'clock.

Stephen and his colleagues usually entertained their clients in the director's dining-room. Wagner ate the same lunch almost every day of the year in a noisy, unfashionable restaurant down the road. He preferred to sit, alone with a newspaper if need be, at a corner table among the office workers, tourists and secretaries. This penchant for anonymity was a hangover from his days as a newspaperman, and enabled him to feel he was not yet off the street, that he was still collecting copy and listening in. To the ebullient patron of the establishment, Wagner was always 'generalissimo'. When Stephen returned from an assignment the tradition was that he would join him there and complain about the menu, the prices and the quality of the wine.

Today, Wagner was shown to his table and ordered his habitual pizza and green salad. Then he called for the house wine and supervised his guest's choice of food.

Stephen came straight to the point. He was not in a mood for pleasantries or gossip. 'So what have you got for me?'

Wagner was the kind of man who needed a favourite son. 'What do you want?'

'I want to get out of here.' The bread stick snapped in his fingers. 'I want to do something I understand.'

'Have you looked at those files?'

'I thought I'd let you sell me the story first.'

'Okay.' Wagner was a player who liked to make a pitch. 'Here's the headline news.' There was, he explained, this snap election on the cards. 'I've had our researchers check it out. The candidate is way behind in the polls, but he's bright and willing to learn, and though he doesn't know it he holds most of the aces.'

'Where is this?'

'Africa,' Wagner replied with satisfaction, taking a sip of wine, and confronting his colleague with silence. He knew he was appealing to Stephen's romantic imagination. Stephen had been born in Africa and had often said how much he would like to return there on business.

There was a photograph on his mother's dressing table of a three-year-old boy in a safari hat standing outside a tropical bungalow next to a naked tribesman with a spear. His father had been relocated elsewhere shortly afterwards, but the memory of the smell, the vastness and the heat, had stayed with him. From time to time Stephen had changed planes there, but never remained long enough to renew the connection. He tried not to seem too eager.

'I didn't know there were any democracies left there.'

Wagner was irritated. 'Come on, Steve. You're making excuses. It's tailor-made for you. What's the matter?'

Stephen saw Isabel in his mind. Perhaps there was, after all, something he could retrieve. How could he begin to explain that confusion?

Wagner saw his hesitation. 'You're thinking about that girl, I can tell.' He shook his head. 'Forget it, Steve.'

Stephen blushed. Wagner was working well today. 'Just to start with, it's a bit difficult.'

'It's always difficult.' Wagner's rough sympathy was surprisingly appealing. 'What you need is to find that old winning streak.'

'Yes,' Stephen smiled reflectively. 'It would be nice to win something for a change.'

'I love the smell of winning.' Wagner raised his glass. 'To victory,' he said. 'Victory in love and politics.'

'Victory,' echoed Stephen, hearing again the ambulance sirens in his mind.

12

The year was growing old and there was death in the air. Isabel, driving up to the hospital, felt the stirrings of an end of season melancholy. The first leaves were yellowing, and on the horizon, across the low brown hills, clouds were massed like mountains; for a moment she could believe she was travelling to some exotic foreign kingdom she had never seen before, but then the reality of her journey returned. As she drove through the weak sunshine, she heard a church bell tolling sadly across the watery valley. The irregular guns of a mid-week shoot were banging away in the empty fields nearby. She felt lethargic with her own sadness and weighed down by the meaninglessness of things.

Paul was sweeping leaves off the hospital path, moving his brush in slow motion like an old man. There was a For Sale sign on the gate she had not seen before. An unsuccessful bonfire smouldered among the trees. She waved as she passed, but her rear view was blocked by the portrait propped up in the back seat and she could not be sure that he had registered her greeting.

No one answered the bell. She pushed in, with echoing footsteps, dismayed as always by the smell of the place. Mary was alone in her office. Isabel glimpsed her through the open door, staring absently ahead. Once, she had taken extra authority from the imposing formality of the office. Now she seemed dwarfed by it and a little bit lost.

Isabel hesitated briefly, then knocked on the door. 'May I come in?'

For a moment it was as though Mary did not recognise her. Then she focused. 'Oh. Hello.' Her voice was very small.

'Excuse me,' said Isabel, still tentative with apprehension.

'Do you have a minute?' With grief, she now knew, there was always the risk of bad timing.

'I'm sorry,' said Mary. 'I was miles away.'

Isabel took off her coat and sat down, hoping to seem natural but conscious of her own profound inner awkwardness. In the distance, a bell rang briefly, then stopped. Mary did not react. Isabel noticed that she was fiddling abstractedly with a garish plastic container. 'Mr Hu was just here,' she explained. 'I have to feed the fish, you see.' She appeared to be studying the instructions on the label. 'I'm terribly afraid I'll kill them.' She sighed. 'I suppose I could give them back to Mr Hu, but in an odd kind of way it's a comfort to have them there.' She began to cry, and fumbled in her bag for a handkerchief.

Isabel sat very quiet and still and let her compose herself. This seemed to be the best kind of sympathy towards someone who had once been so hostile. One of the patients, a mousy-looking girl with a wandering eye, appeared briefly at the window, made a face, and went away. Isabel found it difficult not to smile, and was relieved to find that Mary was now half smiling too.

'I think I'm going a little bit mad myself,' said Mary finally. 'I know it's what I should expect, but it's still a shock. Somehow the training is no preparation for the experience.' There was a new vulnerability in her manner that was rather appealing, as though all her previous enmities had been buried with her brother. 'I looked for you after the funeral,' she confessed, shyly. 'I was so lonely.'

Isabel liked her for this candour, and began to open up herself. 'I had to go away. I didn't mean to, but it just sort of happened.'

She described her visit to Sarabeth. In the end, she had stayed several days.

'The first time you went to that house,' Mary said. 'He was so angry.'

Isabel was surprised. 'Angry?'

'He felt betrayed. He was afraid that the heritage of the

town wasn't interesting enough for you. I remember him saying: "She never writes about us. We're not good enough for her."'

'I don't think it was to do with the house,' Isabel said quietly.

'No, I suppose you're right.' Mary looked down, and did not speak for a moment or two. 'Why have you come to see me?'

'I have something to give you.' She stood up. 'It's out in the car. I'll need your help.'

Mary looked at her curiously. She seemed frightened by the unknown, and Isabel had to reassure her that there was nothing to worry about.

They went outside. Isabel opened the back door. Together they manoeuvred the portrait off the seat. It was still in its protective wrapping. 'I was having it restored. I was planning to give it to Joe as a present, but – ' She stopped, slightly out of breath with the exertion. 'Then I thought I should bring it back where it belongs.'

They carried the picture inside, stripped away the bubblewrap and stood it against the dark wainscot. Mary looked at the proud Victorian couple and seemed to go into a reverie. 'It's odd to imagine that they may have been in this very room.'

Isabel looked up at the coffered ceiling, across at the marble fireplace, and back to the picture. 'Only a hundred years ago,' she said. 'It doesn't seem so long.'

'A hundred years of madness,' said Mary.

'I wonder what it will be like in another hundred years.'

'I'm glad I won't be around to find out,' said Mary with feeling.

Isabel remembered the For Sale sign. 'Has the house been sold yet?' In memory, she heard Curtis's dreams of leaving, and a rush of grief came hurting into her eyes.

Mary did not notice. 'There's a hotel chain looking at it. The government is offering big incentives to the developers now, something called an "interior grant".'

'That's part of the normalisation programme, isn't it?'

Mary suddenly flashed with anger. 'Whenever I hear that word it makes me so cross. You could no more "normalise" this place than you could dress my patients in suits and call them civil servants.'

'I suppose the authorities have to pretend to themselves that something can be done,' Isabel replied calmly.

'There's nothing to be done,' said Mary fiercely. 'Nothing.'

For a moment, silence came between them. Then Isabel resumed, exploring her own thoughts. 'Do you think you will stay here now?'

'Unless I sell the business, I don't have much of a choice.' Mary looked across to her office, as though it was part of another life. 'Mr Hu was here,' she repeated, absently. 'I like him. I think perhaps we'll have to go into partnership. It's probably the best bet for me.' She smiled. 'I'm fond of his girls. They would enjoy running the shop.'

Isabel remembered something. 'Joe was planning to leave, I think.'

'That was just one of his fantasies.' Mary's voice was strong and decisive. 'I can never forget that this is my home.' She looked at Isabel, the outsider. 'What about you?'

'I expect I'll go back to the mainland now.' She became thoughtful. 'My divorce will be through soon. I'll start again. I'll miss it here, of course. It's – it's been very important to me.' Suddenly all her feelings came to the surface in a rush and she remembered Sarabeth's words. 'Look, I know we haven't always got along, and I know you blame me for hurting Joe, but I just wanted to say I hope you understand that I was hurt too.' She heard her exasperation, but did not hold back. 'I can't be held responsible for everything,' she concluded.

Mary did not immediately seem to know how to answer. She stared with embarrassment at the picture. She went distant. 'I appreciate your call,' she said. 'It was a nice gesture.'

Isabel was still stumbling over her own feelings. 'It was just that I wanted – I just – ' She found she could not finish her sentence, and turned away in a blur, angry with herself for the loss of control.

Perhaps it was her sudden inarticulacy that gave Mary confidence, and enabled her to find the courage to speak out. 'You should not feel bad.' She came over and touched Isabel on the shoulder. 'You were not to blame. He only thought he loved you.'

Isabel was pleased by this, and turned to face her, calmer again. 'I think he was in love with the idea of me.' She shook her head at the memory. 'But I should have – ' She hesitated. 'I was not clear in my mind.'

'Well, nor was he,' Mary stared out of the window sadly. 'He knew everything about the town and nothing about himself.' She pronounced this verdict with great finality, then went over to the picture. 'Don't you think we should hang it up?'

'Now?'

'Why not?' She seemed almost light-hearted. 'It will be fun.' She became businesslike. 'There's a hammer in my office. All we need is a nail.' She began to bustle about, while Isabel looked on. In a matter of moments, it seemed, Mary had assembled both hammer and nail. 'So,' she said, as she tested the wire with her finger. 'Where do you think it should go?'

Isabel looked about. 'Over there,' she said, pointing at the fireplace in the hall. 'Don't you think they would want to be over the hearth?'

Mary climbed onto a chair, and Isabel passed her the hammer and the nail. Then, together, standing on separate chairs, they raised the portrait, snagged its wire on the nail, and let it settle into place.

Mary stood back. 'Perfect,' she said, and the delight in her voice was real.

'Welcome home,' said Isabel, with a smile. She felt intensely glad she had collected the picture, and relieved to have made contact with Mary at last.

They stood in the doorway, admiring their work. Outside, in the pale sunshine, there was the sound of a brush being dragged across the gravel. Impulsively, Mary stepped towards her and kissed her. 'Thank you,' she said. There were tears in her eyes.

'I'm glad,' said Isabel, 'I feel better now.'

'If only – ' Mary began, but did not complete her thought.

Isabel guessed what she wanted to say. It was hard not to have some regrets. She stepped out through the front door. 'I'll be at home tonight if you need anything,' she said.

She walked across to her car. Paul came by, trailing his brush.

'Hello, Paul,' said Isabel.

He looked at her very hard. There was a smear of blood on his cheek where he had scratched a spot. 'Who are you?'

'I'm Isabel,' she replied, speaking quietly. 'You visited my house.'

His expression was troubled. She went up to him and pointed at the badge on his anorak. 'I gave you this. Remember?'

'My mummy gave me this.' He sounded quite definite. He let his brush clatter to the ground and fumbled with the zip of his anorak. Inside, fastened to the lining, were several identical badges, each with the logo of Hickey's campaign and the words 'Hope and Salvation'.

'Smile,' he said, pointing to his collection.

She smiled, unable to help herself.

'Happy,' he said. It was not a question.

'Yes,' she said, mainly to herself. 'Happy.'

She got into her car. Paul stood there holding his brush, a weird honour guard. He was grinning at her, strangely conspiratorial, and she could not help smiling back, almost light-headed. At least someone here feels good, she thought, putting the car into gear. Even if they are crazy. She waved. He waved back. 'Smile,' he said.

The girl at the check-in desk was trained to a level of perky banter that was, Stephen supposed, designed to put nervous flyers at their ease. He received her valedictory 'Have a nice day' with the thought that, in the world he was re-entering, even the imagination had become Americanised.

Freed of his baggage, he negotiated customs and airport security and then, with an hour to kill, strolled through the air-side concourse. There was a time when he would have made his way without thinking to the executive travellers' lounge, but today, in better spirits, and finding novelty in life again, it pleased him to window-shop. Christmas was weeks away but already there were fairy lights and spray-on snow in the windows of the duty-free boutiques, as though trade could only flourish in the season of good cheer. When he thought about the parties and the quiet desperation, he decided he would not be sorry to spend those days under a foreign sun.

Beyond, through the walls of plate glass, there was a fine view of the airfield. It was a brilliant autumn morning, reminiscent of those last hot days at the beginning of the school year. Silver jets were lifting into the blue and his spirits soared with each thundering take-off. He felt the breath of possibility again, and was glad to be coming back to a way of life which, with all its drawbacks, he understood. People could say what they liked about his work. What he did was no worse, or better, than most and the compromises involved were no more shameful.

At least he had been pronounced fit for it. The medical centre to which Wagner sent him ('A simple formality') had been almost deserted. There were beer cans and plastic beakers up the staircase. 'We had a leaving party last night, a bit of a beano,' explained the duty nurse, escorting him to a cubicle. 'Just slip your things off and put this on,' she said, handing him a plum-coloured dressing-gown.

He sat in the antiseptic waiting-room with two older men, both studying the financial press. It was odd to be undressed at this hour, like seeing a film in the morning, He accepted a cup of coffee and filled out a questionnaire.

'Dr Mallory.' A tall black nurse with a clipboard was standing in the doorway; as he went towards her she yawned widely and he found himself yawning too. 'Excuse me,' he said.

'Excuse me, Dr Mallory.' She laughed infectiously. 'What's a doctor doing in a place like this?'

'I'm not a "doctor" doctor, if you see what I mean.'

'What kind of doctor are you then?'

'Of politics. Not much use to anyone, really.'

'It sounds very grand to me. Here you are.'

The check-up was a kind of circuit, a series of tests. At each stage, a different nurse evaluated his condition and perform-ance. He began to enjoy the attention.

They tested his eyes. They gave him headphones and tested his hearing. He blew into a tube and they tested his lungs. They attached wires to his body and measured his heart rate. They asked him to pass water, and then they took blood.

'Do you test for everything, as it were?' he asked, as the needle pricked.

'Oh yes,' said the nurse intelligently, scanning his card. 'Especially with travellers like yourself.'

She threw the needle into the bin and suggested he lie down for five minutes. Beyond the screen, two nurses gossiped idly.

'When did he die?'

'Sunday.'

'What has he done with his money?'

'He hasn't left it to me, that's all I know.'

'How did you hear?'

'She told me. "You won't get a penny," she said. The bitch.'

'You deserve better than that, Shirley. After all those years.'

'You don't have to tell me.'

Suddenly the curtain round his bed was twitched back and a middle-aged nurse asked him if he was ready for his X-ray. The voices fell silent and Stephen was left wondering about the little drama of disappointment he had just overheard.

He submitted to the X-ray and then another nurse took him to a private booth with a computer screen, like a video game. This, she explained, was a simple medical survey. 'Just answer yes or no, and when you're done go back to the waiting-room.'

The machine was rather polite. Hello, it said. Are you feeling well today? No, he replied. This answer stirred the programme into a stream of questions. Did he smoke? Drink? Run? Swim? How long did he sleep? Did he drive to work? He answered as pessimistically as he honestly could, hoping to discover the worst. Thank you, Dr Mallory, said the machine. Take care.

He sat in the waiting-room, negotiating with himself about his true feelings.

'Dr Mallory.' It was the black nurse again. 'The doctor will see you now.'

Stephen found himself shaking hands across a desk with a short, red-faced woman in a white coat. She was, he guessed, about forty. Her manner was jolly; she seemed rather stupid. She examined him briefly. 'Africa,' she said, out of the blue. 'How I envy you.'

When he had reported this to Wagner, his boss had laughed out loud. 'I told you there was no choice,' he said.

'So it would seem, Alan.' He shrugged. 'My fate, I suppose.'

He drifted back through the concourse past lines of waiting tourists to the executive lounge. The familiar suite was hushed and almost deserted. A silent television screen flickered in the corner. An officer in uniform was asleep, lolling open-mouthed by the courtesy telephone. A weak-faced man in a double-breasted suit, a diplomat he guessed, was telling his two children about his divorce. 'I love mummy very much, but I'm afraid mummy doesn't love me.'

Stephen went to the self-service bar and poured himself a celebration scotch. Then he found an armchair as far away as possible from the confessional voice of the diplomat and glanced through the international press. The world was full of stories and always would be. It was enjoyable to think that he might occasionally have a part to play out there. He sipped his drink and felt its power within. People said there was no more greatness in the world, that there was nothing glorious to do, nothing inspiring to believe, and only deals, corruption and self-advancement. They claimed there were no gods any more, no heroes, no classics. Everything was a smaller, duller version of what had gone before. Nothing could be changed. There was only the painful task of co-enduring with existence. Probably that was true for the most part. The difference in his mind was that this now seemed a raison d'être, even a high, attractive calling, and if you were willing to take a spin on the big wheel there were still any amount of adventures to be found.

The flight was called. He collected his briefcase and went to look for the departure gate. The moving walkway carried him slowly through the hall. He watched the inbound passengers coming towards him, weary, rumpled, unshaven, standing patiently behind carts of carry-on luggage. At moments like this he tried to find the Zen of international travel, and let his mind become loose, disengaged and unspecific. It was a way of avoiding frustration.

Suddenly, his concentration came back with a rush. Isabel was coming slowly towards him on the other side, half-hidden by a man in a trenchcoat. He began to blush and smile, and was about to wave when he realised his mistake. Close to, the woman's resemblance faded. She was talking to a man, presumably her husband, and seemed unaware of Stephen's embarrassment, though she glanced at him briefly as she passed on the other side. He stood there, not looking back, feeling foolish and confused and discomposed, an apology floundering in his mind.

Of course it could not be Isabel. It was a stupid, an absurd, mistake. How could he have imagined such a thing? For a moment, his mood dipped and his mind went back to the town and those last hours together. It hurt him to admit that she would never believe him.

At the gate, he handed in his boarding pass and went down the tunnel to the plane. The steward directed him to his seat by the window and he settled into a familiar routine. He loosened his tie, took off his shoes, allowed the flight attendant to hang up his jacket, and accepted the complimentary newspaper and the complimentary glass of champagne.

Now the cabin staff were doing the safety drill. He checked, as he always did, the location of the emergency exits and wondered briefly if he would have much of a chance with a lifejacket. The engines started. There was a faint, tilting bump as the aircraft pushed back from the loading bay. The jets were revving and whining, as though all the technology crammed into this machine was being tuned to a pitch of performance. Muzak tinkled overhead. They began to roll forward and then, after a few moments, braked. Looking out of the window, he saw a line of aircraft waiting to depart, taxi-ing on the apron, creaking with gravity.

Again, the revving of the jets. The plane crept forward, paused and crept forward again. Then he could feel the fuselage swing to the right and out of the window he saw a ribbon of lights, the runway. The seat-belt sign pinged twice and they turned again. He watched a flight attendant, taking her seat, cross herself quickly, and wondered how anyone could live with that level of anxiety. The engines roared; there was a surge of power; they began to gather speed. Stephen felt himself pushed back in his seat; now he closed his eyes and felt himself accelerating, lifting, flying.

He looked out of the window. The airport – the wire fencing, the barriers, the security lights, the swivelling radar – was falling away below and the land was quickly becoming a misty patchwork blur. The wing flashed through a scrap of cloud. There was another brief glimpse of the mainland and then they were banking and all he could see was the blue of the heavens and the sun blazing on the wing.

He knew it was only an illusion, but it was an illusion that sustained him within, the belief that here, in flight, he was himself again and that, escaping, he was free.

Robert McCrum
In the Secret State £5.99

The murder of the ex-agent is presented as suicide. The head of the agency is blackmailed into early retirement. The secrets of the Government must be preserved at all costs.

Only Frank Strange can unravel the corrupted loyalties and abuse of secrecy. But can he survive long enough to shatter the conspiracy of silence?

'A notable book, the chase is gripping, the atmosphere of nameless suspicion splendidly sustained.' OBSERVER

'An effortless elegance that puts him immediately ahead of the competition.' AUBERON WAUGH, EVENING STANDARD

'A cracking tale, a sharp young talent.' GUARDIAN

All Pan Books are available at your local bookshop or newsagent, or can be ordered direct from the publisher. Indicate the number of copies required and fill in the form below.

Send to: Pan C. S. Dept
                Macmillan Distribution Ltd
                Houndmills Basingstoke RG21 2XS
or phone: 0256 29242, quoting title, author and Credit Card number.

Please enclose a remittance* to the value of the cover price plus £1.00 for the first book plus 50p per copy for each additional book ordered.

*Payment may be made in sterling by UK personal cheque, postal order, sterling draft or international money order, made payable to Pan Books Ltd.

Alternatively by Barclaycard/Access/Amex/Diners

Card No.

Expiry Date

Signature

Applicable only in the UK and BFPO addresses.

While every effort is made to keep prices low, it is sometimes necessary to increase prices at short notice. Pan Books reserve the right to show on covers and charge new retail prices which may differ from those advertised in the text or elsewhere.

NAME AND ADDRESS IN BLOCK LETTERS PLEASE

....

Name _____

Address_____

_____

_____

_____

3/87